GODLING

BROADFEATHER BOOKS
www.AuthorNicoleConway.com

ARDA

LUNSURAI

AVLAR

NORTHWATCH

HIGHLAND COUNTRY

DAYRISE

OSBRAN

Port Murlowe

Breaker's Cliffs

ALDOBAR

EASTWATCH

Solhelm

FARROW ESTATE

HALFAX

PRISON CAMP RUINS

TWO RIVERS

WATCH

AILSPOT

THE PANTHEON OF MALDOBAR

THE FOREGODS

God of Was: Itanus
God of Is: Enais
God of Still to Come: Milontos

THE OLD GODS

God of Earth: Giaus
Goddess of the Sky: Astaris
The Fates: Viepol

THE LESSER GODS

God of Life & Nature: Paligno
Goddess of Death & Decay: Clysiros
Goddess of the Sea: Undae
Goddess of the Moon: Adiana
Goddess of Mischief: Iskoli
God of War: Proleus
Goddess of Love: Eno
God of Luck: Tykeron
God of Mercy: Ishaleon

This book is a work of fiction. Names, characters, places, and incidents are either products of the author's imagination or used fictitiously. Any resemblance to actual persons, living or dead, business establishments, events, or locales is coincidental. The author makes no claims to, but instead acknowledges the trademarked status and trademark owners of the word marks mentioned in this world of fiction.

Copyright © 2022 by Nicole Conway

All rights reserved.

No part of this book may be reproduced in any form or by any electronic or mechanical means, including information storage and retrieval systems, without written permission from the author, except for the use of brief quotations in a book review.

Cover art by Kiki Moch Rizky

Title and cover and interior design by COVERED BY NICOLE

For Ethan
All of these stories are meant for you.

Life is a strange and difficult thing, but friends will always be waiting for you here within these pages.
And so will I.

Love Always,
Mom

PART ONE

THATCHER

I

CHAPTER ONE

The Ulfrangar had come for Murdoc again.

We'd been dodging those murderous assassins basically since Murdoc and I had first met. They had come after us at the Cromwell estate in Eastwatch, and then again twice in Dayrise. They'd kidnapped me, and nearly killed Reigh by shooting him full of poisoned arrows. They had burned down Ms. Lin's house and left us all running like scared rabbits from one place to the next, fighting tooth and nail just to stay ahead of them.

I guess I should've realized this couldn't go on forever. Sooner or later, we'd run out of places to hide, or they'd finally get us backed into a corner. I just hadn't expected it to happen like this—smack in the middle of a military compound full of dragonriders.

Before, the Ulfrangar had always struck from the shadows. They made stealthy attacks, or used poisoned arrows in the cover of night—usually when we were least expecting it. Not this time, though. There were no combusting dragon-venom bombs, no sudden ambushes, and no explosions of flames. This time, they had come with a blatant threat. An ultimatum:

Murdoc's life or an all-out bloodbath.

It wasn't hard to believe they would make good on that threat. Not when roughly fifty assassins clad in black leather armor and cloaks stood before us, armed and ready. They all wore those signature silver bracers as they remained motionless, blocking the way beyond the gate of the small, slapped-together military fort where Jaevid had sent us.

"Which one of you is Murdoc?" Seasoned Lieutenant Eirik Lachlan demanded again, his gaze panning across the crowd gathered around him at the gate.

My heart hit the pit of my stomach like I'd swallowed a brick of solid iron. My head spun, and my hands instinctively curled into sweaty, shaking fists at my sides. I didn't dare to move, speak, or even glance around to see where Murdoc was. Somehow, doing that felt like I might betray his position. He had to be somewhere nearby, though. He'd come with us to the gate. I knew that much. But what would he do? Was he going to step forward? Give himself up? And if he did, how would Lieutenant Eirik respond? Was he seriously just going to hand him over to the Ulfrangar to be killed?

No, surely not. We'd only just met the lieutenant an hour or so ago, but he didn't seem like the kind of guy to just lie down and submit to the threats of assassins. He was a dragonrider, after all. Not to mention, he had a compound full of his comrades waiting right here, didn't he? We didn't have to give in to the Ulfrangar's demands—not when we could fight. The Ulfrangar were strong, but they were no match for a bunch of dragonriders.

Unless ... there was something else going on here, something I was missing.

That idea closed around my mind like an icy fist, making my head pound with sudden pressure as I stared at all the

Ulfrangar waiting there like dark specters in the night until the gate boomed shut. Even with that barrier between us, I didn't feel any safer.

My thoughts tangled like thorny vines, painful and pricking, as I tried to figure out what I should do. The Ulfrangar agents weren't stupid. They wouldn't do something like this unless they were certain they had the upper hand. I didn't know much about them, but I was sure about that much.

I flinched, every muscle locking solid, as a tall figure stepped forward from our group.

Then I couldn't help but look right at him.

"I'm Murdoc," he replied quietly, his tone strangely calm—almost like he'd already decided he wasn't going to fight this at all. Even his expression, with his head slightly bowed and his gaze fixed vacantly ahead, was all wrong. I'd never seen him make that face before.

I'd never seen him look ... defeated.

Eirik made a thoughtful sound in his throat and studied Murdoc for a long, silent moment. Every heartbeat in my chest made my head throb and my breath come in fast, frantic pants. I couldn't let this happen. I couldn't let Murdoc give himself up. Not like this. Not when things were still so wrong between us. I didn't want to forgive him for being involved with my father's death. Whatever role he'd played in that, I didn't want to let it go. Not yet.

But I didn't want him to die, either.

"Very well," Eirik murmured, flicking a look at the rest of us before nodding back toward his tent. "It seems we have until dawn to sort this out. All of you, come with me."

What? Until *dawn*? That was it? How long was that? A few hours?

My heart gave a painful, wrenching thud in the back of my throat.

I took off right behind Eirik and Murdoc, following them

back through the compound quickly and quietly. The eyes of every dragonrider standing on either side of the rows of tents and campfires followed us the entire way. It took everything I had not to glare back at them. Not out of anger, though. This didn't have anything to do with them. It was frustration, I guess. Humiliation that we were back in the same position once again. I hated this—being cornered by those soulless murderers over and over. Running like scared rabbits from one place to the next. We couldn't keep doing this.

It had to stop.

ONE BY ONE, OUR ENTIRE GROUP FILED BACK INTO EIRIK'S private tent and stood around his desk, solemn faced and completely silent. Isandri, Phoebe, Murdoc, and I waited while Eirik went to go retrieve Reigh from one of the partitioned rooms where he'd been resting. Boy, was he in for a rude awakening.

The tension hung thick and heavy over us, and no one dared to speak. I couldn't even bring myself to look any of them in the eye. Not when my face was still flushed with anger, and my heart was pounding like a war drum in my ears.

Reigh was still fastening his sword belt around his hips as he shambled in behind Eirik, groggy-eyed and scowling with all his red hair mussed up. He limped a little with every other step, as though his injuries were still causing him pain. Based on what I'd seen earlier when I helped him change bandages, I knew Reigh was still in no shape to fight. He'd barely survived from our last encounter with these brutal assassins. They'd shot him full of poison arrows and nearly killed him, and it was only the fast work of Phoebe and Kiran that had saved him. No way was he ready to take them on again.

"What have you guys done now? We haven't even been

here three hours yet," Reigh grumbled as he rubbed at his face. He muttered elven curses under his breath as he staggered over to stand next to me.

Thankfully, I wasn't the one who had to break the bad news to him.

"Seems some of that trouble you mentioned before has already followed you here in the form of a company of assassins camping outside my gate." Eirik's wooden chair creaked as he sat down and placed the black parchment letter from the Ulfrangar on his desk in front of him. He sat and stared at it for a few agonizing, quiet seconds. Then, at last, he looked up at us and sighed. "It's barely four hours until sunrise. That isn't long enough to call for reinforcements, or obtain Her Majesty's permission to strike against those people, even if I sent my fastest riders right now. But you are a Prince of Maldobar, Reigh. Technically, your word is all I need. Assassins or not, I've got dragons enough to scorch them to soot, if that's what you want me to do. All you have to do is say the word."

Reigh's expression darkened, his jawline going tense as every trace of bleariness vanished from his features. He opened his mouth like he might be about to give that order, but Murdoc spoke first.

"Doing that would get a lot, if not all, of your men killed."

"Hah! They can't possibly hope to take this compound with only a few foot soldiers," Eirik balked as he sat back in his chair. He cut his earthy, light brown eyes around at all of us and frowned suspiciously. "Unless you know something you haven't told me."

"The agents outside were likely only sent to get your attention. It's the ones you don't see that are the ones meant to do the real work here. The ones standing at your side, wearing the armor of your comrades, are the Ulfrangar you should fear," Murdoc insisted, his voice far emptier and more monotone than usual. Something about that look in his eyes, like his soul had already separated from the rest of him, set alarm bells tolling in my head. I'd never seen that look before, and it chilled me right down to the marrow.

"Are you suggesting there are Ulfrangar agents hiding within *my* ranks?" Eirik growled through his teeth, as though that suggestion was way over the line.

"No, I'm not *suggesting* anything. I'm *telling* you Ulfrangar do not make empty threats. They don't usually make threats at all. If they've bothered to offer us a chance to avoid bloodshed, you can be certain there are Ulfrangar somewhere in this compound already." Murdoc flicked a glance past me to Reigh, something almost pleading in his eyes. "You don't have a choice. Having me in your company has already caused a lot of people pain and hardship. But I can't live with the knowledge that I've caused the deaths of these men. I am *not* worth the lives of thirty-three dragonriders, and you know it."

Reigh crossed his arms, meeting Murdoc's desperate expression with a stubborn scowl. "I didn't take you for the type to be a martyr."

"I'm not," he snapped, his eyes wide and nearly crazed with urgency. His voice stayed hushed, and he spoke quickly as he took a step closer to square off with Reigh face-to-face. "I'm being realistic. There's no running from this. There's no fighting it. This is their final solution. I've told you all from the start that they would never let me go, and you were the one who barely walked away from it the last time they came for me. Now they'll do what they have to in order to see that my oath is kept, even if that means making an example of every soul in this camp."

"Except that you took no oath," a man's deep, familiar voice interrupted from the doorway.

We all turned to look, gaping in unison at the two, very recognizable figures standing together in the entryway to

Eirik's private tent. An aging human man with graying hair, a neatly trimmed white beard, and cold amber eyes glowered back at us like he'd just caught us all doing something heinous. Right beside him, a petite, staggeringly beautiful woman with long pointed ears studied us, as well. Granted, she didn't look as angry. More curious, I guess. Her silvery-white hair hung in a thick braid far past her waist, and she had one hand on her hip while the other gripped an ornate longbow.

My stomach gave a frantic flip, and I blinked hard a few times just to make sure I wasn't hallucinating. Nope. Definitely not.

King Jace Rordin and Queen Araxie of Luntharda had found us.

CHAPTER TWO

King Jace had mentioned something about going to get his wife when he left our company back in Dayrise. Honestly, at the time, I'd just assumed he was referencing some old, inside joke between Jaevid and him. They teased one another a lot like that.

Staring at the breathtaking elven woman, my brain scrambled at the realization that, no, he hadn't been joking about that at all. Queen Araxie cast her shimmering, multihued eyes around the room at us. Her controlled expression was impossible to read, and her fine robes of vividly colored silks and ornate leather armor marked her as royalty. She didn't look nearly as old as Jace did. But, then again, it was honestly hard to tell. Gray elves didn't show their age like humans did. Er, well, not physically anyway. Their lifespans were supposedly about the same as ours, but their physical bodies didn't wrinkle and sag with time quite as much as they got older. The queen was an excellent example of that. There were a few fine lines around her mouth and in the corners of her eyes, a sort of diminishing thinness to her frame, and a knobbiness to her hands—but none of that took away from her beauty ... or the keen look of suspicion in her eyes when she considered Murdoc.

"Your Majesties, please forgive me, I had no idea you were coming here." Eirik snapped to his feet, stumbling all over himself as he gave a brisk salute.

The old king came closer, and immediately waved him off. "Which is precisely what I intended. I may be past my prime, but I still know how to sneak past Ulfrangar and dragonrider surveillance. What do you think I've spent the last thirty years teaching my sons?" He gave a dry, throaty chuckle. "You've got quite a problem on your doorstep, haven't you, Lieutenant?"

Eirik deflated some and sank back on his heels. "So it would seem. And not much time to fix it. We have until dawn to deliver Murdoc to them."

"Until dawn? She's being generous, then." King Jace kept his piercing stare fixed on Murdoc with purpose as he stepped farther into the tent. "You were still a pup earning back your patronage price. The debt of your defection is not yours to repay. That was why they sent Rook after you. He was your handler. It was his responsibility to hunt you down and punish you for your defection. You were his mistake to correct."

Murdoc stiffened, his face going paler in the warm light of the lamps flickering around the tent. "Rook is dead," he managed in a shaking whisper. "I have no handler. And even if I did, it wouldn't matter. My life is forfeit either way. The punishment for defection is death, even for a pup."

"True," Jace conceded with a knowing smirk. "But it may not be that simple. By the laws of the pack, you should be my heirling now. That status complicates things a great deal—likely far more than you realize. There are great powers at work all around you, pup. This has become far larger than a mere struggle to save your life. Wheels are now in motion that you cannot even fathom, and that dark destiny waiting for you beyond the gates of this modest fort is not even aware of it."

Murdoc's hazel eyes went wide. His mouth fell open, but he didn't make a sound.

What? Great powers? What was Jace talking about? Did this have something to do with Jaevid? He definitely qualified as a great power, but he wasn't even here.

"Make no mistake, your situation is dire. There's no denying that. I'm just not sure you fully grasp what is truly at stake." Jace flicked his gaze back to Eirik. "The boy speaks the truth, though. You shouldn't assume everyone within the walls of this compound is your ally. The Ulfrangar have spent thousands of years perfecting the art of infiltrating every possible court, guild, legion, and tier of society around the world. Normally, they wouldn't want to compromise their agents working within the ranks of an organization as exclusive as the Dragonriders of Maldobar. It's costly and risky to get them there in the first place. Exposing them would mean compromising those individuals that undoubtedly feed them valuable information. But the task of punishing this pup has become a matter of pride now. Their leader, the Zuer, has been shamed in her failed attempts to bring him in. Her reputation now hangs in the balance. Failing this time would call into question her effectiveness as their leader. For those within the pack, weakness is unacceptable."

"You think she's coming here to deal with me personally." Murdoc's voice was barely more than a trembling whisper.

Jace nodded slowly, memories like dark flames dancing in his eyes. "With a gesture like this, demanding your life or an outright battle against a company of dragonriders out in the open? Yes. I do believe the Zuer herself will come for you at dawn. To say that she is acting desperately would be correct, because now her life and station within the Ulfrangar hang in the balance, as well. If she fails to kill you this time, she will have brought great shame upon the Ulfrangar. She will have to endure rivals attempting to drag her from her throne, revolts within her ranks, and eventually her own demise. To get out of this mess with her pride and position intact, she must make a public example of you to the rest of her order."

Murdoc's throat jumped as he swallowed, and once again, I saw real fear seep into the corners of his face. It made my chest go tight, my lungs squeezing around a rising surge of panic that left me numb. That was the same look he'd given me right before he'd told me about his possible involvement with my father's death.

And it filled me with the same cold bite of dread it had then.

Nothing frightened Murdoc—not when it came to fighting. At least, not that I'd seen. We had been up against some pretty terrible odds before, and I'd witnessed him face down our enemies with a defiant sneer even when things seemed hopeless. So if the idea of this woman, the Zuer, coming here was something that scared him ... then we should all be terrified.

THIS NEW REALIZATION ABOUT WHAT WE MIGHT REALLY BE up against settled through the room like a toxic vapor. The Zuer was probably coming here—right to this compound—to kill Murdoc herself at dawn. That meant it was also a fair bet that those Ulfrangar she'd posted outside the gate were probably the best she had. Fighting them would be more dangerous than ever. People would die.

"Running isn't an option. You can be certain they're watching for that. And fighting them head-on will end in a bloodbath." King Jace leveled a harrowing stare upon

Murdoc, all the intensity of those memories still flickering in his steely eyes. "Fortunately, the only question remaining is actually fairly simple, but it's one you'll have to answer for yourself, just as I did. There was a time when I saw my death as a final sort of release from a lifetime of shame, murder, deceit, and cowardice. I ran from the Ulfrangar, and only escaped because a monster in a crown found some use for me as his hired killer. I wanted to die. But when I thought that time had finally come ..." Jace paused, his gaze drawn to the elven woman at his side as though by gravity. The smile that softened all his hard, chiseled features seemed to melt past every cold word that had left his lips. "I was given a new path, instead. A rebirth. A chance to become something better. I didn't know if I would be successful, and I certainly didn't count myself worthy. But it was better to try and fail, than to die in shame."

Queen Araxie smiled back, bumping her arm against his coyly.

Jace leaned down, pressing a kiss against her hair before he cleared his throat and looked back at Murdoc. "I don't envy where you stand now. What lies before you is going to hurt. But I think you've known that all along. And now you must answer that one, simple question. Do you want us to save you? You cannot save yourself from the Zuer's wrath this time—not without significant help." Jace cocked an eyebrow, tilting his head to one side as his expression became curious and pensive, as though he were picking apart every tiny move Murdoc made. "Would you have us hand you over to your certain death? Or are you willing to tempt fate once again, pup?"

I almost missed it. Standing across from Murdoc, I barely caught the flicker of his glance darting in my direction for the briefest instant. I tensed. A hard knot lodged in my throat, making it difficult to breathe. Was he expecting me to say something? To object? Or demand that he continue to fight this?

I tried. But every time I reached for the right words, everything in my mind became so loud I couldn't even hear myself think. That anger and grief welled up too fast, roaring through my head like a tidal wave I couldn't escape. I didn't know what I wanted or how I felt.

I just ... didn't want Murdoc to die.

King Jace seemed to sense the awkward tension rising between us. He cleared his throat again and raised a hand, as though to pause the discussion altogether. "Perhaps we should have the rest of this conversation privately," he suggested. "My dear, why don't you take the rest of Jenna's distinguished hunters outside to ready themselves. Whatever happens next, I think we should all be prepared."

The elven woman cast him a quick, knowing smile before she motioned for us to go with her back outside. Phoebe, Isandri, and Reigh followed wordlessly.

But my feet wouldn't budge.

I stood there, staring at Murdoc as my heartbeat thundered in my ears. He wouldn't even meet my gaze, and kept his face turned down at the ground between us. With his features still swollen and bruised where I'd punched him, his quivering jaw clenched hard, and his broad shoulders curled forward as though he were folding in on himself, I couldn't remember him ever looking so small.

I didn't recognize him at all.

But I knew deep down, like someone had carved it into my brain, that this meant he was giving up. He was going to surrender to those monsters, trembling in fear before them like a scared little kid. Where was the bloody-knuckled brawler I'd known from the prison camp—the one who had beat down any thug who tried to take advantage of us? Where was the coldly defiant warrior who had fought

Rook? The strong and capable duelist who'd taught me to fight?

I couldn't find that person anywhere as I studied his face.

And I hated it.

Words burned through my chest, confused and angry like a tangled rat's nest of red-hot wire. I sucked in deep, furious breaths. I wouldn't let him do this. Murdoc would *not* just give up. Not now.

But before I could say anything, Jace's voice growled my name like a warning. "Thatcher. You need to step outside."

I cast the old king what was probably an extremely inappropriate glare of defiance. Step outside? But this wasn't—

"Go, Thatcher," Murdoc muttered, his voice tight and shaking as he glared up at me suddenly. "This has *nothing* to do with you."

CHAPTER THREE

I stood outside Lieutenant Eirik's tent, staring at the closed flap. It was just a piece of heavy canvas, but it felt like a door that had just been slammed right in my face. Now I was on the outside, cut off from even being a part of the conversation that would decide Murdoc's fate.

And I didn't know what to do. I didn't know what to say, or think, or feel. Jaevid's words burned through my memory. No one knew for sure if Murdoc had really been the one to kill my father that night in Thornbend. I should've guessed it was a possibility long before Murdoc ever brought it up. But did that really absolve him of being involved in it at all? Should I just let it go? Act like it didn't matter? Should I even want him to live?

Boot steps approached, crunching over the ground and finally stopping right next to me. "Thatcher?" Reigh asked. "You all right?"

I bowed my head some. "No."

"Afraid Murdoc's going to give up and turn himself in?" he guessed.

My head hung lower, and I couldn't even muster up the nerve to answer. I guess I didn't have to, though.

Reigh clapped a hand on my shoulder and gave me a small shove. "Come on. You can mope all you want over there with the rest of us."

I followed him around to the side of Eirik's tent where Isandri, Phoebe, and Queen Araxie were gathered around a campfire ring. They sat on a few wooden crates and boxes that had been dragged close to the fire's edge as makeshift chairs, their faces lit by the warm glow of the flickering flames. Phoebe looked every bit as miserable as I felt, and Isandri had a crease of worry in her brow. Only Queen Araxie seemed calm and unconcerned as she used a long metal poker to stoke the flames.

They all looked up as we approached and sank down into the two remaining seats, but no one said a word. Nothing but the crackle and pop of the campfire, and the occasional distant sound of growling dragons or voices of soldiers, filled the heavy silence. Minutes passed, maybe longer, and all I could do was sit there, numb and motionless. I stared into the glowing embers while my thoughts ran wild, imagining every terrible thing that might happen in the next few hours. What was going on back in the tent? What was Jace saying to Murdoc? Would anything the old king said change his mind at this point? Or was Murdoc too far gone to be convinced to fight the Ulfrangar again?

Was ... was it my fault? Because of the fight we'd had? Because I hadn't talked to him so we could try and fix this?

We sat that way, the atmosphere thick with anxiety, until at last, Queen Araxie gave a heavy sigh. "My, my. I've been told so much about the tenacity and courage of Jenna's hunters, but you are all rather grim."

"There's not much to be tenacious about until we know

what's going to happen with Murdoc," Reigh grumbled, sitting slumped forward with his cheek resting on his fist.

"I see. And you truly believe it's his choice to make?" The queen's opaline eyes shone in the firelight, reflecting in colors of silver, purple, blue, and green as she studied me.

"Well, it is certainly not ours." Isandri scowled disapprovingly. "We cannot force him to continue fighting this fate if he does not wish to."

"Is that so?" Araxie's smile was cryptic and still aimed directly at me. "It is my belief that we all need a little forcing every now and then, should we begin to lose our way. That is the function of friendship, I think. To help keep one another on the right path when our courage fails and our hope withers."

My mouth scrunched, screwing up involuntarily, and I looked away. I didn't want her to see me gnashing my teeth so my conflicted emotions wouldn't show.

"Jace has told me a great deal about you all. You've been through a lot in quite a short time. You've endured much," she continued quietly, her tone gentler. "I know it is not common in Maldobar for children to be taught about the ancient gods. We have tried to keep such beliefs and practices alive in my homeland, but as I'm sure you now know, some things have diminished over the years. I had never heard the tales of the godling children until now, and if it weren't my own husband telling me, I'm not sure I would have believed it."

I didn't dare to meet her stare as I rubbed at the back of my neck and mumbled, "I'm still not sure I even believe it."

She gave a light, melodic laugh. "You sound so much like him."

"Like who?"

"Jaevid."

I stiffened, my gaze snapping up to lock with hers just in

time to see a warm, almost motherly grin spread over her features. What? She thought *I* was like Jaevid? No—no way. He was the greatest hero Maldobar had ever known. There was no way I'd ever be anything like him.

"He was about your age when I first met him. Maybe a little older. But every bit as unsure of himself as you are now," she recalled fondly. "He doubted his birthright, too. He worried that his power would not be enough. And yet, he made everyone around him want to be better. I wonder if that is how Murdoc has felt, if being around all of you has made him desire to become better?"

My mouth clamped shut and I had to look away again as my heart gave a painful twist deep in my chest.

"I see great pain in your eyes, young man. Sorrow and betrayal. And in that way, I see myself in you, as well." There was a strange, cryptic edge to her tone as she gradually panned her eyes back down to the fire between us. "Did you not know about your friend's past?"

"No, he knew. But they had a pretty intense fight a few days ago, apparently," Reigh piped up, and I'd never wanted to hit him more in my entire life. "They haven't spoken since."

My mouth pinched up and I shot him a glare of warning. He didn't even know what our fight was about, right? He'd still been out of it thanks to getting shot full of poisoned Ulfrangar crossbow bolts. So Jaevid must have told him about it. Or Phoebe. Or Isandri. Ugh!! I didn't know who'd run tattling to him, and it didn't matter. It wasn't his story to tell to Queen Araxie.

"Ahhh, I see." Her shimmering, multihued eyes narrowed a little. "You must be asking yourself if you want him to live or not, then."

Every muscle in my body went stiff as I sat, biting down hard against the urge to storm off. I didn't want to sit here and listen to them try to pick me apart. Queen Araxie didn't even know me. We didn't have anything in common. She'd been born royalty, trained as a powerful warrior, and ultimately been a champion to her people in the Gray War.

I'd shoveled a lot of horse manure. Nothing about our paths were the same.

"I know *exactly* how you feel, Thatcher," she insisted as though she could somehow read my mind. "This might come as a surprise to you all. You're all too young to remember the Gray War when Maldobar fought my homeland of Luntharda. It was a brutal and devasting time. And when I first met Jace, all those years ago, I hated every breath he took. I wanted him to die. I wanted to be the one to end his life for all the pain he'd caused my family." Her expression had gone distant, as if the storm of battles past had carried her mind far away.

"Why?" Phoebe asked, her voice hushed and anxious.

"Because he nearly destroyed my entire family," the queen answered matter-of-factly. "He came with Jaevid to Luntharda, standing at the lapiloque's side as though he were a trusted friend. I couldn't understand it. How could Jaevid—the one sent from the god of all life to deliver us from decades of evil—choose the man who had murdered all of my brothers to be his ally? How could I be expected to help that man, too?"

"You mean ... Jace *murdered* your brothers?" Reigh's mouth hung open. I guess he hadn't heard this story before, either. Maybe it wasn't one they liked to share beyond the members of the royal family.

I couldn't believe it. Was that something Jace had done while he was still an Ulfrangar assassin? Or had it happened after he'd already defected and joined the dragonriders? Either way, how in the world had she wound up marrying the guy who killed members of her own family?

The queen leaned back in her seat some, her long white

braid swishing at her waist as she nodded. "Yes. And it filled my heart with anger and resentment for many years. I hated Jace. We fought many times on the battlefield before I actually spoke with him, or even saw his face beneath his helmet. That day he spoke of, the day he nearly died, *I* was the one who had cut him down. It was in the midst of a fierce battle. I shot his dragon down. I avenged my family." Her lips pursed some, seeming to pinch sourly at that particular memory. "But it did not fill me with the peace and satisfaction I had hoped for. And when I finally saw his face—when I looked into his eyes—I didn't find the monster I wanted so desperately to see. I saw a profoundly broken and empty man who had never known happiness or hope. I saw that he hated himself far more than I ever could. He didn't expect me to change my mind, or accept him in any way. He didn't want me to see him for anything except the murderous beast he believed he was."

My mouth twisted to one side as I thought that over. It definitely sounded a lot like the situation I was in with Murdoc now. Well, sort of. I hadn't hated him right away. But there were some eerie similarities. I was asking myself constantly if I wanted him to die or not, and what kind of relationship we should have. Could I ever call him a friend again? Should I? I didn't know.

That's why I had to ask her, "Why did you forgive him?"

Queen Araxie cast me a wistful, misty-eyed smile, almost as though she were staring at a version of herself from years ago. "Out of spite, at first," she answered with a soft little laugh. "Jaevid insisted that I spare him, so I was forced to tolerate his presence. Jace wanted me to hate him, and it seemed to bother him a lot more if I acted indifferent about his presence than if I lashed out at him. But the more I got to know him, the more I began to see glimpses of his true heart. He claimed to be this disgusting monster, but where before

I'd only seen the actions of a bloodthirsty murderer, I began to recognize a man's desperate and misguided attempts to stay alive. I saw how a lifetime of violence and hatred had nearly crushed him down to nothing. He didn't think his life had any value at all anymore. But more than anything else, I saw sorrow unlike anything I'd ever witnessed in his eyes—just endless, spiraling, confused anguish. And it broke my heart. I felt truly sorry for him."

I stared back at her, trying to process all that. I couldn't do it—not without picturing Murdoc in my mind. I knew that expression she was talking about. I'd seen that exact same look in Murdoc's eyes many times. Hopeless sorrow. Hatred for himself. An endless spinning vortex of shame that might consume him completely.

"I had grown up with a beautiful family that loved and cherished one another. I had lived in a palace, surrounded by fine things, and never known hunger or true fear until I was much older. The war was a faraway thing my parents worried about," the queen went on, finally glancing away to the rest of my friends. "But even Jace's life before the Ulfrangar was difficult. He was orphaned young, raised by an elder brother who was killed in the crossfire of the same war we would eventually fight one another in. It's as though our paths were destined to intertwine. The more I began to realize that, the easier it was to start letting go. He'd done terrible things, yes. But the world had done terrible things to him, as well. Standing before me was this shattered husk of a man who probably wouldn't even fight back if I decided to take my revenge and kill him once and for all. I decided ... I didn't want that. I found myself enjoying his clumsy attempts at kindness. I liked his crooked smile, and sarcastic laugh. I liked how easy it was to fluster him with any hint of flirting, and I couldn't ignore how my soul felt drawn to his. And when I saw him start to hope for the first time, to trust in me like no one else had, I knew ... I didn't want to hate him at all. I loved him."

Phoebe shifted uncomfortably, her cheeks flushing bright pink as Araxie's stare now settled on her. She kept her eyes fixed down at the toes of her shoes as she wound a lock of her bright red curls around her finger over and over.

"You're all quite young, but I learned long ago not to doubt the strength or heart of those destiny has chosen, regardless of their age. You must understand, though. Families, friends, lovers—all are structures built upon the same foundation. Trusting one another. Understanding that we are all imperfect and broken. Communicating our feelings. Forgiving each other our faults, but holding one another accountable to be better in the future. That is how we make each other stronger and more certain going forward. That is the only thing that will save Murdoc's life, and none of it is his to choose."

Queen Araxie looked over to the front of Lieutenant Eirik's tent, the light from the fires wavering over her face in a way that made her seem timeless, the sculpture of a long-forgotten goddess. "My husband does not understand this. He can't understand it because he sees things only from his side of the situation. I don't fault him for it, though. And I'm not saying that you must forgive Murdoc even if you don't want to. But believing that his path forward is his to choose without consequence to anyone else isn't necessarily true. Becoming a part of this group, your friend and brother in arms, means Murdoc's life is no longer his alone. His actions impact all of you, and he needs to be reminded of that—gently, of course."

Araxie spoke like she was still talking to all of us. She hadn't even mentioned my name specifically during that little speech. Even so, I got the impression there was only one person she believed should be the one to go in there and talk to Murdoc.

I frowned down at the campfire again, anger still prickling through my chest with every breath. Why did I have to be the one to go? Wasn't Phoebe, you know, in love with him or something? They'd done a lot of weird hand-holding recently, and with all the blushing, it seemed like a fair guess that something was up between them. She should do it, right?

And wasn't Reigh supposed to be the one in charge of our group? He'd let Murdoc come with us in the first place. They argued a lot, sure, but Murdoc had always deferred to Reigh as our leader. Shouldn't he be the one demanding Murdoc stay alive until the job was done?

Okay. Fine. I knew why it had to be me. I just ... wasn't ready. Not yet. Murdoc might not even listen to me at all. He'd already told me this wasn't any of my business—that it had nothing to do with me.

"If you are feeling as conflicted as I once did about letting go of those past hurts, then it might be good for you to hear from someone who has been through the same thing: I have not once regretted offering forgiveness. But there are many times when I have regretted holding grudges." Queen Araxie whispered, a somber heaviness in her voice that made me shiver. I didn't even have to look to know that she was staring straight at me again. "It's the words not spoken that haunt us, young hunters. It's the things we wish we had been brave enough to say to the people we hold most dear that follow us like dark shadows all the way to our graves."

4

CHAPTER FOUR

My heart sat like a heavy, cold stone in my chest as I looked toward the canvas-flap door to Eirik's tent. My thoughts had been so scrambled and chaotic before, like snowflakes whipping around in a blizzard's fierce winds. Now it was as though the storm had cleared. All those worries and frustrations slowly drifted to quiet stillness in my mind.

And in that silence, I was lost.

I knew what I had to do, but that didn't make it any less terrifying to think about. That ominous voice screamed in the back of my mind, telling me I wasn't ready to talk to, fight with, or even look Murdoc in the eye yet. Just the thought of doing any of those things made my stomach bind up and wrench like I might throw up. I couldn't decide if it was from anger, terror, or a scorching mixture of both.

I still wanted to hate him. I wanted him to hate me back. I wanted us to yell at one another and maybe even exchange a few more punches. Maybe then that smothering pressure would break.

It didn't make any sense. But I didn't have a choice now.

There wasn't time to hesitate. I needed to go into that tent, right now, and figure out what was going on. I'd never even heard what Murdoc's answer was. Had he really decided to surrender? Or was he going to try something else, something that might save him from the Ulfrangar's wrath?

Whatever it was, I needed to find out. I needed to hear it straight from Murdoc's mouth. After everything we'd been through, he owed me that much, at least, didn't he? And I owed him, too.

I owed him some honesty.

Sucking in a deep breath, I stood up and squared my shoulders.

Everyone around the campfire stared at me, but none of them spoke or tried to stop me as I walked away.

When I reached the door to the tent, I almost smacked right into Jace and Eirik. They emerged suddenly, their expressions grim and cold with focus. I scrambled to move aside, letting them storm past. They didn't even glance my way as they started for the front gate of the compound.

Oh no. What was happening? Where was Murdoc? Why wasn't he with them?

My skin crawled as a cold sweat ran down the sides of my face. My muscles flinched hard at every sound or movement as I looked at the tent's door again. Was he still inside? Or had he left? Had Jace and Eirik sent him away? Just what the heck was going on here?!

Storming into the tent, I stopped short in the main room where Eirik's desk stood, still bathed in the weak glow of the lantern light. The room was empty. There was no sign of Murdoc anywhere. Panic jabbed at the pit of my stomach and my pulse throbbed in my throat as I rushed from room to room, searching for any sign of him.

Bursting into a partitioned room at the back of the tent, I finally found him. Murdoc sat alone on the edge of a cot before one of the small wooden stoves, his cross-sheath already buckled across his back and his head hung low toward his chest. His black hair fell down almost to his chin now, hiding most of his face from view, but I could still see his jaw clench some as my footsteps crunched over the ground toward him.

"Murdoc?" I asked hoarsely.

He didn't look up.

"Look, we ... we really need to talk." My voice cracked a little, probably betraying the fact that I was a complete nervous wreck. My stomach gave a queasy twist like I might be sick.

He still didn't reply. He didn't acknowledge me at all, like I might as well have been invisible.

Like he didn't care.

And that—Gods and Fates, it stoked the flames of my anger back to life full force. I couldn't stop it then. The words poured out as I took an angry step closer to him. Every bitter word I'd wanted to yell at his back. Every stupid worry that kept pricking at my brain like thorns. It all broke past my lips in a rush. "I won't forgive you, Murdoc. Not if you do this. If you go out there and give yourself up to the Ulfrangar, if you let the Zuer kill you, I will *never* forgive you for anything ever again. I'll hate you till the day I die. I'll tell everyone what a coward you were to just lie down before them like a dog. And someday, in the afterlife, I will hunt you down and hit you again. I swear it."

Murdoc's head slowly raised and turned, his gaze panning up to meet mine. His eyes twitched with a mixture of shock and anger. He opened his mouth as though he might try to argue, but I didn't give him the chance.

"Maybe you did kill my father. Maybe you didn't. No one seems to know, and ... and I can't live the rest of my life wondering. So, I've decided to believe it *wasn't* you. As far as

I'm concerned, it was someone else who murdered my father. And I don't ever want to hear you say anything different," I growled, my face flushed so hot it made my lips feel numb. "You probably think that's stupid and naïve, but I don't care. It's my choice, just like my decision to count you as my family now. You're my brother. And I need you to freaking act like it."

Murdoc's mouth snapped shut and his eyes went wide.

"I need my brother to stay alive. And whatever I have to do, whoever we have to fight to make sure that happens, I'll do it." My voice shook some, and I looked down as the ground seemed to spin from all the rage and pain that had burst to the surface at once. "I can't lose you, too. Don't you get that? We've come this far because we stayed together and watched out for one another. Don't throw it all away now. Don't bow to them. Because if you do, I'll have no choice but to stand alone."

The cot creaked, and I glanced up to find Murdoc standing before me, his expression still tense and his brow knitted with uncertainty. He stepped closer, a full four or five inches taller than me. Once again, it made me feel like a pathetic little kid sniffling before him. Great.

"Thatcher, I—" He hesitated, seeming at a loss for words. Then his hand fell onto my shoulder and squeezed it some. "I am so sorry. For whatever part I played in what happened to your father, for betraying your trust and not telling you sooner, for letting you down over and over ... please forgive me."

I shrugged away from him and turned my back. I didn't want him to see my face screw up as I asked, "Does this mean you're going to surrender to the Ulfrangar?"

Murdoc didn't answer right away. I could feel his gaze on me, watching my every move like a lion sizing up an injured fawn.

"It's not that simple," he answered quietly. "Not anymore."

"What's that supposed to mean?"

His broad shoulders moved, flexing with a heavy breath. "It means, according to King Jace, there's someone else who has a claim on my life, too. Any decision I make might be irrelevant."

"But that's what you want, right?" I spun to face him again. "After everything we've been through, after how hard everyone has worked to keep the Ulfrangar from getting to you—you'd really just walk out there and surrender to them?!" My voice grew louder as my clenched hands shook at my sides. "We've been looking out for each other for almost a year now, right? You know you've been like family to me. I've told you that over and over. I've fought for you—Reigh, Isandri, Judan, and even Jaevid have, too. But it's like it all means nothing to you, and I really hate the way things are now. I really hate *you*. Or, no, maybe just the old you that did all those awful things before we met. And the worst part is, I don't know if you changed because you wanted to, or because I did some godling magical stuff to twist your thoughts and force you. I-I ... I never meant to do that. I never meant to warp your mind, o-or—"

He didn't make a sound as he surged toward me like a lunging wolf, grabbing my arm and forcing me to look him square in the eye. "Curse it, Thatcher! Just shut up! You have no idea how long I wanted to run, how many times I watched chances slip through my fingers when I might be able to escape them. I let the fear of what they might do keep me there," he snarled, bearing down harder as I tried to pull away. "It was you that night, Thatcher. You did make me defect, but it wasn't because of any stupid divine magic. You were just ... the first one who had ever talked to me like I was a person and not a monster."

I IMMEDIATELY STOPPED STRUGGLING AND STARED BACK AT him. Wait—really? Was he serious? No one had talked to him like he was a regular person? Even in the Ulfrangar? Hadn't Rook been, er, well, as nice as a handler could be to him?

I did recall overhearing some of the conversation between him and the other assassin on the night we'd first met. That guy hadn't called him anything except "pup." He'd shouted commands at Murdoc like he was an attack dog. Until now, I hadn't thought about what that might mean.

"I guess I never told you that before. I was embarrassed. Ashamed, too. You talking to me like that was bizarre, and yet, it was all I'd ever wanted for as long as I could remember. I'd worked, suffered, and killed to be treated like a person by the other members of the pack. I wasn't considered worthy of being treated as anything other than a semiconscious blunt object. Pups aren't people. They're raw clay. Crude weapons still being honed for the kill. Nothing more. Then you came along and did it on impulse, like it was nothing, while I still had a blade to your neck." Murdoc's expression fell, his own frustration seeming to fizzle as he slowly released his hold on my arm. Then I saw it again—that same look Queen Araxie had talked about. That hollow stare of an empty, broken man who had nothing left to hope for.

"You talked to me. You trusted me. You listened to me. You defended me before Queen Jenna, even though you barely knew anything about me," he said quietly. "You treated me like someone who had value, even though I was the last person in the world who deserved it."

"Well, there's no way I would have gotten out of Thornbend alive without you. And in the prison camp, you saved my life more times than I could count. It wasn't like I was going to just kick you aside the first chance I got and go on my merry way," I muttered.

"I know. But you could have, and no one would have blamed you for it. You didn't owe me anything. I was—am still—a criminal on the run. It's okay if you hate me, Thatcher."

I hung my head, taking a step back and rubbing my arm. Fates, he had a grip like a vice. I'd probably have a nice big bruise there. "I-I ... I don't. I'm sorry, I didn't mean that. When I get upset, I say stupid things. I just don't want you to give up. We got into this mess together. That's how I want to end it."

Murdoc stepped back, too. With his head bowed so low, all his shaggy, black bangs hid most of his face. "I-I don't want to die." His voice scraped and halted, like he was fighting to keep it together.

I froze.

"I don't know why you and the others want me around. I don't understand why you keep giving me second chances. Over and over," he rasped, biting hard at each word. "I haven't brought you anything but pain and suffering. I'm not worth it. I don't deserve that sort of ...."

"Mercy?" I guessed when his voice faded to silence.

Murdoc nodded.

I crossed my arms, taking a few seconds to consider my next words a little more carefully. "No. You don't," I decided aloud. "But I'm not sure anyone does, honestly. When it boils down to it, we're all jerks sometimes, so just get over it already. You don't get to decide if you're worth it or not. The people doing the fighting to keep you alive, the ones who care about you, that's something *we* decide."

He made an annoyed sputtering sound like he was choking on his own spit. "H-How can you—"

"No! I'm serious, Murdoc. You may be a big, brooding,

grumpy, violent, stubborn pile of horse flop sometimes," I paused, just for effect, and shrugged. "But you're *our* big, brooding, grumpy, violent, stubborn pile of horse flop. Never forget that."

Murdoc finally lifted his head, giving me one of his classic, blood-chilling scowls. "Oh, trust me, I won't."

I got a little thrill of terror up my spine when he narrowed his eyes slightly.

Oops. Too much?

Oh well. He did owe me a few punches, after all. I figured he'd settle that score sooner or later. "Come on. You need to tell me and everyone else what's really going on here. I saw King Jace and Lieutenant Eirik leave. I take it they have a plan of some kind?"

His brow creased, expression becoming distant and thoughtful again, like he was silently trying to figure out what was wrong with me. Good luck with that one, buddy. If not even Jaevid could figure that out, I doubted anyone could.

"Not a plan," he corrected. "More like a desperate idea."

I deflated. Right. Well, desperate ideas were sort of our specialty at this point. I guess I shouldn't have been surprised. "Your face looks awful, by the way," I added as he followed me from the room. I made extra sure I was moving along at a healthy distance when I made my jabs at him this time. If he came at me for revenge, I wanted a head start.

Not that it would help much, but a guy could try.

"I'm sure," he grumbled. "You hit *decently* for once."

"Yeah, well, this jerk I know has been teaching me some stuff," I baited again as I stopped at the tent's main door and held the flap back so he could go out first. I made sure to stay well out of arm's reach, though.

"I didn't think it was possible, but you're even more obnoxious than usual today," he muttered as he stomped by.

"There's that horse flop charm."

He gave me another squinty, wrathful glare over his shoulder. "This ends badly for you, you do realize that, right?"

"Yep."

"Good," he grunted, and I could have sworn I saw one corner of his mouth twitch into a smirk. "As long as you're aware."

CHAPTER FIVE

I made a point not to glance up at the sky as Murdoc and I stepped out into the chilly night air. My stomach clenched and cramped with dread, too afraid of spotting traces of scarlet sunlight blooming on the horizon to even dare looking. I knew it had to be getting close to sunrise. We'd flown for a while just to get here in the first place. How long did we have left until the Ulfrangar decided to make good on their threat? Hours? Minutes?

The commotion in the compound made for a good distraction, though.

Everywhere I looked, dragonriders were mustering arms, collecting their gear, and assembling in front of their tents in full armor. Their mounts gathered in, too, occasionally growling and snapping at one another as they assembled in the middle of the compound. Had Eirik given them orders to prepare for battle? Were they really going to fight the Ulfrangar? What did that mean for us?

I glanced sideways at Murdoc, but he didn't say anything and kept his grim scowl trained ahead to where the rest of our companions were still sitting around the campfire.

"Oi! Look there, I told you! That's him!" a voice called out suddenly. We both turned to look as a pair of younger dragonriders walked up, waving to get our attention. Both of them seemed to be a little older than Murdoc, maybe in their early twenties, and they smiled broadly at him. "Hey there! Fancy seeing you here! Been a while, yeah? Are you working for the royal court these days?"

Murdoc's eyes narrowed suspiciously. His hand edged toward the hilt of one of the longswords strapped across his back. "Who are you?"

"It's Sam and Kellan. Don't you remember? We saw you come in earlier, but didn't get a chance to say hello before the lieutenant dragged you off." The taller of the two men stopped abruptly, seeming to sense our apprehension. That, or he'd noticed the ominous and slightly terrifying scowl on Murdoc's face. "You're Fenn, aren't you? Fenn Porter? It's been a while!"

Murdoc hesitated, his scowl becoming more of a confused frown. "No. I think you have me confused for someone else."

"See, Kellan? I told you, dummy," the other rider snorted. "He's far too young. Just looks a bit like him, that's all."

The first rider, Kellan, flushed and waved his hands apologetically. "Ah. I see. My mistake. Gods and Fates, you do look like him though. The spitting image! You some relation to them? The Porters, I mean."

"Don't be daft! How would he even know who they are?" The second rider, Sam apparently, scoffed and gave his friend an elbow to the side. "Come off it. The boy obviously has no idea what you're talking about, and we're supposed to be mounting up. Let's go."

Murdoc's face paled a little, watching them walk away with his mouth hanging open some. A haunted sort of shock slowly crept over his sharp features like a fog bank drifting in from across the sea. It seemed to douse any hint of light in his eyes. For a moment, I thought he might run after them. Or start screaming.

But he didn't. Murdoc just stood there, slack-jawed, as more and more of that stunned uncertainty creased his brow and drew his thin mouth into a tense, hard line.

Maybe I shouldn't have been so surprised. Murdoc didn't have a family—at least not one he'd ever been able to find. It must've been like ripping open an old wound to have someone ask him that, especially when he was already reeling from the situation we were in now.

I bumped him with my elbow, trying to break his trance. "That was kinda weird, huh? You okay, Murdoc?"

His mouth clamped shut. "Y-Yeah," he answered quietly.

"Were they talking about the same Porters that we had stayed with?" I wondered aloud, not really expecting him to have an answer. There must've been hundreds of people in the kingdom with that family name, right? What were the odds?

Murdoc's broken whisper was so faint I barely heard him at all. "I ... I don't know."

REIGH WAS ON HIS FEET, STILL LIMPING A LITTLE AS HE paced back and forth near the campfire. He stopped when he noticed us approaching, his expression going blank in surprise. I guess he hadn't expected I would actually get Murdoc to come out and face us again. Bravo to me, I suppose. Too bad I didn't feel very proud of that fact. Yeah, Murdoc and I were back on speaking terms. For now, at least. But things were still tense between us. Worse than tense, really. Weird. Uncomfortable. Painfully awkward. And I didn't know how long that would last, or if it would eventually go away. Maybe it wouldn't.

I frowned and looked away, silently hoping Reigh and the others would be able to pick up on all that without me having to explain it. We had bigger problems to deal with at the moment.

"What's the plan here, Murdoc? Where are Jace and Eirik?" Reigh questioned as soon as we stopped at the fireside. The rest of our friends, along with Queen Araxie, stood up and gathered in closer to listen.

All I could do was shrug.

Next to me, Murdoc slowly shook his head and muttered quietly, "I don't know. He asked Eirik to divert attention by calling the camp to arms so he could make a stealthy escape by shrike without the Ulfrangar taking notice. I don't know why, or where he's going. King Jace was ... unusually cryptic. Probably afraid of who else might be listening in on our discussions."

"A wise decision considering you both believe there are Ulfrangar hidden within the ranks here," Isandri said approvingly. "We must assume everything we do and say is being watched."

"Right, fair enough, but that still doesn't answer my first question." Reigh flinched some, his voice hitching when he crossed his arms. His injuries were still severe. I'd seen that much firsthand. But he seemed determined not to let anyone else see how much pain he was still in. "I'm not sure if you've noticed, but we don't have a lot of time left here."

"I just said I don't know," Murdoc growled through his teeth. He cut a wrathful look up at the rest of our group through his lengthy bangs. "He made it sound like me walking out there to surrender wasn't an option because ... because there are other figures, powerful people, claiming ownership of my life now. I don't know what he meant, but if you're wanting me to make wild guesses, I'd assume that's who he's gone to talk to."

"*Other* powerful people?" Phoebe echoed, her delicate features creased with bewilderment. "Is he talking about Jaevid, maybe?"

"Possibly," Reigh mused as he rubbed his jaw. "He'd certainly qualify as powerful. But I'm not sure he'd ever declare ownership over anyone's life."

"I would agree." Queen Araxie ran a thoughtful hand along the arc of her bow. "It is not like my beloved cousin to make such claims."

"Queen Jenna?" Isandri guessed.

Reigh's mouth scrunched and he shook his head. "I doubt it. But, then again, she might be willing to make a few drastic claims in order to get the Ulfrangar off our backs. And we are technically in her personal service right now, so ... maybe?"

There was something distinctly dissatisfied in Queen Araxie's expression as she studied Murdoc. She went on rubbing her fingers along the intricate engravings on her bow, her lips pursed and multihued eyes as sharp as razors. "It is too far to reach the royal city before dawn, even on a shrike. They are faster than a dragon, yes. But the distance is too great. There are only a few places my husband might go and be able to return here before the sun rises."

Murdoc's shoulders trembled some as his gaze slowly panned up to meet hers, but he didn't say a word.

"Back to Dayrise, if he pushed it," Reigh mumbled. "Osbran isn't that far away. Port Marlowe, as well, but I don't know who he'd want to see there. Barrowton is too far. He could probably get there, but he'd be hard pressed to make it back in time."

Great. I couldn't think of anyone in those places King Jace might be going after. At least, no one who might also put a claim on Murdoc's life. Of all the likely candidates, Jenna seemed the most plausible. But Jaevid might be the only one in the area—if he hadn't already departed for Halfax with Phillip, that is.

"I don't guess you have any idea who he's going after? Someone powerful enough to give the Ulfrangar pause? Someone close by?" Reigh eyed the elven queen, his tone edged with suspicion, like maybe he thought she was holding out on us. "No creeping suspicions whatsoever?"

The queen straightened some and cast him an admonishing glare. "My husband has many secrets, young prince, and I've never pressed him for them. He has always told me when he was ready, I very much prefer to let him do it on his own than trying to pry it from him against his will."

"You trust him that much?" Murdoc sounded genuinely surprised. "Even knowing he was an Ulfrangar?"

Her smile was as cryptic as it was enchanting, making her strange eyes reflect the light of the campfire in hues of yellow, deep blue, and radiant red. "What is love if it has no trust? My faith in him far surpasses any uncertainty I might feel."

Murdoc's eyes widened and his mouth mashed into a crooked, bitter line. It only lasted a second, maybe less, but I definitely saw his gaze dart away toward Phoebe for an instant. He drew back slightly, shoulders curling in and jaw clenching hard as he turned his face away. "Look, I know what you all want from me. But I-I … I can't let Lieutenant Eirik send his men out there to fight the Ulfrangar," he faltered, seeming to force every halting word. "If you choose to stand with me before them, I can't stop you, but I also can't be responsible for the deaths of more innocent people. I can't live with knowing the finest soldiers in Maldobar sacrificed themselves for my sake. Please, Reigh, don't … don't let them do that. Not for my sake. Order Eirik to call them off and let me go out alone. If King Jace makes it back in time with someone he thinks can force the Ulfrangar to spare my life, then … so be it. But these are good men with families and children. They shouldn't be led to slaughter for me."

Reigh arched an eyebrow, giving an exaggerated slow blink and small shake of his head in surprise. "Wow. I'm so glad I wasn't the only one standing here for that display. Jaevid might not believe me later if there weren't lots of witnesses to back me up."

"What?" Murdoc's scowl was desperate as he glared back at Reigh in defiance. "Are you mocking me?"

"Not at all." Reigh chuckled and stepped forward to clap a hand onto his shoulder. "It's just all that 'don't let these people die in vain' self-sacrificing talk—I think that might be the most dragonrider-sounding speech I've ever heard!"

"I agree," Queen Araxie chimed in, grinning fondly. "If I didn't know better, I might have assumed it came from the lips of Jaevid himself."

Murdoc's head bowed lower and lower until most of his face was hidden by his lengthy bangs. His ears gave him away, though. They'd turned bright red. "I-I ... no, I'm nothing like him."

Queen Araxie stepped closer and stretched out a hand, lifting his chin with two of her fingers so that he was forced to look her in the eye. "No, you aren't. Not yet. But give yourself this chance to try, young one. Who knows, perhaps a destiny tied to the wings of a dragon will lift you higher than you have dared to imagine."

"Remember, the name of the game is shock and awe. If King Jace is correct, then we'll only have one shot at this." Lieutenant Eirik spoke quickly as he led the way through the compound.

Huddled behind him like a flock of ducklings, Isandri,

Reigh, Murdoc, and I passed the rows of armored dragonriders and their snarling mounts. Some of them were already taking off into the night in pairs of two, disappearing like massive scaled phantoms into the star-speckled sky. With any luck, the Ulfrangar would take notice that there weren't any dragonriders left here.

Well, except for us, of course.

My sweaty hand stayed clamped around the hilt of my xiphos blade as I tried not to look too hard at any of the men we passed. If I stared too long, I might start to wonder if they were one of the hidden Ulfrangar spies or not. I couldn't bear to let my mind go racing out of control down that road right now.

Focus, Thatch. Now wasn't the time to get queasy. I had to keep my eyes on our goal. All that mattered was clearing the Ulfrangar's potential battlefield—removing the dragonriders from the equation so they couldn't be used against us. That's why Eirik had given them all the order to go to Osbran immediately. There, they'd be too far for any of the Ulfrangar agents that might be hiding in their ranks to be of any use against us.

Or so we hoped.

"Queen Araxie and your artificer, Phoebe, are already in the towers. I suspect they'll have better range from there," Eirik continued. He kept a fierce pace until we reached the large gate that led out of the compound. The gate was still closed, giving us a small barrier between ourselves and the Ulfrangar forces waiting just on the other side.

"Reigh, you and Vexi are with me so we can make our move from the air. We will put down a perimeter of flame to contain the Ulfrangar within the area and prevent their escape." He turned to face us with a fiercely determined expression. "The rest of you, stall for as long as you can. We'll be watching for your signal."

"Assassins. Poisoned arrows. Slimy scumbag traitors hidden in our own ranks," Reigh fumed under his breath and spat on the ground. "You know, I actually miss when it was just crazy Tibran invaders. At least then you knew who your enemies were. They even had the decency to form nice, organized lines. Made them a lot easier to roast with dragon fire, too. Ah, the good old days."

"Yes, well, the nature of our enemy tends to change with the times. Welcome to life on the frontlines, Your Highness. Say your farewells quickly. We're out of time." Eirik cracked a smirk before he took the helmet from under his arm and slid it down over his head. He gave a hand signal to a few other riders who were waiting nearby, motioning for them to open the gate, and then started walking away toward his dragon.

Reigh faced us, giving me a long, reluctant stare with his mouth skewed to one side.

What? Was there something he wanted to say to me? Or was he just standing there thinking I wasn't up to this fight?

Uggh. Probably the last one.

He wasn't wrong, of course. But I was counting on a little divine magic to even the odds, or at the very least, buy us some valuable time.

"I'm no good at goodbyes, so let's just say good luck for now and leave it at that, okay? Watch your backs. Try not to die," Reigh mumbled at last. His gaze drifted between us and finally settled on Isandri. There was something strangely tense and apprehensive in his expression as he watched her, but I couldn't even begin to guess what he was thinking then.

There wasn't time to try, either.

Reigh gave a nod and turned away, crossing the short distance to climb into Vexi's saddle. It took him a minute to pull her away from Fornax and Shalni. They'd been snuggled up close to one another basically since we'd arrived, preening their scales and making deep purring sounds. Lieutenant

Eirik had mentioned that his dragoness, Shalni, had lost her rider in battle just like Fornax had. That thought made my heart twist painfully. What if they had been together in the final battle? What if they'd been partners or related somehow? Maybe it was better not to know.

Raising my whistle to my lips, I called Fornax over long enough to give him a parting scratch under his chin and to give Reigh and Eirik a chance to get airborne. My big orange dragon's scaly ears swiveled forward at the sound of my voice, and his sightless, milky jade eyes looked all around as he lumbered forward. The tension in the air, all the clinking of armor and shouts of the riders preparing for flight, must've been familiar—and not in a good way. Poor guy.

"Just keep to the plan, buddy. I know you want to fight right alongside me, but you have to hang back and watch over Phoebe. If anything goes wrong, I'll call for you." I gave his bony, horned brow a pat. "But remember, don't leave her behind. She's not like the rest of us. She doesn't know how to fight, so you've got to protect her. Think you can handle that?"

He smacked his jaws grumpily and blasted a snort right in my face. It blew my hair back and made me smile. I didn't blame him for being sulky about it. I would much rather try scorching all those Ulfrangar from the safety of his saddle. But we'd already tried that—several times in fact. And, yeah, it had worked in the moment. But it had almost gotten Reigh killed, burned down buildings, and ultimately only encouraged the Ulfrangar to hit us with even more brutal attacks.

This was the end-game. If we really were going to finish this once and for all, then we needed the Zuer to make an appearance. And if we were waiting for her with dragons ready to light her up on sight, we all felt pretty certain she wouldn't be dumb enough to storm straight into the fray. We had to play this *very* carefully.

"All right, just be ready. There's only one door in and out of this tower, so don't let anyone else get in there. If you smell or hear someone getting close, you've got my permission to toast them good." I gave his saddle one last, quick check before I patted the side of his strong neck and backed away. "Stay safe, big guy."

Fornax gave a low whine and dipped his head some, curling his tail around his legs. Next to him, Murdoc's much younger dragon scooted in closer and rubbed his head along Fornax's side as though trying to console him. Lieutenant Eirik had insisted on keeping the smaller dragon hidden here, as well. His hide might not be thick enough to stop Ulfrangar bolts from close range. Best to keep him tucked away safely unless we got desperate for reinforcements.

I had to look away. I hated this—being separated from him when we were both about to be in real danger. What if he needed me? What if I needed him?

My gaze snapped upward, sucking in a sharp breath as a deep rumbling filled the night air. It seemed to shake the entire compound and made the earth shudder under my boots. All at once, every dragonrider still lingering there under Lieutenant Eirik's command surged skyward. They took off like a flock of massive, scaled eagles, wings spreading to the early dawn. After doing one slow circle, I watched in tense silence as they veered away to the south—toward Osbran.

Then we were alone. Three of us on foot, two in the sky, and two in the tower against fifty armed-to-the-teeth Ulfrangar assassins and the Zuer. We did have a few dragons at our disposal. No problem, right?

Gods and Fates, we were going to die.

CHAPTER SIX

The sky burned deep scarlet as the first sliver of the sun peeked over the far mountains. It melted away the stars and offered just enough light to see as Murdoc, Isandri, and I stood at the gate of the dragonrider compound. Our time was up. And our answer to the Ulfrangar's threat would be crystal clear:

If they wanted Murdoc's life, they'd have to fight us to the last breath for it.

"Leave the Zuer to me," Murdoc warned as the gate before us groaned open. "Keep the rest of her forces back for as long as you can. If I can kill her, they will lay down arms and surrender to me. The law of the pack demands that anyone who defeats the Zuer has the sole right to claim the seat of power." His chest rose and fell with a deep, steadying breath. "I was only a pup, so they might decide I'm unworthy. But I don't think a pup has ever challenged a Zuer like this before, so I don't know for certain what they'll do."

"You really want to become the next leader of the Ulfrangar?" Isandri asked with a snort and devious grin.

"No—although it might be convenient for as long as it takes to order them to stop trying to kill me," he sighed like he'd seen that question coming a mile away. "After that, I'll happily leave them for Her Majesty to sort out."

She gave a breathy chuckle and sank lower into an aggressive stance, brandishing her gleaming staff. "Regardless, we are at your side."

I drew my xiphos and glared straight ahead as the opening gate revealed the line of ominous dark figures waiting on the other side. I couldn't tell that any of them had moved an inch all night. Creepy. Were they in some kind of trance? Or was it just another part of Ulfrangar training to be able to stand in one spot for hours on end without even scratching your nose?

"One way or another, we're ending this today." Murdoc's voice thrummed with a deep growl as he took a step forward.

The hiss of the wind through the prairie grass filled the silence as we stood, tense and ready, and glared straight ahead at all the Ulfrangar. With their faces mostly covered by black shawls and cowls, only their eyes were visible. The wash of the crimson light from the rising sun reflected off their silver cuffs, making them seem to glow deep red. Not a single one of them moved or made a sound. They didn't so much as blink. Fates, it's like they weren't even alive—like they might as well have been made of stone.

A tingle of fresh terror prickled up my spine as we waited. Seconds passed. Then minutes. My chest ached from how my heart thrashed hard against my ribs. What were they waiting for? For us to make the first attack?

At last, Murdoc called out across the distance between us, his shout echoing over the dew-laden grass. "You came here with an ultimatum—my surrender or a fight to the death. Now you have my answer. I will not ask the dragonriders to fight on my behalf, but make no mistake, I will *not* go peacefully. I will not surrender. If you want my life, you'll have to rip it from me here and now."

A cold gust of wind made my skin prickle. It rippled through the Ulfrangar's dark cloaks and carried in a bank of low fog, making them seem like a legion of dark spirits hovering not fifty yards away from us. Not one of them moved or made a sound.

Dread squeezed at my heart like the jaws of a steel trap, growing tighter and tighter until I could hardly breathe. I stole a sideways glance at Murdoc. He stood tense, one of his longswords already drawn, with his jawline went solid and his gaze narrowed straight ahead. Sweat drizzled down the sides of his face and his brow twitched some, as though he might snap at any moment and surge forward to attack.

Then, on the very back row of the Ulfrangar's ranks, something moved in the dim morning light. A shadow blurred through the mist, making it curl and shift. One by one, the lines of assassins before us began to part, stepping aside to make way for one figure to approach. Tall and slender, I couldn't tell anything about the individual that slowly approached thanks to the long cloak they wore. But it wasn't like the uniform the rest of the Ulfrangar had on. This cloak had been fashioned from a wolf's pelt, with fur as black as pitch and the head fashioned into the cowl. A single silver eye had been painted into the center of the wolf's head, and beneath it, a slender chin, black-painted lips, and stark pale skin were all I could see.

My stomach dropped to the soles of my boots. Was this really the Zuer?

"Well, well, well. When I saw all of your dragonrider friends depart, I assumed you might try to run again. Color me impressed. You've more audacity than I expected." A smooth, feminine voice cooed from beneath the cowl. Those dark-painted lips bowed into a cunning sneer as she stopped ahead of the rest of her hunting party. "What a waste. I saw your potential from the beginning. You might have gone far under my tutelage, pup. But now your fate is sealed. Step forward and die with whatever honor you may have left. There is no need for these fools to suffer for your betrayal."

Murdoc's chest seized with a shaking breath. His body gave a jerking flinch and his face went pale, as though just the sound of her voice caused him physical pain. Doubt fractured over his features, and in an instant, I knew.

He wasn't going to be able to do this. Not on his own. I didn't know this woman, or what she might have done to him in some wicked, twisted past he'd buried deep. But it was as though she had a hook set deep in his mind, and she could use it to pull him wherever she wanted.

"Hey!" I snarled suddenly, stepping forward and ripping my xiphos free of its sheath to aim the point straight at her. "Don't you dare dismiss me. You're the one whose fate has now been sealed. Ishaleon, God of Mercy, stands for this pup!"

"Adiana, Goddess of the Moon, stands for him as well!" Isandri hissed as she sprang forward, spinning her staff and cracking it off the ground once. The impact sent out a bolt of crackling, sizzling power that lit up the pale dawn with a radiant silver glow.

The Zuer's dark lips parted in a wide, delighted smile. "Ah, yes. The godlings have rallied around you, I see. Such passion. Such devotion. And yet, all in vain. Do you think my pack has not felled gods before?" She stretched out an arm from beneath her heavy, wolf-pelt cloak. The black, oiled leather armor shone as she raised a hand out to the side. "Allow us to demonstrate."

A snap of her fingers cracked through the cold morning air.

And in an instant, all hell broke loose.

Blood ran down the side of my face and seeped past my clenched teeth, thick and warm. My pulse kicked fiercely in my chest, keeping rhythm with the swing of my blade as I pulled from every combat lesson Murdoc, Reigh, and Jaevid had ever given me. Parry up. Defensive stance. Press in for strike one. Sidestep. Dip low and strike two. Parry left. Now make the kill.

Back-to-back with Murdoc, Ulfrangar closed in from every side. Crossbow bolts howled through the red twilight. One punched through my crude armor at my shoulder, making my vision go white with pain for a second. But I didn't stop. Focus. Control. I couldn't lose it now.

Three Ulfrangar fell. Then two more.

Murdoc spun in a blur of deadly motion, every strike flawless and precise. Isandri flipped and wove through her enemy's assaults, jabbing the brutal, tri-dagger tip of her staff easily through the Ulfrangar's leather armor. Another crack of her weapon off the ground sent out a blast of divine energy that blew a few of them off their feet.

Before me, an Ulfrangar surged in, dipping under one of his comrades as fast as a shadow. He lifted a crossbow and leveled it right at my head. I tensed. Curse it! I'd let him get in too close!

TWANG!

The Ulfrangar's eyes went wide over his face-wrap. His body lurched and went stiff, then dropped right where he stood. A slender arrow, fletched with colorful feathers, stuck out of his back.

I chanced a look up at the tower, barely able to make out the silhouette of a woman standing in the small window. Queen Araxie. W-Wow. I guess those stories from the Gray War about her deadly aim were all true, after all.

A pang of pain sizzled down my arm suddenly, making my fingers go numb so that I nearly lost my grip on my blade. I sucked in a sharp breath, biting down hard and taking a tactical step back. Was that arrow in my shoulder poisoned? Was it starting to take effect? Phoebe had said before that the toxins they used would cause paralysis. How much time did I have until I couldn't even move anymore?

I blinked hard and shook my head, trying to clear the fog that made my thoughts go hazy and my ears ring. No—I wouldn't lose focus. Not now!

"Flip parry!" Murdoc shouted suddenly over the clang and clash of his longswords.

I set my jaw and dropped to a knee, immediately making a sideways swing. My xiphos smashed against an enemy blade howling in from my left just as Murdoc leapt into an aerial backflip and landed in front of me, slicing through another assassin to my right. We moved in unison, me scrambling to keep up with Murdoc's lethally efficient pace, as we kept the Ulfrangar at bay. But I could feel each of my swings slowing. My grip faltered as my hand went numb. The poison was spreading. I couldn't even feel the bolt of the arrow embedded deep in my shoulder now.

"I-I'm hit," I managed to wheeze as I forced another whirling strike. "Call it down."

Murdoc turned and our gazes locked for an instant, then he shouted up toward the sky, "LIGHT IT UP!"

Isandri let out a yowl of affirmation that pierced the dawn like the screech of an eagle. A flash of sterling light exploded from amidst the throngs of Ulfrangar, and she broke skyward through a hailstorm of crossbow bolts in her winged feline form.

With a final deadly jab to an Ulfrangar, dropping the assassin where he stood, Murdoc leapt toward me and landed on a knee right at my side. I gulped in a deep breath, pulling all the frayed threads of my focus inward as I squeezed my eyes shut. I stretched out a hand over us, a groan of pain leaking past my lips as the sudden rush of divine power burst from somewhere deep inside me. It hit like I'd been struck by lightning, blowing through all my mental fortifications immediately, and radiating outward in a rush like wind in a wildfire. A wavering globe of golden light bloomed outward from my hand, closing around us like a dome of raw energy.

My body shook. My lungs spasmed for every tiny, desperate breath as it felt like my mind was being stretched inside out. But I couldn't let that shield drop. Not yet.

WHOOOOM!

Fire exploded into the air, pouring from the sky in two plumes that encircled the area around us. Flames, arrows, and swords smashed against my divine shield, making it ripple and waver. But nothing broke through. Ulfrangar screamed, catching sprays of burning dragon venom and trying desperately to douse it before it ate through their armor. More of Araxie's arrows from the tower rained down two and three at a time, dropping one assassin right after another.

I let out another rasping cry of pain as my palm burned like I'd dipped it in molten metal. My vision doubled and went blurry. A little longer—I just had to hold it for a little bit longer. The more Ulfrangar they could take out without having to worry about hitting one of us, the easier the fight would be. We might actually stand a chance. I could do this. I wouldn't fail. Not when I'd already come this far.

Out of nowhere, the burning in my hand stopped. I blinked, my vision suddenly clearing.

"THATCHER!" Murdoc shouted my name, but it sounded strange. Or maybe that was just the ringing in my ears growing louder. His blood-spattered face had gone white with horror as he stared at me.

Wh-What? What was happening?

Behind him, my shield of divine energy melted away like snow in sunlight, seeming to break down around something long, dark, and spear-shaped that had punctured straight through it.

But ... how? Nothing had been able to pierce my divine shield before. What was happening?

Murdoc bared his teeth in fury and growled a curse, looping an arm around my shoulders as my legs suddenly buckled. He thrust his sword up in a frantic parry, barely managing to block an incoming sword point as he slowly let me down to sit on the ground. "Stay with me, Thatcher! I've got you! Just hang on!"

Stay? What did that mean? I looked down as he reached for my stomach. That's when I saw it—the point of that dark spear that had rammed through my divine barrier was now buried deep into my gut.

Oh ... oh no.

The pain hit me so abruptly I couldn't even react. I couldn't scream. I couldn't breathe. Bitter cold washed over me like I'd been shoved beneath the surface of an icy river. I stared at the deep crimson blood soaking through my breastplate in shock. My hands trembled as I reached for the shaft of the spear. As soon as my fingers brushed the surface of it, the entire weapon dissolved into a curling black mist and disappeared, leaving nothing but an empty hole in my armor behind.

Still sitting on the ground, I struggled to look up again. My head bobbed as tremors of agony made every muscle in my body spasm. Standing not even twenty yards away, the Zuer curled her fingers in a gesture that summoned a wisp of dark smoke. One jerk of her wrist made the mist solidify, and the spear appeared in her grasp. One corner of her dark-painted lips twisted up into a pleased grin.

"What a mighty gift you have, little godling. But I have

mighty allies, as well. You are not the only ones with godling power at your disposal." she cooed with a voice like warm venom. "Iksoli sends her love."

7

CHAPTER SEVEN

Iksoli? This was her doing? But how?

It didn't make any sense. How had the Zuer managed to pierce my shield? How had she survived Eirik and Reigh showering everything in dragon fire? Was she telling the truth—was it really a manifestation of Iksoli's divine power? Did this mean they'd been working together all along? Or was this some new deal they'd struck?

I scrambled to make sense of the storm of questions whirling through my head as everything around me grew dim. I slumped back and hit the ground next to Murdoc, as my breaths came in shallow, desperate puffs. Everything seemed to grow colder and farther away, as though I were looking at the world through frosted glass. Voices echoed around me. Shouts of panic and rage. The Zuer's wicked laughter.

Oh gods, was I ... dying?

No! I couldn't die! Not now—not like this! I couldn't let everyone down. What if they needed my help?

And Murdoc. He still stood over me, his arms and legs now marred with deep cuts and slashes and crossbow bolts bristling from his leather armor. He snarled like a beast as he forced the Ulfrangar to back away from me with wild swings of his swords. That idiot. If I died, he might do something really stupid and get himself killed, too. He might stand there over me, defending my lifeless body until the Ulfrangar cut him down, as well. Then who would be left to fight Iksoli? Isandri couldn't handle it all by herself. She'd need his help.

No. Murdoc wouldn't die here. I wouldn't let that happen. My hand shook as I reached for the whistle buried beneath my breastplate and tunic and put it to my lips. My vision swerved and dimmed as I blew hard blasts into it, sending up a shrill call above the chaos.

An answering roar like a low roll of thunder resounded over the battle.

Through the wall of flames glowing in the early dawn, a massive dark shape rose up over the wall of the compound, stretching leathery wings wide to the scarlet sky. Fornax bounded over the wall with one beat of his wings, landing with a boom on the other side and baring rows of jagged fangs. His green eyes glowed in the light of the fire as his ears swiveled, tracking the sound of my call.

Four Ulfrangar standing close whirled to face him and raised their crossbows, taking aim at my dragon's head. Even standing so close, Fornax couldn't see them to know he was in danger. I started to blow another signal on the whistle, but before I could even catch my breath, another dark shape dropped from the sky with a *BOOM!*

A second dragon landed right in the fray, crushing one of the Ulfrangar under his weight and snatching another in his jaws. Murdoc's young drake, Blite, flared his spines and flung the assassin around like a rag doll before slamming him into the ground with a gory *crunch*.

Ouch.

The remaining two Ulfrangar fired their crossbow bolts at the younger dragon, one catching him in the side and making the dragon screech in pain. Fornax dove in suddenly, making wild snaps with his jaws and ripping another assassin off his feet.

Glancing back to the tower, I could barely make out the flash of coppery red hair fluttering in the wind through my daze. It was enough, though. Phoebe was there, and she had my goggles. A little aerial sight-assistance was all Fornax needed.

"Enough!" The Zuer's voice snapped out across what remained of her minions like the crack of a whip.

Everything stopped.

The Ulfrangar rushing in to attack Fornax and Blite withdrew immediately at her command. The ones battling against Murdoc bounded back and froze in defensive positions. The flurry of crossbow bolts buzzing through the air stopped. In an instant there was an eerie silence, filled with nothing but the crackle, hiss, and pop of the burning dragon venom.

Through the curling smoke and dancing flames, the Zuer's dark silhouette emerged like a prowling demoness. She spun that magical spear over her hand again and again, her face angled straight at Murdoc. Lifting her empty hand, she made a taunting, curling motion with her fingers as though to call him forward. One small, upward tilt of her head revealed a staggeringly beautiful face. Gods and Fates, she seemed a lot younger than I expected. And her eyes—they *glowed*.

My breath caught, and I winced. Was I seeing things? That couldn't be. But ... I'd seen eyes like that somewhere before, hadn't I?

Murdoc stood over me with a crazed look of fury twisted over his features. He still gripped a longsword in each hand, the blades dripping with blood, and turned to face the Zuer. His chest heaved with every ragged, growling breath as he stared her down like a cornered feral wolf.

"I am pleased, pup. The tales of your strength and defiance were not merely fanciful exaggerations, but I've tolerated more than enough arrogance and defiance from you," she seethed as she whirled that wicked black spear. "I have not come this far to be undone by some pathetic human whelp."

Murdoc's hazel eyes flashed with reflections of the flames as he gave each of his longswords a similar flourishing spin over his hands. "Then why don't you stop playing games and fight me yourself?"

There was something ancient and ethereal about the way she gazed across the distance at Murdoc, like a dark goddess stepping from beyond the Vale to meet him. "As you wish," she purred delightedly.

DARK BLOOD RAN THROUGH MY FINGERS AND OUT ONTO the grass as I gripped my stomach. The world spun and swirled, dimming in and out of focus. Every heartbeat ached, thudding slower with each second. But I couldn't look away. Murdoc was right, I had to hold on. I had to stay awake.

I-I ... had to ...

Before me, Murdoc and the Zuer dueled like something from an ancient fable of gods and heroes. She moved with inhuman speed, seeming to blur from one place to another like a phantom, all while brandishing that spear. Sometimes it would vanish into smoke, only to reappear in her other hand. Other times, I could have sworn she could make herself vanish for an instant, too.

Murdoc bore in hard, his teeth bared and his body drenched with sweat and blood as he matched her every move. His swords hummed through the air, ringing in a dark deadly melody as they clashed with her spear, her reinforced bracers, and glanced off her armor. He snarled and barked cries of frustration, ducking and weaving around her relentless assaults.

The way they pitched, dodged, spun, and leapt at one another with flawless, lethal grace—it almost seemed like a dance they'd rehearsed a thousand times.

The coppery warmth of blood filled my mouth as I coughed. Wiping my chin, I stared in horror at the smear of fresh crimson on my palm. My chest gave a shudder, and all of a sudden, I couldn't breathe. I sputtered and wheezed, falling forward as the coldness paralyzed me.

I barely managed to catch myself with one elbow, fighting to keep my head up. Gods, no! Not like this! I couldn't die—not yet. Not until I knew Murdoc would be okay. I needed to see him end this, to see him win his freedom. I needed to know he'd be okay, and that someone would be able to take care of Fornax.

"Thatcher!" Murdoc's desperate shout pierced the air as he suddenly looked my way just in time to see me flop limply onto my side. His guard dropped for an instant.

And that was all the opportunity she needed.

The Zuer smirked as she rushed him with a brutal assault, using the shaft of her spear to crack him across the face. The blow sent him staggering back, and she swept his feet with another whirling strike.

Murdoc landed flat on his back at her feet. The impact knocked one of his blades from his grasp, sending it sliding over the ground, far out of reach. He let out a yell of rage as he raised the other one, barely managing to put up a frantic parry and deflect another strike of her spear.

The Zuer laughed, her eyes shining with vicious pleasure as she stood over him like a cat over a caught mouse. She rained down blow after blow, toying with him, and preventing him from even trying to get to his feet again. "Rook taught you well," she snickered. "But make no mistake, your life is *mine*. Now, do as you're told and die."

Rearing back her spear suddenly, she took aim right at his chest. The brutal, barbed tip gleamed in the light of the rising sun.

Murdoc's eyes went wide.

I reached a shaking, blood-smeared hand toward him. N-NO!

WOOOSH!

Out of nowhere, a violent rush of wind kicked up around us. It howled through the battle like a stormfront, making all the flames swirl higher and higher. But they didn't spread. Instead, it almost seemed like the fire's flickering was growing *slower*. But why? How was that even possible?

With a deafening *WHOOM,* all the flames surrounding us suddenly froze in place and turned gray, like curled statues of silver glass.

The Zuer stopped mid-attack, the point of her spear less than an inch above Murdoc's heart. Her head snapped up, looking straight at me. No, not me. Her glowing gaze peered farther, focusing on something *beside* me.

I could barely lift my head enough to see the shape of a tall figure in a long, hooded cloak stepping past me across the grass. With wide shoulders flexed, the figure made a gesture with each hand that sent out another burst of wind.

SMASH!

It shattered every one of the frozen, silver flames like someone hurling rocks into a field of glass sculptures. Glittering shards peppered the grass and began to melt away.

The Zuer straightened, her gaze narrowing upon the figure with no traces of a smile anymore. "You," she seethed accusingly. "I might have known."

The figure didn't stop, the lengths of that long cloak

twisting and billowing in the crisp wind with every precise step toward her.

Was this another Ulfrangar? Someone else they'd brought to ensure their victory? With the cowl pulled down low and the figure's face pointed back at the Zuer, I couldn't tell.

Every assassin it passed took a calculated step back, but never dropped their guard. They kept their bowstrings taut and blades raised, their heads slowly moving to watch the figure stride by like a shark gliding silently past a reef.

Then the figure stopped. Its head turned some to consider Murdoc lying there on his back, gaping in shock. Even from a distance, I spotted two eyes glowing like tiny specks of candlelight underneath the hood. Locks of golden hair like bolts of satin hung down to the figure's chest. A narrow face and pointed chin appeared as it turned slightly to consider me, as well.

My stomach dropped.

Was that ...? No, it couldn't be. I was seeing things. Or maybe I was already dead, and this was some sort of weird hallucination I was having in the afterlife. It couldn't possibly be real—because there was absolutely no reason Arlan the Kinslayer would ever come here to fight for us.

Right?

No. Absolutely not. Everyone had insisted that Arlan didn't want any conflict with the Ulfrangar. He'd even said something like that himself when we'd met him in Dayrise. He didn't want to get involved with assassins. He didn't deal in murder.

So ... what was he doing here? How had he even known where to find us in the first place? Just what the heck was going on?!

Arlan gave me a brief, unconcerned glance before looking toward the Zuer again. The wind billowed in the lengths of his cloak and blew through his hair, but his smooth, ageless features never moved. He never made any expression at all, almost as though he were staring at her through a mask.

"Zarvan," the Zuer snapped from beneath her own hood, her voice spitting the name as though it were something foul.

Uhh, what? Zarvan? Who was Zarvan?

One corner of Arlan's mouth curled into a smirk. "I see you've not forgotten me, Sadeera. Good. Then you know why I've come."

The Zuer stood eerily still, studying him carefully. Her chest rose and fell, each breath deeper and faster than the one before. Her leather gloves squeaked as she clenched her hands into fists around the shaft of her spear.

I bit back a shout of alarm as she suddenly snapped her head back toward where Murdoc still lay at her feet. Wrath warped her beautiful features, as though she were silently weighing the option to end his life now or not. Oh gods, if she did, there was no one close enough to stop her!

"Pathetic," she seethed, "And here I had given you sole credit for masterminding such elaborate and convenient escapes from my pack again and again. I assumed Rook's training was to thank for it. Now I understand. You've had *help*. Clever. And yet immensely disappointing."

"You assume too much," Arlan countered, his tone still chillingly indifferent. "Do not mistake me for one who meddles in the mire of your barbaric pack. I did not come here for his life, dear sister." His brows drew together, and he slowly raised his hands. Currents of silver energy licked like sterling flames around his fingers as he narrowed his eyes. "I came for yours."

The Zuer brushed back her cowl, revealing a smooth, pale face as flawless as a fine porcelain mask. Hair like bolts of fine white satin hung down her back, and had been braided up over her long, pointed ears on either side of her head. Her black-painted lips pressed together bitterly, and her golden eyes shone like embers in the weak light of the dawn as she stared straight at Arlan.

Wait—did he say *sister*? Gods and Fates—the Zuer was an Avoran elf just like Arlan? And they were ... *brother and sister?!*

"What an interesting sentiment," she sneered, matching the cold hatred of his tone. "You know, I did wonder which slimy rock you'd hidden yourself under. Tell me, little brother, how long have you been down here wallowing in the affairs of these mortals? You look positively awful."

"I might ask the same of you." Arlan's tone cut with a venomous edge. "But, then again, the rags of lowland murderers suit you so well. Perhaps you should consider wearing them at court."

The Zuer's veneer of calm indifference shattered. In an instant, her features twisted into a look of pure wrath and she sprang over Murdoc, hurling her spear at Arlan in one lethal, fluid motion. The weapon streaked over the blood-spattered grass, aimed straight for his head, and leaving a trail of curling black smoke behind it.

Arlan didn't flinch. He didn't even blink. Standing tall and composed, his expression sharpened as his chin tilted slowly down to level a dominating snarl upon the Zuer. As fast as a viper's strike, he snapped a hand forward with his fingers spread wide.

The spear froze right before his open palm, suddenly halting in midair. Silver light crackled around it, shimmering like it'd been caught in an invisible forcefield.

Holy. Gods.

Arlan glared past the weapon as it hovered before him, slowly rotating. His eyes smoldered, but they weren't gold like they'd been before. Now, they shone with the same eerie, sterling light as that strange magic he used. "Do not toy with me, Sadeera," he warned. His lip twitched, curling into a snarl as he gave a gesture with his outstretched hand. "I am not one of your mindless pups."

CRACK!

The spear burst into a shower of silver light with a concussive pop.

"*You*," she seethed, her face twitching with fury.

"Yes, dear sister." Arlan licked his teeth like a dragon preparing to feast. "Come, let us finish what we started all those years ago."

PART TWO

MURDOC

CHAPTER EIGHT

I'd heard many stories of the Avoran elves, their incredible magical power, and their floating glass kingdoms throughout my life. All of those tales, usually whispered by merchant caravans around campfires, or woven by storytellers in tavern halls, had sounded a lot more like fables or myths than anything that might actually be true. After all, the Ulfrangar had not taught me much about them beyond a loose grasp of their language and strong advice to avoid them at all costs.

Now, shambling to my feet to watch the two ancient elven beings duel in the scarlet light of the rising sun, I could better understand why. This was why no one dared to cross the Zuer. This was why Arlan had been able to move with such obscurity and ease through society. The Avoran elves never left their homeland unless they were forced to—and that was a good thing. Normal weapons were nothing but a joke to them. Child's play compared to the force of their magical explosions and arcing beams of ancient power.

My heart pounded in my throat as I struggled to keep up with their blurring movements, both figures weaving and dancing around one another like striking serpents. The crackle and hum of each spell sent a current of power through the air that made every hair on my body prickle. I stumbled back as a bolt like a tongue of silver lightning snapped off the ground less than ten feet from me. One of my boots snagged across the body of a fallen Ulfrangar, and I flailed my arms to try to keep from falling.

"Watch it, pup," a gruff voice barked as a strong hand grabbed my arm to steady me.

I yanked away on pure instinct and whirled around, dropping into a defensive position with my longsword raised. Adrenaline poured over me like molten metal as I braced for combat, preparing to face another Ulfrangar assassin bent on killing me.

It wasn't.

King Jace frowned down at me from the back of a shrike, one of his eyebrows arched in a completely unimpressed expression.

What the—what was he doing here? When had he come back? Was he the one who'd brought Arlan here?

"Go get your dragon," he ordered. "This is our chance. We need to clear out while we can."

Another bolt of raw magical power sizzled through the sky and cracked off the ground behind him. It made the shrike screech in panic and flutter its translucent wings.

"Hurry it up, kid!" Jace yelled. "Unless you want to stand here and die on principle!"

Right. Good point.

I started for Blite at a sprint, but I only made it a few steps. Realization hit me like a kick to the face. Wait. No. I couldn't go yet.

Where was Thatcher?

Whirling around, I searched the area where I'd see him fall. Curse it all, he'd been struck by the Zuer's spear. I didn't know how bad it was, but I was willing to bet he couldn't get up on his own dragon without some help.

And I was not about to leave him in this hell hole by himself.

"Blite! Follow me!" I shouted as I forged back into the chaos, ducking stray bolts of magical power and scattering Ulfrangar who had begun trying to take cover, as well. Not that there was anywhere to go. I slashed my sword through one that dashed too close, giving it a brutal jerk and yank before I turned to squint against the glare of the magical battle raging between Arlan and the Zuer.

They clashed like two angels, bodies glowing with radiant power as they hurled their scorching assaults back and forth. At this rate, they'd leave this whole place nothing but a field of ash and bones.

I had to hurry. I had to find Thatcher—*now*.

Blite appeared at my side, cupping one of his wings over me and whining. Behind us, Fornax let out a string of panicked, barking cries and swung his head around. His big, sightless eyes blinked and swiveled, searching as his nostrils puffed. He was looking for Thatcher, too. Calling to him.

I scanned the battlefield, looking for any sign of him. His cloak. That mess of hay-colored hair. Anything.

The flashing light of another magical explosion shone off his armor. There! Thatcher lay only twenty yards away or so, resting on his side, and not moving or flinching even when the sky erupted with the force of those magical assaults around him.

Not good.

"Go back!" I shouted to Blite. "Get Fornax out of here! He can't navigate without your help!"

He growled disapprovingly and nipped at my cloak, trying to drag me away.

I shoved his head away and glared at him. Now wasn't the time for this. "Do as I say! Go!"

Blite's ears drooped. He blinked and gave a low whine, then turned away to bound back across the battlefield toward Fornax, making urgent, cawing sounds the whole way. Good enough. If he could get Fornax clear, maybe Phoebe and Araxie would be able to evacuate with Jace. Isandri, Reigh, and Lieutenant Eirik were already clear.

That just left the two Avoran sorcerers and a few dozen panicked Ulfrangar standing between Thatcher and me.

Better odds than I'd had all day.

"THATCHER!!" I YELLED HIS NAME AT THE TOP OF MY lungs, pumping my legs as fast as possible to cross that distance. I hit the ground on my knees beside him, taking him by the shoulders and carefully rolling him onto his back.

He coughed and choked, blood oozing from the corners of his mouth, as he lay limp on the ground. He stared back at me, his face already ashen and his eyes glazed. "M-Mur ... Murdoc." He coughed again as he tried to speak.

"It's okay. You're going to be just fine, Thatcher," I rasped as I looked him over. Merciful gods. The ground before me was soaked with blood—*his* blood.

Gods and Fates. He wasn't going to last much longer. I had to hurry. I had to do something—anything!

I looked around for someone, anyone, who might be able to help. A blinding light bloomed over the battlefield suddenly, forcing me to shield my eyes and turn away. When I dared to squint back in the direction of Arlan and the Zuer, I found both standing nearly nose to nose, wreathed in a rippling, crackling globe of power. Arlan snarled as he held the Zuer off her feet, gripping her by the throat and yelling in his native tongue. There was no mistaking the twisted look of rage, like a man crazed by the need to make her suffer, as another blast of power sent out a low, concussive shockwave.

The Zuer's form burst into a cloud of silver mist, vaporizing her before she could even scream. I threw myself over Thatcher to shield him as the wind and humming force of power washed over us like a pounding ocean wave. It lit up every nerve in my body with a rush of stinging pain like the prick of a thousand needles.

Then ... silence.

I sat up again, gritting my teeth as the lingering ache from that final blast throbbed all the way to my bones. Was it finally over? Was she gone?

"F-Fornax ..." Thatcher sputtered weakly. "Wh-Where's ..."

Oh gods. I had to get him out of here. I had to find some way to stabilize him.

"He's fine, I promise. But you have to stay awake, okay? Focus on the sound of my voice. Concentrate. What's your full name?" Panic took my mind like a pond freezing at the first breath of winter. My hands shook as I scrambled to drag his upper body into my lap and wrestled to unbuckle his breastplate. That spear, whatever it was, had punched straight through the steel of his armor and into his abdomen like it was nothing. The wound was deep, and had obviously nicked something crucial.

"Th-Tha ... Thatcher R-Ren ... ley." his voice slurred until he coughed again. Staring up at me, his expression pale but strangely calm, he gave a faint, delirious smile. "W-We won ... right?"

I put a hand over the wound and tried applying pressure—anything to slow the bleeding. "Yeah. We did."

"G-Good." His body relaxed some, arms and legs going slack as he blinked owlishly up at the sky. "I ... I'm c-cold."

I bit down fiercely, trying to keep my emotions in check. Trying to hold it together. "I know, just hold on. Help is coming. Keep talking to me, okay? You need to stay awake." I gulped against the rising knot of heat and pain in my throat. It made my chest ache and my eyes well up. "How old are you? What's my name? You remember it, right?"

"S-Six ... teen," he rasped faintly. His eyes fixed suddenly, and his pupils dilated. "I-I ... I don't ... p-please take c-care ... of ..."

His expression went distant. His chest gave a weak shudder and went still.

"Thatcher?! Thatcher!" I shook him. I smacked his cheek. I yelled in his face and jostled him. Anything to get a response.

Nothing.

O-Oh gods. Gods, no. No. *NO!!*

"HELP! SOMEBODY HELP HIM!" My throat burned as I screamed. "SOMEBODY PLEASE!"

Everything seemed to stop as I sat there on my knees with Thatcher lying limp against me, yelling to the calm morning sky as loudly as I could. It was as though the whole world had gone still and silent. And I was alone.

Completely and totally alone.

Thatcher had been my friend when I didn't deserve it. He'd been my little brother when I had no family.

If he was gone ... I had no one.

"Thatcher," I begged, grabbing fistfuls of the front of his tunic and bowing my head so that my forehead rested against his. "You can't leave. Not now. Not after all this. Where am I supposed to go? What am I supposed to do? Please ... please don't leave me."

"Move aside, boy," a deep voice spoke over me.

I looked up, clutching at Thatcher's body with one arm and snatching up my longsword with the other as that primal, protective instinct took over. "Get back! Don't you dare touch him!"

"Take care what you do with that blade. You've no enemies here now." Arlan the Kinslayer glowered down from where he stood right over me, his long pale golden hair blowing loosely around his broad shoulders. He winced and hissed an elven curse through his teeth, staggering a bit as he knelt down right at my side.

No enemies? What about the other Ulfrangar?

One glance around answered that question. The grassy prairie outside the dragonrider's temporary compound was now littered with motionless bodies dressed in black and silver. Merciful Fates, he'd ... killed them all. And he'd done it so quickly, cleanly, and without a single weapon of his own.

A chill of primal fear stirred in my chest and tingled up my spine. This man—whoever or whatever he was—held power unlike anything I'd ever imagined could be possible.

Arlan's brow shone with sweat and his sharp jawline went rigid as he stretched out a hand toward Thatcher's body. His nostrils flared some, as though he were fighting to keep his composure.

"Stop. Can't you see it's too late?" My voice shook, cracking as I forced out the words. "H-He's ... he's gone."

"Not quite," Arlan murmured, his scowl sharpening as he sucked in a deep, preparatory breath and rested his palm over the wound on Thatcher's stomach. "Be ready."

Be ready? Ready for wha—?

A flare of silver light glowed from beneath Arlan's hand, shocking the air around us with a strange gust of stark, bitter cold. The usually golden rings of his irises shifted, matching that sterling light as he bared his teeth and furrowed his brow. A grunt of pain leaked through his clenched teeth as he leaned into his hand.

"Come on. Do not fail me now," he snapped angrily, but I

couldn't tell if he was fuming at Thatcher or himself. He made another low, agonized sound as his knuckles blanched and the veins stood out against the side of his neck.

"Arlan!" A frantic, female voice called out suddenly.

I looked up just in time to see Garnett running for us over the body-strewn battlefield. Flushed and breathless, she gripped an axe in each hand as she jogged to a stop. Her face paled as soon as she spotted Thatcher, and she let out a shriek of horror. "Oh, stones, no! Thatcher! What happened?!" Both her axes hit the ground at her sides and she clapped a hand over her mouth.

"Garnett, you must pull it out," Arlan barked through his teeth, never looking away from where he still forced his hand down against Thatcher's body. "Now!"

Garnett didn't hesitate. She fell to her knees and grabbed the crossbow bolt still lodged in Thatcher's shoulder, giving it a twist before she ripped it free. I cringed back as a beam of radiant, sterling light streamed from the wound, lighting up the dreary dawn.

What the—?!

The light grew brighter, and the flesh around the arrow wound turned a strange shade of ashen, stony gray. Then, little by little, it began to heal. No—not heal. This was something else. It's as though the wound was disappearing completely.

I gaped at Arlan, trying to make sense of it. I'd heard stories of healing magic, mostly in stories about Jaevid Broadfeather. He'd been the chosen champion of the God of Life, and had been gifted with powerful healing abilities because of it. I'd also heard tales and legends of the might of the Avoran elves. Their kingdom was said to be steeped in ancient, pure magics beyond anything the lower kingdoms could even begin to fathom. But this was ... I-I didn't even know what to call it.

I flinched back, nearly coming out of my own skin in

surprise as Thatcher's body suddenly tensed and seized once. His mouth opened and he sucked in a deep gulp of air. He blinked hard a few times, almost like he was trying to clear his vision. Then his eyes rolled back and he slumped against me, still wheezing in slow, steady breaths as though he'd fallen asleep.

H-Holy ... gods. He was alive!

As soon as Thatcher took that breath, Arlan jerked back and pulled his hand away. His palm smoked like he'd lit it on fire, and he cradled it to his chest as he doubled over and groaned in pain. Rocking back and forth, I heard him muttering faint words in the Avoran tongue. I wasn't as fluent in that language, but I caught enough to be able to tell he was spitting strings of curses that might have made a demon blush.

"Arlan! By the stones, man, what did you do?" Garnett whispered brokenly. Her expression was still blank with shock as she gingerly touched Thatcher's neck to take his pulse. "Did you bring him back from the dead?"

"No," he managed weakly. He let out another sharp, hissing curse of pain and fell back to sit on the grass beside us. "Nothing so grand as that. He had not yet passed into the Vale, but his spirit was fading. A few more seconds and he would have been beyond all help. I cannot bring anyone back from the dead. It is, however, still within my abilities to alter the threads of time in a very limited capacity."

Oh. Right. Because there was nothing grand at all about manipulating *time*.

"You mean ... you altered time around Thatcher's body to undo his wounds?" I guessed, trying to make sense of what I'd just witnessed. When I said it out loud like that, it sounded even more ridiculous.

"In simplest terms, yes," Arlan confirmed. He kept his face angled away from us, but I could still see his cheek moving as he winced in discomfort. Whatever he'd done, time-altering power or not, it had clearly taken a toll on him.

"He will be all right, then?" Garnett asked worriedly as she scooted in closer, now running her hand across Thatcher's cheek. She nibbled at her bottom lip as she brushed some of his bangs out of his eyes.

Heh. Too bad he was unconscious for all that. He might've thrown up from anxiety if he'd known the girl he liked was petting him like that.

Arlan nodded and rubbed his forehead and the bridge of his nose with his good hand. He still held the other one close to his chest, his hand clenched into a shaking fist as though he'd burned it. "Yes, the boy will recover. The wounds are gone, but he's lost a significant amount of blood. He will need to be taken somewhere secure to rest and recover." His voice hitched as he finally held out the hand he'd used to cast his magic and tried extending his fingers. His controlled, calm demeanor cracked again, his expression twisting in pain. He let out another low, agonized moan and shut his eyes tightly. "A-As will I, it seems."

"You've gone and used too much of that high elf power, haven't you?" Garnett scolded quietly. "Can you walk? Or do I need to send for Howlan and Violet?"

He shook his head, making a few smooth locks of his light golden hair swish loose from where he'd tucked them behind his pointed ears. "I'll manage. Send word for the others to wait for us in Osbran. I suspect a certain dragonrider commander will have a long list of questions for me as soon as he arrives there. Perhaps I'll indulge him a little."

Garnett pursed her lips unhappily, her soft violet eyes studying him carefully as he slowly got to his feet. "Pardon me for speaking out of turn, but in light of all this, I'm not so sure toying with Jaevid Broadfeather is such a good idea."

"You're absolutely correct, dear Garnett." Arlan's thin

mouth curled slightly at one corner, briefly giving her a bemused half-smile. Then he turned and began staggering away toward the compound's open gate. "That's why I intend to be easily found and completely hospitable."

"And what if he wants to have you arrested?" she called after him.

I could have sworn I heard the strange elven man chuckle, as though he found that idea adorable. "He can certainly try."

9

CHAPTER NINE

Arlan, Garnett, and I sat sat outside the gate of the former dragonrider compound, staring at the smoldering field of Ulfrangar corpses. Thatcher was still unconscious, so I had to carry him down to the gate on my back. Not so easy given my own injuries, and the fact that the surge of battle-fueled adrenaline had left me weak and unsteady on my feet. Still, as I sat there, I had to wonder how, by all the gods, I was even breathing at all. Destiny? Divine providence? Sheer dumb luck?

A little of all three?

Thankfully, after only a few minutes, King Jace arrived with a cavalry in the form of eight Gray elven scouts all riding shrikes. They picked us up right outside the compound, and immediately took off for Osbran like a formation of speedy, mirror-scaled dragonflies.

Before noon, we'd landed outside a decent-sized tavern on the edge of the small, rural city. Compared to somewhere like Dayrise, Osbran was barely more than a collection of thatch-roofed buildings smashed into the crumbling ruins of an old fortified city. One of the walls had fallen probably hundreds of years ago, and the city had apparently begun to spill over the old boundary there to extend a little bit beyond. It looked a little like a bowl that was cracked open on one side, so the contents of houses, shops, farms, and fields poured out over the sweeping prairie between the knobby, bare-rock hilltops.

I didn't know much about the place, except that it was small and mostly made up of folk who lived off the weaving industry. The farms around it tended flocks of sheep and goats, and many of the businesses within it catered to that by making fabrics and threads that could be supplied to merchant caravans moving across the kingdom. It was supposed to be a quiet, quaint place. Not somewhere you'd expect to find trouble.

Not until we arrived, anyway.

As we landed in the muddy street in front of the tavern, I spotted several groups of locals—farm hands and shepherds, most likely—watching with mixed expressions of worry and fear. Older men scratched at their beards and leaned together to whisper, eyeing us and keeping a firm grip on their staffs. Not that I didn't understand their concern. These people probably hadn't seen a company of elven warriors on shrikes since the Gray War, and I doubted it called back fond memories.

"Take him inside," King Jace instructed as he stepped over to help me unfasten Thatcher's limp body from the back of another shrike. "The others are already here waiting, and a healer is on the way."

"What about the dragons?" I asked as I jostled Thatcher some, trying to get his weight balanced on my back again.

"I'll see to that next. Most of the dragonriders formerly at the compound are scattered throughout the surrounding farmland, taking shelter where they can for now. There's no fort or tower to house them here, but the common folk have been accommodating so far. Hopefully that luck holds out until we can come up with a better plan. I'll return tonight with more information."

"And what about him?" I asked, lowering my voice and tipping my chin toward where Arlan was also dismounting from a back of a shrike.

King Jace joined me in staring distrustfully at the elven man who, ironically, had just saved mine and Thatcher's lives. I didn't expect that grace to be given freely, though. He was still a crime lord, and I wasn't stupid enough to believe for one single second that he didn't have an ulterior motive for intervening on our behalf. He was up to something. I just hoped, whatever it was, it wouldn't require me to sell my soul to yet another wicked entity in this gods-forsaken kingdom.

"I've no right to detain him here. In Luntharda, I might try to hold him long enough to question him about who and what, exactly, he is. But I can't do that here in Maldobar, and I'm not sure that killing the Zuer qualifies as a crime in anyone's book. So, he's not done anything that even warrants me even alerting the local officials," Jace sighed and sank back onto his heels some. "We have no choice but to let him go, for now."

The old king rubbed at his short, white beard as we watched Arlan speak a few words to Garnett, then he strode off into the city without ever looking back. Every step he took away from us made my toes curl inside my boots and my stomach writhe in apprehension. It felt wrong to just let him slither out of sight like that. Then again, he'd mentioned he intended to stay in Osbran, at least long enough to talk to Jaevid. Maybe we'd get some real answers out of him, after all.

"Rest while you can, Murdoc," Jace warned as he flashed me another critical, appraising glance. "You should be safe here for a few days, at least. The city's overseen by Count Wilmot. A good man, by all accounts, but I don't know him personally. You would do well to tread lightly and not burn anything to the ground, if you can manage it."

I snorted and started shuffling off toward the front steps of the tavern, lugging Thatcher along like a scrawny backpack. "No promises." I only made it a few paces before something burrowed deep into the pit of my gut, twisting and gnawing, and forcing me to stop. I turned to give the king one last look.

"Thank you," I murmured, and lowered my gaze in submission.

He gave a squinty, puzzled frown.

"I don't know how or why, but I know you were the one who brought Kinslayer there. If you hadn't, the Zuer would have killed me. She would have killed all of us. So ... thank you."

"Ah." He gave a stiff nod and quickly looked away. "Don't take this the wrong way, but I didn't do it for you. You're not the only one who's been watching the shadows since the day you left the pack behind, and to be perfectly honest, I owed Rook the courtesy of finishing what he'd started. By taking the risk and trying to get you out of their grasp, he did what I never had the courage to even try to do for him. I wasn't about to let his dying effort be in vain."

I studied Jace's profile for a few seconds, watching the way his brow puckered as his frown deepened, and the way his eyes went steely as though he were trying to keep the memories at bay. Finally, I turned and started for the tavern again, leaving him in that heavy silence.

I did understand why he'd done it. I knew full well what kind of hell he'd lived through all these years, dreading that every step he took might be the wrong one that led him back into the path of the pack. Time didn't make it easier. It didn't make the fear go away. He'd spent a lifetime held hostage by that dread and quiet suffering.

Now, we were both free. Well, hopefully, anyway. Time would tell.

Now, thanks to Arlan the Kinslayer, time was something we had on our side.

I HIT THE FRONT DOOR OF THE RUN-DOWN OLD TAVERN AND inn with a sigh that made my chest ache and my back throb under Thatcher's weight. Just a little farther. Then I could put him down and let him get proper treatment and rest. I might even be able to steal a little of both for myself, as well.

The wooden boards of the front porch creaked under my weight, and I had to balance Thatcher's weight just right in order to get an arm free so I could try opening the door.

Another smaller and much faster hand beat me to it.

"I got you, love," Garnett announced as she held the door open so I could stagger inside.

"Not going with Arlan?" I murmured, wondering if I should even be using his name or not.

"He prefers to be on his own. Not that we don't try to help him, but he's a stubborn one." She shrugged, and I could have sworn I saw a hint of worry crinkle her features as she stole a glance up at Thatcher.

Ahhh, so that was it. The *real* reason she'd stayed behind. Miss Crime-Lord-Informant had a new tell of her own, and his name was Thatcher Renley.

Ugh. Why did that sort of make me want to throw up?

The tavern-keeper met us just inside the door, flustered and looking like he might be a heartbeat away from fainting. The short, heavyset man had more hair in his bristly red mustache and thick eyebrows than he did on the rest of his entire head. He stammered through an explanation of which rooms upstairs had been prepared for us, looking concerned when he noticed Thatcher was still unconscious and flung over my back like a caught goat. "They paid for four rooms, but I've opened up an extra just in case. Then you're on a mission for Her Majesty? To retake Northwatch? Gods and Fates, isn't that dangerous? You're hardly more than children!" He fretted and dabbed at his sweat beading on his brow with a handkerchief.

"We appreciate the hospitality." I nodded and started for the wide staircase at the far end of the bar.

"Of course, no trouble at all! We're always happy to assist Her Majesty in any way," the man continued to ramble, following us all the way to the bottom of the stairs. "My daughter, Evie, should be somewhere up there helping, and the healer should be here any moment. I'll send him right up when he arrives, don't you worry."

Garnett did a much better job of thanking him profusely before she bounded after me up the stairs to the second floor. She certainly had a knack for handling people. A useful skill, and not one I possessed in any capacity whatsoever. Well, unless they came at me with a blade. That I could handle proficiently enough.

But according to Thatcher, I needed to try "smiling more." Hah.

The tavern itself wasn't all that large, with only two floors in all. Overall, it had a much more modest and rustic feel, but it was clean and smelled of fresh cut pine logs, spiced ales, and something delicious baking in the kitchen behind the long, high-top bar. The floor above had eight rooms for rent, and it was easy enough to track down which ones had been opened for our use. As usual, I just had to follow the ambient sounds of chaos and arguing.

"Reigh Farrow! Are you even listening to me? You're in no shape to be walking anywhere! I can't believe Kiran even let you leave Ms. Lin's house like this. You've torn nearly all your stitches and you're bleeding all over your clothes." Phoebe fussed like an angry sparrow, her voice echoing down the hallway before I even got to the top of the stairs. "Go back and lie down right now. So help me, I know where you keep your chaser root tea, and I *will* sedate you if that's what it takes—HEY! Don't make that face at me; I'm just trying to keep you alive! Isandri didn't put up any fuss at all, but you're acting like a big baby."

"Lively, isn't she?" Garnett giggled as we made it to the landing.

I just smirked. Phoebe had always been excitable, but now that she and Reigh had arrived at a mutual understanding, she'd been much less cautious around him. A good thing, too. That bratty, stubborn kid needed someone to thump him upside the head now and again. Not that it helped much. It was entertaining to watch, though.

As soon as we rounded the corner, I spotted that familiar mane of wild red curls at the other end of the hall. For whatever reason, the sight made all the muscles in my body want to go slack and the last little bit of my energy fizzle away. My head and shoulders drooped, and I practically had to drag my feet like someone had filled my boots with lead.

We were all here. We were all safe.

That was all that mattered.

"Murdoc!" Phoebe gasped when she saw us. Tears welled in her eyes as she ran to meet me. "You're alive!" She reached out like she might embrace me, then stopped short. Her expression tensed, closing up as she quickly looked away, like she was afraid I might lash out at her or something if she touched me. Then she noticed Thatcher where he lay, still unconscious, and draped over my back. Her wide blue eyes glanced between us like she couldn't decide what to panic over first.

"He's okay," I tried to calm her before she jumped to the wrong conclusion. "Just unconscious."

"O-Okay," she gasped, still blinking back tears as her cheeks flushed pink. "Oh gods, he just looks so pale. Are you sure he's all right?"

I nodded. "It might take him a few days to get back on his feet, but he should be fine. Just tell me where I can put him down. He's supposed to rest."

Phoebe led us farther down the hall, to a room across from the one where I spotted Reigh stretched out on a small bed. With his torso wrapped in fresh bandaging, he lay on his back and scowled up at the ceiling with his arms crossed. Isandri stood over him, one of her biceps also wrapped in bandaging, and frowned down at him as though she were daring him to try and get up again. I guess Phoebe had her working as reinforcements to make sure he stayed put.

"They're, um, they're bringing us some more clean hot water, rags, and bandages," Phoebe rambled as she rushed in ahead of us to pull back all the blankets on the bed, except for one white sheet. A good call, since getting Thatcher cleaned up was going to require dealing with his blood-drenched clothes. It'd make a mess everywhere. "They said the healer should be here soon, too. But, um, I'm not sure how long he'll take. Kiran showed me a few things while I was helping him take care of Reigh and Judan before, so I can at least get everyone ready and—"

"You're doing a great job," Garnett consoled, patting Phoebe on the back and smiling broadly. "And now I'm here to help, too. Just tell me what you want me to do."

Phoebe's smile was still teary and twitchy, like she might break down crying at any moment. I guess it'd been hard for her to watch everything from that tower—too far to do much except fire from Thatcher's crossbow whenever she got a clear shot. Thatcher had also given her his goggles, hoping she could at least help Fornax orient if things got dire. In the end, none of that had helped much. I'd known from the start that once the battle started, regardless of whether or not the dragonriders were removed from the equation, we were going to be in for a bloodbath. Mostly, I think positioning Phoebe in the tower like that was Reigh and Eirik's way of putting her as far out of harm's way as she would allow. She had flat out refused to evacuate with the rest of the dragonriders.

"O-Okay, yes, thank you," she managed in a trembling voice. Her gaze met mine for an instant before she quickly looked away again.

My heart twisted painfully. I didn't understand why—why was it so hard to look at her now?

Turning around, I sat on the edge of the bed and leaned back so Garnett and Phoebe could help slide Thatcher's limp body up onto the mattress. Once they had him sprawled out, they immediately got to work removing the rest of his armor and bloody clothes. Once again, I was a little sad he wasn't conscious enough to be aware of it. He would have blushed as red as a beet if he'd known Garnett and Phoebe were stripping him down to his smallclothes like that.

I'd have to remember to tease him about that later.

"Is the room next door one of ours, as well?" I asked as I stood and started to leave. I wasn't much use here now, after all. Might as well give them some space to work.

"Oh, um, yes. And there's a washroom at the end of the hall." Phoebe looked up from where she'd been wrestling one of Thatcher's boots off. "It's not very big, but they said we could use it. I-I, um, I asked Queen Araxie if she would go and find some new, clean clothes for everyone. She should be back any moment. Oh! And I asked if they could bring us up something to eat. You know, because I sort of thought everyone might be too tired to sit downstairs."

"I'll pass on the food for now. Thanks, though." I looked

back long enough to cast her what might have been the world's most pathetic excuse for a smile.

It must've looked as half-hearted, exhausted, and pained as it felt, because Phoebe's expression immediately shifted from that reluctant, evasive anxiety to concern. "Murdoc ...?" She said my name in that soft voice again—the one that passed through my body like a tingling heat and made every corner of my mind go silent.

Great. No way I could keep a straight face now. Or a smiling one, in this case.

I waved a hand, hoping she'd take that as assurance that I really was fine. Seriously, I was. But it didn't seem like she was buying that, either. Her little eyebrows rumpled together suspiciously.

"Let me know if you need any more help," I sighed.

Turning away I let the door close behind me as I stepped back out into the hall. I rubbed my face with my hands, massaging my temples as I tried to shake off that feeling. What was wrong with me, anyway? She'd said my name a thousand times since we'd met. Why was it different now? It was getting harder and harder just to have simple conversations with her. Was I losing my mind?

Urggh. I didn't know. The only thing I was certain of was if she kept on doing that, looking at me with those sad doe eyes and whispering my name in that tone, sooner or later ... I might do something stupid. As in, completely irresponsible, recklessly selfish, Reigh-level stupid.

And no one was prepared for that kind of disaster—not even me.

CHAPTER TEN

I almost smacked right into a young woman carrying a big bucket of steaming hot water when I stepped into the tavern's small washroom. She gave a yelp of alarm and froze like a spooked squirrel, staring with wide eyes at my slashed-up, blood-spattered state. Right, so, I probably did look somewhat horrifying like this. Hence the trip to the washroom.

"Sorry," I muttered and moved out of her way.

"Not at all! You just ... surprised me a little. My apologies." She hurried past, still giving me a wary side-eye as she carried the bucket away in the direction of Thatcher's room.

The tavernkeeper's daughter? The one he'd mentioned was named Evie? Seemed like a fair guess. And with those slightly pointed ears peeking out of long, ash-colored hair ... she must've been a halfbreed like Jaevid. Interesting.

Now that I had the washroom to myself, I took my time stripping off my own tattered, bloodstained tunic, pants, armor, and even my socks and smallclothes. Blood oozed from the open slices and gashes I'd gotten in the fight. Fortunately, thanks to my armor, none of the crossbow bolts had managed to pierce through all the way to my skin. The rest of my injuries were minor. A few stitches and some bandages after I'd rinsed myself clean, and I'd be fine.

A large copper basin sat waiting in the corner of the small, dimly lit space. It was already filled with fragrant, steaming water, and I hissed through my teeth as I sank down into it. I cursed when the water washed over a much deeper cut that sliced across my upper back. It stung a lot worse than the rest, although it was hard to tell just how bad it might be. If it hurt that much, though, I'd probably need more than few stitches to close it up.

I rinsed myself off as best I could and dunked my head under a few times, trying to scrub the grit out of my scalp and the grime from my skin, before I finally climbed out. There were a few clean but well-worn towels set on a shelf behind the basin, and I swiped one to dry off and ruffle some of the water out of my hair. I didn't have any new clothes to change into—not that I wanted to since I still had injuries slowly oozing blood—so I pulled my smallclothes back on and wrapped the towel around my waist. Good enough.

Poking my head outside the washroom to check, I waited until I was certain everyone else was otherwise occupied to gather the rest of my stuff and make a speedy dash down the hall. I speedily made my way into the room next to Thatcher's and shut the door. Now maybe I could rest some while I waited for the healer to show up.

I dropped my stuff at the foot of one of the two untouched beds, and let out a deep breath. The narrow room itself wasn't anything grand or lavish, which suited me fine. A window on the longest wall let in a few rays of weak midday sun, and two small beds were set on opposite ends of the space with a washstand, little table, and two chairs in between them. It smelled faintly of soap, like someone had scrubbed the floors recently, and the quilts folded neatly on each bed looked a little threadbare, but also clean.

A small round mirror hung behind the washstand, and a glimpse of my reflection in that old glass made me freeze in place. I didn't remember how I'd looked before we left Halfax months ago. I didn't usually pay attention to that sort of thing. Even so, I was willing to bet it wasn't this bad. Dark circles hung under my eyes, and my hair had grown out so long it covered my ears and came down to my neck. A few more weeks and I'd either have to cut it or tie it back like Thatcher did.

Eh. Definitely cut it.

There were still a few green-and-yellow-colored bruises on my face from where Thatcher had punched me. I'd gotten a little thicker through the chest, and a dusting of dark stubble flecked my chin, neck, and jaw. It made me look older, and not in a good way. That combined with everything else—my ragged hair, weary drooping eyelids, and body slashed with fresh and recently stitched wounds from our other encounters with the Ulfrangar—made me look like I'd just crawled out of a gutter somewhere.

It wasn't so far from the truth, I guess.

Standing in nothing but my smallclothes and the towel, I let my gaze wander from one horrific scar to the next that marred nearly every inch of my skin. I couldn't remember how I'd gotten some of them. The worst ones, though—the thick, raised, gnarled, scars on my wrists and neck—I knew all too well where those had come from.

My heartbeat slowed to deep, aching, hard thumps as I stared at those marks. Somehow, now that the Zuer was dead and the Ulfrangar had no reason to hunt me any longer, I expected to feel something. Free, I guess. Or relieved. Maybe even happy.

But now, looking at those marks on my body, I didn't feel

any of those things. I only saw the truth of what I was still etched into my being forever. The Zuer was gone. The pack wouldn't pursue me now. And yet, I didn't feel anything except ... lost.

I shivered as a strange numbness like lukewarm water settled through my mind, leaving me adrift and wondering what I was supposed to do with my life now. Who was I supposed to be? Where should I go? I'd done the impossible and escaped the Ulfrangar. I'd gotten my freedom. Now, I just wasn't sure what I was meant to do with it.

The obvious answers were that I'd go to the dragonrider academy and follow Thatcher wherever else he went. But part of me knew that couldn't last forever. He wasn't like me. Sure, he was gawky and awkward now, but he'd grow into himself. He'd eventually stumble across a girl who found his baby-face and bumbling, naïve kindness endearing. Then he wouldn't need a brother-figure staring over his shoulder all the time. I'd have to move on, too. I'd need to build a life of my own somewhere.

For now, the fact that I was even standing here still felt unreal—like a dream I'd suddenly wake up from at any moment. I still didn't understand most of what had happened. I couldn't begin to comprehend why Arlan the Kinslayer had actually shown up to fight the woman who was apparently his sister. I didn't even know how he'd gotten there in the first place. Had King Jace brought him? Or had he used some of that magical power to somehow cross the distance? Had he simply agreed to help us for the chance of fighting the Zuer? Or had he and Jace struck their own, separate bargain? How was it that an Avoran elf had become the leader of the Ulfrangar? And if she was really dead, did that make Arlan the new Zuer?

All were excellent questions that I had no hope of answering at the moment. Right then, I didn't even have the will to try. I wandered to the bed farthest from the door and sank down onto it, letting my elbows rest on my knees. I didn't want to think anymore. My head swam every time I closed my eyes, as though my brain was bobbing and bouncing around in my skull like a rowboat on a stormy sea. Sleep—I just wanted to sleep. And to know that when I woke up, the world wouldn't be burning down around me again.

Hah. Fat chance, right? If I'd learned anything over the last several months, it's that wherever Thatcher Renley went, disaster was bound to follow at an alarming speed. And, naturally, I'd wind up caught right in the thick of it.

Still, even knowing all that, ... I couldn't think of anywhere else in the world I'd rather be.

I don't know how long I sat there like that, tossed amidst my reckless thoughts and trying to decide if it was worth it to try sleeping. I wasn't sure if I could, or if I'd just wind up lying there for hours, worrying over things I had absolutely no control over, and thinking about everything I should have been doing right then. Ugh. Maybe a sleeping remedy was in order, after all. I wondered if Reigh had any packed away in his bag of medicinal tricks.

A soft knock on the door made me look up.

"Murdoc?" Phoebe's quiet voice called from the hall. "Are you, um, is it okay if I come in?"

"Yeah. It's okay," I answered on pure reflex, without really thinking at all.

And by the time Phoebe cracked the door open and peeked inside, it was way too late. As soon as she realized I was sitting there in basically just my underwear, her face blushed almost as red as her wild storm of curls and she immediately slapped a hand over her eyes. "O-Oh! I'm so sorry, I-I didn't know you were still—ah!"

Crap. What the heck was wrong with me? "S-Sorry!" I quickly snatched my pants off the pile of filthy clothes on the floor and pulled them on.

"No! No, I should have realized you were—gods, I'm really sorry!" She panicked, her eyes still pinched shut as she floundered not to drop the armload of bandages and medical supplies she'd been carrying.

"It's fine. Totally my fault. I wasn't paying attention." Great. Now my whole head felt like it was on fire. "I, uh, I'm decent now." Sinking back down on the edge of the bed, I buried my face in my hands so hopefully she wouldn't see me blushing like a moron.

Her light footsteps approached and stopped before me. "Murdoc?" she asked softly. "Are you okay?"

I rubbed at my cheeks still finding a few tender spots from those bruises around my nose and cheekbones. "Yeah," I lied. It didn't seem right to burden her with any of my issues.

She didn't answer for a moment, and I had to wonder if she could tell I was bluffing. "The healer's here. He's, um, he's checking on Reigh and Thatcher first," she said at last. "You got hurt, too, didn't you? Can I take a look? I'm not a healer, but Kiran was teaching me a little about it before."

I lifted my head, meeting her worried, raindrop-blue gaze. She had her bottom lip drawn into her mouth, nibbling at it, and her little ginger eyebrows were drawn up in concern.

"Okay," I surrendered.

Neither of us spoke as she began looking over the new cuts and wounds I'd gotten during our battle. Lucky for me, most of them were trivial. The injuries I'd sustained while taking that godsgrave potion were a little more worrisome. They'd been deeper, and despite Reigh constantly funneling those healing remedies down my throat, they were healing a lot more slowly. The one on my side stung when she lifted my arm and carefully prodded it with her fingers. It made my breath catch and I gave a small grunt of pain.

"That hurts?" she asked, leaning around to peer into my face as though trying to detect whether or not I was fibbing this time.

"Y-Yeah. A little."

There was no mistaking the worry in her face as she ducked back around me and tested the area around it with her fingers. "It's hot to the touch, too. I think it's getting infected. We should ask the healer for some medicines, and you need to rest."

"Well, I'll be happy to as soon as people stop trying to kill me every few hours," I chuckled weakly.

She didn't seem to find that as funny. The bed jostled as she climbed around behind me, examining my back. Knowing what she'd find back there made me cringe and I shut my eyes tightly. I bowed my head as embarrassed heat bloomed in my cheeks again.

"Oh, Murdoc. This cut across your shoulders, it's ... it's really deep. I'm so sorry, we'll definitely need to stitch it, but I don't have any way to numb it." Her voice trembled a bit as she pushed the cloth against it again. "We should wait for the healer. Maybe he has something for the pain, so it won't hurt as much."

"It's fine, Phoebe," I said, trying to keep my tone as gentle as I knew how.

"But, no, Murdoc, it isn't!" she protested, beginning to sound a little panicked now. "It's got to be almost half an inch deep, and—"

"It's okay. Really. I ... I don't have much feeling left back there now, anyway," I murmured.

She didn't make a sound for nearly a minute, but I could barely sense the tickle of her fingertips moving across my back. She traced the old stripes left by years of whelpers' and handlers' whips. Sword cuts and blade marks from training duels, many of which I didn't even remember. After a while, it all ran together, blending into one long tapestry of violence and agony I'd assumed I would never escape. The layers upon layers of scarring there had made the skin rough and thick, and I'd lost a lot of the sensation there because of it.

Finally, I heard Phoebe whimper, "The Ulfrangar did this to you?"

"Yes."

She went quiet again. Her hand moved to my shoulders, then up into my neck. I couldn't resist the urge to let my eyes roll back when she combed her fingers through my hair. No one had ever done that before. But it felt so ... *good*.

A little too good, I guess, because a deep sigh left my chest.

I heard her laugh softly. "You scared me a little, at first, you know. When we first met, I mean."

I frowned. I had scared her? Why? It's not like she'd known who and what I was then. And as far as I could recall, I'd never raised a hand against her before.

"Why?" I dared to ask.

"I don't know. Maybe because you were so quiet and serious all the time. Also, in case you hadn't noticed, you're about twice my size, so ..." She let her voice trail off, as though she were thinking. "But I guess most people are a lot taller than me, so maybe that's not exactly fair to say. Well, other than Garnett. I can't believe I'm taller than her! I've never been taller than anyone except, you know, little kids."

I bowed my head to hide my smirk. "Some people assume you're a little kid, too, probably."

She swatted the back of my head and stormed off the bed, coming back around to stand in front of me with her arms crossed and her cheeks puffed like an angry chipmunk.

"Don't be rude! I'll have you know, I am *seventeen* years old! Everyone just assumes I'm a lot younger because I'm short. I know I'm not as tall or mature-looking as other girls my age, but I—"

"Not so scared of me now, are you?" I teased.

She put her hands on her hips. "No, I'm not. Not even a little," she declared. It was hard not to find that fiery little glare of hers amusing. And cute.

"Good," I chuckled.

"Also ... I know you now," she added, her tone softening some again as she scrunched her mouth and looked down. "I know you'd never hurt any of us."

My heart did that squeezing, fluttering thing that made my body tense again. She didn't sound so certain about that last part, maybe because ... I'd already hurt her once. Not physically, of course. But still.

I'd pushed her away. I'd rejected her feelings. I had lots of good reasons for it, of course. And not all of those reasons had changed. I still had nothing to offer any girl that might be interested in me. Didn't that matter to her? Didn't she want a normal life with someone who could secure a good living, provide a safe home, and offer her a future she could rely on? Sure, I might wind up a dragonrider at the end of all this. All that promised was a decent salary and the assurance that I would be traveling under military orders around the kingdom for a while. And not even that future was guaranteed.

I was still a former Ulfrangar pup, a murderer in the eyes of the kingdom, and I wasn't stupid enough to think there wouldn't be some punishment in store for everything I'd done in their name. Unlike Jace, I hadn't wound up a king who was far beyond the grasp of the normal legal system. Jaevid might be able to keep me out of prison, but I wasn't counting on that. Not when Queen Jenna heard about all the people who'd died and the homes that had been damaged during all this.

I mean, gods, Thatcher had almost *died* because of me.

Thinking about that, about those few seconds when I'd thought he was gone, hit me like an iron fist to the chest. My body tensed, and my head bowed lower. All that confusion, frustration, panic, and pure terror surged through my brain like flood waters cracking through a dam. I couldn't stop it.

"Murdoc?" She did it again—said my name in that small, breathless whisper.

I looked up at her, and that last feeble thread of my sanity snapped.

"Are you okay?" she asked, her tone insistent. "And don't brush me off this time."

My mouth screwed up. I wanted to look away, but I couldn't. Her expression of genuine worry held me captive. She wanted to know how I really was ... and I didn't have the mental fortitude to even try lying to her right now.

"I-I, I don't know," my voice shook and I sucked in a sharp breath, trying to steel myself. It didn't work. "I almost killed him, Phoebe. I thought I did. Thatcher, he was dying right there in front of me and I couldn't do anything. I couldn't save him. If Arlan hadn't—I-I don't know what I ..." I stopped short, my mouth clamping down hard against the rising lump of pain and grief that lodged at the back of my throat. It made every word burn like dragon venom. My eyes welled. I bowed my head lower, praying she wouldn't see. "Now I don't know what's going to happen. I don't know if I owe my life to Arlan as payment, or Jace for arranging all this, or both. I don't understand why any of them wanted to help me. I don't know if I've just traded one form of slavery for another."

"Murdoc, I—"

"Don't." I cut her off immediately.

"Don't what?"

"Don't tell me you're sorry," I snapped hoarsely. "Don't tell me that it wasn't my fault, or that I did the best I could, or that it's going to be fine. Just *don't!*" The words just kept coming. The more I tried to stop, the louder and more broken my voice became. "Thatcher, he ... he wouldn't have even been out there if it wasn't for me. He never would have gotten hurt—none of you would have!"

My hands drew into fists, clenching so hard it made my whole body shudder and my knuckles go white. Tears ran down the end of my nose and dripped onto the wood floor at my feet. It should have been me. If anyone had deserved to be lying there on that battlefield, bleeding out, it was me, not Thatcher. I'd almost lost my best friend. I'd almost watched him take the fall for my sake. And I'd been completely helpless to stop it.

My voice caught, strangled by a sob as I buried my face in my hands. "I-I can't do this. I can't be like the rest of you. I don't deserve ... I ... I-I'm ... not worthy of ..."

Phoebe hugged me.

She wrapped her arms around my head, burying my face against her soft purple tunic, and held me tightly against her. "I wasn't either. Don't you remember? I was a Tibran. I did terrible things, too, Murdoc. But you were the one who taught me how to start moving on," she murmured against my hair. "Now you have to try, just like I did. You can't give up—not when you're so close."

I dragged her in closer, squeezing her back as hard as I could. "I-I'm ... I'm scared," I admitted, the low, rasping words like poison on my tongue. Not so long ago, saying something like that would've gotten me beaten within an inch of my life.

Ulfrangar were not allowed to be afraid.

"Shhh. You're safe now, Murdoc," she cooed gently and

pressed her lips against my temple. "It's over. Everyone's okay, and you're safe right here with us."

My eyes closed as I relaxed into her embrace, taking in deep breaths of her scent. It reminded me of the soothing, cozy smells in Ms. Lin's house—of warm cinnamon, nutmeg, honey, and sweet cream. Cozy. Inviting. Safe. Comfortable. Phoebe was all those things ... and so much more.

I didn't know when it had happened. I guess it wasn't something that had come about suddenly. It must have grown gradually, little by little, since the moment I'd first met her. But somewhere along the way, I'd ... fallen for this girl.

She was all the happiness I'd ever wanted and couldn't have. She was more resilient than I'd ever be, stronger than I'd ever given her credit for, smarter than anyone else I knew. I'd never deserve her.

But I had never wanted anything more than to call her mine.

Grasping my face in her small hands, she turned my head back so I was forced to look at her. She smiled as she brushed her thumbs along my cheeks and wiped my eyes. "You need to rest. I'll go and speak to the healer. Maybe he has something that will help you relax so you can get some sleep."

I nodded—unconvincingly, I guess, because she scowled and pursed her lips.

"I mean it, Murdoc. How long has it been since you had a decent night's rest?" She fussed and continued to pet my face, brushing my bangs away from my eyes, and running her fingers along my brow and cheeks.

I would've kept on arguing with her all afternoon if it meant she'd keep doing that. Soft, gentle touches like that were still so ... strange. But I liked them.

Or *her*, I guess was a better way of putting it. I liked *her*. A lot. Too much.

"Go ahead and lie down," she went on scolding me. "Not

on your back, though. We still need to have a look at that cut on your shoulders. Probably the one on your side, too, I think. I really do think it's getting infected. Fates, between you, Thatcher, and Reigh, we'll be stuck here for a week trying to get you all put back together."

I didn't have the willpower or the energy to protest. Crawling the rest of the way up onto the bed, I collapsed on my stomach with a heavy grunt and lay still. All those clean sheets and soft blankets seemed to swallow me whole, and for a moment, I couldn't think about anything except sleep. Sleep, and Phoebe. I wanted to ask her to stay here, with me. Then I'd know she was safe.

But regardless of how unfathomably kind she was to me, I had no right to ask her for anything like that. Just wanting her to be close—wanting her to be mine—wasn't enough. Phoebe was, without a doubt, the most beautiful person I had ever met in my entire life. Inside and out, there wasn't a single part of her that didn't resonate with goodness and light. She deserved the absolute best that the world could give her.

... And even if she'd never admit it, even if she didn't want to hear me say it, I knew that was never going to be me.

11

CHAPTER ELEVEN

The Gray elf spy network from Luntharda had done a fantastic job getting us set up with everything we needed in Osbran. At King Jace's request, they had arranged for us to have a place to stay at the tavern, as well as all the supplies we would require in terms of medicines, food, and gear. Honestly, I was surprised at how thorough they'd been in their preparations. They'd even arranged for Blite and Fornax to stay in a farmer's barn, scarcely a quarter mile away from our tavern. It wasn't ideal, but the farmer seemed eager to take in dragonriders—either for bragging rights, or for a little extra coin. Perhaps both.

Somehow, though, I doubted the now one-handed prince would be very thrilled to hear that things were going so well with his network in his absence. He hadn't liked being left behind in the first place, and knowing he'd missed out on all this—a grand battle with the Ulfrangar, the Zuer, and seeing Kinslayer wage magical battle. Well, I wasn't about to volunteer to be the one to fill him in about it later, that's for sure.

Hmm. Actually, that sounded exactly like something

Reigh should do while I watched from the opposite side of the room, well out of arm's reach.

The healer, an elderly man with distinctly half-elven features, hobbled between our rooms while Phoebe fluttered around him nervously like a scarlet butterfly. He cleaned and redressed Reigh's wounds, stitched up the places where Isandri and I had a few fresh gashes from sword cuts, gave me a few herbal remedies for infection, and gave Phoebe instructions on how to look after all of us—which essentially boiled down to "don't let them do anything else stupid."

Talk about an exercise in futility.

There wasn't much the old man could do about Thatcher's condition, though. Thanks to Arlan, there weren't any visible wounds on his body to treat anymore. He'd lost a significant and nearly lethal amount of blood, though. The only treatment for that, apart from a few herbal concoctions and a few food choices that would help speed things along, was making sure he stayed off his feet for a few days.

Easier said than done, though.

Thatcher awoke late the next morning, delirious and asking about his dragon. He fretted over me, too, and wouldn't lie down and be still until I came in to prove I wasn't actually dead. I guess the last thing he remembered clearly was the Zuer standing over me with that spear. Ridiculous kid. *He* was the one who'd almost died. Couldn't he worry about himself for once?

The only thing that kept him in the bed, where he was supposed to be, was Garnett. Not that she forced him. But since he was still only wearing his smallclothes under the blankets, he didn't dare to get up while she was sitting in there with him. I had to wonder if not fully redressing him was a tactical move on her part. After all, Queen Araxie had come by at some point early in the morning with fresh changes of clothes for all of us. So, was this her passive-aggressive way of making sure he followed the healer's orders and didn't go wandering off? If so, it was working brilliantly.

She stayed around the tavern for several days, mostly helping Phoebe and the healer. But after two nights, and the growing confidence that none of us were going to die, she finally confessed that she needed to return to her duties. Arlan was still in the area, and there was a lot of loose ends to tie off after what he'd done at the dragonrider compound. What those loose ends were, exactly, she didn't say. I knew better than to ask, though. I might not have been as keen as she was when it came to reading people, but I could tell from her shifty demeanor and reluctant mumbling that something wasn't quite right.

"I'll be in touch as soon as I can," she promised on her way out the door, casting one last, distinctly sad smile in Thatcher's direction. "I know Arlan will be wanting to speak with you all once Lord Jaevid has arrived and you're all up to it. Just try to stay out of trouble till then, eh?"

"Heh, yeah, well, no promises," Thatcher called back. His forced chuckle sounded more like the despairing squeak of a mouse getting stepped on.

I guess that meant he still hadn't worked up the nerve to tell her how he so obviously felt about her. Ugh. At this rate, he never would.

Not that it was any of my business, I guess. I still hadn't spoken to Thatcher beyond a few, muttered passing words since, well, those few, slurred words we'd exchanged when he nearly died right in front of me. I didn't know what to say to him now.

Before the battle, when he came to clear the air and insist that I not surrender to the Zuer outright, I'd known it wasn't the end of that conversation. There was a lot more that needed to be said—a lot more I should be able to tell him now. But just the thought drove me farther and farther away from everyone as the days dragged on. I didn't know how angry he still was, or what he wanted from me anymore. I didn't know if we were still friends like we had been before, or if he wanted space.

And based on the pasty, wild-eyed way he looked at me from a distance, like someone about two seconds away from throwing up, either he felt the same way ... or he was dealing with some extreme food poisoning. He didn't demand that I leave his room whenever I wandered in to see how he was doing, though. I wondered if that might be a good sign ... Hmm.

The next few days passed slowly, bringing with them another storm that choked the sky with thick, gray clouds. Low rolls of thunder and occasional gusts of howling wind stirred over the bleak landscape, and cold rain ran in rivers down the muddy streets outside the tavern. After nearly five days of it, however, I found myself growing restless. There wasn't much space to escape the ambient noise of the tavern and the rest of our group, who'd gone back to their normal antics now that everyone was on the mend. But the foul weather had also forced the gathering audience of locals who hung around outside, hoping to spot a dragonrider or a member of the royal family, back to their homes. That was probably for the best. We were supposed to be meeting with a certain famous war hero any day now, and I doubted he would want to stop and sign autographs on his way inside.

Sitting beneath the shelter of the tavern's slumped-roofed front porch, I took my time cleaning all the pieces of my leather armor and weaponry. Most of what I had was still stained with dried blood, but I'd been able to find a small bottle of oil and a few rags so I could begin getting everything polished back to pristine condition. On the far end of the roof, a dozen or so little copper cups hung on a thin chain. The rain spilling over them made an odd noise, and after a while, I decided I sort of liked it. Something about it was almost musical, and strangely soothing.

The front door creaked open, but I didn't need to look up to know who came tromping out to stand over me. I knew Reigh's restless, frustrated sigh right away. "Still no word from Jaevid," he muttered.

"It's a long flight here from Halfax," I reminded him. "Even for a dragon. The weather will likely slow him down, too."

"Yeah. True. But I'd thought he might at least send a letter ahead if he got delayed, or that we'd hear something from Jace by now." He strolled over to stand in front of me and lean back against the porch's rickety railing. "You, uh, you doing okay? After everything that happened, I mean."

I glanced up, arching an eyebrow. What was this? Concern for my wellbeing? Since when? "Fine," I said, looking back down at one of my now mostly-clean longswords. "You?"

"Relieved, I guess. Confused, but I'm betting we all are," he admitted. "It's easier knowing the Ulfrangar are finally off our backs now. But Kinslayer showing up to fight like that? I knew Jace was up to something, but Gods and Fates, I had no idea he'd go that far." The young prince shuddered, as though the memory of that battle still made him uneasy. "I saw some incredible things in the Tibran War, you know. I guess I did some of them myself while I was Clysiros's harbinger. But I've never seen *anyone* use power like that before. I didn't even know it was possible. I mean, he killed her without even drawing a weapon. Is that something all Avoran elves can do?"

I frowned down at the freshly polished blade of my sword, scrutinizing it while I mulled that question over. "I don't know. The Ulfrangar don't teach much about them, except that they are an ancient, powerful, and highly secretive people. They don't welcome outsiders, and they usually don't leave their own borders, which makes their social circles extremely difficult to penetrate. I've heard stories that suggest they can live for thousands of years, and can perform feats of magic thought to be impossible everywhere else, but many people here in Maldobar still dismiss that sort of thing as nothing but fairy tales. It makes it difficult to discern what's a real account, and what's just someone's imagination running wild."

"Well, I dunno about you, but it seemed pretty real to me." Reigh shook his head, making his thick mop of dark red hair swish over his brow. "I thought it was strange that Kinslayer didn't have any guards or lookouts when we first met him in Dayrise. Isandri and I kept expecting to spot people posted outside, keeping watch for him. But there was no one. Now it all makes sense. He didn't need any backup, just like he didn't need a weapon the other night."

I had to agree. And the more I thought about it, the more I found myself questioning if getting involved with Kinslayer had been a smart move, after all. I wasn't stupid enough to think he'd intervened like that out of the goodness of his heart. He had a motive—a reason. We just hadn't figured it out yet.

"Congratulations, by the way," Reigh said with that smug little grin that always made me want to punch him in the face.

"For what?" I snorted and went back to polishing the hilt of my sword.

"Your sudden career change," he said evenly, giving a flourish of his hand. "You're officially not an assassin anymore, and I also hear you've finally accepted that drake as your mount. From cold-blooded killer to dragonrider—it's so appropriately *dramatic* for you."

I stopped, slowly letting my glare settle on him. "What is that supposed to mean?"

He snickered. "Oh, you know, because you're always walking around with this ominous scowl, lurking in the shadows, and doing that whole 'me-against-the-world' silent brooding thing. Guess you'll have to leave all that behind for a dragonrider's cloak, right? Ahh, when I picture you, standing there in formation with the rest of us as a fledgling in dragonrider training ... I just get all warm and fuzzy inside." He gave a little mocking, fake sniffle and pretended to wipe a tear away.

I blinked, staring at him as I tried to remember a time when I'd wanted to hit him more than I did right now. Hmmm. Nope. This was it. This was the closest he'd ever come to having my fist through his front teeth. I looked away and considered my next words carefully. He was a prince, after all, even if he was a complete idiot.

"I suppose you're right." I managed to keep my tone controlled and casual. "And you know what else?"

He was still giving me that stupid little smirk. "What?"

I let a cold, calculating, and brutally vicious smile curl across my face as I stared at him, doing everything I could to channel all the excitement of a fox entering a coop of sleeping chickens. "I'm *really* looking forward to the first time I get to spar against you."

Reigh's smile vanished, his expression going slack with sudden realization.

My smile widened. "I think it'll be a really *educational* experience for everyone, don't you?"

JAEVID BROADFEATHER FINALLY ARRIVED EARLY THE NEXT afternoon. By then, the storm that had settled over the city had intensified. The air had turned bitter cold, and the rain that still fell in buckets across the prairie had now turned to sleet.

The low *WHOOM, WHOOM, WHOOM* of dragon wingbeats drew everyone out of their rooms and into the hall. I stole a peek out one of the second-floor windows just in time to see the massive blue king drake touch down right outside. Finally. Perhaps now we would find out what our next move should be.

Mavrik shook himself, snapping his jaws and squinting through the falling slurry as Jaevid quickly climbed down from the saddle and sent him off with a pat on the neck. The massive dragon spread his wings and gave a low growl as he launched skyward again, soaring away until he disappeared above the cloud cover.

It was probably a good idea not to have a dragon that size hanging around close by. The locals would absolutely recognize him, which was bound to draw even more attention to our current location. Not to mention, I doubted there was a barn in the city big enough to accommodate a beast that big. Maybe he'd made other arrangements elsewhere for him?

By the time we all got downstairs, Jaevid was already stepping in the front door. He shook the ice off his shoulders and slid off his helmet, raking his shoulder-length gray hair away from his face with a weary exhale. Tired lines creased the corners of his eyes as he stared around at all of us, hesitating a moment like he was trying to remember why he'd come in the first place.

I did feel a little sorry for him. If rumors were true, he'd left his wife and a new baby at home to go soaring around the kingdom, trying to clean up the messes we left behind while we pursued this so-called hunt for Queen Jenna. Then there was the mess in Halfax where he was basically functioning as crowd control for the Court of Crowns, and the fact that he was supposed to be the Academy Commander at Blybrig. The poor guy couldn't catch a break, it seemed. The true plight of being a kingdom's most famous war hero—everyone expected you to solve any new problems that popped up.

"I'm glad to see you're all on your feet," he said at last. "Some of Eirik's men flagged me down a few miles outside the city. They're preparing to move back to the compound once the storm lifts. I understand there was some trouble there?"

"You didn't get the details?" Reigh asked in surprise.

Jaevid's expression tightened with suspicion. "Not a lot of them, no. Why? What happened?"

Thatcher and I exchanged a tense, sideways glance.

"Oooh boy," Reigh grumbled and shuffled over to one of the dining tables set closest to the tavern's hearth. "Might as well get settled in, Jae. You're gonna want to be sitting down for this one. In fact, let's see if we can't just get some dinner and drinks over here, yeah? This may take a while."

It took about three hours, actually. Jaevid had already been told that there was an altercation with the Ulfrangar at the compound, but since he had yet to speak with King Jace about it, he didn't know the gritty details. I couldn't bring myself to meet his gaze as Reigh explained what'd happened. Or, at least, he tried. There were a lot of gaps since we still didn't fully understand what we'd seen go down between Arlan and the Zuer. It was a safe guess that they had known each other, and might even be related. But what that actually meant in terms of who they were, and what Arlan's real motives were for wanting her dead, was a mystery.

At the end of it all, Jaevid sat back in his seat and stared dejectedly straight ahead. He didn't say a word for a few minutes, and we all sat in uncomfortable silence while the flames crackled and popped in the hearth nearby. I didn't envy his position one bit.

"So, the Zuer is dead," he surmised, glancing in my direction as though looking for verification.

I didn't dare to say a word. Whatever had happened on that battlefield between Arlan and the Zuer was far beyond my understanding. Yes, I wanted to believe she really was gone and my days of being stalked by the pack were over. But I also knew hope like that could be dangerous—especially for someone like me.

"Yeah, as far as we know," Reigh confirmed. "But at this point, what can we say we really know about Kinslayer at all?"

A fair point, and one Jaevid seemed to appreciate as well. His chair creaked some as he leaned forward to rest his elbows on the table and rub at his eyes. "And you believe Jace had something to do with Kinslayer interfering in this battle?"

Reigh gave a flustered snort. "Well, *we* certainly didn't call for him."

"I see." Jaevid sat for a moment, the firelight flickering off the polished pauldrons of his armor. His tight frown made the scar slashing over his eye from his brow to his cheek crinkle some. His mouth pursed and quirked to one side, as though he were chewing on the inside of his cheek while he thought.

To be honest, I'd never studied him all that closely. I'd seen his face a thousand times in statues, mosaics, and tapestries throughout the kingdom. But sitting across from him at the table, watching as he massaged his temples and kept his eerily pale, silver-blue eyes focused on the half-empty ale mug in front of him, I wondered what he must be feeling about all this. He didn't look nearly as old as I'd assumed. In fact, it seemed like he might only be a few years older than I was—well, physically anyway.

But that was another, very long story.

"How are things in Halfax? Is Jenna doing okay?" Reigh asked in a not-so-discreet attempt to lighten the mood.

It didn't work.

Jaevid groaned and sat back in his chair, beginning to unlace his vambraces and pieces of interlocking plate armor and toss them into a pile next to his chair. "They're ... no less complicated than before, although tensions have eased a bit now that Phillip has come home and the Court of Crowns is on a temporary hiatus while she recovers," he replied. "But you know your sister. Her Majesty was less than thrilled to hear about what's been happening with all of you, and especially with the complications coming from Northwatch and nearly losing Judan to the switchbeasts. In light of the rising threat, and the need to have dragonriders properly stationed in that part of the kingdom, she's ready to handle the situation a little more aggressively."

"*More* aggressively?" I blurted. What the heck was that supposed to mean?

Jaevid dropped his pauldrons into the growing pile of armor at his feet with a *thunk* and sighed. "That's the main reason I rushed here so quickly. Queen Jenna would like to send her thanks for your assistance, but she now believes this problem is too big for you to solve. She doesn't want you getting hurt any more than you already have. Two days ago, a decree was sent out from Halfax calling on dragonriders from the other three watches to send a portion of their forces here. They'll be gathering at the compound two nights from now to stage an all-out aerial assault upon Northwatch. The intent is to take it back, even if that means razing it to the ground."

Phoebe covered her mouth to stifle a horrified gasp.

Isandri's expression blanked, her mouth falling open as she stared at Jaevid.

"They're going to burn all of Northwatch to the ground?

But what about the people in the city?" Thatcher protested. "They can't all be criminals and thieves, can they?"

"By all accounts, they are," Jaevid replied somberly. "Phillip's account of what he saw there was most distressing. Some of Judan's agents have verified it, too. There's no other option at this point. Allowing the city to be controlled by mercenaries, murderers, and thieves is not an option."

Isandri's chair gave a sharp squeal across the stone floor as she suddenly snapped to her feet. "Devana is no mercenary! She is not a thief! And she is still being held captive there! Would the queen also sentence her to death? To leave her to burn along with the rest of the filth that has tortured her for so long? Is that what serves as justice in Maldobar?"

No one said a word.

Standing with her shoulders flexing as she took in rapid, furious breaths, Isandri's eyes shone with welling tears that sparkled in the firelight. Her ebony cheeks flushed deep scarlet, and her face twitched with a raw frenzy of emotion.

Next to her, Reigh reached out to gently grasp one of her wrists. It made her flinch, at first. Then her leanly muscled frame seemed to relax a little.

I couldn't help but narrow my eyes, watching her chin tremble and her strange, lime-and-yellow-colored eyes search Jaevid with chaotic determination. This wasn't the first time she'd gone leaping to Devana's defense, as though she'd known her personally somehow. In Dayrise, she'd had a similarly emotional response. Sure, there was the connection of both her and Devana being godlings. This seemed more intense than that, though. After all, she hadn't been quite that attached to Thatcher.

No, this seemed ... personal. *Extremely* personal.

Hmm.

Jaevid gave her a sympathetic nod. "I understand all that, Isandri. Truly, I do. But Devana is also locked in a nearly impenetrable tower designed to be a war fortress that is now, as best we can guess, controlled by either a devious goddess or a similarly powerful sorceress calling herself Iksoli. I cannot, in good conscience, send all of you to that place to even attempt a rescue ..." his voice trailed off, becoming meaningfully quiet as his glacier-hued eyes slowly panned around at all of us with purpose. "But I also can't stop you if you decide to try it anyway."

CHAPTER TWELVE

"This is unfathomable," Isandri hissed angrily. Sitting with her arms crossed, tucked into the bell sleeves of her silken robes, she glared down at the tabletop with her cheeks and tips of her long, pointed ears still flushed in anger.

Jaevid had left us sitting alone at the table long enough to take his belongings upstairs to a room. Or, at least, that's the excuse he'd given. I had a feeling his intention was more along the lines of plausible deniability when it came to whatever stupid, reckless, and poorly-thought-out plan we came up with in the next few hours.

"It's far too dangerous," Phoebe worried.

"It's basically suicide," Thatcher whispered in agreement.

"It's typical Jaevid-level insanity," Reigh muttered, his chin resting on his fist. "Not that I'd expect anything less. He's right, though. This is on us now. We don't have a lot of time to figure it out. If we want to try to get into Northwatch and rescue Devana, we need to be ready to go by tomorrow night at the latest. That'll give us one full day to get there, find her, free her, and get out before the dragonriders unleash all hell on that place."

"It's doable," I decided aloud. "Risky. There won't be any room for mistakes or detours. But it's doable, providing we get the right information beforehand. How familiar are you with the layout of that tower?"

I looked up, waiting for one or all of them to reply. At one point or another, Isandri, Reigh, and Phoebe had all been in Northwatch's dragonrider tower before. We already had a description of where she was, thanks to Phillip. But actually navigating there would be the crucial key. We needed someone who knew the fastest, most discreet way in and out.

"I was not permitted much time outside of my cell," Isandri said, her expression still riddled with distress. "They kept prisoners like myself and Devana under extremely tight security. Whenever we were moved, we were blindfolded, so I've no recollection of where we were within the tower."

"I wasn't free to roam without a security officer," Phoebe murmured. "And I was only allowed in certain areas of the tower, even with that supervision. I might be able to find my way back to that cell block, if I had to. Maybe."

"I can," Reigh said, his voice low and heavy.

Thatcher shot him a meaningful look. "I don't know if that's a good—"

"It's fine," Reigh snapped, keeping his face angled down so none of us could read his expression. It didn't matter, though. I could still see how his knuckles blanched as his hands closed into fists. "I've been through the high security cell blocks from the outside. I remember the way. I can get us there."

"You're sure?" I pressed. If this was his stubbornness and pride talking again, he needed to understand that all our lives hung in the balance.

Reigh's light amber eyes burned with quiet wrath as he shot me a scathing glare. "Considering I've had nightmares about it every night for the last year—yeah, I'm pretty freaking sure." Several tense seconds ticked by before his posture finally relaxed. His mouth twisted to one side as he sank lower in his seat and let out a shaking exhale through his nose. When he spoke again, his voice had lost all its fire and venom. "It's basically burned into my brain at this point, whether I like it or not. So don't worry about it; I can get us there."

"Okay," I said, before anyone else could object. If he was determined to do this, I wasn't about to try to discredit his ability—not when we had no other alternatives.

"Then there's just the matter of actually reaching the tower," Isandri reasoned, tapping her chin thoughtfully. "A dangerous endeavor, even with the cover of darkness."

"They'll spot dragons from miles away, and that might tip them off to the dragonriders' coming, so that's out," Reigh agreed.

"Oh, well, I think I can probably help with that." A merry, sing-song voice giggled from behind our table, nearly making Thatcher shoot straight out of his boots as he scrambled to stand up.

We all turned to find Garnett standing right behind us, her hands planted confidently on her hips and her violet eyes glinting with excitement. "Look at you lot! Like a bunch of kittens caught in the cream! Up to no good, I take it?"

Thatcher's face lit up and he immediately straightened in his chair, staring at her like a blind man seeing his first sunrise. Or a starving puppy seeing a freshly grilled sausage.

Yeah, more like the latter.

A smile stretched from one of his cheeks to the other, and I had to actively resist the urge to bury my face in my palm as he eagerly scooted to the edge of his chair. "Garnett! You're back!" he practically cheered.

Gods preserve me.

"I am. And look at you—back on your feet where you belong, I see," she said, matching his enthusiasm in a way that made me a little sick to my stomach.

If Thatcher had a tail, it would've been wagging fast enough to start a whirlwind. "O-Oh. Yeah, I'm feeling much better now."

"Good. Not a moment too soon. Now that everything's calmed down a bit, there's quite a lot we need to talk about. Arlan's requested a meeting with you all—and Lord Jaevid, of course," she announced merrily. "Tonight, preferably, if that suits you."

ARLAN THE KINSLAYER WANTED TO MEET WITH US tonight? Hmm. I couldn't help but shift uncomfortably at the thought. He certainly hadn't wasted any time.

The scar across Reigh's nose crinkled as his expression tightened into a squinty, suspicious frown. "That didn't take long. Jaevid's barely been here a few hours. Spying on us?"

Garnett's grin was as sheepish as it was prickly, as though she didn't appreciate that brazen accusation. "Yes, well, I like to think I can be as sneaky as the next person, if the occasion calls for it. But a massive blue dragon flying over isn't exactly a secret, now is it? Doesn't take much spying to pick up on that."

Reigh pursed his lips sourly. I guess he didn't have a witty retort for that.

"You really think you can help us get into the tower?" Thatcher pressed, momentarily stunning me with his ability to stay focused on the problem at hand. Wow. Maybe he was growing into this role of being the underdog, dragonrider hero, after all?

Naah. Not a chance.

"I absolutely can!" Her thick braided pigtails swished as she bobbed her head. "Engineered every one of those tunnels myself. Providing no one has gone back and messed up all my fine work, they should be easy enough to access."

"The tunnels?" Reigh's eyebrows rose. "You can't be serious. They're a death trap—especially now. They're bound to be riddled with—"

"—Nothing you lot can't handle, I'm sure," she interrupted, waggling a finger at him. "Besides, you said it yourself, going in above ground stands a greater risk of being spotted and tipping off the whole city—and this Iksoli person—about what's coming their way. This is the fastest and most discreet option, and there's an access entrance not three hours' flight from here. I've been studying all those lovely maps my agents got ahold of. I know this territory backward and forward."

Hmm. She did have a point. Moving underground meant that, even if we were met with some kind of resistance or conflict, we could still keep it quiet. We could snuff out any opposing forces, be they mercenaries or common bandits, without compromising our position. But still ... something nagged at the back of my mind.

"And Kinslayer is willing to allow you to go skipping off to help us like that?" I dared to ask. After all, she seemed to be one of his more valuable agents. I wondered if he'd really be willing to let her do something that dangerous.

Garnett's cheery demeanor dimmed and she fidgeted with one of the ends of her pigtails. "It's not really his decision to make. I'm his employee, not his slave. He doesn't claim any ownership over the people who work for him, and he's always been very clear about that. He protects his workers and contacts, and pays us well, but he isn't going to try to stop us from doing what we want unless it harms his business."

Ahh, so that was it. He'd positioned himself more as a benevolent, understanding figure to his agents, then. A curious choice from a man who dealt in the illegal trade of secrets, information, and illicit goods. No wonder they were so loyal to him. The Ulfrangar had used fear as their unseen tether to force the loyalty of their members. Apparently, Arlan had a different theory about how to ensure his people did as they were told. Interesting.

"I'd like to help you, if I can. And it sounds as though you need it," Garnett continued. "You're not wrong, the tunnels can be quite dangerous. It's easy to get lost if you don't know the right way, and stones only know what or who is hiding down there now."

"Like underbeasts?" Phoebe asked with a shudder.

"Or more of those switchbeasts," Reigh agreed.

There were a lot more problems to consider, things that I wasn't sure Reigh or anyone else standing there in our midst had even considered yet. Dangers that had stared us in the face already. But before I brought any of that up, I wanted to hear what Arlan the Kinslayer had to say. He might be able to solve some of them. More than anything, though, I wondered if he would bother mentioning them at all, or if he was happy to let our little band go stumbling off to our doom in ignorance.

I wanted to see who's side he was really on, and maybe even figure out which angle he was playing. I had a lot to thank him for, and he might even claim ownership over my life—which I undoubtedly owed him—but I also knew his reputation in the criminal underworld.

And it wasn't nearly as generous and understanding as Garnett seemed to think.

"We need to plan to leave tomorrow night, just after nightfall. We can take the dragons to the tunnel entrance," Reigh decided, keeping his voice hushed. "With so many dragons already in the area, I doubt anyone will even notice."

"I take it we are not going to mention any of this to Lord Jaevid?" Isandri asked, an edge of concern in her tone.

Reigh shook his head. "Absolutely not. He'd be duty-bound to try and stop us—he knows that as well as I do. Jenna would never approve of this. Lucky for us, I'm betting he'll have his hands full when all those dragonriders start arriving. We can slip out, no problem."

Garnett clapped her hands, looking pleased as she rocked up onto her toes. Reaching into her belt, she took out a single piece of crisply-folded parchment and handed it to Thatcher. "Right, then. Please pass the word on to Lord Jaevid, if you don't mind. We'll be expecting you later this evening."

Thatcher blushed like an idiot as he took it. He stammered and choked, looking like he might suddenly faint and drop right where he was standing from pure anxiety. "I, uh, yes. Okay. See you later then."

I could spot the silent panic in Thatcher's eyes from ten paces away. Unbelievable. Ugggh. Gods. Send this kid some help, please.

"Watch yourselves, yeah? And don't you go running off to have all the fun without me." Garnett said, giving us all another broad grin and wink as she patted one of the axes hanging at her hips. "If there's gonna be any more beast and baddie-slaying, I want more than just a few test swings this time."

Reigh arched an eyebrow and flicked a disconcerted sideways glance in my direction. "Riiight. Yeah, we'll try to, uh, refrain from ... all the ... *fun*."

I turned away, trying to stifle a laugh by covering my mouth. Instead, I somehow managed to choke on my own spit while I snorted and nearly gagged myself. Fantastic. Well, at least as far as stupid antics and general idiocy went, I was in good company. That was more than I'd ever been able to say about the people I lived with before all of this.

So, for whatever it was worth, I'd take it.

PART THREE

THATCHER

CHAPTER THIRTEEN

As soon as the tavern door shut behind her, I thought of about fifty things I should've said to Garnett. Like how she looked really pretty today, and how I loved that her smile made that rune tattooed under her eye crinkle a little, and that she told the funniest stories I'd ever heard. Now that she was gone, it felt like all the warmth and light had been sucked out of the room.

I sank back in my chair, ignoring the lingering hint of tightness in my chest whenever I took a deep breath. It was the only thing still holding me back after ... well, after everything that'd happened in that fight with the Ulfrangar. To be honest, so much of that night felt like a muddied, hazy blur of pain, confusion, and fear. I had a hard time figuring out what was real, and what was just a nightmare.

I wanted to ask. But the only person who would know for sure, was standing a few feet away, his arms crossed and his expression drawn into a forbidding, thoughtful scowl as he stared at the door Garnett had just gone through. Murdoc was keeping his distance. Even I could tell that. Things were better-ish between us, although I still didn't know where we stood, exactly. I'd said a lot of things to him before that battle with the Ulfrangar. And then I'd nearly died, I guess. It was a lot to process, and we hadn't gotten a chance to talk about it alone.

Maybe tonight, before we got started on this mission to rescue Devana, I could find a good opportunity to pull him aside and we could ... I don't know ... talk.

Frowning down at the clean, neatly folded piece of parchment in my hand, I winced against that pain in my chest as I sighed deeply. "I'll go give this to Jaevid and break the news," I volunteered as I stood, forcing what I really hoped was a believable smile back at everyone.

I guess it wasn't, though, because they all frowned back at me.

Great.

"I can do it, if you'd rather not," Reigh offered glumly, leaning into his elbows and letting his head drop some.

"No, it's fine. I'm not much use when it comes to battle planning anyway, right?" I waved a hand dismissively. "Be right back."

Okay, so maybe it was an excuse to get some air. I hadn't been left on my own much so I could think things over since we'd gotten back from the compound. Or, well, since way before that, actually. Everything was moving so fast. We blurred from one crisis to the next, and I could barely keep up. We had one problem solved now, yes. Er, well, hopefully, anyway. But there were still so many unanswered questions about Devana, Iksoli, what was happening in Northwatch, and myself.

And to make it all worse, we now had a very fixed deadline before it was all bathed in dragon flame.

It made my brain throb as I climbed the steps back to the hall where our rooms were reserved. Tracking down Jaevid's room took a few minutes. I expected to find him busily working to arrange his gear or checking weaponry. Instead, I found all of that piled in the hall outside like he'd dropped it and gone inside. Strange.

I knocked on his door. "Um, Jaevid? Sir? It's Thatcher. I have a letter for you."

No answer.

Oh no. This couldn't be good. Was he hurt? Had something happened? Immediately, memories of how I'd been abducted by the Ulfrangar flashed through my mind. I couldn't let anyone do that to him, too.

"Jaevid?!" I whipped the door open and stormed in, realizing halfway into the room that I didn't even have a weapon.

It didn't matter, though.

Sitting on the foot of the bed, leaned over with his face in his hands, Jaevid didn't even look up when I suddenly burst in. "Yes, Thatcher?" he muttered, his voice low and so muffled by his hands I barely heard him. "What is it?"

"S-Sorry, I-I ... you didn't answer, so I thought you might be in trouble or something," I stammered.

"I'm fine." He still didn't look up.

Fine? He didn't sound fine. I mean, he wasn't hurt anywhere that I could see, but he also looked like he might be in the middle of a mental breakdown, so ...

I closed the door behind me, giving us a little privacy before I walked over to stand next to him. "I'm sorry if this is way out of line, sir, but you don't *seem* fine. Sort of the opposite, actually. Is there, um, is there anything I can do?"

He let out a long, heavy sigh that made his broad shoulders flex and relax. "No, Thatcher."

I glanced down at the letter in my hand. Now definitely didn't seem like a good time to hand him this. It could wait a few more minutes—or a few hours, if he needed it.

"I'm sorry none of this went according to plan." Hedging a little closer, I sat down beside him on the edge of the bed.

"You and Queen Jenna put your faith in us, and we made a real mess of things."

Jaevid lifted his head some, his chin now resting in his palms. At least now I could see his eyes, though. Too bad they looked droopy, bloodshot, and every bit as miserable as I'd feared. The creases around them were deep and weary, like he'd spent the majority of the last few months scowling more than sleeping.

"Please ... don't. I'm the one who should be apologizing to you, Thatcher," he murmured.

"O-Oh! No, I'm fine now, really. And the stuff with the Ulfrangar wasn't really you're fault anyway—"

"I don't mean about that," he said quietly. His eyes fell closed and his dark brows knitted deeply. "I hate that I'm here. I hate every step I take, everything I must do. Every second that passes feels worse than the one before. But I can't do anything about it. I can't leave."

Huh? He didn't want to be here? I leaned over some, trying to get a better look at his expression—to understand what he really meant. "Why?"

A look of anguish ghosted across his sharp features an instant before he bowed his head again. "I had to fly past my home twice. Once carrying Phillip to Halfax. A second time coming here. Both times, all I could think about was how badly I wanted to turn back. My wife is there, with our baby, and ... I can't go to her," he confessed, his tone utterly broken. "I keep remembering how, many years ago, she told me that her own mother had warned her against marrying a dragonrider. That it would only lead to pain and separation. I wanted so badly to prove her wrong. But where am I? Sitting here, repeating the mistakes of hundreds of dragonriders before me."

"Then go home, idiot," a deep, grouchy voice huffed from the doorway.

Jaevid and I both looked up to find King Jace standing there, dressed out in the colorful silken ensemble of a Gray elf scout, with his arms crossed and one shoulder leaned against the doorframe. The old king's disapproving scowl made my insides cringe up with that same sort of feeling I got whenever my father caught me slacking off during my chores. Yikes.

"You know it's not that simple," Jaevid grumbled back.

"Isn't it, though?" Jace countered. He pushed away from the door and ambled in, stopping only when he stood right in front of us. "I seem to have forgotten the moment when you were told to solve every single problem that arises in this kingdom, Jae. You're one, very young man. And you need to go home. Now."

Jaevid's tone tightened, snapping with anger as he glared up at him. "How can you say that? You know as well as I do that the dragonriders—"

"—will be just fine in your absence," Jace cut him off, matching his angry tone with a similar growl. "Look at you. Your head's not in this fight, anyway. What good are you? You and Jenna chose the men to place in command over the dragonrider ranks, but as best I can tell, you don't trust them to actually do their jobs. If the Dragonriders of Maldobar can't handle taking one city without you holding their hands like a nanny, then what good are they?"

Jaevid's mouth snapped shut, but his lips pinched and mashed together as though he were fighting to keep his temper in check.

After what was probably the most uncomfortable few seconds of heated silence I'd ever experienced in my life, King Jace finally shook his head. "Listen, if you're really worried about it, take my shrike back to your estate, lend Mavrik to me, and I'll see this done. You seem to have forgotten you're not the only dragonrider standing in this room. You at least trust me to handle it, don't you?"

All the anger seemed to fizzle from Jaevid's face at once. His posture relaxed, becoming almost defeated as his shoulders dropped and his arms relaxed. "I can't ask you to do that."

Jace cast him a knowing, half-cocked smile. "You don't have to. That's the beauty of me still technically being your senior officer. Granted, I'm an unseated one. But I'm old enough now to be able to tell you with all certainty when you're making a big mistake. Take it from a father who has already made his share of them—the moments you let slip by because you chose your job over your family cannot be replaced. The job won't mourn you when you're gone, Jae. There'll be a new Academy Commander to take your seat before it even gets cold. But the people you love will be the ones laying flowers on your grave and speaking your name for generations." He stepped closer and leaned down, putting a hand on Jaevid's shoulder. "So go pack your things, go home, kiss your wife, and hold your baby."

I WAITED OUT IN THE HALL, STILL HOLDING THAT LETTER from Arlan the Kinslayer, so the two men could talk a little more while Jaevid packed up his belongings and redressed in his armor. Giving them some space seemed like the right thing to do, especially after seeing Jaevid so broken down. I'd grown up hearing stories and legends about Jaevid's adventures—about all his incredible feats to save Maldobar from not one but two deadly wars. Somehow, seeing him that way, stirred up a courage in my chest I hadn't felt since he'd given me that necklace. I fiddled with it, wondering at the things he had done and witnessed while he wore it, and feeling much less ridiculous about all my fears and worries.

After all, if the great Jaevid Broadfeather got homesick, maybe it wasn't so bad for me to be nervous about storming a tower full of mercenaries and cutthroats under the mind control of a crazed goddess.

"Give Beckah our love. And I apologize in advance if I mention this to Araxie in a way that even *hints* you might need help with the baby. I think we both know she will be knocking down your door within hours if it means getting to play grandmother again," Jace said as the door opened again and he and Jaevid came out into the hall, too. "And be sure to leave a word with that dragon of yours to go easy on me. It's been a while since I was in the saddle."

Jaevid gave a tired laugh. "I'll try. But you know he won't."

They went on saying their farewells and exchanging a handshake before Jaevid dipped his head at me, ruffling my hair some on his way past as he headed for the stairs. I watched him go, wondering if there was anything else I could or should have said to him. Maybe I needed to go thank him before—

King Jace cleared his throat. "Well, well, well. Looks like you're *my* problem now."

I winced and turned to face him. "Uh, y-yeah. I guess so."

"Is that for me?" He held out a hand for the letter.

"Um, well, technically it was for Jaevid, but I guess … yes?" I quickly passed it over and took a *big* step back. You know, just in case he wasn't nearly as calm about receiving word from Arlan the Kinslayer as Jaevid had been before.

Also, he terrified me a little.

Okay, a *lot*.

It only took him about two minutes to read it, his sharp, light amber eyes scanning the page as his eyebrows rumpled together and his lips pursed thoughtfully. When he'd finished, he folded the letter up again and tucked it into the fine leather breastplate fitted over his colorful robes. "Very well, then. Seems Kinslayer wants to hold audience with us at sunset. Does the rest of your merry band know about this already?"

I nodded.

"Good. Then I suggest you get some rest while you can," he said as though it were a warning. "Whether you realize it or not, every time you cross paths with that man, you're going into the lion's den. Now isn't the time to be sluggish or distracted."

"Sir—um, I mean—Your Majesty ... sir," I managed to squeak. "Can I ask you something?"

His eyes narrowed dangerously. "As long as it's not something stupid. And just call me Jace. Got more than enough people clucking around here like a yard full of hens calling me that. Makes me twitchy."

"Right. Um, Jace ... sir," I tried again, a little less squeaky this time. "You were the one who went to get Arlan, weren't you? You told him what was happening between Murdoc and the Zuer, right?"

He blinked, his scrutinizing expression seeming to size me up like someone trying to select which pig they were going to butcher for dinner. "And if I was? Is that a problem for you?"

"N-No! Not really, I just ... wondered how you knew where to find him, and ... well, um, ... why you did it." I floundered and waved my hands, stealing another quick step back. "Before, at Eastwatch, you were ready to have Murdoc executed. Then you went to all that trouble to save him. I guess I'm just confused."

The king stared me down for what felt like a terrifying eternity during which I sweated rivers down my back and couldn't keep my stomach from feeling like a spinning whirlpool. Gods and Fates. I shouldn't have said anything at all.

"I supposed I'm confused, too, kid. But I've watched you all rally around that kid, one after another. Rook died for him. A dragon chose him. So, I guess all of that combined tends to sway a person's mind." He rubbed the back of his neck and looked away, still frowning thoughtfully. "That, and it's hard not to look at him now and not see a much younger version of myself. He's come a long way. But make no mistake, he still has a long way to go. The life he had before—it's not something you just slough off and forget. He'll be recovering from it for the rest of his life. Make sure you don't forget that."

I swallowed hard. "I won't, sir."

"Jace," he corrected with an irritated growl.

"Oh! Right. I mean, Jace, sir."

He groaned and rolled his eyes. "No wonder Jae was at his wit's end. Fates preserve me."

CHAPTER FOURTEEN

Thanks to the miserable weather and pouring, sleety rain, it was difficult to tell when, exactly, sunset was. But as the sky grew dim, and everyone grew more anxious, we all gathered in the tavern downstairs and prepared to go meet Arlan the Kinslayer once again.

Murdoc grumbled quietly, standing near the door and helping Phoebe tie on her cloak so that it hid the small dagger belted to her hip. Reigh and Isandri sat near the hearth, already dressed to go and muttering to one another in low voices. She flicked me a meaningful look when I came downstairs, as though silently asking if I was all right. I forced a smile that probably wasn't fooling anyone.

I'd wanted to try talking to Isandri before we left, to find out if she was all right after that sort of heated moment when she found out what was going to happen to Northwatch. But there hadn't been a good chance. Or, rather, there hadn't been an opportunity when Reigh wasn't lurking somewhere nearby her. Whether it was just friendship or something else budding between them, they definitely seemed to be spending a lot more time talking.

And I wasn't even going to try to guess what was happening between Murdoc and Phoebe. Nope. No way.

Glancing between each pair, I found myself standing awkwardly at the bottom of the stairs ... alone. I'd almost made up my mind to sit down on the bottom step and wait when the door swung open and Jace came in wearing a long rain-drenched cloak. He stuck his head inside long enough to glare around at all of us and give one solemn nod.

Time to go.

With my insides frantically tying themselves up into a thousand knots, I pulled on my own cloak and followed behind everyone else out into the frigid rain. Mud squished under my boots and the bitter wind stung at my face. I wished immediately I'd bundled up with more clothes. I could only hope we weren't walking all that far.

The feel of my teeth chattering and my fingers going stiff as my nose went numb brought back flashes of memory like splinters in my mind. It'd been a storm a lot like this one when Rook and the Ulfrangar had marched me out of Dayrise. I'd almost died then, er, well, the first time. Reigh had said I was severely hypothermic. I would've died of exposure in another hour or two if Isandri hadn't found me in the back of that upturned wagon.

I stumbled, almost tripping as those distracting thoughts overtook me. Gods, I had to pull it together. I couldn't go into a meeting with Arlan like this. Confidence—I had to project confidence!

Jace led the way as the night closed in, driving the few villagers and commonfolk who were willing to brave the weather back into the warmth and safety of their homes. We passed empty, muddy streets, closed shops, and windows lit by soft golden light. Smoke drifted up from the tall chimneys, and muffled laughter echoed from beyond bar and tavern doors.

We trudged along for nearly a mile before Jace finally threw up a hand, signaling us to stop. At a crossroads on the far eastern edge of the city, we squinted through the pouring rain. The cottage stood on a busy corner only about a block off Osbran's main road. The stacked stone sides were mottled with frozen moss, slimy mushrooms, and splotches of brown lichen, and the thatched roof shed the frigid rainfall into a growing moat around the outside.

At first brush, it looked every bit as run down, soggy, and miserable as the rest of the city. But looking more closely, I noticed that its windows also shone with inviting light, smoke curled from its crooked chimney, and a little wooden placard hanging on one of the porch posts read "Bookseller – Inquire Within" in curling green letters. Bookseller? I'd never heard of a shop that only sold books before, but something about it made me smile.

Everyone began to cross, making their way up the weathered stone steps and under the low porch roof to the front door. An old copper bell hanging over the door jangled as we entered, and the heavy smells of ink, old parchment, and dried herbs seemed to wrap around me like a friendly hug. Warmth radiated from the large, raised hearth on the far wall, and an iron kettle whistled where it hung over the low embers.

"Fates. It's incredible," Phoebe whispered in awe as she turned in a slow circle, drinking in the walls that were lined from floor to ceiling in bookshelves and cubbies. Every single one was crammed with tomes, scrolls, stacks of clean parchment, or ink bottles.

"It is, isn't it?" An older human woman in a long, billowy dark purple dress laughed merrily from behind a long counter set up right next to the crackling fireplace. With large round spectacles perched on the end of her nose and her long, somewhat wild golden hair beginning to turn a frosty white around her temples, she leaned against the counter and stroked the back of a black kitten with large, oddly yellow eyes. Portions of her hair was braided with colorful beads, charms, little feathers, and flowers woven into it. More trinkets like that, including a few more pairs of those large glasses and even a few tiny bottles of what looked like ink hung on beaded strings around her neck.

Her skirt fluttered as she whirled around the counter, sky blue eyes looking us over one at a time as she fished through one of the many pockets of her long white apron. "My, aren't you all a proper mess? Here to see Arlan, I take it?"

"We are," Jace confirmed, seeming a little tense at the sight of her rummaging through her pockets like that ... until she pulled out what looked suspiciously like a cookie.

Yep. Definitely a cookie.

"Very well, then. Wipe your boots and take off those drippy cloaks, if you don't mind," she said before taking a bite. "Then it's the fourth book on the far shelf just over there."

Wait, what? Fourth book? What was that supposed to mean? Who was this lady? And did she have any more cookies or was that the last one?

And why was her cat staring at us like that? Its eyes followed every move we made, and its ears perked curiously, almost like it could understand everything we said. Weird ...

After we'd all shrugged out of our rain-soaked cloaks and wiped our muddy shoes off on the small rug right outside the door, everyone followed Jace down the long shelves of books to a narrow one squished in the corner of the room on the other side of the hearth. He counted down four spines until he arrived at one particularly thick tome bound in dark burgundy leather. He and Murdoc exchanged a dubious glance before he grasped the spine and began to pull. Something clicked inside the shelf, like the heavy metal *thunk* and clack of a door lock.

The shelf swung in like a big, thick, book-laden door, groaning on old hinges.

Whoa.

Phoebe was practically convulsing with excitement as she squirmed her way to the front of our group so she could peer through into the next room. It made Jace grumble in disapproval, but he didn't try to stop her. Or maybe he couldn't.

She was pretty fast, after all.

"Well, then," the familiar tone of Arlan the Kinslayer carried in from the dim space beyond. "Don't just gather at the door. Come in. You're right on time."

THE INSIDE OF ARLAN'S, ER, SECRET OFFICE WAS DEFINITELY not what I'd been expecting from a guy who supposedly made his living doing bad, illegal things. Granted, that was beginning to become sort of a theme with him. It made me wonder who he really was, exactly. Was all of this a disarming front meant to put us at ease? Or was this his true personality, and all the crime stuff was just something he did to make money?

Regardless, as I stumbled along after the rest of our group into his hidden room behind the bookcase, I once again stared around in amazement at every crowded corner. His room shared the same fireplace as the storefront, although you couldn't see through it to the other side. Pretty clever. A long velvet sofa and several fancy-looking chairs with clawed feet and big, intricately embroidered cushions were pulled close to it. A low, marble-top coffee table was stacked high with books and papers, some of which were held open with weights that looked suspiciously like enormous gemstones. Those weren't real, right? No way. They couldn't be.

More overloaded bookshelves covered most of the walls, but there were a few empty spaces packed with framed maps, oil portraits, and iron sconces lit with flickering candles in colored glass globes. A chaise lounge with a blanket and a pillow had been pushed to one corner of the room like an afterthought, and a large mahogany desk was set to face into the room with a wingback chair pulled up to it.

Like before when we'd met Arlan in Dayrise, his desk was also covered in stacks of books, scrolls, quills, and ink bottles. Some of the tomes lay open, while others had been set aside with twenty or so strips of ribbon slipped between the pages to mark certain passages. A few empty bottles of wine were scattered here and there, and an untouched plate of sliced bread, cheese, and grapes sat on a little round pedestal table next to his desk.

Arlan himself stood at one of the far shelves, perusing the spines of some of the books before he plucked one from the collection and turned around. "I'm pleased to see you've all recovered," he said without ever looking up. Opening the book, he thumbed through the pages as he strode right past our group and sat back down at his desk. "Although, I can't help but notice the esteemed Academy Commander has elected not to join you. I trust he's in good health? Or has Her Majesty's most recent call to action concerning the fate of Northwatch summoned him away?"

Geez. He already knew about that? How? Had Garnett told him?

I glanced around, taking in the cluttered, dimly lit room again. But I didn't see her anywhere.

"Neither, actually. He's gone home. It's long overdue," King Jace announced. "Hopefully, you'll accept my presence as a substitute."

Arlan finally looked up, his peculiar eyes glowing just as brightly as the coals smoldering in his fireplace. "Jace Rordin, formerly known as Rift among the ranks of the Ulfrangar, although much more recently a Seasoned Lieutenant for the dragonriders, who now sits enthroned as Luntharda's king. I suppose you'll suffice, since I'm also told you are the one who brought warning to my agents of the Ulfrangar's movements."

Jace tilted his chin up, a defiant smirk playing over his features. "Well-informed, aren't you?"

Arlan looked back down at his open book as though he'd already lost interest. "Frighteningly so, My King. Now, if you would be so kind, move whatever might be in the way and have a seat at the hearth. I'll be with you momentarily."

It took some light stepping and awkward shuffling to get through all his stuff—the stacks of papers and books on the floor, random artifacts, stone figures, and a folded-up painting easel—to get back to the sitting area. I took one of the chairs closest to the fireside and watched, chewing on my cheek, while Arlan took up his quill and scribbled a few things onto a piece of parchment he had spread out on his desk. The feather tip scratching on the paper and the soft crackle and hiss of the fire filled the awkward silence while we waited. Finally, he closed the book, folded up the parchment neatly, and sealed it with a drop of red wax. His long golden hair swished at his back as he strode by, opening the bookshelf just long enough to pass the letter to the merry, cookie-eating woman outside.

"See that Violet takes this directly to the Zuer, Larisse," he ordered.

She answered, confirming his request around what sounded like another mouthful of food. Probably another cookie. Not fair.

Then it hit me so suddenly I choked and wheezed—did he just say ... *Zuer?!*

No. No way. Not possible. I was hearing things, I had to be.

Looking around, I found all my companions staring straight ahead with blank looks of absolute shock. Oh gods ... I wasn't just hearing things. He'd really said Zuer—as though that was a person who was still *alive*.

My gaze immediately locked onto Murdoc. All the color had drained from his face, and he sat eerily motionless, not blinking or breathing at all. What did this mean? Was the Ulfrangar going to continue to hunt him? Was he still in danger? Had they seen us come here? They'd attacked us the last time we met with Arlan, so I sort of doubted his presence was going to deter them. Or maybe it would after what had happened a little over a week ago? Gods, I didn't know.

My stomach cramped and my hands clenched at the arms of the chair as I bit back the urge to yell—to demand to know just what the heck was going on here.

Calm—we had to stay calm. Now wasn't the time to freak out. Deep breaths. Control the panic.

Arlan had just begun to pour himself another glass of wine when Jace suddenly snapped up from his seat and spun to face him, teeth bared in anger like a bristling wolf. "You spared the Zuer? After all that?" he growled.

The elven man swirled his glass, studying it with a keen, scrutinizing frown before he finally came over to sit down in our midst as though nothing were wrong. "No. I simply appointed a new one."

"You ... *WHAT?!*" Jace thundered.

Arlan took a sip before he finally glanced up at the raging king. "If you don't mind, sit down, and we will discuss this at length. It was not a decision I arrived at lightly, and with some contemplation, I think you will agree it was the appropriate course of action."

Jace licked his teeth behind his lips and slowly shook his head. "Oh, I very much doubt that."

"Do you?" Arlan arched an eyebrow, looking wholly unimpressed. And after what I'd seen him do with his magic on that battlefield, I could appreciate why. Arlan's gaze fixed upon Jace, a hint of disapproval crinkling his ethereally perfect features. "I understand your concern, Your Majesty. Truly, I do. But I would like to invite you to consider the situation a bit more deeply. On the surface, yes, the Ulfrangar are a consistently malevolent presence. They deal in death and contracted murder as a specialty," he said, his tone as collected and precise as ever. "But as an organization, you know as well as I do that the Ulfrangar have been in existence for many centuries. Their network spans kingdoms and empires far beyond these borders. They're interwoven into cultures and communities that are otherwise closed to the outside world. Yes, their treatment of their initiates is harsh and violent. Their purpose is no less unsavory. But they are profoundly structured, and can be reasoned with, when necessary."

Reigh spoke up, matching Arlan's expression with a frosty glare of his own. "Make your point."

Arlan's mouth pressed into a tense, dissatisfied line. "My point, Your Highness, is very simple. Dismantling the Ulfrangar will not eradicate the demand for the services they provide. Right now, they are a superior force in that world. An apex predator, if you will. And one that we now have the ability to communicate openly with and, to a degree, influence. If you remove them from play, others will seek to take their place. New organizations that we have no understanding of or influence over will arise to seize the opportunity of controlling that market. Currently, we know who and what the Ulfrangar are. We know how they operate. We can anticipate their movements and actions, with a tactical choice of successor to the Zuer, we can even sway them if needed. A known enemy can be an effective tool if used properly."

"A choice of successor? So, then, ... you don't intend to

take on that role yourself?" Reigh sputtered. "Not in *any* capacity?"

Arlan made a scoffing sound and wafted a hand. "Of course not. I've no interest in the business of paid assassination, lucrative though it may be. And they have no desire to be led by someone who is not a true member of their pack. That is why I summoned the remaining elder hunters of the Ulfrangar here this morning, to strike this bargain with them. In exchange for advocating my position and passing the role of Zuer on to another, I made a few simple requests. They found my terms agreeable, and so the deal was struck."

"And what terms were those?" Jace snapped bitterly, his face still flushed.

"First, that the claims against yours and Murdoc's, lives would be forever forfeited. You are, as they say, free men henceforth," he explained with a satisfied smile. "Second, that *I* would be the one to decide the successor to the role of Zuer, that being my right as the one who has slain their previous one. And lastly, that the existing understanding of the boundaries between our two organizations would now be more defined and solidified. I will not encroach upon their work or hinder their agents, and they will show me the same respect and never target my affiliates or interfere with subjects of my business dealings. Should they receive a contract for someone of interest to me, I reserve the right to declare that person off limits—within reason, of course."

"And they agreed to this?" Murdoc asked, his voice shaking and hushed.

Not that I didn't get why. Out of all of us, he undoubtedly felt the sting of this situation more than anyone. It seemed like Arlan had a handle on it, though. In fact, by the sound of things, he had the whole pack sitting and rolling over like trained dogs now. Impressive.

And ... sort of terrifying.

My stomach fluttered a little, realizing probably way too late the sheer magnitude of the power this man now had. He had friends in all the most critical and convenient places, and was well on his way to making himself untouchable. He had the Ulfrangar underfoot. He had connections in every noble house and court.

Gods and Fates, he might even be more powerful than Queen Jenna.

"They did," he confirmed evenly. "They are happy not to have an outsider presiding over their organization. And I'm equally pleased to finally have the relations between us crystallized and mutually understood."

I guess Murdoc couldn't take it anymore. He sat forward in his seat, staring Arlan down with an expression of absolute terror, like he was just waiting for the axe to drop. "You expect me to believe that's it? That I'm walking out of here a free man? We both know I owe you my life. But you're letting go of your claim over me? Just like that?"

Arlan's cold stare made my stomach flip and twist up again. That look, like the mysterious, unpredictable gaze of a tiger lurking in our midst, chilled me to the marrow. At any moment, he might snap. He could destroy every last one of us with a snap of his fingers.

But he didn't.

"Trust me, the exchange was more than fair. By luring one of Sadeera's aspects into the open where I might dispel it, you've more than compensated me for any claim I might have over you," he replied. "My own agents have not been able to accomplish that very task despite trying for a great many years."

"Sadeera?" Jace crossed his arms. "You're referring to the former Zuer?"

Arlan dipped his head slightly, his golden eyes shining just as brightly as the flames flickering in the hearth. "Yes ... and no. She was posing as the Zuer of the Ulfrangar, and likely has been for quite some time. But what you saw to be a physical woman was, in fact, a very complex manifestation of magical power. A duplicate, if you will. She's conjured a great many of them—no small feat, even for an individual of our heritage. The amount of magical power required, along with the rare artifact necessary to accomplish the ritual, is staggering." He took a long sip from his wine glass and slowly licked his lips. "Because of that, she is very careful with them, and luring one of them out into the open so that I might destroy it has been frustratingly difficult."

"So this aspect ... it wasn't a real person? Just a duplicate of someone else? This Sadeera person?" Murdoc pressed.

His quiet answer was barely more than a whisper over the rim of his wine glass. "Yes."

CHAPTER FIFTEEN

I frowned as my mind raced, trying to quickly assemble all the pieces to this puzzle. The Zuer had been a woman named Sadeera—another Avoran elf. Er, well, sort of. According to Arlan, she wasn't even a real person at all. She was something he called an aspect, which as best I could tell, meant she was some sort of magical duplicate. I guess she was able to give those aspects commands, or control them somehow, even from far away. Was the actual Sadeera even in Maldobar? Or was she still in Avora?

Fates, this was a lot more complicated and involved than I'd ever imagined.

"And this Sadeera person, the real one, you're related to her? You called her 'sister' before," I recalled.

Arlan's eyes flicked up, catching the firelight like two golden mirrors, although the rest of him never moved. He stared at me as he answered, "She is, indeed, my sister."

"She called you by a different name," Murdoc added. "Zarvan."

The elven man shuddered some, looking away and sucking his teeth, as though the sound of that name left a bitter taste in his mouth. "I'd thank you never to speak that name again. The life attached to it ended a very long time ago—long before any of you were ever born," he snapped coldly. "My personal history is irrelevant, and entirely beside the point. I called you here to discuss another matter. A business opportunity, if you will. Garnett has informed me that you hope to infiltrate Northwatch tower and rescue Devana before the proverbial hammer drops. No small task."

Jace shook his head and pinched at the bridge of his nose right between his eyes. "Are you kidding me, Reigh? You're going in there after that woman? Have you lost your mind?"

"We got a clear account from Phillip about her situation in there. She's being held prisoner by this Iksoli person," Reigh reasoned, his expression softening as his gaze drifted over to Isandri. "It's important."

"It better be," Jace snorted. "Since you'll likely get yourselves killed trying it."

Arlan gave a deep, bemused chuckle. "Now, now. Perhaps not. Garnett has expressed her intentions to go along with you, and I've suggested that I might be able to provide some additional assistance to you, as well ... for a price, of course."

Murdoc's eyes narrowed. "What kind of assistance?"

"Information, primarily." Arlan gave a sweeping gesture to the cluttered room around him. "It is, as they say, power. And I've quite a lot of it at my disposal. You've neglected to ask some very significant questions regarding the individual who calls herself Iksoli. What I know would give you an edge—a degree of assurance to your success, as well as caution to prevent any unfortunate casualties."

"What is it you want in exchange?" Jace asked, shifting to stand with his arms crossed over his chest.

Arlan took another sip from his wine glass. "There is a certain artifact located in that tower, one brought there by the Tibran Empire, that I would like to collect. It has immense significance to my people, and power that no person outside Avora would be able to utilize without killing themselves."

Jace's forbidding frown deepened. "And ... that would be?"

"The lowlanders, such as yourselves, call it the Mirror of Truth. It has a different name in Avora, naturally. I would like to have it secured so that my people can go in and extract it," he replied.

Reigh made a sputtering sound. His eyes went wide, face going nearly as pale as milk. He sank back in his seat, staring at Arlan like he was seeing a phantom. "What, by all the gods, would you want with that thing?"

"Ahh, so you've seen it, have you?" Arlan's expression softened, becoming somewhat intrigued.

"Yeah," he rasped, his voice quaking some as he breathed in hard puffs through his nose. "Yeah, I've seen it. I've seen it suck the souls right out of people if they try to tell a lie while looking into it. Is that what you'll do? Interrogate people with it?"

"Rest assured, young prince, I've no interest in using it in the same, barbaric manner the Tibrans did," Arlan assured, his nose wrinkling as though he found the idea disgusting. "They defiled it with their blundering attempts to wield it's true power. The Mirror of Truth, as you call it, is not a mirror at all. It is a means of contact, a holy relic used to commune with one of our patron deities. There are three, all identical in make, and each one is tethered to a separate entity—beings that your people here, in the lowlands, refer to as the foregods. The one you know as the Mirror of Truth is tethered to Itanus,"

Arlan stopped, taking a final drink from his glass and setting it aside. He wafted his hand, as though brushing the subject aside. "There's no point in explaining it further. Not at the moment, anyhow. I realize the object is far too large for you to remove yourselves. I would merely like to have it located so that my people can go in and extract it later. All I require of you is your assurance that you will move it to a securable location, and then relay that to my network. Easy enough, wouldn't you agree?"

"Yeah, except the part where we're on a time crunch in case the dragonriders decide to make their strike early and douse the whole place in dragon venom," Murdoc muttered. "Will the mirror even survive being burned if it gets caught in the crossfire?"

Once again, Arlan's cold smile curled over his thin lips, and sent a fresh jolt of terrified chills up my spine. "Absolutely."

No one spoke for almost a minute, each second passing with the weight of a brick being stacked on my head. Making another deal with Arlan, especially one like this, left a bitter taste in my mouth. I didn't know anything about this Mirror of Truth, but it sounded like something dangerous. What did Arlan want to do with it? Probably something bad, right?

Jace finally puffed a growling sigh. "This is your call, Reigh. You know what you're up against in that tower. I hate to lay it all at your feet, but it's your life you're gambling with by going in there in the first place."

"We'll do it," Reigh blurted suddenly.

Everyone stared at him.

Arlan's eyebrows rose. "Oh?"

Sitting tense and stiff in his chair, Reigh kept his gaze locked onto the floor as his chest heaved in slow, furious breaths. "Yeah. We'll secure the mirror. Now, tell us what you know about Iksoli."

"To understand Iksoli, you must understand what, precisely, the gods are," Arlan began. Setting his wine glass aside, he shuffled through some of the books and loose pieces of parchment scattered across the coffee table until he tugged one small, slim tome bound in faded green leather. The golden leafing upon the cover had all but been worn away, making it pretty much illegible.

His thin lips pursed thoughtfully as he flipped through it, his vibrant eyes scanning each page with startling speed. Was he really able to read that fast? No way—that was impossible, right?

"Ah, yes. Here it is." He opened the book to a page with an intricately drawn diagram. It looked sort of like a ladder, or maybe a lattice, with little scribbled words and tiny pictures all around. But the language wasn't one I recognized.

"The divine hierarchy," Murdoc muttered as he leaned over to steal a look.

I stared at him. Wait a second, he could actually read whatever language this was? How? Had the Ulfrangar taught him that?

Arlan's smile was cryptic again, and it made my skin crawl. "Indeed. I realize this is not something commonly studied by the lowland kingdoms. But perhaps now you can all see the importance," he said smoothly. "Those with a limited understanding of the divine realm often lump all of the gods together, as though they are all of the same power and presence. But in truth, there is a very distinct recurrent evolution to their essences. They are a separate race unto themselves, although their life cycles are much different than what we experience as mortals. They begin as godlings, juvenile beings of limited divine power, still struggling to establish their place and define their essence. As they grow over the ages, they mature, expanding and assuming the mantle of their true power."

"You mean, the gods all began, as sort of people? Like us?" I asked.

Arlan shook his head. "Not precisely, but it is comparable. Your situation, being bound completely within a mortal body, is slightly different. But the essence you possess, your spirit, is that of a godling. A young deity still sorting himself out."

"O-Oh," I managed to wheeze. "I get it."

I absolutely did *not* get it.

"With the passing millennia, godlings like you are expanded even further. Their interest in the toils and ventures of mortals wanes, until, at last, they are stretched even into the fabric of reality—existing far beyond the realm of mortal understanding. Instead of a powerful being with relatable sentiments, reactions, and comparable feelings, they become a cold, indifferent, and distant presence that cares nothing for the mortal world. They exist above it, beyond it, and through it, even unto the farthest reaches of the universe."

I had to remind myself how to breathe and blink at the same time. That was going to happen to me? I was going to ... expand into ancient, omnipresence god-form? Just the idea made my brain scramble. I stared at Isandri, who looked similarly overwhelmed and mildly panicked. She gnawed at the inside of her cheek, her vivid eyes darting back and forth as though she were frantically trying to process all this.

"Taking that into consideration, what you are dealing with now from the entity calling herself Iksoli, is another godling of the same caliber as you," Arlan said, staring straight at me for a few seconds before shifting his focus to Isandri. "Devana, as well. You are the next generation of your species. There is one other, but he has not yet made himself known to the world. I have my people watching him closely, however. It won't be long, I'm certain."

"You mean, Iksoli ... she's a godling, too?" I just had to be sure I was hearing all this correctly.

"Precisely," Arlan confirmed. "But an unfettered one. While you, Isandri, and Devana have found yourselves bound in mortal flesh, Iksoli has no such constraint. Her powers have become more affirmed, as well, and I suspect your time spent in mortal flesh is to blame for your delayed progress in that regard." He gestured to Isandri and me with a sweep of his hand. "Devana, also, has likely suffered some difficulty in controlling and calling forth her abilities. The tyrant Argonox attempted to forcefully expidite this process, and in so doing may have fractured her very essence. Now Iksoli has preyed upon her, as well."

"Not that I'm not enjoying story time, but how does any of this help us fight Iksoli?" Reigh demanded.

"Have patience, young prince. It is because you rush so recklessly through life, and do not take time to know your enemy before you engage it, that you have suffered so much already." Arlan's expression cooled, obviously not pleased to be rushed, and he raised a finger. "First, now knowing that you are dealing with a rival godling, you can be assured that her powers are likewise limited to the constraints that would hinder any deity. It has long been understood that one god cannot use their power to injure another. They are impervious to that sort of harm, but rather struggle for dominance in a space. It's not unlike the struggle between two children trying to shove one another out of a chair. The one who earns the seat is dominant, and the other is forced out."

"Then how is it that Iksoli is controlling Devana?" Reigh countered. "If she's holding her prisoner, and using her power to control other people's minds—"

"Not *using*," Arlan interrupted to correct him. "Mimicking. That is the basis for all of Iksoli's divine power. She is, as best my research can establish, a goddess of mischief and chaos. Her power lies in deception, illusions, and mimicry."

"It makes sense," I murmured, talking more to myself than to the rest of them. But when I looked up, even Arlan was staring at me with a puzzled expression. "I-I mean, just based on what Duke Phillip told us about his encounter with her. He said she touched him in order to get control over him. So maybe that's how she does it? Maybe she has to make physical contact to copy someone's power and that's why she's keeping Devana prisoner?"

Arlan tapped his pointed chin. "A worthy guess. I would advise you to take special care, then, not to let her touch you, or she may turn your own powers against you, as well."

Wow. Now there was a terrifying thought. Not really because of mine, honestly, but Isandri's powers were pretty incredible.

"One touch, and she could turn any one of us," Murdoc pointed out, panning his gaze around at our group in solemn realization.

My stomach dropped. Gods—he was right! What if Iksoli turned Murdoc on us? Or Reigh? I'd only barely managed to drive her out of Phillip's mind. The longer I thought about it, the more this felt like a mission doomed to failure. Now I understood why Queen Jenna was ready to just burn the whole place and call it a day.

"This will be dangerous," Isandri whispered. "Far more than we anticipated. Reigh, you needn't endanger yourselves for this. Going there—freeing Devana—is my responsibility. I can go alone."

My heart gave a furious jolt. "*Your* responsibility? I'm a godling, too. Not to mention, I'm the one Devana has been calling for this whole time. I'm all for minimizing risk, but why is this all on you?"

Isandri snapped a wrathful glare in my direction, all those

frantic emotions bursting back to the surface just like they had the last time we'd discussed Devana's fate. But this time, she didn't shout. She didn't storm away. Her head bowed some, and her gaze drifted to the staff in her hand as her features fell into a look of quiet anguish. "Because ... she was my sister." Her eyes closed and her brow wrinkled, as though each word stung. "Not by blood. And not just by divine connection. It was more than that. We ... grew up together. Devana was brought to the temple seven or eight years before me. The priestesses had raised and taught her after her parents left her there, as well. Her abilities were much different—softer, I suppose. At first, the priestesses let us study together. But when it became clear that my own abilities would be more aggressive, more suitable for battle, they separated us. I didn't see her very often after that. Only once a month, on a full moon, when I could make myself invisible. I could sneak through the temple grounds to visit her."

"Then the Tibrans invaded your kingdom," Murdoc guessed.

Isandri nodded, making her long black hair swish where it fell to her waist. "They burned our temple and killed the priestesses. I nearly died as well, trying to defend it. They must have thought me dead. That's the only reason I can fathom they didn't take me captive like they did Devana." Her shoulders rose and fell with a deep, unsteady breath. "For a while, I followed the Tibran movements as they conquered. I tried several times to rescue her, but eventually, they captured me, as well."

Reigh tilted his head to one side, studying her with a fractured expression. "That's why I found you in that prison cell," he murmured quietly.

She stared back at him, tears welling in her strange, lime-and-yellow eyes. "Yes." She sniffled some, her lips thinning as she turned her face away and wiped her cheeks with a shaking hand, as though she didn't want anyone to see her that way. "I should have been able to protect Devana. Instead, I failed her and the rest of the people who had cared for and raised me. Now you understand why I must set her free. I will not give up. I will not abandon her."

"Neither will we," I promised. "We started this together. That's how we should finish it. Right, Reigh?"

His crooked grin never quite reached his eyes as his gaze stayed fixed on Isandri. "Yeah. You're right. So, no more of these rogue warrior antics. If anyone here is going to die doing something insanely dangerous on their own, it's gonna be me. Got it?"

Isandri flicked him an exasperated look, then smiled faintly as she rolled her eyes and shook her head. "Very well, Reigh. If you insist."

16

CHAPTER SIXTEEN

We sat with Arlan for a long time, probably hours, going over as much information as we could about the specifics of divine magic, Iksoli's identity, and what we could do to get Devana out of her grasp. Bottom line? Yeah. It wasn't going to be easy. But with some preparation, it might be possible. We just couldn't afford to make any wrong turns—literally.

There were a lot of "don'ts" that we had to consider. Don't get lost in the tunnels, obviously. Don't let any of the cutthroats or vagabonds we might come across live long enough to tell the tale about our arrival. Don't get sidetracked. Don't let Iksoli touch us. Don't get lost in the tower. And, most importantly, don't die.

"We'll have to split off into two teams once we get inside the tower," Reigh considered aloud. "That's the only way to get this done as fast as possible and with the least confrontation. One team will be focused on getting Devana, the other on securing the mirror. Crap. I hate irony."

Murdoc arched an eyebrow, as though silently asking what he meant by that.

Reigh just shrugged. "Trust me, the last time I split up with my allies in that place, it did *not* go well. But it's not like we have a choice."

"I can take a group to secure the mirror." Murdoc insisted. "Phoebe, can you get us to where that thing is kept?"

She flinched in her chair, suddenly sitting up straighter as she stammered, "I-I, um, yes. Yes, I think so. The divine artifacts were kept in the same area, under tight security, but I did have access a few times. I think I can find it again."

Murdoc nodded, then glanced back to Reigh. "Garnett can come with us, too, so we have enough muscle to move the mirror if we need to. That'll put you, Thatcher, and Isandri headed for the cell block where Devana is. Phillip said he came across her in the cells near the base of the tower, right? That should help to narrow your search."

My heart gave a painful throb and twist in my chest, feeling like a soggy sponge being squeezed in someone's fist. Murdoc was going with Garnett? In a separate group? What if something went wrong? What if they were attacked? I'd be too far away to help them—I might not even know they were in trouble at all.

My mouth screwed up and I looked down, biting back everything I wanted to yell in protest. I didn't like it. Not one bit. But what could I do? Deep down, I knew Murdoc and Reigh were right. We couldn't go running all over the tower in one big group. We'd get spotted, overwhelmed by Iksoli's mind-controlled army, and probably killed without finding the mirror or Devana. Splitting up really was the best option.

I just ... didn't like it *at all*.

"Once we've accomplished what we came for, the fastest point to evacuate from is the passage on the roof of the tower. That's where we can call down the dragons to airlift us to safety before the rest of the dragonriders come in for their assault." Reigh rubbed at his chin and jaw, his gaze distant as he stared into the flames flickering in Arlan's hearth. "Gods and Fates, I can't believe I'm about to do this again. This is either the most severe form of divine punishment or ... I don't even know what. Torture, I guess? Someone remind me to punch Jaevid later for ducking out right before we do this."

Murdoc looked to me, somehow managing not to look the least bit worried about any of it as he spoke. "Blite won't be able to take any additional weight apart from mine. Fornax can carry two, right? Vexi, as well. And Isandri can fly on her own. So we should be set for departure if you can take Devana as your passenger. We don't know what state she'll be in, so we need to pair her with someone who can hold her in the saddle, if necessary. Reigh, you can take Garnett. Isa can take Phoebe, since she's the smallest and lightest—that way carrying her doesn't slow us down. I think we can anticipate some pushback. By that point, the word will be out and the whole tower will know we're there, so we need to be prepared for a fight. Unless, of course, liberating Devana eliminates Iksoli's control over her minions. That would be ideal."

"Yeah, but let's face it, we are *not* that lucky," Reigh snorted.

Nope. Definitely not. I had to agree with him there.

"There's only one access point to the roof, so it should be easy to bottleneck there if you are pursued," Jace mused. "As far as I know, there haven't been any altercations with aerial forces coming from the tower. I'll try to confirm that for you before you depart tomorrow night. No promises, though. Asking too many questions may give you away."

A few seconds of heavy, suffocating silence passed before Reigh finally slapped his knees and stood. "Well, then. Not to rush out, but I've got a lot to prepare—a few panic attacks and mental breakdowns to have—before we make this grand suicidal gesture. You understand."

Arlan smirked as he settled back into his seat, crossing his legs and giving a flourish of his hand. "Of course. I wish you all the greatest success in your mission. And do look after Garnett. She tends to get a bit carried away, and I would be greatly displeased to hear of her coming to any harm."

"We won't let anything happen to her," I promised as I stood up, too. Ugh. It sounded stupid even as the words left my mouth. I wasn't even going to be in the same group with her. How could I guarantee she would be okay?

Thankfully, no one called me out on that as we all prepared to leave. Stepping back through the door hidden behind the bookcase, the smell of the bookseller's shop and the cold rain, mingling with the ambient aroma of freshly brewed tea, washed over me. It made my soul feel calmer and heavier all at the same time.

I almost didn't notice the cookie-eating woman leaning on her countertop, talking to someone else and petting the black kitten. A much shorter, gingery-blonde someone else who made my heartbeat skip and stall like it might suddenly launch right out of my chest.

"Oi! There they are!" Garnett called out cheerily and practically skipped over to greet us. "And with such long faces. Not good news, then?"

"Oh, you know, nothing any more hopeless, dangerous, and totally mad than usual," Reigh grumbled as he skulked by on his way to collect his cloak.

Garnett clapped him on the back as he passed. "Oh, now, it can't be all that bad. Besides, you've got me to help this time!" She stroked one of her axes and grinned, making that rune under her eye crinkle and her lavender eyes sparkle. "I only got a few good swings in last time, and you weren't even there to see them. Just wait, young prince, I'll have those odds evened right up for you."

I wasn't sure if he was just dreading going back to Northwatch tower, or tired from trying to keep up with Arlan's mind games for so long, but Reigh did *not* look convinced.

I tried not to dwell on the fact that Garnett didn't say anything to me, or even glance in my direction, as we made our way out of the shop and back into the gusting storm. Maybe that was for the best, though. My head was a mess, trying to sort through all the information Arlan had given us about the gods, what it meant to be a godling, and what we might expect from Iksoli if we encountered her. We were the same thing, basically. Godlings. The only difference was, being trapped in a mortal body limited what I could do with my powers. Iksoli didn't have those same limitations, and that put Isandri and me at a definite disadvantage.

Not a great way to start out.

But I told myself that wasn't the point. We didn't have to beat or destroy Iksoli. We just had to maneuver around her, slip free of her grasp, and be gone before she could stop us. An open fight was not the goal. Simple, right?

Oh, gods help us.

I COULDN'T FIGHT THAT SINKING, SECLUDED FEELING AS MY steps slowed and I fell to the back of our group. Looking ahead, I watched the rest of my companions forging on ahead through the stormy night, braving the wind and pouring rain, toward the tavern. Murdoc and Jace walked together in the front, muttering quietly. Most likely going over plans, or Ulfrangar stuff, or ... well, who knew, honestly. They had a lot in common, I guess. Part of me was glad to see Murdoc interacting with someone who'd successfully made the transition from assassin to normality. It might be good for him. But another part wondered if that lingering strangeness between us was permanent, and a few indifferent conversations were as close to friendship as we'd ever get now.

Behind them, Reigh and Isandri strode along silently, side-by-side, but didn't seem to be saying a word to one another. It seemed like they did that a lot, now. Isa usually hung around not far from his side ever since he'd nearly been killed by the Ulfrangar's poisoned arrows. I wondered if that was out of guilt, or if she was just worried about him. Both, maybe.

Phoebe and Garnett, on the other hand, were chattering away as happily as two songbirds. A few locks of Phoebe's wild red curls had escaped the cowl of her cloak and blew around her face as she smiled down at Garnett. She went on and on about her ideas for ... well, everything. New weapons for Murdoc. New dragon saddle designs. Something about a replacement hand for Judan. She raved about Arlan's collections of books and artifacts, and Garnett agreed to take her back sometime so she could chat with him more casually about some of the things he had in his office.

By the time we got back to the tavern, I'd fallen several paces behind everyone else. The rain had soaked through my cloak and ran down my neck and back, making me shiver. I wanted a hot bath, something to eat, and to sleep for the next week. But that wasn't going to happen. And there was something else I wanted even more.

As everyone else went inside, I stopped at the base of the front steps and stared at the open door. My mouth pinched up, and I stole a glance back over my shoulder at the dark silhouette of the old barn nearby. It was barely visible through the gusting sleet and darkness. A single lantern hung over the door, it's faint yellow light shining through the gale like a guiding star.

Before I could even think about it, I started walking there. I probably should have ducked inside just long enough to tell someone where I was going. But, then again, they might not even notice. Everyone had been pretty distracted before. Besides, I didn't want to have to explain myself. I just wanted a few minutes to think. And more than anything, I wanted to see my dragon.

I hurried through the darkness, my boots sloshing in the mud all the way to the barn door. The big lantern creaked as it swung back and forth, blown in the angry winds. It gave me plenty of light to see as I unlatched the barn's side door and ducked inside. Pulling the door closed behind me, I took a moment to catch my breath. Water dripped from my cloak and hood, pattering on the stone floor. I took in a deep breath, drinking in the smells of old hay, grain, and the familiar musk of horses.

The inside of the barn was nearly pitch black, with only one small, glass lantern hanging on another hook just inside. I brushed back the cowl of my drenched cloak and took the lantern down, holding it ahead as I made my way farther inside. It didn't take long to find where the dragons were roosting. This barn wasn't as big as the one we'd used at Ms. Lin's new farmhouse, and it barely had enough open space in the center for Fornax and Blite to curl up together. It did seem a lot cleaner, though. The floor was patched together from large, flat stones that had been filled in with sand around the edges, and a fine layer of hay was scattered about. Big sacks of grain were stacked along one wall, and barrels were arranged in a far corner. A small workbench was set up with basic farrier's tools—nothing fancy, but enough to trim and clean hooves, brush down horses, and maybe do some light repairs to saddlery or wagons.

All of it brought back my own private storm of memories as I walked forward and finally stopped right in front of the small mountain of black, orange, and red scales. Fornax lifted his head and his scaly ears perked at the sound of my footsteps. His big nostrils puffed in deep breaths, probably able to tell it was me just by my scent alone.

"Hey, big guy," I said as I stretched out a hand to rub the end of his snout. "Are you doing okay, in here?"

He gave a low, satisfied grumbling noise as he snuffled through my hair and along the front of my tunic.

I leaned forward and let my forehead rest against his. "I'm sorry I didn't come sooner. It's been a little ... complicated," I whispered. "I guess I almost died again. And this time, it didn't scare me as much as it did before. I haven't told anyone, but it almost felt ... okay. I don't know why. I guess it could be because I'm not supposed to be in a mortal body in the first place, but to be honest, that just sounds really weird and ridiculous. So maybe I'm just getting tired of constantly being in survival mode. Or I'm getting jaded. I don't know."

I sighed deeply, stepping back and setting the lantern down on the floor nearby. I'd hoped saying that out loud, to someone who wasn't going to yell at me for it, would make me feel a little better about it. Nope. No such luck.

Unbuckling my soggy cloak, I dropped it next to the lantern and tried to shake some of the water out of my hair. My damp tunic stuck to my skin and left me shivering. I let out a totally undignified yelp as a big scaly tail suddenly snaked around my legs and dragged me forward. I stumbled and fell, landing on my hands and knees in the hay right against Fornax's big, scaly chest. He lowered his head, curling his neck around me and sandwiching me in that space between his neck and shoulder.

Then he started to purr.

His big, milky jade eyes rolled closed and he let out a blasting, snort of a sigh that stirred up the hay in front of him.

It was kinda hard to argue with that—mostly because he was squishing me and preventing my escape. I didn't struggle for long, though. Not when his scaly hide was so warm compared to the cold night air and all my soggy, rain-drenched clothes. The thrumming rhythm of his purr against my ear made every tense muscle in my body relax. I didn't feel so squished, then. More like ... embraced. Or aggressively cuddled.

Yeah, definitely that.

I let my head loll back against his chest as I stared up into the barn's wooden rafters and beams. The whoosh of the storm outside seemed to grow farther and farther away as my eyelids drooped. I rubbed my fingers along Fornax's smooth, warm scales.

"I don't want to be a god," I whispered to myself. It was easier to say it knowing none of my friends—Murdoc and the others—were around to hear it. "I have all these questions now, and no one to answer them. If this is the last time Ishaleon is going to be reborn, then what happens after I die? Will I even remember my mortal life? Or any of my other mortal lives? Or will I just wake up somewhere as a god and not remember anything about who I was before?"

I hoped not. Gods, I hated that idea. But it wasn't like I had much choice in the matter.

A long, exhausted sigh slipped past my lips and I closed my eyes. "I wanted to ask Arlan. He seems like the kind of guy who might actually know. He knows a lot about the divine stuff. But asking in front of everyone like that—I just couldn't. Everything still feels so weird and wrong. Murdoc's avoiding me. I act like an idiot every time I try to talk to Garnett." My voice slurred as the exhaustion overtook me, dragging me under to the deep rumble of Fornax's purring.

Maybe tomorrow would be better. Maybe I'd wake up feeling clearer and more confident. Talking to Arlan always seemed to shake me up, mostly because he knew things that, quite honestly, terrified me. Things about the gods, the past, and the fate I seemed to be hurtling toward. I didn't like that idea—that feeling like I had no real control over what happened to me. Like it was all decided and I was just following along. I just wasn't sure how to change it. All I could do right now was take the next step, and hope for the best.

Even if all those steps seemed to be leading me straight for disaster.

CHAPTER SEVENTEEN

"THERE YOU ARE!"

I jolted awake, floundering on my bed of hay and dragon scales as an angry voice boomed through the barn. Oh dear sweet gods, what was happening?

"Wh-What is it? Iksoli? Are we being attacked?" I rasped groggily, scrambling backward over the ground. I backed right into one of Fornax's horns and doubled over, whimpering and clutching the back of my head.

Murdoc loomed over me like a tower of wrath, his hair and clothes soaked, and one of his eyes twitching. "You stupid, air-headed, little—what the heck is wrong with you?! You came out here and fell asleep without telling anyone where you were going? Do you have any idea how long we've been looking for you, you idiot?" he shouted.

"What?" I winced, the back of my head still throbbing. "O-Oh. Oh, fates, I ... I'm sorry. I didn't think anyone would notice if I—"

"You didn't think anyone would notice if you, the reason most of us wound up involved in this mess in the first place, decided to go missing in the middle of the night on the eve of the fight for our lives?" he finished for me. "Thatcher, by all the gods, you better stay down because if you stand up right now, I will punch your face inside out and break every bone in your body." He shut his eyes tightly and slowly shook his head, licking his teeth behind his lips like he could already taste blood.

I did not dare move a muscle, mostly because I'd seen him do that to someone while we were in that prison camp. No way was I ready to volunteer for a repeat of that performance. "I-I really am sorry, Murdoc. I ... well, everyone seemed busy. And I've kind of been in the way, lately. I'm not much good for battle planning anyway, so I honestly didn't think it would matter if I came out here for a little while," I confessed, probably sounding even more pathetic than I felt. Ugh. He was right. I should have at least mentioned it.

His eyes popped open suddenly and he stared down at me with an accusing scowl. "What do you mean you've been 'in the way?'"

Great. Why did I have to say it like that? Why did I have to say anything at all?

"Nothing. Just forget it. I didn't intend to cause any more problems. I'll come back in," I checked my hand to make sure the back of my head wasn't bleeding. "Just give me a few minutes to—"

"Thatcher," Murdoc growled my name like a curse through his teeth.

I sat, backed up against Fornax's side, and glared straight ahead so I didn't have to look him in the eye. What more did he want me to say? I'd apologized, hadn't I? Did he want to fight again—is that why he was pushing this?

We stayed that way for what felt like a few centuries, with him glaring at me and me glaring at the toes of his boots because I was too big of a coward to look him in the eye. Finally, Murdoc let out another deep, growling noise and stepped forward. He shoved a hand down into my face like he was going to help me up.

"Look, we ... we need to have a conversation. And it sucks, because I'm exquisitely terrible at this kind of thing, as you well know. But I can't keep tiptoeing around, not knowing where I really stand."

Oh no. Not this. Not now. Reluctantly, I seized his hand and let him drag me back up to my feet. I tensed up a little, you know, just in case he did decide to hit me.

He didn't, though.

"I don't know what's going on here anymore, Thatcher, and my head hurts from trying to figure it out," he said, blurting it out like the words had been hung in his throat for days. "All I know is that I hate this. I hate the way you've been slinking around like a nervous cat whenever I'm in the room, keeping your distance, being so quiet, and giving me all those weird looks. I hate that we can't just talk about things anymore, and you're acting like you're alone in this mess. Maybe you'll never trust me again, not like before, and I get that. I don't blame you for it at all. But I at least need to know if you hate me still. I need to know what *this* is." He motioned to the empty space between us. "You said I was like a brother to you, but do you actually mean that? Or was that just the adrenaline talking? Are we friends? Acquaintances? What?"

I opened my mouth, but nothing except a few panicked, squeaky choking sounds would come out at first. "I-I don't hate you," I sputtered at last. "Really, I don't. I know I've been sort of ... withdrawing. I don't know why, except that the whole godling thing is just really ... overwhelming. My power didn't stop the Zuer from almost killing me. What if it doesn't protect us from Iksoli, either? What if someone else gets hurt or killed?"

Murdoc looked down, his wet bangs falling so that I

couldn't see his face. I could still hear the frustration in his sharp, quiet tone, though. "Yeah. I've been thinking about that some, too. You're right. You almost died. And if it wasn't for Arlan showing up like that, having the powers he does, you might be gone. But, Thatcher, none of that is within our control. One or both of us might die in that tower, your powers might be enough, or they might not. We don't know." His shoulders rose and fell with a heavy breath. "Fortunately, this all boils down to one, very simple question: do you want to go in there and try to save Devana or not? Cause with or without us, Isandri is going. And if she goes, Reigh goes. But their choices don't have to impact ours. We can leave, if that's what you want. So, what's it going to be?"

I hesitated, my thoughts racing as I pieced all that together. Before I could really understand it, however, my head bobbed and words spilled out. "Yes. I want to go with them."

"Why? Just because they're your friends and you don't want them to go alone?"

"No," I realized aloud. "I want to see her. Or, them, I guess. Devana's been crying out for me this whole time. Iksoli's been targeting me. I want to know why. I want to stop whatever plan this is she's trying to concoct in that tower. I don't want her to hurt anyone else."

Murdoc looked up at me again, seeming satisfied. "Then we go. And maybe we die, maybe we don't. We can try to be prepared, take precautions, and play this as smart as we possibly can, but it's going to be risky. There's no way around that."

"I know."

"Good." He pursed his lips and shrugged. "So, what does this mean for us? Where do we stand? Are *we* good, or not?"

An uncertain, twitchy smile spread over my face. "Yeah. We're good."

"All right, then." He made a popping sound with his lips and turned around, waving a hand for me to follow. "Come on. We've got work to do, and you get to apologize to everyone else for making them freak out and think you'd been kidnapped or something."

I cringed as I jogged over to catch up, stopping only to grab my cloak off the floor. "R-Right."

"Reigh's probably going to hit you, so prepare yourself."

I chuckled as I fell in step beside him. "I bet it doesn't hurt nearly as bad as when you punch people."

"Nope."

Hesitating at the barn door, I glanced back at Fornax. He'd already gone back to sleep. "You know what I think when I look around a place like this?" I realized aloud. "That I would give anything to have nothing more to worry about than Master Godfrey yelling at me to muck stalls faster."

Murdoc gave a low chuckle. "Yeah. That guy was a jerk."

"I kinda liked him, though."

He rolled his eyes. "You like everyone."

"Not everyone," I corrected.

Murdoc flashed me a challenging smirk. "Oh yeah? Name one—*one* person—that you don't like."

It didn't take me even two seconds to come up with that answer. "I don't like Arlan."

Murdoc's brows rose in surprise. "Is that so? Why not?"

My mouth scrunched as I looked away. "He gives me a bad feeling, I guess. I can't really explain it. Maybe that's wrong to say, since he's the one who saved my life. But something about him just ... I don't know, it's like that feeling you get when you're standing in a dark room by yourself, and you think someone might be watching you."

"Fair enough," Murdoc agreed with another soft laugh. "For the record, he creeps me out, too."

Reigh didn't hit me when I got back to the tavern. He did yell a lot, though. Nothing new there. Granted, he did come up with some pretty creative names to call me.

Isandri and Jace just smoldered ominously in a corner, dripping wet and eyeing me like they might both try to corner me in a dark alley when I least expected it. Yikes.

The person who actually hit me was Phoebe—which I wasn't expecting. She smacked me upside the back of the head, and glared so hard it made a little wrinkle pop up between her eyebrows.

"Do you have any idea how upset you made everyone? All night we've been searching while you just snoozed away in that barn," she fumed, jabbing an accusing finger in the center of my chest. "The nerve. You had us all thinking Iksoli had come for you or you'd been abducted again! Garnett's still out there looking for you in this horrible weather! She was beside herself with worry, and now we don't—"

Everyone, even Murdoc, jumped as the tavern door flung open and cracked off the wall with a *BANG!*

Garnett stood in the doorway, breathless, wide-eyed, and absolutely drenched from head to foot. Her wet hair stuck to her cheeks and shoulders as she sucked in panting breaths. Our gazes locked, and I knew right away.

Ooh no. Trouble. I was in trouble.

So. Much. Trouble.

I'd only just begun to realize that this was my one and only opportunity to start running so maybe I'd get a head start when she hit me like a charging bull. Garnett moved incredibly fast, like a blur of dwarven fury, and she wrapped her arms around my waist and tackled me straight to the ground. I hit the floor with a "OOF!" that knocked the wind from my lungs and left my vision spotting.

I expected to get smacked again—much more painfully this time since, you know, Garnett was probably stronger than Murdoc and basically everyone else I knew. I tensed up, shutting my eyes tightly, and bracing for it. Would it be my face? Stomach? Surely, she wouldn't go for the groin. I mean, she was probably really angry, but that was—

"You stupid, *stupid* man," Garnett gasped suddenly.

Oh gods. This was it.

She grabbed my face in her hands, practically sitting on me as she leaned down and pressed her mouth against mine.

My eyes popped open wide. My arms and legs went stiff. I didn't dare to move, breathe, or do anything at all.

Wh ... What? She, uh, she was ... really? No. No way. This had to be a dream, or a hallucination. Or maybe Murdoc had actually hit me back when we were standing in the barn, and I was now dead. Or he'd punched me so hard I'd been knocked into a different reality altogether. Yeah. That was probably it.

I mean, because she'd also called me a *man*, and literally no one had ever called me that before.

Kid? Yep.

Brat? Definitely.

Idiot? At least five thousand times, probably.

But never a man.

"Careful, Garnett," Murdoc snickered as he strode past, stepping over my legs on his way to the stairs. "We need him alive, remember? Don't send him into a heart attack."

She snatched back, still mashing my cheeks with her hands as her rain-soaked hair and clothes dripped all over me. I was honestly surprised every drop didn't sizzle when it hit my face because ... well, it felt like someone had lit my entire head on fire. Gods and Fates. Had she really just ... kissed me?

"Don't you ever do that again, you hear me? Honestly! You scared us all half to death. I was ready to have Arlan's entire network scouring every gutter in the kingdom trying to find you," she scolded.

"Ahm shorree," I tried to apologize, but she still had my face all smooshed.

"Oh, I'll bet you are. We ought to have you wearing a bell like a goat from now on. Honestly, what—" Garnett stopped and snapped her mouth shut, seeming to suddenly realize the, uh, several other people in the room who were staring at us. She jerked her hands back, releasing my face and quickly scooting off me to get back to her feet.

I just lay there for a few more seconds, still wondering if this was a dream or not. If it wasn't, then for the first time in my entire life, a girl had just kissed me. On purpose. In front of witnesses.

I don't know what it was—fear of the fact that I might be about to die tonight, a sudden boost of confidence and courage, or just sheer panic—but as I got to my feet, I felt a heat rise in my chest like a roaring forge. If today really was the last day of my life, and we got ourselves killed tonight when we tried to sneak into that tower, then by the Fates, I was going to make it count.

I turned to face Garnett, who was still dripping a puddle on the floor and frowning sourly up at me. Her nose wrinkled some, mouth pinching up like she might be about to start yelling at me again.

Nope. She'd thrown down the gauntlet. Now I was picking it up.

I stepped toward her and snagged my arms around her, drawing her in before she could protest, and planted a returning kiss against her lips.

When I finally drew back, Garnett blinked up at me with her face flushing bright pink and her eyes as big as two lilac moons. She didn't say a word, which suited me fine. There was something I had to say first.

"I am really sorry for ducking out last night without telling everyone," I panted, my head swimming a little from adrenaline. Oh gods, I wasn't about to pass out, was I? Better do this quickly, then. "And also, I like you—a lot. And not just as a friend. I think you're beautiful, and amazing, and I *romantically* like you. So ... yeah. I just wanted to make sure that was ... you know, clear."

"Wow," Reigh blurted, almost like he hadn't meant to say that out loud.

"All right, you kids, knock it off with that," Jace grumbled from the corner. "Just because Jaevid's gone doesn't mean you get to act like a bunch of rabbits in springtime. Break it up."

Murdoc gave a suppressed, snorting laugh. He held a hand out to Reigh and wiggled his fingers.

"Ugh, you've got to be kidding me." Reigh growled elven curses under his breath as he reached into his pockets and took out a few coins, smacking them angrily into Murdoc's palm.

Wait a second, were they *betting* on me? For what?

Before I could ask, Garnett slipped out of my grasp and darted for the stairs. Phoebe immediately bounded after her, practically glowing with excitement as she dashed by. Footsteps thumped rapidly along the hall. Then a door slammed somewhere upstairs. I stood in awkward silence, staring up at the ceiling, as I heard the muffled sound of voices ... followed by a chorus of two girlish squeals of delight.

18

CHAPTER EIGHTEEN

There wasn't much time to relish in the victory of my very first, successful, attempt at kissing a girl. Sinking down into the nearest chair, I tried to breathe through the shock of what I'd just done. Gods and Fates, what had I done?

"We'll set out just before nightfall," I overheard Reigh muttering quietly to Jace as they walked past, Murdoc and Isandri close behind them. "Anything you can do to make sure no one questions our movements through the area would be appreciated. With any luck, maybe this storm will lift and then we won't be flying in slop."

Jace shifted the weight of the bag he had slung over one of his shoulders as he made his way toward the door. "I'll do what I can, but I wouldn't count on the weather easing any. This time of year, slop is about all we get. Count it as a blessing, though. It'll make you harder to spot from the ground." The old king paused at the door, glancing back at me and smirking some. "Watch out for one another. I don't know how long it might take for me to be able to meet with you again once it's done and the siege of the city begins, but I would suggest not lingering anywhere near Northwatch. I'll come looking for you here."

Jace and Reigh went on talking even as they headed out the door. Murdoc and Isandri followed, listening, but not saying much. Finally, the tavern grew quiet and still. It must have been very early in the morning. I couldn't tell, exactly, because of the weather. The lingering storm made everything seem so bleak, gray, and dim. But after a while, the tavern-keeper came down from their private quarters on the top floor, along with his daughter, and they began opening up their business and making preparations for the day. They offered to serve breakfast for us, but with nerves making my stomach churn and my thoughts tangle up like old fishing nets, for once, I didn't feel much like eating. No one else did, either, although Phoebe gratefully accepted some tea with honey.

Most everyone took a few hours upstairs to rest since, you know, they'd spent most of the night running around in the storm looking for me. Oops. But with all our plans made, and a decently clear idea of what we had to do, there wasn't much else to prepare. All my weapons were ready. I had two cartridges of bolts for my crossbow, my xiphos was cleaned, I'd checked over Fornax's saddle, and had almost thrown up from anxiety a few times—so I was ready to go. Now, all that was left was to wait for the perfect time to make our move.

Murdoc had already cleaned all his weaponry and checked over his leather armor, making sure it all fit perfectly into place, before he took a seat by the fire with his feet kicked up on a tabletop and sat, staring into the flames and rubbing his fingers together anxiously. Isandri settled into the chair next to his, her arms folded into the big, bell sleeves of her robes as usual. The light from the fire danced in her eyes as she ran one hand along the smooth, wooden pole of her staff.

Nearby, Phoebe pored over the tiny little bits and pieces

of something new she was crafting. Some of the parts looked suspiciously like they'd come from the trap she had made for Phillip. I guess she was repurposing them? It didn't seem like a good time to ask, though. She'd pulled all her wild red curls into a massive bun on the back of her head and leaned in close, fidgeting with tiny tools as she squinted at her work.

Reigh slept for a few hours, then got up and began feverishly writing out a few letters. He quietly passed them off to the tavernkeeper when he thought no one was paying attention. Farewell letters in case we died? I wondered if I should do that, too. Except, I didn't really have anyone to write to. Pretty much anyone I knew who would have cared if I died or not was already sitting in the room.

Speaking of which, Garnett was the last to come down stairs. By the look of it, she'd spent some time brushing out and re-braiding her hair and had changed into a different set of much more complex and hardy leathers. She'd buckled on pieces of plate armor that fit the curves and contours of her frame, and had her two double-headed hand axes belted to her hips.

Her cheeks still seemed a little rosy when she glanced my way. That look in her eyes, like there was something she wanted to say but wasn't sure how, stirred up a fresh wave of panic in my gut. It took everything I had not to let it show. Cool—I had to play it cool. Confidence. Dragonrider-level confidence.

I managed a somewhat-twitchy smile at her, which only made her duck her head and blush harder.

Great. I'd probably embarrassed her by doing all that and saying those things in public. But, to be fair, she'd started it. She had kissed *me* first. Was I not supposed to react to that kind of thing?

Uggghhh. None of this girl-stuff made any sense to me at all.

As the hours passed, the mood got heavier. The already faint light outside grew dimmer. Low rumbles of thunder sounded in the distance like the growl of a beast. Cold shivers ran through my body, making me shudder and my skin prickle. At last, I looked up and locked gazes with Reigh from across the room. He didn't say a word. He didn't have to. I could tell just by the look on his face, like a somber finality had settled over his brow.

It was time.

I nodded once, and slowly stood up. Buckling on my now only slightly damp cloak, I pulled the hood down low and fastened my crossbow to the holster Phoebe had made that fit against my hip and leg. Then I started for the door. Murdoc was at my side before I could blink, and Isandri and the others weren't far behind. We gathered by the front door of the tavern, greeted by a blast of icy, frigid wind and the howl of the storm.

While everyone waited under the shelter of the porch, Murdoc and I struck out for the barn where I'd spent last night sleeping. The freezing rain lashed at my face and stung my eyes, but I barely felt the cold now. All I could feel was my heart pumping hard and fast, throbbing in my fingertips as I helped him roll the barn's big door open far enough that the dragons could exit. Then I pulled my whistle out from under my tunic where it hung, still strung on the resin cord of Jaevid's necklace. I blew a few signaling blasts.

Fornax answered with a deep roar. The ground shook under my boots as he lumbered forward, snarling into the sleet and blasting a snort of disapproval at being forced out into the weather. Murdoc's smaller drake made a similar squawk of distaste and hunkered back, squinting out through the gale at us reluctantly.

"I know it's lousy, guys. Sorry about that," I said. Rubbing my hands along Fornax's horned head, I stole a sideways look at Murdoc as he did the same to his dragon.

The young drake scooted toward him sideways like an eager puppy, whining and dipping his head in submissive excitement. He sniffed through Murdoc's hair and nipped at the end of his cloak, swishing his tail and keeping his small ears pinned back.

"Blite, right?" I'd heard Murdoc call his dragon that in passing.

My sulky friend shrugged. "Yeah. I'm not good with names."

"No, I think it's a good one." I patted Fornax's neck and sighed. "Time to go, huh?"

He sighed, too. "Yeah. I think it is."

"Hey, Murdoc?"

"Yeah?"

"Try not to die, okay? I know we won't be together for this mission. I probably won't have any clue where you are in that tower. Do me a favor, and don't get killed. We're supposed to go to the dragonrider academy together after all this is done, and I'm not doing that without you."

He turned to face me, his features locked in a stubborn glare. "On one condition—you don't die, either. I mean it. I already watched you almost die right in front of me one time. Don't do it again. Got it?" He stuck a hand out like he wanted to shake on it.

I grinned and grasped his hand as tightly as I could. "Deal."

PROGRESS WAS SLOW THROUGH THE ROUGH AIR, AND FLYING in the failing light did not make it any easier. Hunkered low against Fornax's back, I was only able to see thanks to the goggles Phoebe had made for us. They shielded my eyes and let me get a clearer look around at everyone in our formation. To my right, Reigh and Phoebe sat astride Vexi. The sleek, green dragoness had come soaring in as soon as she heard the commotion with Fornax and Blite. According to Reigh, she'd been wild before she chose him, and so it wasn't uncommon for her to prefer roaming over being cooped up in barns and tight spots for long periods of time. She never went far, though, and always kept an ear turned his way.

On my left, Murdoc and Blite soared in close enough to draft off my wing, which helped the smaller dragon keep up with our greater speed through the storm. Isandri did the same, streaking through the wind and slurry on her graceful dark wings like a diving falcon. And Garnett, well ...

I looked down, feeling that knot of excited heat in the center of my chest at the way she had her arms wrapped tightly around my waist while she sat in the saddle behind me. I'd, um, made a few suggestions when it came to our passenger assignments. I mean, it made sense that Fornax and I should be the ones to carry her. We had the better saddle set up and Fornax was bigger and stronger than the other two dragons. Plus, Garnett was the one showing us where to go to find this hidden access tunnel, so she needed to be sure she was in the lead and could give directions to everyone else.

Yes. It all made perfect sense.

Okay, fine. Vexi probably could have carried her, instead. But a girl wanting to sit next to me in any circumstance was kind of a first for me, so I wasn't about to let this opportunity slip by.

So here we were, me sitting in front gripping the saddle handles to steer my big orange and black dragon, and her pressed right up against my back. Her arms hugged me around the middle, warm and sturdy. Part of me wished I could reach down and take one of her hands in mine.

Buuut now did not seem like the right time for that. Later, though. Definitely later.

We zoomed low over the rolling farmland outside of Osbran as darkness took the kingdom like the grip of an iron fist. Heading west as fast as we dared, the dark shapes of the exposed, dark rock clusters passed by like phantoms in the whiteout of the falling sleet. Thunder rolled in the stormy sky overhead, making my heartbeat skip every time. I bit down hard to keep my teeth from chattering, and tried to keep my gaze focused on the path ahead. Sometimes the ghostly shapes of other dragons would appear through the low clouds, soaring by but never coming close enough to make out any detail. According to King Jace, there would be more and more of them as the night went on. The riders were departing in waves, making their way from all corners of the kingdom to rally at the military outpost nearby. That's where they would launch their assault tomorrow.

There wasn't a single minute to waste.

I urged Fornax on, pushing him to pump his large wings faster as we dropped down to soar less than two hundred feet off the ground. We had to be getting close. We'd been at this for almost three hours. How much farther would it be? With the wind in my face, I couldn't ask. Garnett probably wouldn't be able to understand a word I said in this weather.

I knew she had to be getting anxious, too, though. Every now and then, she would lean to peek around, looking around at the landscape and features in the area. Finally, I felt her give me a little squeeze and pat on my shoulder to get my attention. I looked down, my gaze tracking the direction where she pointed to a cluster of large, black boulders piled in a crude C-shape. It didn't look any different than any of the others we'd passed already, but if she was sure this was the right spot, then I was willing to take her word for it.

I threw up a signal to the others and started a steep turn,

arcing around the hilltop. Fornax flared his wings, coming in for a swift landing and catching the ground with his clawed hind legs. Vexi touched down in perfect formation right beside us, and Blite touched down a little behind. The smaller dragon shook himself and growled, lashing his tail and flexing his shoulders as though Murdoc's added weight was still difficult for him to manage. Hopefully that would improve as he got older.

Isandri bounded in front of us, shifting forms mid-stride and brandishing her staff as her brightly-hued eyes scanned all around for any signs of danger. Even in her human shape, there was something distinctly feline about how she prowled around on the balls of her bare feet, her dark purple and green robes billowing around her lithe frame. She stood poised, waiting while the rest of us climbed down from the saddles and unloaded our gear. We didn't have much to take apart from our weaponry—a few rations, a bundle of torches, and some small packs of medical gear for each group.

Garnett didn't wait for me to help her down from the saddle. She unbuckled herself and bounded off, landing in a crouch and slowly rising to fix a focused glare upon the cluster of boulders before us. "All right, then. Everyone keep a distance and I'll give it a look. No telling what might come popping out of there once we throw the hatch."

Gathering before our dragons, the rest of us watched in silence while she forged ahead to the base of the rock formation. It didn't take her even two minutes of digging around in the mud and moss to find a small crevice between two of the rocks. Reaching her arm inside all the way to her shoulders, she quirked her mouth, sticking her tongue out to one side while she felt around.

Something gave a loud, metallic *CLUNK*.

Murdoc and I exchanged a glance.

"Hah! There it is," Garnett announced proudly as she

pulled her arm out of the hole and bounded over to a mossy slope on the other side of the cluster of boulders. She hooked her fingers along the bottom of a narrow hatch door hidden seamlessly amongst the rocks, roots, moss, and mud. She gave a little grunt as she lifted it, her impressively muscular shoulders flexing as she hefted it upward until a stabilizing mechanism caught it and held the door ajar.

Whoa.

It wasn't all that big of a door. Maybe five feet wide and seven feet tall. Somehow, I'd pictured it being a lot larger—big enough to fit a monster or war machine through. But this was a lot more discreet, almost as though it'd been placed here for something other than just moving Tibran military forces around. Spies, maybe? Or infiltration behind enemy lines?

"It was meant to be a sort of emergency exit," Garnett explained, as though she could easily read the confusion on my face. "A smaller offshoot passage leading to one of the main tunnels. It could be easily collapsed if needed. We didn't build too many of them, though. Argonox wasn't a fan of wasting time and materials on things that would make things safer for his forces. I managed to convince him that, in the areas where our tunnel construction was rushed and I wasn't able to take the necessary precautions to ensure they wouldn't collapse, having a few pathways out might spare him the lives of his key engineers—namely me. I refused to dig one more foot until he started allowing at least a few emergency safeguards for my teams."

"I can imagine how well he took that," Reigh muttered as he stepped past her and leaned in to peer down into the tunnel beyond the hatch.

"Oh, stones, it made him furious! He was ready to have me strung up and tortured for my insolence. But I was in the rare position of having a teensy bit of leverage against the madman, since he saw fit to murder the rest of my people. He didn't have a Plan B to take over the construction of his tunnels, and they were supposed to be the key to overtaking Maldobar and avoiding open conflict with the dragonriders—a fight he must have known he would ultimately lose. Hard to match that kind of air power." She grinned up at Fornax, something softly affectionate in her expression. "I've never been so glad to have all my plans made useless."

"Is this going to be secure for us to move through?" Murdoc asked, shuffling over with the others to peer through the gaping, dark maw of that open hatch.

"As safe as any other. According to the maps my people lifted off Iksoli's forces, the main tunnel this passage connects to is still open and operational. If it's lasted this long, it should be fine," she explained. "Now, then, I suppose we should light a torch or two, yeah? My eyes are keen to the deep places of the world, but I rather doubt the rest of you will fare so well."

Reigh made a face as he followed her instructions, ducking under the cover of the open hatch door and pulling one of the torches from our bundle. "For the record, I hate everything about this," he complained as he lit it.

"Just let me take the lead and stay close and quiet," Garnett warned, already disappearing down into the darkness of the tunnel. "This isn't the sort of place you want to go strolling around without your guard up and your wits about you."

19

CHAPTER NINETEEN

Stepping through that passage into the deep, smothering darkness of the Tibran tunnels felt like we'd all just been swallowed whole by a giant serpent. The walls were muddy and slimy at first, and the temperature plummeted as the tunnel delved down farther and farther into the earth. It twisted and seemed to wind back on itself so that I lost all sense of direction immediately.

Fortunately, Garnett didn't seem the least bit unnerved by it. She walked along at the head of our group, Reigh following close behind her with a torch raised to cast a warm yellow glow around so the rest of us could see. With Isandri, Phoebe, and I in the middle, Murdoc brought up the rear of the group with another torch—just in case. The wavering light revealed an exposed smooth dirt ceiling, reinforced every now and then by a wooden frame. I'd expected to see roots poking through, or even a worm here and there. But there was no sign of life anywhere. The hard-packed floor was barren and the longer we walked, the less moisture seemed to hang in the air. I guess that meant we were traveling down a lot deeper than the rain could soak through.

Somehow, that wasn't exactly comforting.

The smell of rich, moist earth changed the farther we went. I caught the wafting scents of something almost mineral-like, sort of like the inside of an old well. The air grew colder still, until I could see my breath, and the tunnel didn't twist or curve quite as much. With my thoughts racing and my heart beating wildly, I couldn't tell how long we had been walking before Garnett threw up a hand in a signal for us stop.

Dead ahead, the tunnel came to what looked like another heavy hatch door made of thick wooden beams bound together with iron plates. Jogging the distance, Garnett left us standing and waiting for her signal while she checked the door over thoroughly. Then she motioned for us to follow.

"This should take us into the main tunnel system," she whispered. "Once we're inside, we need to be on our highest guard. Stay very close. No noise. No talking. Eyes and ears open. If you even think you see something odd, get my attention. All right?"

We all nodded.

"Good. Now, wait here. I'll scout ahead a bit and make sure it's clear." She took in a deep breath, seeming to collect her nerve before she turned back and slowly began to unlatch the door. She pressed against it little by little, easing it ajar an inch at a time, before she finally dared to poke her head out and take a look around.

Slipping through the door, Garnett disappeared into the dark beyond without a sound. I gripped the handle of my crossbow, ready to draw in a moment's notice. Or run. Whatever the occasion called for.

Minutes passed. Or maybe it was only a few seconds. I couldn't keep focused when every faint noise of a boot on the stone or someone swallowing made me flinch. My chest hurt thanks to how my pulse kept thrashing hard, and my hands shook, although I couldn't tell if it was from the cold or the adrenaline. Both, probably.

I almost came out of my skin as Garnett's head suddenly popped back through the doorway, glancing around at all of us and giving a quick, silent nod. All was clear. So far, so good.

We emerged out into the main tunnel one at a time, moving as quickly as we dared without running the risk of making too much noise. As soon as my boots hit the solid stone of the main tunnel, I couldn't stop my mouth from falling open as my gaze drifted up to the tall, cavernous ceiling overhead. Fates, it must have been thirty feet or more. And judging by the almost patterned-looking slashes and cuts in the rock on every side of the passage, it looked like it had been made by something ... *chewing* the stone.

My stomach dropped.

An underbeast? That was the only thing my panicked brain could come up with. Not a lot of animals spent time chewing their way through solid rock. At least, not that I knew of.

Garnett had talked a lot about the underbeasts, and how Argonox had stolen them from her homeland and brought them here to dig these tunnels. She'd described them as big, brutish, strong, and without any eyes. They could apparently dig very fast, and I guess I'd pictured something a tad smaller than ... whatever behemoth of a monster had left this kind of a tunnel behind. No wonder the one we'd stirred up while we were rescuing Phillip had sounded so massive. It had nearly shaken down the entire cavern right on top of us, and we'd never even glimpsed it.

I prayed we never would.

We walked in the near dark of the tunnel, keeping to one side and picking our way very carefully. Garnett's demeanor seemed to grow colder and more distant with every step, her usually smiling face now sealed in a look of determined focus. Her jaw stayed set, and she already had one of her hand axes out and clenched tightly in her fist as she moved ahead of us as quiet as a fox. Every movement was calculated and precise, as though she'd slipped into survival mode and was only focused on the way ahead. Her forehead shone with a sheen of fresh sweat, and it made a few stray locks of her hair stick to her brow and cheeks. Every few yards, she panned her gaze methodically all around, searching every dark corner that our torchlight didn't reach.

But so far, nothing raised any alarm.

I dared to hope. If we could do this—if we could make it all the way to Northwatch tower without being detected or running into any of Iksoli's forces—then maybe we stood a chance of pulling off this rescue without any catastrophes. We could get this done and be long gone by the time the dragonriders decided to incinerate that place.

I should have known better, I guess. Things never went that well for me. And down here, miles away from the surface and any form of help or rescue, we were far more vulnerable.

This deep underground, if something did go wrong, no one would be able to hear us scream.

Hours dragged on as we trekked through the darkness until, at last, Murdoc jogged to the front of our group to catch up to where Garnett was still in the lead. He took her arm to get her attention and tipped his head back down the line to the rest of us. "Let's take a breather," he whispered. "We're no good to anyone if we show up with everyone dead on their feet."

Oh, thank the gods.

I sagged on my feet, wiping sweat from my brow onto my sleeve. I would've given anything to sit down long enough to peel my boots off and rub at my sore heels. Keeping this pace was hard enough in armor and carrying all our gear, but after the surges of adrenaline had left my muscles shaky and cold, it was getting harder and harder to keep my senses sharp to anything that might be around us, hiding in the dark. Thankfully, I wasn't the only one losing steam. Phoebe blinked owlishly, leaning against me a little as she panted. Of all of us, she was probably the least physically prepared for it. Hiking into battle hadn't exactly been one of her hobbies before all this.

"It'll be okay," I whispered to her. "We've got to be getting close now, right? Just a little farther."

"How close are we to the tower?" Isa asked, dropping into a crouch to run her hands along the rough stone floor as though she were trying to get a sense of her surroundings. Her brow scrunched sourly as she shook her head and flicked a meaningful glance up in my direction. I guess whatever abilities she might have been able to use on the surface wouldn't work down here. Were we too far from the moon? Would she be able to use any of her powers as long as we were down here?

Garnett glanced down our line, her expression a mixture of apprehension and worry, as though she didn't like the idea of staying in one place for too long. "The emergency access tunnel we entered through is a good twenty miles from Northwatch," she whispered back, shifting her focus back to Murdoc. "Of course, the paths themselves aren't a straight shot, but I would guess we're still a good three or four miles from the tower itself. Maybe a touch more."

Twenty miles? Gods and Fates. No wonder my back and feet were killing me.

"It doesn't get any safer from here," she warned as she

spun her axe over her hand a few times. "You can bet there'll be a lot more of Iksoli's mind-controlled minions the nearer we get to the city. She's smart, keeping her forces in close. She must be on guard since we took the Zuer out of play. I'm betting she'll have things locked down nice and tight around the tower."

Great. Well, that sounded ... fun.

I helped Phoebe ease down to sit on the floor so she could rest. Reigh spoke to her quietly, seeming to notice that of all of us, she seemed to be struggling the most to keep up the pace. He and Isandri hovered over her, offering her a few sips from a waterskin, while Murdoc stood over them like he was supervising.

I glanced at Garnett, but she still stood facing away down the tunnel ahead, bristled and gripping her axe like she was ready to hurl it at a second's notice. Probably not a good time to check on her. Not while she was this focused, anyway.

Picking up Reigh's torch, I wandered a few feet away— not too far—and held it up to get a better look at the area around us. The sheer scale was still staggering, and my brain boggled at the idea that the Tibrans had built all of this in such a short amount of time. The looming ceiling was still thirty to forty feet tall, and the tunnel must have been twenty feet wide. Big enough to march a line of soldiers through, even on horseback. Granted, I imagined getting horses through the dark on this uneven ground would've been a challenge. Unless they'd been thoroughly conditioned not to spook.

I stopped, squinting across the width of the tunnel as the torchlight glimmered off something metallic. Weird. What was that?

I stole a look over my shoulder at my companions. They all seemed pretty occupied. I probably should have been resting, as well. But my curiosity got the better of me. Just one quick look, then I'd go back and sit down. Besides, it's not like the rest of them couldn't see where I was with the big burning torch in my hand, right?

Right.

I picked my steps carefully as I crossed the width of the tunnel, making my way toward that metallic object shining and reflecting the torchlight. Was that gold? Or brass?

I stopped when the dark shapes surrounding it came into view. My mouth opened slightly and I stared in silent awe at the cluster of skeletons dressed in Tibran armor lying around something that looked like a huge crossbow on wheels. Or, at least, it had been once. My torchlight had caught off one of the brass fixtures on the arms, and now that I stood much closer, I could see that the back half of it was smashed to splinters. Likewise, some of the skeletons looked like they'd been crunched, as well. Their armor was bent and cracked, like something huge had mashed it underfoot.

"The Tibrans used those to shoot down dragons," Reigh explained in a low whisper as he suddenly appeared at my side like a phantom from the dark.

I gasped and flinched away, biting back the urge to hit him for sneaking up on me like that. Geez. "I-I ... figured," I managed to wheeze quietly.

"We should go back and get the others ready to ..." his voice trailed off as his eyes narrowed, head tilting to one side. He stepped away toward one of the fallen skeletons sprawled nearby, still dressed in its rotting clothes and dinged-up bronze armor. Crouching down, he pulled something from around its neck. A necklace?

"Weird," he murmured as he held it up into the light of the torch in my hand. Hanging on a thin gold chain, the small emblem in the shape of a hand with an eye in the center, sparkled and glittered.

"What symbol is that?" I asked quietly.

Reigh just shrugged. "Never seen it before. No telling, though. The Tibrans took people from kingdoms all across the world. It could have come from anywhere."

My mouth scrunched as I watched Reigh tuck the necklace into his pocket. Something about that symbol put an uneasy shiver up my spine. Even if I was sure I'd never seen it before, it gave me a bad feeling. Like maybe we shouldn't take it with us.

I didn't say anything, though. After all, if that symbol meant something bad, maybe it was a good idea to let someone like Arlan look at it and tell us what, exactly, it was. He seemed like the person who might actually know that kind of thing, especially if it came from somewhere far away from Maldobar.

"Let's go," Reigh urged, still keeping his tone quiet as he nudged me with his elbow and gestured for me to pass the torch back over. "And, uh, hey ... good luck. You know, in case I don't get a chance to say it later."

I stared at him. Why did this sound so much like one of those deathbed speeches? Like maybe he thought he wasn't going to make it out of that tower, so we might as well end things on a nice note with everyone?

"Yeah, well, good luck to you, too." I frowned and looked away. "I'm not sure luck has anything to do with this, though."

He gave a faint, humorless chuckle and started walking ahead of me. "You're probably right. It's good, though, 'cause when it comes to luck, I've never had any."

I was about to remind him that I didn't, either. My hometown got burned to a crisp by Tibrans, my father had died, I'd wound up being best friends with an assassin, had found out I was actually some kind of reborn deity who really sucked at using my powers, had almost died several times, and now I was about to try and sneak into an enemy-occupied death tower with no idea whether or not I could count on my divine powers to protect me and everyone else in my group. Talk about no luck.

Before I could even get a word out, a sudden sound made both of us pause halfway across the tunnel. It started out distant. Faint. Like maybe it was far away. But as we both stood there, my blood rushing and all my extremities going numb, it grew louder.

And louder.

Oh gods, was that ... people screaming?

"Hide!" Reigh barked through his teeth, dropping his torch and seizing my arm. He dragged me back to that heap of skeletons and we dove in, hiding as best we could against the bones and debris.

Across the tunnel, the rest of our group scrambled to their feet at the noise. Garnett and Isandri ducked into a small crevice in the wall, all but vanishing from sight. Murdoc doused his torch and grabbed Phoebe, sprinting for a large fallen boulder we'd passed a few yards back and leaping behind it.

I held my breath.

The screaming grew louder, intermingled with the sounds of footsteps and the clunk and clatter of armor. The light of our abandoned torch flickered and wavered, illuminating a crowd of people dressed in patched-together mixtures of armor. They ran past, tripping and falling over one another like startled sheep.

Merciful Fates. What was happening? What were they running from?

I clamped a hand over my mouth to keep myself from making a sound as one of them fell right in front of my hiding place. The man let out a garbled yell, pitching and flailing, as something big landed right on top of him and bit down into his shoulder. I recognized the creature's pitch-black fur, bulbous white eyes, six powerful legs, and long, whip-like tail.

Every muscle in my body froze solid. I didn't dare to move, breathe, or even blink.

That was a switchbeast.

20

CHAPTER TWENTY

No—not just one. There were more switchbeasts running after the group, taking them down one at a time like lions on the hunt.

They sprang and latched onto the fleeing fighters, gripping them in razor-sharp talons, and sinking their quill-like teeth into them. Some of the monsters crawled along the cavern walls, able to move as easily as they did on the ground.

Sprawled on his belly next to me, Reigh's face drew into a fierce scowl. His hands slid slowly down his sides, moving to the hilts of his two elven-styled blades. I shot him a desperate look, barely managing to shake my head once. No. We couldn't attack them. We had to stay still and silent. They might continue on without even noticing us.

My heart kicked at my ribs, like a horse bucking in a stall, as the switchbeast not even six feet away from us tore into the man it had pinned down, then looked up. In the wavering light of our discarded torch, I got a clear look as the monster panned its gaze around, long tail slowly swishing as its many shoulders flexed under short, silky black fur. Its jaggedly pointed ears swiveled and flicked, nose wrinkling as it sniffed the air.

I held perfectly still.

Next to me, Reigh seemed to have stopped breathing completely.

No sound. No movement.

The switchbeast let out a sudden, piercing yowl and darted forward to continue the chase. It disappeared into the dark, scrambling up the walls and forging after the rest of the fleeing fighters—mercenaries, or whoever they were.

I dared to let out a slow, shaking breath.

Reigh made a gesture over his mouth, signaling for me to stay silent, as he slowly began to move out of our hiding spot amidst all the bones and bits of armor. I watched down the tunnel, straining to see any sign of the switchbeasts in case one of them had fallen behind or was doubling back our way. Nothing. Just darkness and the fading echoes of screams.

"Come on, we have to get out of here—*now*," Reigh urged, his voice barely audible thanks to the thrashing of my pulse in my ears as he helped me wriggle free of the bone pile.

Across the tunnel, Garnett and Isandri were already emerging from their hiding spot, staying completely soundless as they waved us over frantically. I could barely make out the blanched look of terror on Phoebe's face as she and Murdoc peeked over their boulder and immediately began running to rejoin, too.

I stopped and bent down to grab the torch as we ran by. We still needed at least one to make sure we didn't trip over any of the rubble or uneven places on the tunnel floor.

Just as I seized the wooden handle, something dark dripped onto the floor right next to the flame's flickering light. Three dark splotches dotted the stony ground. Huh? Was that water?

I dipped my fingertips into them near the light

No. Not water.

It was clear, but sticky almost like sap or snot. And it reeked with a sharp, musky odor. Was that ... drool? It reminded me a little of dragon venom except it didn't burn when air touched it.

I looked up, trying to peer through the dark to see where on the ceiling of the tunnel it might be coming from.

I almost didn't see it. But my one quick glance overhead and the sparkle of the torch's glow off the stone must have coalesced at just the right instant. Something shifted in the dark and then held perfectly still.

I froze, my gaze now locked onto a large, dark shape on the ceiling. The glimmer of the torchlight briefly reflected over what I could have sworn looked like two big eyeballs.

Then a maw bristling with thousands of needle-like teeth appeared.

Oh gods.

Reigh stopped a few feet away and whirled back to stare me down with a crazed expression, like he was ready to drag me along if I didn't start moving. He hadn't seen it. He didn't know. But I guess he could read the terror on my face even from a distance.

Immediately, Reigh's gaze darted upward, following my line of sight. Then his eyes went wide, too. His mouth twisted into a snarl. Moving slowly, he sank down into a defensive position and reached back to the two, curved blades sheathed at his hips. The metallic hum and scrape of the scythe-like weapons leaving their sheaths made the rest of our group stop and turn, just in time to hear him growl in a quiet, low voice, "No. Sudden. Moves."

He was right. I didn't know how intelligent those creatures were. Maybe it didn't realize we'd spotted it, yet. I clenched my teeth, keeping my eyes fixed on that spot—the pair of big white eyes staring down at me. *Think, Thatcher. You can do this. No panicking.*

It was too far up. None of us could make a successful swipe at it with a sword. And if it sprang, it might take a bite at one of us. One tiny prick of one of those fangs is all it would take. My hand drifted slowly to my crossbow.

I'd have to take a shot.

My mind seemed to go strangely quiet, as though every racing, terrified thought had been dissolved away like mist in the morning sun. Reigh's pupils narrowed, going as tiny as pinpricks in terror as I set my jaw and unhooked the leather strap that held my crossbow to my hip. One movement. One shot. That's all I'd get.

No time to second guess it.

Overhead, the switchbeast gave a low, probably suspicious hiss.

I sucked in a sharp breath and held it.

Now or never.

I dropped to a knee and ripped the crossbow free, finger already poised on the trigger as I leaned back and aimed for the darkness right between those two eyes. My finger squeezed against the warm metal of the trigger. The thick, taut bowstring fired with a *THUNK*, sending the bolt howling through the gloom.

THERE WASN'T TIME TO MAKE SURE THAT I'D ACTUALLY HIT it. I turned and ran, seizing Reigh by the collar on the way by and dragging him along as I sprinted for the rest of our group.

A piercing yowl and *THUD* from behind sent a fresh wave of terror through me, giving me a new burst of speed. When I finally dared to look back, I found the switchbeast pitching and flailing on the ground, making sickly gurgling sounds until it went still.

"Nice shot," Reigh gasped as he stopped next to me, still gripping his weapons. "For a moment there, I thought for sure we were—"

A low, answering chorus of eerie yowls echoed from down the passage.

Oh no.

We ... we had to ...

"RUN!" Garnett shouted, already sprinting ahead as fast as she could.

Was she serious? Run where?! We couldn't possibly beat those things on foot!

We didn't have much of a choice, though.

I bit back a curse as I took off after her. Everyone else followed, dashing as fast as we could along the tunnel. Isandri's form shimmered as she changed into her feline form, her feathered wings unfurling and giving off a radiant silver light that was not stealthy at all. That ship had sort of sailed now, though. The evil, venomous, six-legged cat was out of the bag, and it definitely knew we were here.

Isandri dipped her head, performing a maneuver she'd used on me once before at the Cromwell estate. She scooped up Phoebe with her snout and tossed her up on to her strong, feline back. Bounding forward, Isandri gave a low growl of frustration as another split in the massive tunnel came into view ahead.

"Left!" Garnett shouted.

We all headed for the path to the left, scrambling over a place where the floor had buckled and left big boulders and chunks of uneven stone cracked upward. We passed more skeletal remains of Tibran soldiers in the rubble. More smashed war machines.

And all the while, the screeching and hissing of the

switchbeasts grew louder at our heels. They were gaining fast. We wouldn't make it. We had to—

A sharp pain shot up through my leg and I fell, my head cracking off the stone floor as something dragged me backward. I kicked and fought, rolling over to find a switchbeast with its claws embedded in my calf. Curse it! Without thinking, I raised my crossbow and fired three bolts right at the monster.

THUNK—THUNK— THUNK

The switchbeast shrieked and let me go, scrambling back and pawing at where my arrows had lodged into its chest. Then its head snapped up, baring those needle-like fangs and coiling its muscular shoulders for a vengeful lunge.

THUNK!

The final bolt lodged deep into its open mouth and the switchbeast dropped right where it stood.

I spat at it and started to stagger up, biting back a cry of pain as blood oozed from the deep claw-punctures in my boot.

"Thatcher!" Murdoc shouted, running at me with his longswords already drawn. His expression went blank suddenly, a primal sort of fear draining all the color from his features as he stared past me.

I looked back down the tunnel behind us. There, just beyond the range of Isandri's celestial light, the glow of dozens of more eyes winked in the gloom. More climbed along the wall and skittered across the ceiling.

My blood seemed to freeze solid in my veins as I squeezed my crossbow desperately. There were ... more. A *lot* more than before. The noise must have attracted them. Now there were too many for us to fight like this. Not without one or several of us being bitten.

As the hoard of switchbeasts closed in, we grouped together around Isandri. She spread her gleaming wings over us, Phoebe still clinging to her back as she snarled and bared her fangs at the encroaching monsters. Murdoc took a defensive stance on my left. Reigh stood at my back, and Garnett held her axes at the ready on my right. We could make a stand—but it wouldn't last long. We'd be overwhelmed in seconds. We didn't stand a chance.

"How far to the tower?" Reigh shouted.

"A mile and a half, at least!" Garnett called back.

"Good. Thatcher, you and Isa take Phoebe and go! We'll hold them off!" Reigh ordered. "Go!"

Was he freaking kidding? That would never work!

"I'm not leaving you here!" I snarled.

"Listen, you idiot, either you go now, or we all—"

BOOOOM ...

A low, concussive sound like the heartbeat of the earth itself made the ground rumble and shake under us. Even after the sound faded, the vibrations still shivered all the way up from my feet to the top of my head. The writhing hoard of switchbeasts all went eerily silent. They froze, their big white eyes blinking and their bodies shifting uneasily.

"Wh-What ... was that?" Reigh gasped hoarsely.

BOOOOM ...

A second tremor hit, nearly knocking me off my feet this time. I slammed into Garnett, faltering on my injured leg. She looped an arm around my waist and held me up, her expression closed and grim as she stared ahead at the hesitating swarm of switchbeasts. Her throat tensed as she swallowed.

There was no denying the look of pure, mortal dread in her eyes as she looked up at me and whispered one, breathless word.

"Underbeast."

CHAPTER TWENTY-ONE

Underbeast.

That word cut through my mind like a blade through warm butter. I stared back at Garnett, waiting for some clue or indication of what to do. Why were we just standing here? Wasn't this our chance to run for it?

BOOOOM...

Another tremor, louder and more violent than the rest, shook rubble and dust from the ceiling that fell in a clacking shower around us. Murdoc coughed. I had to shield my eyes. Not even fifty yards away, the writhing, twisting hoard of switchbeasts still hesitated. The shuddering of the tunnel shook a few of them off the ceiling, sending them crashing into the ones below. A few of the ones on the walls scurried away, running like startled lizards back down the tunnel they'd come out of.

"It's coming!" Garnett cried, hauling me along as she whirled around to the rest of our group. "Run! Go, go, go!"

Pushing away from her, I hobbled as fast as I could, wincing and cursing with every step. Murdoc tried seizing my other arm and looping it around his shoulders, but I shrugged him off, too. We didn't have time for that. Either I made it or I didn't. I wasn't going to risk slowing anyone else down because of it.

Behind us, a cacophony of dismayed yowling broke through the tunnel. Oh gods, were some of the switchbeasts still willing to chase us? We'd never be able to outrun them like thi—

CRACK—BOOM!!

We all staggered to a halt and scrambled back as another massive tremor dislodged a huge chunk of rock from the ceiling and sent it smashing down in front of us like a small moon. It blocked the way ahead and choked the air with dust.

Then the rock *moved*.

No. Not a rock. This was ... something else. Something enormous.

It rose up, unfurling before us like a colossal god, wreathed in the swirling clouds of dust. A blasting snort like a gust of wind blew the dust clear enough for a massive snout to appear, followed by a head and body covered in thick, leathery hide. Huge jaws snapped with four muscular mandibles, each one lined with jagged teeth as big as my arm. There were no eyes on its flat bony skull, and its hulking body had only two arms as thick around as tree trunks. Each arm had a big, paddle-like paw with thick claws caked with dirt and rock. The ground shook as it crawled forward dragging its long, eel-like lower half behind it.

Garnett stood in front of us, her arms spread out wide with her axes still gripped firmly in her hands. She gaped up at the towering behemoth, but it only lasted a second. She glanced back at us, locking gazes with me ... and then Murdoc. She nodded at him slowly, and something came over her features—a grim sense of resolve I didn't understand—and Garnett stepped forward with her strong shoulders tensed.

A shrill note went up through the cavernous tunnel, echoing off the stone walls like an eerie melody. Was she ... whistling? She was! It was the same sort of method I'd developed to communicate with Fornax.

Garnett made the sound again, stepping closer to the underbeast with her axes still at the ready. Its huge head swung down in her direction, blasts of its breath whipping in her hair and sending all the loose dirt and pebbles around her skittering away.

"That's right, you big beastie," she growled bitterly. "You remember who I am."

The underbeast let out another booming cry that made my brain scramble and my vision spot. Its slithery hind quarters writhed, bashing against the sides of the tunnel as it reared back and opened its jaws. Garnett bolted forward as fast as a flash of lightning, diving into a spin with both of her axes primed for an attack as the creature's giant head descended toward her like it meant to swallow her whole.

Reigh let out a yell and charged in, too.

Murdoc snarled, baring his teeth and flashing me a quick, determined glare. "This is where we part ways. We'll hold it off as long as we can! *GO!*"

What?! No! I wouldn't leave him to be—

"We must hurry!" Isandri yowled. With Phoebe still clinging to her back, she bounded forward and spread her wings, letting out a grunt of effort as she seized the back of my cloak in her teeth and broke for the open air. Our weight slowed her down and made her flight erratic, but she managed to zoom around the monster's bashing head, dodging flying boulders and sprays of rock and rubble. She zipped over the underbeast's shoulder and darted down its back, barely making it to the tunnel beyond before my cloak ripped and I fell.

My arms and legs flailed as I plummeted about eight feet

and landed with a *thud* on the tunnel floor. I rolled a few feet, finally stopping flat on my stomach and wheezing for breath.

"Get up! Now! We must make it to the tower before it is too late," Isandri hissed as she landed beside me.

"W-Working ... on ... it," I rasped as I staggered back to my feet and began to shamble along beside her down the dark tunnel ahead. A mile and a half—maybe. We could make it there.

I glanced back over my shoulder, unable to see anything except the massive pitching creature moving like a writhing worm, cracking down more hunks of rock as it bellowed. I couldn't spot any sign of Murdoc or any of the others. I didn't know if they'd make it. Even if they somehow managed to get past the underbeast—what about the switchbeasts? Would they all flee the much larger predator or not?

Tears welled in my eyes as I turned away and continued on, biting down hard against the coppery flavor of rage that burned over my tongue. They *would* make it. They had to. Garnett knew those monsters better than anyone. Murdoc was the strongest person and the best fighter I knew. Reigh never gave up—ever—even when all the odds in the world were stacked against him. He was way too stubborn to die.

They would all make it to the tower, too.

I refused to believe anything else.

THIS WASN'T HOW IT WAS SUPPOSED TO GO.

Phoebe was meant to go with Murdoc's group in search of the mirror. Reigh was supposed to be with us, looking for Devana. He'd been through those base level tunnels before. He had a much better idea of where to go. Now we had it backwards, and I didn't know what that might mean for our plan. Did Phoebe even know where to take us once we got into the tower? I wanted to ask, but as I jogged on, gritting my teeth against the shooting pain from the wound on my leg, it didn't seem like a priority just yet. First, we had to actually reach the tower. Then we could worry about where to go inside of it.

One crisis at a time, as Murdoc liked to say.

The sounds of combat slowly faded behind us, replaced by our panting breaths and the scuffle of our footsteps over the stone. Sweat made my clothes feel damp and heavy and my bangs stuck to my forehead. My head pounded, and I'd probably cracked a rib or something when I fell from Isandri's grasp. Small problems, though. Well, comparatively, anyway.

Still in her feline form, Isandri didn't seem much better off. Her wings slumped and her feline mouth gaped as she panted. Maybe staying in that form for so long was exhausting to her, as well.

"Isa, please, just put me down. I can run on my own. You need to conserve your strength," Phoebe insisted after we'd been stumbling along for almost an hour. "We must be getting close now, right?"

She was right. It shouldn't take this long to walk a mile and a half, even if the terrain was rough and the tunnel zigzagged some. We should be getting close. Gods and Fates, without Garnett, we really had no idea where we were going now. What if we passed the entrance and didn't even realize it?

"Let's stop, take another breather for a minute, and think this through," I suggested, stumbling to a halt and doubling over to try and catch my breath.

"There is no time," Isandri objected, snapping her jaws angrily.

"Then we will *make* time," I fired back. Trudging over to the side of the tunnel, I leaned back against it for support as I slowly sank down to the floor to sit. "I need to do something about my leg or I'm not going to be any use running around Northwatch. And Isa, if you need to rest ... you've got to do it right now. We're gonna need all our power once we get inside."

She sent me what I can only describe as a scowl of utter feline disapproval. She slicked her ears back and snorted, looking away and swishing her long tail before she finally came stalking over. She folded her luminescent wings in tight to her sides and crouched down close beside me long enough for Phoebe to slip down from her back.

While Phoebe pulled another torch from our supply bag and lit it, Isandri stomped over and plopped down close by. Her form shimmered, giving off a shower of sterling light as she resumed her elven form, sitting beside me, with her knees drawn up to her chest and her arms wrapped around her legs. Her staff lay on the ground beside her and she glared straight ahead—but it wasn't a pouting or sulky look. The creases in her brow were drawn upward, and her eyes darted quickly back and forth as though in silent desperation.

I guess I wasn't the only one worrying about the rest of our friends. I couldn't imagine what she must be thinking, although I was willing to guess it had a lot to do with a certain redheaded prince. She'd left him behind once before, in a situation sort of like this one, I gathered. He'd stayed behind to fight. She'd gone ahead and escaped.

I wondered if, for her, this was like reliving a nightmare.

"Here, I can take a look at your leg," Phoebe offered. She scooted over close and took out one of the emergency medical kits we'd brought along.

"It was a scratch, not a bite. It just hurts a little," I told her, trying not to wince as she unlaced my boot and rolled up my pantleg to get a better look. "No time for stitches."

"I'll just bandage it tightly, then." Phoebe's lips pressed

together, obviously not liking that she couldn't be more thorough in her treatment.

"Phoebe?" I cleared my throat some, already hating that I even had to ask this question. There was no way around it, though. Of the three of us, she was the only one who knew anything about Northwatch. "Do you know what the entrance to the tower looks like from, um, *underground?*"

She winced some, brows crinkling up into a look of distress. "I-I ... no, I never saw it from underground before. I'm sorry. I don't know where we are, or how to get there from here."

Great. Well, that wasn't the news I'd been hoping for.

"What about if we get inside? I know you were supposed to go with Murdoc and the others, but do you think you can take us to the place where Iksoli is holding Devana? Cell doors with those symbols on them?" I tried again. "They were supposedly near the bottom of the tower, right? So, we don't have too far to go once we get inside ... hopefully."

Her head raised slowly to look me in the eye. She drew her bottom lip into her mouth, her gaze distant as though she were thinking hard. "I ... maybe. I went down there a few times. Not for Devana, of course. Lord Argonox had me examine a few other magically gifted people he had captured. He was always wanting us to find ways to extract their abilities or harness them somehow. But it was only twice—once for a man and then ... once for Reigh."

"But it was the same place?" I pressed. "The cell block that Phillip talked about?"

She nodded slowly. "I think so. But I only ever went there from my workshop, not from other places inside the tower. If I found my old workshop, I might be able to navigate there. But it's hard when I'm starting at a different point. Lord Argonox didn't let us have free range. I lived in my workshop almost all the time. Every now and then I got to go down to the manufacturing levels to inspect progress on the machines I'd designed, critique them, and watch tests. Except for the few times I was sent to the cell block to examine Reigh and that other man, I didn't get to go out. And even when I did, there were armed guards chaperoning me."

"So, if we find your old workshop, you can probably find the cell block we need," I surmised aloud.

Phoebe nodded again. "Yes."

"How far up the tower is it?" Isandri asked. "We don't have time to take a long trip out of the way."

Good point.

"Um. Not that far, I don't think. Maybe two or three floors up?" Phoebe guessed, fidgeting nervously as she glanced between us. "The higher levels were reserved for officers, experimentation rooms, and other things I didn't have access to."

"Okay, then. That's our first goal." I looked over at Isandri, who had leaned forward some to rest her chin on her kneecaps. "Now we just have to find that tower entrance, somehow slip inside without anyone noticing, and not get attacked and killed on our way through it."

Uggh. If I was the one trying to come up with plans, we really were in trouble. Maybe if we sat here for a few minutes, caught our breath, and let Isandri rest while Phoebe patched up my leg, the others would catch up to us.

A guy could hope, anyway.

Glancing across the tunnel, I caught another glint of metal sparkling in the light from our torch. More Tibran skeletons dressed in armor, no doubt. There were a lot more of them scattered around now that we were getting closer to the tower. I wondered what would happen to all of the gear and weapons that were just lying around. There must have been hundreds of suits of armor, swords, shields, and all kinds of stuff the Tibrans had left behind.

An idea hit me like someone had slapped me in the face with a dead fish.

Sweet Fates. I knew how we were going to sneak into that tower. I knew how we were going to pass through it unnoticed. It was an awful, truly terrible idea. But I knew it would work—

Because I'd seen it work before ... on the night my village burned.

22

CHAPTER TWENTY-TWO

"This is not going to work," Isandri muttered as she buckled the Tibran breastplate on over her robes.

Rummaging through the pile of bones and armor, I tossed her a set of greaves and vambraces, too. "It did last time. Plus, if the people here fighting for Iksoli are really under her mind control, they're probably not going to look too closely. Did you see the ones who ran past us during that switchbeast attack? Most of them were wearing patched-together bits of old Tibran stuff, too."

"He does have a point." Phoebe's voice echoed from under the helmet she'd pulled down over head. It fit her about as well as an empty bucket. Honestly, she was so petite that all of the armor was bound to be hilariously too big for her, but we didn't have a lot of time to be choosy. Hopefully, no one would look at her closely enough to notice.

"Last time? You've disguised yourself this way before?" Isandri arched an eyebrow as she held up the vambraces.

I turned my face away just in case I couldn't keep it together. I didn't want either of them to see any signs of weakness right now. "Yeah." I cleared my throat a little. "Murdoc, he, uh, he had us dress in Tibran armor to escape my village. It worked, mostly."

I could feel Isandri's probing stare without ever having to look her way. "Mostly?" she pressed.

"Well, right up until the tide of the battle turned and the dragonriders arrested us because we looked like Tibrans." I forced a chuckle that seemed to snag in my throat. "Look, I know it's not fool-proof. But it's the best we can do right now."

A warm hand touched mine. "Thatcher," Isandri said quietly. "You don't have to do this. I can go on alone. This was never meant to be your burden. Devana has called out for you, yes. But you are not responsible. Not like I am. You can take Phoebe and be—."

"And be a coward?" My mouth screwed up and I lifted a defiant glare up at her. "I've been running ever since this all started, Isandri. I ran from my home and left my father to die. I ran from Phillip. From the Ulfrangar. From the underbeast. I've stood behind stronger people like Jaevid, Murdoc, Reigh, and even you, letting you all fight my battles for me. I ... I'm not doing it anymore. Iksoli has wanted to get to me from the beginning. I'm going to grant that wish and give her all of my attention she can stand."

Somber understanding shone in the depths of Isa's otherworldly eyes. She seemed to look through me—past my flesh and down into my soul—and sank back onto her heels with a small, relinquishing sigh. "Very well."

"If it helps, in the event that I get killed doing this, you can say you tried to talk me out of it, right?" I forced a half-grin.

She shook her head and turned away, going back to fastening on the old Tibran armor.

No one said much else as we finished strapping on all the bits and pieces we found among the bones. I had to help

Phoebe tighten hers up a little, and I found a light short-sword she could easily carry. Now, if no one paid much attention to the fact that she was about the size of a fourteen-year-old, we'd be fine. Honestly, I didn't know how old she actually was, but now wasn't the time to ask her about it.

Striking back out down the tunnel, I held the torch aloft to light the way as we took off as quickly and quietly as we could. Keeping Phoebe between us, Isa prowled along behind us with her staff at the ready, eyes narrowed keenly through the slit in her helmet's visor. I kept a hand on my crossbow, just in case.

We'd been going for less than an hour before more noise echoed down from the passage ahead. I threw up a hand and motioned for everyone to get against the wall. This time, it wasn't screaming or yowling. This sounded like ... conversation. People talking loudly. Shouting commands to one another. Footsteps on the stone and the clunk and clatter of armor.

Isa and I exchanged a look.

Roughly two minutes passed and the noise didn't seem to be getting any closer—more like it was focused in one spot, dead ahead. An outpost? Or a mercenary camp? Or were we at the base of the tower?

Only one way to be sure.

I gave Isa a slow nod, handing off the torch and motioning for her and Phoebe to stay put. Her eyes squinted up in a disapproving glare, so I gave my very best "no seriously, I've got this" look with my eyes widened and made the stay here gesture again.

She took the torch and growled something softly under her breath—probably a curse in her elven language.

I crouched down, moving as carefully and silently as possible with one hand on the wall to keep track of my location as I crept away from the wavering torchlight. As soon as

I was back in the pitch black of the tunnel, I spotted it—the faintest glow in the distance. If it weren't so dark, I never would have noticed. Ahead, the passage curved to the right rather sharply, and around that bend there seemed to be some sort of light source. The closer I got, the brighter it was. The voices grew louder, too.

At last, at a point where the ground made a sharp angle upward, I went down on my belly and crawled up the incline. Peering over the edge, I kept myself crammed into the shadows as much as possible as I gaped in awe at the open chamber ahead of me. It must have been a hundred feet across, at least, with a ceiling that spanned upward nearly as high. Four other tunnels met here, all leading off in different directions. But that wasn't what made my breath catch and my toes curl up inside my boots.

The chamber was filled with at least fifty armed men. They were separated out into smaller groups, almost like they were trying to organize themselves into hunting parties or something. Crap—did that mean Iksoli already knew we were here? Or had the commotion with the underbeast just drawn their attention enough to try and hunt the thing down themselves? Either, way it was a big problem—because also in the middle of the chamber was a large rectangular wooden structure like scaffolding that spanned from floor to ceiling. Cables ran down the sides of it on massive ironwork gears, and the top part disappeared into a large shaft cut into the ceiling overhead.

Wait a second ... I'd seen something like this before, hadn't I? Yes! In Eastwatch tower. There had been an elevator made of wood and metal with a broad platform that could be raised and lowered through the entirety of the tower. Jaevid had warned us about it—that being careless around it was a fantastic way to get killed. It was for moving crates and gear, not people, so it wasn't exactly made with safety in mind. But that's exactly what these guys were using this one for.

As the platform appeared from the dark open shaft overhead, slowly descending the wooden framework to the ground, I could make out the shapes of more people wearing hodgepodge assortments of armor standing inside it.

Okay. Well. We'd found the way into the tower, so that was one problem solved. This new issue, however, was going to require a change of plans.

Oh, and an insane amount of luck.

I BEGAN SCOOTING BACK DOWN THE INCLINE, FINALLY daring to get on my feet and make a dash back to where Isandri and Phoebe were waiting once I was sure I was out of sight. It took a few seconds of panicked gasping before I was able to explain to them what we were up against. Meanwhile, Phoebe's face went ghostly white and she chewed on her bottom lip, looking like she might faint on the spot as I described everything.

"So they did extend the elevator shaft, after all," she whimpered. "I told them it was dangerous until the tunnels were completed in the surrounding areas. Any tremors or explosions might cause the framework to become compromised. But Argonox didn't like hearing any of my suggestions when it came to the safety of his workers and soldiers. They were all just expendable to him."

"How are we going to get past all those mercenaries?" I asked, looking to Isandri in hopes that she would have an idea.

"I could transform and fly you both up there," Isandri suggested. "If your estimation is correct, it is a long way up, but I can manage it."

"Except everyone will definitely see that," Phoebe pointed out. "They'll be trying to shoot us down. And then the entire tower will know we're there."

Hmm. She was right. Simply storming in there and making a run for it wasn't going to work, even through the air. Isandri was fast, but not when she was loaded down with passengers.

"We look like them now, don't we? Dressed like this, how do we know they wouldn't overlook us entirely if we simply walked in?" Isandri glanced between us, as though expecting someone to object.

Only, I didn't have a good reason right off the top of my head for why that *wouldn't* work. That had been sort of my idea from the start. But it felt a teensy bit riskier now that I knew we would be standing amongst at least fifty-or-so armed fighters under ambient light where one of them might notice that, you know, we were definitely *not* part of their ranks.

Yeah. This felt like one of those moments where Murdoc would have called me an idiot.

"What if ... we don't try to hide it when we enter?" Phoebe said suddenly.

"I'm not sure we could hide it, even if we wanted to," I reminded her.

She waved a hand. "No, no. I mean, what if we try to get their attention on purpose. You said it yourself, we just saw a bunch of switchbeasts hunting down people dressed like us. What if we ran in, screaming and warning them that there's been an attack and there's an underbeast in the tunnel? Draw their attention that way?"

"And if the others are following us farther behind? We might be sending enemies straight into their path," Isandri warned.

Phoebe glanced fretfully back down the way we'd come. "I know. But maybe they can hide just like we did before."

Isandri did not look convinced *at all*.

"I don't like it any more than you do," I muttered as I bent over and began pulling off the bandaging from inside my boot where Phoebe had wrapped up my leg. "But this is the best chance we've got. We have to get to that elevator, and I'm fresh out of ideas."

"If you can get us onto it, I'm sure I can get it to work. The mechanics are fairly basic," Phoebe said, as though hoping to give Isandri a little hope that we weren't completely out of our minds.

I held up the bloody strips of gauze. "Sounds like all we need now is to make some makeup adjustments."

I HAD NEVER IMAGINED THAT ACTING IN ANY CAPACITY might be one of my finer skills. I couldn't even recall having ever tried it before now. But as I ran headlong up the incline again, screaming my head off while dressed in Tibran armor smeared with my own blood, and sporting an extremely authentic and convincing leg wound from a switchbeast, I realized I might actually pull this off. If being a dragonrider didn't work out, maybe I could give stage performances a try.

I reached the top of the tunnel's incline, stopping with Phoebe and Isandri right behind me, and yelled, "THE UNDERBEAST IS IN THE TUNNEL!"

Every single swordsman, cutthroat, and mercenary assembling in that chamber stopped dead in their tracks and stared at me in stunned silence.

I took that opportunity to limp dramatically forward and stumble, collapsing into a heap. Isa and Phoebe rushed forward to catch me, hauling me back up and looping my arms around their shoulders to begin dragging me away toward the elevator.

That's when they all began to converge upon us—drawing blades, nocking arrows into bowstrings, raising shields, and storming straight in our direction.

I braced. On both sides of me, Isa and Phoebe stiffened and squeezed harder at my arms. I held my breath.

The armored mob ran past us, clambering down the passageway and off into the tunnel beyond. Nearly half the chamber emptied out, and as we staggered for the elevator, no one tried to stop us. I added in a few groans and wails—just to really sell it. Phoebe and Isandri laid me down slowly on the platform and motioned to the guy operating the crank system to begin lifting us up.

I dared to let out a shaky exhale.

So far, so good. But we weren't clear, yet. There was still a lot of ground to cover between us and Phoebe's workshop.

As soon as I was sure we were high enough up that no one on the ground might see, I sat up and got busy wiping as much of the blood off my armor as I could. Isandri crouched down next to me, eyeing the rickety elevator distrustfully. Not that I blamed her in the slightest. The way the thing lurched and rattled, chains groaning and clanking loudly as we slowly climbed higher and higher toward the open dark chasm above, didn't inspire much confidence.

"This should take us to the base subterranean floor of the tower," Phoebe whispered, her voice trembling. "Th-There, um, there were some cells down there. But they were mostly for high-profile prisoners, not the magically-gifted ones, I think." She pinched her eyes shut and took a few deep, shaking breaths. "I-I'm trying to remember, I'm sorry."

"How do we get to your workshop from there?" I asked, reaching out to grasp one of her hands to give it a reassuring squeeze. "You can do this, Phoebe. Just try to remember."

"I-I ... well, there was a window in my workshop. A small one. I needed some ventilation for some of the things I had to work on. I could see out. It was a long way to the top from there—I-I only went up a few times. I think my workshop was ... on the second floor." She opened her eyes again and stared at me, anguish drawing her features tense. "I'm sorry, I just keep thinking about Murdoc and the others. Gods, what if we sent all those mercenaries straight at them? What if they were injured and ... and we just got them killed!"

I gave her hand another firm squeeze. "Phoebe, if there's one thing I know for sure, it's that no one is better at killing things than Murdoc. I once saw him kill a man with one punch. Literally—it was one hit to the face that broke the guy's jaw and I guess gave him brain damage or something. It was horrible, but at the time it also sort of kept us from being beaten to a pulp in a prison camp. Anyway, my point is, injured or not, I don't think the people who just ran down there can take him down. And he's got Garnett and Reigh with him. They're going to make it."

She stared at me through the visor of her helmet with her big blue eyes rimmed with tears. Bobbing her head a little, she sniffled and lifted it long enough to wipe her eyes on her sleeve. "O-Okay. You're right. He's ... stronger than anyone else I know."

"Yeah, he is." I looked back to Isandri, who was staring up at the slowly encroaching dark hole as our platform ascended into it. "Now, what do we do when we get to the subterranean floor?"

"There should be a staircase leading upward. It's part of the original tower," Phoebe explained.

"Yes," Isandri growled low. "I am familiar with it."

I blinked in surprise. "You are?"

"I was held there for a time. That is where I first met Reigh. Our area of cells were different. The doors did not have runes or marks upon them. They were secluded, and there were no guard patrols watching us. I think it was where they sent the prisoners they either intended to execute ... or allow to die slowly of their injuries or neglect. I was relocated there after Argonox concluded that my powers would not be useful to him, and my will could not be broken to his will. I was blindfolded for my transport, however. I don't remember how to navigate those halls."

"We won't have to," Phoebe assured us. "We just need to get to the stairs, and that shouldn't be so hard to find. We go up and start searching at the second floor. I'll know right away if it's the one where my workshop was."

Getting to my feet, I pulled my crossbow from its resting place, belted at my hip, and held it at the ready. "Good. Let's do this as fast as we can. In and out."

"And when we encounter Iksoli?" Isa flicked me a wary look.

I spun the cartridge on my crossbow, making sure it was already primed with a bolt ready to fire. "Then we give her the reunion she's been waiting for, and a whole lot more."

PART FOUR

MURDOC

CHAPTER TWENTY-THREE

I'd imagined my death a thousand times. Being caught in the dark at the end of an Ulfrangar blade. Being beheaded in a city square by an executioner's axe. Being shot full of arrows by a city guard. Being incinerated by a dragonrider's flame. And more recently, being cut down in a duel against the Zuer.

But I had never imagined it might go like this—miles underground in a Tibran tunnel, overrun with switchbeasts crawling the walls like cockroaches, and ducking the body slams and the snapping maw of an underbeast.

Never let it be said that the Fates aren't creative with their destinies.

I kicked into a side roll, ducking another sweep of the underbeast's lashing tail. The thing crawled along like a salamander missing its hind legs, bellowing and threatening to shake the entire tunnel down on top of us. Boulders the size of buildings broke loose from the ceiling and smashed down into the crawling onslaught of switchbeasts. Most of them had fled in the presence of this monster, but the few that remained made lunging strikes at us whenever they got the chance.

I dipped and dodged, weaving around the hailstorm of flying debris, snapping switchbeast jaws, and the thundering crash of the underbeast slamming its head into the ground. It made wild snaps at Reigh, Garnett, and anything else that got too close. Without eyes, I could only guess it oriented by sound or maybe smell, although the latter seemed less likely for a creature that lived underground.

A squeal and crunch made me look back, just in time to watch a switchbeast that had come too close disappear down the monster's throat, crushed in those four mandible jaws.

My pulse raced, and I made another driving strike with my swords, scrambling through the underbeast's tree-trunk-sized stomping legs. I cursed, feeling the steel of my weapons glance off the monster's thick, leathery hide. Gods and Fates, it must have had skin five inches thick. I couldn't get through to pierce anything vital. And by the look of things, Reigh and Garnett weren't having much luck, either.

Garnett screamed dwarven curses as she hurled one of her axes, sending the weapon howling through the air and catching the underbeast in the soft meat of its throat. It sliced through the thick hide, but not deep enough to even make the monster bleed. Curse it.

I set my jaw and tried again, angling my blades in a frantic downward thrust with all my strength against the beast's hide. My strike stuck in less than an inch before the blade slid askew and sent me floundering backward. Mashed against the stone, I cringed as the underbeast slammed into the tunnel wall, barely missing me with its massive leg. Curse it all to the abyss! Nothing made a spit's worth of difference! Was there any way to kill this thing before it caused a cave in or smashed us all to jelly?

"Murdoc!" Reigh shouted suddenly.

I spun to see him standing atop a fallen switchbeast, his elven kafki blades still jabbed deep into its back. He glared past me at the underbeast, blood dribbling from what I sincerely hoped was a claw-swipe and not a bite mark across his forehead.

"Ever heard tales of my sister fighting in the Tibran War?" He growled as he prowled closer, his chest heaving with panting breaths.

I arched a brow. Now really wasn't the time for—

He spun his blades over his hands once, giving them a testing flourish before he flicked me a meaningful look. "I'm gonna give it the bitter bite. Cover me."

The bitter—oh gods, no.

"Reigh!" I shouted after him. That idiot! Was he completely insane? Did he *want* to die?

He took off toward the monster at a sprint, spinning and weaving through its roiling fit, until he came to a skidding halt right in front of it. The underbeast's massive head cranked around, nostrils flaring and four jaw-arms opening wide. Reigh dropped down into a crouch, curling his body into a ball with his arms and legs tucked in tight.

I ran for him. No way would I let him try this. There was stupid, and then there was—

My body flew backward through the air, tossed end over end as the underbeast's head slammed down into the ground before me. I hit the ground yards away, my blades knocked from my grasp. Flat on my back, I wheezed and groaned. My vision swerved and tunneled, spots like fairy lights dancing before my eyes as I tried to move. My head lolled as I dragged myself to my hands and knees, looking up just in time to see the underbeast gulp down the idiot prince whole.

"REIGH!" I shouted, my voice broken and hoarse.

Nearby, Garnett's face went white with terror. She'd seen it, too.

A thousand thoughts took my mind like a winter storm. Gods, how would we tell Jenna? Could we even recover his body? Or were we all about to meet a similar fate?

The underbeast rose up, rearing back with its jaws snapping with another shattering cry. Its mighty claws raked trenches in the earth, crushing more switchbeasts underfoot. It floundered like a beached fish, suddenly pitching into a mad frenzy. What the—?

BOOOOM!

A thrash of its body sent a shower of rocks and earth plummeting from the ceiling directly before it. Garnett dove toward me, and I surged forward to catch her hand and drag her out of the way as the passage caved in. I yanked her behind me, trying to shield her with my body as rubble showered over us. The beast bellowed, rattling the earth and slamming its head back and forth between the sides of the tunnel.

BAM—BAM—BAM!

Gods, what was it doing?

With another deafening bellow, the monster threw its head back as a gurgling spray of something black spewed from its mouth. Its mandibles opened wide as its body jerked erratically. I tucked my head down and shut my eyes tightly, curling as closely as I could against Garnett, as it suddenly pitched forward and hit the ground with bone-rattling force. One of its passive paws crashed into the stone wall right next to us, missing us by only a foot or two.

Then silence.

A second past, and I couldn't hear anything except the hiss and rattle of bits of rock and dirt still showering down from the ceiling. No angry roars. No thrashing. No shrieks of switchbeasts. Just my own heartbeat still pounding like a war drum in my ears.

I slowly lifted my head and squinted back over my shoulder. There, amidst the debris and curling plumes of dust, the underbeast lay on its side ... motionless. Its jaws were splayed open, a long prickly tongue lolled out amidst rivers of that black stuff. Its blood?

Pulling away from the wall, I dared to face it. I didn't have my weapons—they were lying somewhere in the chaos—so I bent down to slide the dagger free from where I always kept it tucked in the side of my boot. Prowling forward, one cautious, slow step at a time, I watched the creature for any signs of stirring. Its sides didn't heave with any breaths. Its hide didn't so much as twitch.

Was it ... dead?

I scrambled back, nearly tripping over my own feet as a sudden spray of that black blood spewed from the underbeast's neck with a sickly, slapping burble. Its throat split open like an orange peel as something sharp poked through from the inside. I gripped my dagger harder, ready to fling it at a moment's notice.

Prince Reigh Farrow crawled out of the underbeast's throat, soaked with black blood, and gasping for breath like a newborn calf. He wrenched himself free, still gripping his blades in his fists.

Holy. Gods.

"Reigh!" Garnett shrieked. She bounded past me and seized him by the elbow, helping him squirm the rest of the way out of the monster's corpse. "Are you all right?"

Reigh sat, a dripping, slimy mess, and panted for a few seconds with a look of catatonic shock on his face like he couldn't believe he'd survived. That made three of us, I guess.

Finally, he let go of his weapons just so he could try wiping some of the bloody slop away from his eyes. "That ... was ... so much ... worse ... than Jenna ... made it sound," he coughed and spat out mouthfuls of the blood. "Have I mentioned ... I really *hate* ... Northwatch?"

Garnett doubled over, catching her weight with her hands

on her knees as she laughed. "Stones, man! Who does something like that? You are one reckless fool, Reigh Farrow."

He flopped back onto the ground with a sticky slapping sound and lay there, arms and legs sprawled wide, and slowly shook his head. "You ... have no idea."

"Maybe they'll stop and wait for us farther down the tunnel?" Garnett suggested as we all sat, staring across the now barricaded exit behind us. Not that we'd planned on making a retreat that way when all this was done, but now it wasn't even an option.

"I doubt it. They were running with the fear that either the underbeast or some of the switchbeasts might be right on their heels. I doubt they would stop unless they had no other choice," Reigh said, still trying to wipe the monster's blood from his face and hands.

Rummaging through the debris, I unearthed my longswords from where they'd been knocked from my grasp. One of them had been pinned under a good-sized rock and was now bent enough it wouldn't slide into the sheath on my back again. Ugh. Useless. I tossed it down and put the other one away. Fortunately, that one was only slightly dinged, so at least I wasn't empty-handed now.

"Is the entrance to the tower something they'll be able to find on their own?" I asked as I turned to rejoin them.

Garnett grunted, her foot planted on the underbeast's neck for leverage as she wrenched her second axe free of its leather hide. "Probably," she huffed as she tugged. "It's not like there are signs with big arrows pointing the way. But five tunnels converge there in a fairly large chamber. I'm sure that ought to tip them off."

"We can only hope," I muttered.

"Regardless, we now have a problem. They're traveling with Phoebe. She knows the tower better than I do, probably. Maybe she can get them to the cell block where Devana is—which is good news for them. The bad news is, I don't have a clue where the Mirror of Truth would be held in that place." Reigh grunted as he stood, combing some of his now slimy hair away from his face. "I've seen the mirror once, but it was in an underground chamber or something. Hilleddi was using it to interrogate people."

Garnett nodded like that made sense. "Argonox didn't like to move his more precious captured artifacts out in the open. He moved them underground, where they were less likely to be stolen or damaged if there was an attack."

"Any chance it might still be down here somewhere?" Reigh guessed, his tone hopeful.

She sighed as she clipped her axes back into place on her belt. "I doubt it. On the eve of the battle at Halfax, Arognox wanted everything locked down inside the tower and secured—artifacts, valuable prisoners, and people he considered especially useful assets like me. I guess he knew the tunnels could be collapsed or infiltrated, but the Maldobarian architects who designed the watches built them with the intention that they would be difficult to siege."

"And you have no idea where he would've wanted these artifacts secured inside the tower, then?" I pressed. "Think, Garnett. Because the only other choice we have is searching the tower from top to bottom on foot, which will take more time than we have. I'm not sure how your boss deals with not receiving payments he wants, but I'm willing to bet it's unpleasant."

Her mouth mashed up sourly and she crossed her arms, beginning to pace back and forth. "I'm thinking, I'm thinking. Just give me a moment, will you?"

"Think while you walk. Or better yet, run. We've got to try to catch up to them if we can," Reigh urged.

I had to agree. If there was any chance at all of catching up to them and swapping back to our original groups, we had to seize it while we could. Unless Garnett had a sudden stroke of genius about how we could find the mirror in this rat's nest of a city, we were going to be kicking in doors up and down that tower until we found the right one. Not ideal.

Pulling another torch from our supplies—one of the only two I had left—I took a second to light it before we all took off at a jog. Garnett led while Reigh and I matched pace behind her, keeping our eyes and ears attuned as best we could for the approach of anything else that might want to eat, bite, or kill us. Not an easy task, considering the way Reigh's blood-drenched boots sloshed with every step. There was nothing stealthy about our approach whatsoever.

And suddenly, that didn't matter.

Light appeared ahead of us down the tunnel, coming closer—fast. The sound of footsteps echoed over the walls, along with a ruckus of angry shouts and the metallic clanking of armor.

Oh no. What now?

Reigh growled an elven curse and motioned for us to hide. Only, where the heck were we supposed to hide? Looking around, there weren't any convenient crevices or piles of Tibran rubble. No boulders or shards of old war machines.

I spun back to face him. "There's nowhere to—"

Reigh was gone.

I looked around for Garnett.

She'd vanished, too.

What the—?

My pulse roared in my ears as I whirled in a circle, searching every dark shadow. But there was no sign of them. How ...? Where ...?

I opened my mouth to call out for them, but something clamped down around my face, gagging me before I could make a sound. I dropped my torch as two large, hairy legs tipped in shiny black claws snatched me up and spun me like a sausage on a spit, wrapping my middle with something stringy and sticky as I wrenched and fought. I couldn't even yell out as I was yanked upward to the ceiling of the tunnel and held there.

Looking to my left, I finally spotted Reigh and Garnett. They'd been bound up just like I was, their mouths gagged and arms pinned with what looked like ... was that spider silk?

My head snapped to the other side, looking to my right as something enormous, black, and covered in glossy hairs clung to the ceiling right next to me on eight long legs. The biggest spider I had ever seen stared directly at me like something straight out of a nightmare. Fates, it must have been the size of a horse. It peered at me with two big, dinner-plate-sized yellow eyeballs facing front, and numerous ones along the side. They blinked in a sort of rippling pattern, seeming to consider me curiously.

Then the massive spider took one of its legs and held it over its mouth.

Wait a second—was it gesturing for me to be quiet?

No. Not possible. I was imagining things. I had to be. There were no spiders this size in Maldobar. Not that the Ulfrangar had ever told me about. I hadn't heard anything about Argonox bringing giant spiders along with his forces, either.

Even if he had, and one had taken up residence down here in these tunnels ... as far as I knew, spiders of any size did not *shush* people.

My gaze snapped back downward as light bloomed through the tunnel, growing brighter and closer as the voices became louder. A mob of mercenaries roughly twenty or thirty men strong stormed by, their weapons already primed and as they called to one another, barking orders for forming ranks. They stormed past right below us, but never looked up in our direction.

Dread poured through my body, leaving me breathless and limp as I hung, suspended by the spider's silk. Had those mercenaries already found Thatcher and the others? Had they killed them and now they were coming for the rest of us? Or taken them prisoner? Gods, what if Iksoli already had them? What would happen to them? Would she torture them?

I shut my eyes tightly, fury like molten metal surging through me at the thought. No. I wouldn't accept any of that. Not until I'd seen their bodies myself. They were still alive. They were somewhere ahead of us. They were fine.

They had to be.

CHAPTER TWENTY-FOUR

"Lukani! You put us down this instant!" Garnett's voice hissed angrily. Somehow, she'd managed to work that spider silk gag out of her mouth. She glared at the creature, her violet eyes practically glowing with wrath. "I mean it! What are you even doing here?"

The spider made a sound sort of like a sad puppy's whimper, coiling back and rubbing two of its front legs together sheepishly.

"Don't you dare make that face at me," Garnett growled. "Put us down right now. Arlan is going to be ready to spit fire when he finds out you've snuck off again. Honestly, who do you think he'll blame for this?"

The spider went on making sad, squeaky sounds as it slowly lowered us to the tunnel floor one by one. I stared in complete awe as the creature scurried down the wall and stepped onto the ground before me, changing shape mid-stride. Its outline wavered, rippling and warping like a reflection through curved glass, until it took the shape of a young boy. Or, rather, he appeared young. Maybe twelve or thirteen at most, with a lithe build and boyish face. But since his features weren't of any race I could name or remember from all my Ulfrangar training, I didn't dare assume.

His skin was a strange, emerald green hue, and his large ears sloped to sharp, knife-like points. Similar to an elf's, but much more ... exaggerated. He wiggled them like a fox as he crept closer to me on bare feet, dressed in nothing but a pair of dark purple silk breeches and a broad, woven leather belt. He pulled a curved dagger and bent over me, studying me with bizarre yellow eyes and feline-like vertical pupils.

I drew back on instinct, panting through my nose as my gaze flicked between him and the blade.

He smiled broadly, tilting his head to one side and tossing some of his long black hair away from his face in the process. "It's okay. I won't hurt you, human," he announced, his accent strong and a little similar to others I'd heard from Damaria. He spun the blade through his fingers with an effortless speed I had to admire. Then he cut down the front of the spider silk that still held my arms in place before quickly bounding over to do the same to Reigh and Garnett.

"What are you?" I demanded as soon as I could pull the sticky, silken gag out of my mouth.

Lukani flicked a long, lion-like tail tipped in a tuft of black fur that emerged from a slit cut in the back of his pants. He opened his mouth, a haughty grin already curling over his childlike face, but Garnett cut him off.

"He's a menace, that's what he is," she grumbled as she snatched the silk away from her arms. "Wildshapers is what people call them outside of Damaria. But in their homeland, they're called Rajinna. They seldom ever leave their cave-cities, let alone make it all the way to other kingdoms. But Arlan stumbled across Lukani being trafficked by slavers. We've been trying to get safe passage back to Damaria, and the location of a Rajinna tribe to take him in, but it's not been easy now that the Tibrans have stirred everything up in a nasty way."

Reigh frowned at the boy ... or whatever he was. "How did you get down here?"

"Oh! That wasn't so hard. I just had to blend in a little," Lukani rocked back on his heels, swishing his tail while he spun his dagger around his hand a few more times. His form wavered again, rippling and warping into the shape of a switchbeast. He gave a convincing hiss that sent Reigh scrambling backward and ripping one of his kafki blades out.

"You stop that," Garnett scolded as she picked more spider webbing out of her hair. "Scaring folk with your clever shapes. It's just rude."

"He can shapeshift like Isandri?" I asked, studying his new form for any clue that he wasn't authentically a switchbeast. There wasn't any—not that I could see. Impressive.

"No, not exactly," Garnett sighed. "Isandri can take one alternate form because of her godling powers. Lukani, and every other Rajinna, can change into an animal they've seen before. Some especially clever ones can also change into people, but only ones they've already seen. It's a good trick, but it's gotten them into a lot of trouble in their time. That's why Arlan says their tribes have become so reclusive and wary of outsiders—they fear being abused for their power."

Lukani's image flickered again, blurring back into his green-skinned, somewhat elven-looking form. He sat in a squat, lips pursed unhappily as he crossed his arms. "Are you going to send me back?"

"Now, I can't very well do that, can I? The tunnel's caved in so there's no going back that way." Garnett put her hands on her hips and stared him down like an angry mother hen. "You've got to stick with us. If anything happens to you, Arlan will have my head on a pike. Stones, and after all the trouble he's gone to finding you a way back to Damaria. Why would you want to follow me down into this pit?"

"You said you were going to the tunnels," the boy sulked, looking down. "I wanted to see them. Besides, you would've gotten seen if I didn't come, right? I saved you from those people!"

Garnett threw her hands up and rolled her eyes, muttering angrily in dwarven as she stomped off down the tunnel.

Right. Well, I guess that meant we were dragging this kid along with us. Fantastic.

Snatching up my torch again, I started after her. Reigh wasn't far behind.

Aaand neither was Lukani. He bounded ahead, fast as a cat on his bare feet, and swishing his long, lion-like tail, grinning proudly to himself the whole way. I tried not to reflect too deeply on the fact that we'd just been forced to babysit, as well. At least his shapeshifting ability might come in handy, and he seemed fairly competent with that dagger.

We pressed on, taking up a faster pace as we trekked the tunnel toward the tower. After only a few minutes, Reigh gave a whistle to call our attention over to one side of the tunnel. We'd been passing more and more Tibran ruins, long forgotten down here in the dark. The remains of soldiers, their skeletons still dressed in armor and gripping weapons or clinging to the rotting remains of war machines. Not unexpected, but a harrowing reminder of where we were headed, nonetheless.

Off to the left, Reigh crouched down over a pile of gray bones clustered together. I held the torch higher, trying to get a better look on my way over. Then he held up a very familiar breastplate. I stopped dead in my tracks. That was ... Thatcher's.

My pulse raced for a moment, sending a fresh wave of

panic through my body. My thoughts raced, trying to make sense of it.

Then Reigh held up other pieces of his armor. And the Tibran bones, they weren't lying neatly in their skeletal arrangements anymore—as though they'd been disturbed. Many of them were missing pieces of armor. Three helmets. Three breastplates, sets of greaves, vambraces, and belts.

It clicked in my mind and sent a smirk curling across my face. Aaah. So *that's* what he'd done.

"Why would Thatcher take off his armor? Or do you think those mercenaries took him and stripped him of it?" Reigh guessed as he stood again.

"No," I corrected. "He changed. He and the others have dressed themselves in Tibran armor to try and blend in."

"Clever," Garnett said approvingly. "They might be able to sneak their way in."

I wasn't ready to start jumping to that conclusion just yet. After all, this was Thatcher we were talking about. Sneaking into anything was not his strong suit. "Maybe. It'll help. But we'll have to see. Something sent those fighters our way—tipped them off to our presence. We need to assume they know we're here and move with caution."

"Agreed." Reigh stepped back and rubbed the back of his neck. "Fates, I still don't know how we can even find the mirror. That tower's going to be a hive of terrible things that all want to gut us alive."

Garnett raised a finger. "Actually, I've been thinking on that. I might have an idea. Granted, it's not a great one. But it's worth a shot, I think."

I made a sweeping motion with my hand. "By all means."

"When Argonox began restructuring portions of the tower, turning the former soldier bunk rooms into prison cells and the like, he had blueprints made for the builders.

Diagrams of what he wanted in the new constructions inside. If we can find those, we can narrow our search."

"Makes sense," Reigh murmured, his demeanor becoming grim and focused as he stared at the armor scattered on the ground before us. "I don't remember a lot from when I was in there. I was ... in and out of consciousness most of the time. But on the eve of the last battle for Halfax, I know Argonox was doling out orders to lock down the tower, like Garnett said. The vaults are going to be our best bet."

"You're sure about that?" I pressed, not entirely convinced. I knew a little about the state he'd been in during that battle—the kinds of torture the Tibrans subjected their captured enemies to. He was probably in agony and drugged out of his mind.

Reigh fixed me with a harrowing glare like the soul had been sucked straight out of him and left nothing behind but hate and venom. "Yeah. I'm sure."

Hmm. Good enough for me, then. "All right. So, we find these blueprints. Then we find whatever vault Argonox might have wanted his divine artifacts placed in."

"Finding the blueprints should be easy enough. Argonox didn't trust anyone, not even his own people. He kept all sensitive information under lock and key, where no one could have access to it without his supervision. I'd bet my life they'll be in his old office," Garnett pointed straight up. "At the top of the tower."

"Well, this is going to complicate things," Reigh grumbled softly as we crouched at the edge of a steep incline in the tunnel path.

Peeking over the edge, the chamber ahead of us was slightly less populated now, probably, thanks to that group that had gone storming down the passage earlier. But there was still a gathering of twenty or thirty armed men between us and the freight elevator that led from the tunnels up into the tower itself. Not to mention, based on what I could see from this distance, it didn't look like the elevator was even down here now. They must have raised it up. That presented its own problem, since we didn't exactly have time to sit around waiting for them to decide to lower it again. Maybe they never would. What then? We had to get up into that tower soon.

"We can take them. There's not that many." Garnett wiggled with excitement where she lay next to me, her purple eyes sparkling.

She was probably right about that. But fighting them would draw attention—specifically, Iksoli's attention. We needed to move in shadow and silence for as long as possible. Once she knew we were here, I had no doubt she'd dedicate every sorry soul in this place to killing us. Not ideal.

On the other hand, the right kind of distraction might be just what we needed.

"What's at the top of that elevator shaft?" I asked, looking to Garnett. "Do you know?"

Her mouth mashed into a thoughtful line. "It goes to the base level of the tower. It's still underground, but it was part of the original structure. A dungeon, I suppose. Or something like it. I went up there a few times, and best I can remember, the room is, mmm, probably less than half the size of this one. Circular with some halls leading off of it, but I never went down those. The central staircase that spans the length of the tower ends there, as well."

"She's right," Reigh answered darkly. "The elevator goes up the full height of the tower, too. Just like it did at Eastwatch. In fact, the dungeon where they had you imprisoned there isn't unlike the room that tunnel opens up into. The watch towers are all designed basically the same way."

Perfect.

"How long can that kid hold one of his shapeshifting forms?" I whispered.

Lukani popped up between us like a daisy, beaming proudly as he whispered back, "Depends on the size. Bigger ones are harder. I can't hold those shapes for more than a few minutes. Small ones are easy, though. I can stay that way for almost a full day now."

I ignored the seething look of absolute rage Garnett was giving me from behind him as I asked, "What about a dragon?"

Lukani's eyes went wide, practically sparkling with enthusiasm as his mouth made an O-shape like he hadn't thought about that before.

"Absolutely not—are you mad? You can't send him in there! He'll be shot full of arrows in seconds!" Garnett fussed like an angry squirrel.

"Which would be a problem for most things, but not a dragon. Regular arrows won't pierce their hide. Crossbows might, but only at close range. He won't need to get that close," I reasoned.

Her eyes narrowed suspiciously. "That close for what?"

"To fly us up that elevator shaft ... and light this place up with dragon fire on the way so no one follows."

Garnett's mouth fell open.

It wasn't the most discreet approach, true. But we were running out of options in that respect. As long as we were going to send up an alarm through Northwatch of our arrival, we might as well make sure we closed this area off so we weren't dealing with more of Iksoli's fighters pouring out of here like ants from an anthill.

Dragon fire was, essentially, the best way to be sure of that.

"Oh, please, Auntie G. Oh, please, oh please, oh please," the boy whirled to face Garnett, his long, pointed ears drooping as he begged. "I've never gotten to do a dragon shape before!"

Garnett cast me another smoldering, withering glare. Hmm. I might have to watch my back for a little while, until she cooled off. Otherwise, she might try planting an axe in it when I wasn't paying attention.

"Fine," she snapped sharply. "But if something happens to him and he's injured, you'd better believe I'll be telling Arlan it was *your* fault."

I smirked and panned my gaze back across the chamber before us. "Fair enough."

25

CHAPTER TWENTY-FIVE

We took the room in a flurry of shining golden scales and blistering flames. Clinging to the back of Lukani's dragon form, we tore through the air and headed straight for the elevator shaft. Men scrambled beneath us, screaming in panic and running for cover as he bathed the ground with sprays of burning venom. Arrows zipped past us, humming through the air and glancing off his scales. Flat against his back, I wasn't sure if anyone on the ground would even look closely enough to see us. Hopefully, they'd been a little too worried about burning to death to notice.

Flaring his wings wide, Lukani landed on the scaffolding like a bat on the wall of a cave. The wooden framework creaked and cracked, beginning to list dangerously to one side. I clenched my teeth, gripping the scales and horns of his back as his body flexed and moved, beginning the awkward climb upward. Below us, the scaffolding broke away and shattered, wooden beams falling like tree trunks to smash on the stone floor far below. Flames roared high and choked the air with smoke and heat.

Reigh snarled a curse as Lukani floundered to one side, barely managing to hang on as we climbed up to the opening of the elevator shaft above. It wasn't much more than a hole cut into the stone overhead, but it was our only way out of this hell pit and into the tower.

As Lukani's clawed front legs struck solid stone, finding purchase and sparking over the dark rock, the rest of the wooden framework cracked and broke away below, landing with a *SMASH* and shower of sparks. No one would be following us now. Not this way.

"This was a bad idea!" Reigh shouted over the chaos, keeping his own white knuckled grip on the dragon's hide as we slowly ascended.

Lukani crawled through the vertical elevator tunnel, his wings tucked in tight and his jaws still dripping with burning venom that lit the path ahead. Chancing a look up, I could spot the round hole where the passage opened up overhead. It wasn't far. Maybe a hundred more yards. We would make it.

Bursting out of the passage like a demon crawling up from the abyss, a volley of arrows pinged and clattered off Lukani's scales again as he hauled himself out of that hole. He roared and threw his head back, plated chest heaving in a deep breath before he sent out another blistering spray of acrid, burning venom around the much smaller stone chamber.

Men screamed as flames filled the tighter space, catching most of them in the initial blast. We'd barely managed to scramble off Lukani's back when his form wavered and he shrank back down to his normal, childlike size. He wobbled on the edge of the open pit, arms flailing and barely managing a small yelp of alarm before I lunged and seized one of his arms to drag him back onto solid ground.

"Make for the stairs!" Garnett shouted, already sprinting for a passage to the right.

There wasn't time to question it. We were now fully

relying on hers and Reigh's ability to navigate this place. That didn't inspire a lot of confidence, and I silently wished I'd been paying more attention to the layout of Eastwatch tower when we'd been there. At the time, I'd had other things on my mind.

With Garnett in the lead, we dashed for the stairwell and charged headlong up it, taking the steps two and three at a time. But after about ten floors, we began to lose steam. Especially Garnett, who thanks to her dwarven ancestry, was at a slight disadvantage when it came to leg and step length. We'd already been sprinting for hours now. Sooner or later, we were all going to reach our limit.

Garnett slowed and finally came to a stop, resting her weight against the wall as she struggled for breath.

We didn't get to stand around wheezing for long, though. Reigh and I had barely jogged to a halt behind Lukani, when the door at the next landing burst open ahead of us with a *BANG!*

More men dressed in patched together pieces of armor stormed out into the stairwell. They stumbled some, seeming shocked to see us. Then they raised their blades and charged.

I didn't hesitate for a second. Drawing my only remaining longsword, I surged over the distance to meet them halfway. My lips drew back into a snarl as I spun through a sequence of assaults, cutting through the first two before I locked blades with a third.

It took Reigh a few seconds longer to react. Typical. But he appeared at my side with his twin, scythe-like blades whirling. Garnett stormed in last, yelling as she hurled one of her axes ahead of her. It hummed as it spun end over end, lodging dead center in one of the fighters and dropping him like a tree immediately.

A hauntingly familiar, piercing shriek sent a shiver of primal terror up my spine. I hesitated and looked back—just in time to see a switchbeast bound over my head and pounce onto another one of our enemies, bearing him to the ground with its fangs already clamped onto his neck.

The sound of a switchbeast's cry sent several of the swordsmen fleeing back the way they'd come, and I could have sworn I saw Lukani's toothy, feline mouth grinning as he sprang after them.

Okay. Garnett could fuss all she wanted about having him here, but that kid had been more useful in the last ten minutes than anyone I'd ever met. As far as I was concerned, he could follow us around for as long as he wanted.

We cut through the ten or so swordsmen like harvesters reaping wheat, leaving nothing but broken bodies behind. Garnett gave a shrill whistle to call Lukani back, and he loped along behind us in his yellow-eyed switchbeast form with his massive, six-legged body easily scaling the stairs. Four more floors. Then six. Sweat soaked through my tunic and ran down my face, drenching me completely as we forged ahead. I hadn't asked how tall the tower was in all, but after a while I lost count of what floor we were on anyway.

More fighters appeared, bursting through doorways along the stairwell and storming for us. Most of them took one look at us, blood spattered and yelling in fury with a switchbeast behind us, and immediately ran screaming in the opposite direction. The ones who didn't and held their ground, didn't last long. We were going to make it. The odds were in our favor now. We had the momentum. We had the advantage. We could do this.

We ran until my feet went numb, winding around the tower as the stairs seemed to spiral up and up for an eternity. It was a blur of mad running, desperate fighting, and the constant slow burn of rage in my blood.

Glimpsing an occasional barred window, I caught hints of daylight outside. This was it, the day of Queen Jenna's attempt to retake the city. At sundown, this place would be nothing but flames and carnage.

Faster—we had to go faster. We had to get this done.

"There!" Reigh shouted suddenly.

Up the stairs ahead of us, a larger landing led to an open, arched doorway. Or, at least, it had been open. An iron-gated door now blocked it, appearing to have been bolted into place as a security measure after the Tibrans had taken occupation of the tower. Beyond it, the dim hallway looked abandoned. I guess if this door had been shut and locked since the war, no one had been able to get inside. A good thing for us. It meant the rooms beyond wouldn't have been looted or ransacked already by the thieves and cutthroats living here.

"Great." Reigh growled as he seized the iron bars in his hands and shook them. The door rattled some, but held firm. "What now? If Argonox was using the former Colonel's office here for his own, it's at the end of this hall."

"Stand aside, Your Highness. Let me show you how it's done." Garnett muscled her way to the front of our group and put her hands on two of the bars. Widening her stance, she clenched her jaw and her gaze went steely with focus. Her sturdy shoulders flexed, hard muscles going solid on her arms as she let out a low, grunting exhale. The metal groaned under her hands, creaking and slowly bowing outward as she pulled the two bars apart like she was parting a curtain. She pulled them far enough apart that we'd easily be able to slip through now.

Sweet Fates. Maybe I didn't want her putting axes in my back, after all.

Standing back, she dusted her hands off and gave a little bow. "Princes first."

Reigh snorted. "You're a little terrifying, you know that?" he quipped as he stooped over and slid sideways through the freshly-bent bars.

"I do know, actually." She chuckled and hopped through the gap next. "Keeps all you human folk from pushing me around, though. Handy for a young dwarven woman just trying to make her way here. Now, which way did you say it was?"

Reigh motioned to the left. "End of the hall. There's probably an even bigger locked door there, too, so maybe do some stretches and limber up. Don't want you pulling any muscles out here."

Garnett just laughed as she trotted proudly on.

Lukani slipped through the bars next, and I waited until he was well clear, taking a second to check down the stairwell both ways, before I followed. Something nagged at the back of my mind—a whisper that made me hesitate. My skin prickled with that eerie feeling, as though I was being watched by someone—someone I couldn't see.

We'd come through the entire tower, up every flight of those god-forsaken stairs, but we hadn't seen any sign of Thatcher and the others. Shouldn't we have seen something? Some sign? Or heard them? I'd expected to meet with more resistance than this, or at the very least, to detect some sign that the others had passed us or gone the same way.

"Murdoc, come on!" Reigh shouted down the hall.

I shook my head, trying to clear those thoughts. I couldn't get distracted. Not now—when we were this close. Once we knew the location of the mirror and had it secured, then finding Thatcher and the others was priority number one.

I couldn't speak for the others. I knew the plan was to meet at the top of the tower and leave before the dragonriders came to destroy this city and everyone in it. But I wasn't going anywhere without the rest of my ... family.

26

CHAPTER TWENTY-SIX

CRACK!

With one mighty swing of her axe, Garnett easily cut through the door lock on Lord Argonox's private quarters. We all crowded in close, weapons at the ready, as the hinges creaked and the massive door slowly swung open. The cool air rushed out, and I winced at the smell of old, rotted blood that hung thick in the air. A smell I knew all too well.

All the little hairs on the back of my neck stood on end as I stepped across the threshold, my boots leaving prints in the fine layer of dust. So ... this was what the personal quarters of a tyrant looked like. Not what I expected.

Everything about the room was a contradiction. The fine furnishings stained with dark splotches—probably the source of the smell. Porcelain teacups, crystal goblets, empty bottles of liquors and wines lay aside shackles, torture implements hung on gilded pedestals on the walls, and an array of different sized skulls displayed on shelves. An oil-painted portrait of the man himself dominated an entire wall, hanging in a massive golden frame, and flanked on either side by gold-plated sconces.

I'd never seen Argonox in the flesh before, but the painting didn't look at all how I'd imagined him. He was a lot younger, clean-cut, and better looking than I'd imagined someone who had conquered and devastated nearly every known kingdom in the world would be. If the picture was accurate, he must have been somewhere in his early thirties, at most. His dark black hair was cut short and efficient, he was clean shaven, and there was something strangely disarming about his deeply set blue eyes. I would have assumed he was a prince or some royal, not a soulless murderer.

"He was a monster unlike any other," Garnett whispered.

I flinched, looking down from my trance to find her standing right beside me, staring up at the portrait, as well. Her violet eyes studied the image, her expression closing up like a flower folding in on itself at nightfall.

"You hear stories of wicked people, but it's a much different experience to actually look one of them in the eye. One moment he'd be smiling, talking in such a friendly way. And he was charming, so you ... you forgot who he really was. He could do that—manipulate people so easily. Make them drop their guard. Make them relax and trust him. Then in an instant, he would ... change." Her eyebrows drew up, expression tensing with fear. Her eyes went wide, as though the memory of that man was still all too real for her. "It's like he became someone else. Someone evil. He would snuff out a life, listen to the screams of people begging him for mercy, and never stop smiling. I used to wonder where he came from. How does a person become that way? What has to go wrong in their lives for them to feel ... nothing? No pity. No empathy. No reaction to brutality and violence at all."

"It starts when you're young," I murmured. "Someone has

to break those things in your soul, and what grows back is twisted and wrong."

"Like the Ulfrangar do to their people?" she asked.

I swallowed hard.

Her strong hand reached out to grasp mine firmly. "I know you've been worried that Thatcher's power compelled you to spare him. That it wasn't a choice you made on your own. But I don't think that's true. I think his power healed everything in you that the Ulfrangar had broken before. Those things in your soul that had grown back wrong. He made them right again, so now you can do good and be the man you were meant to be from the start. That's what a God of Mercy would do, don't you think?"

"Found it!" Reigh called from where he'd been digging through a small cabinet in the corner of the room. Each of its drawers had been locked, so it had taken him a while to pick each one and work his way through.

The rest of us looked up from where we'd been scouring the other corners of the room for some sign of the blueprints like prairie dogs.

"You're sure?" Garnett rushed over, vaulting over the sofa on her way to check the roll of papers he held up.

Lukani ... well, he hadn't really been helping all that much. He had gotten distracted by the collection of skulls, and was looking over each one of them curiously. He glanced over from where he'd been busy poking his fingers through the eyehole sockets, seeing the papers, and giving a snort of disinterest.

Crowding together, Garnett, Reigh, and I carefully unrolled the thin, weathered papers and spread them out across the desk.

"You're right," Garnett confirmed, her voice shaking a bit with nervous excitement. "This is them—the plans for restructuring the tower. Look there, you can see where the experimental wing was. There are the high security cells, too. That's probably where Devana is being held. Stones, it's a long way from that central chamber where we first popped out of the elevator shaft. I hope they can find their way that far."

I leaned in to get a better look, noting where she pointed to a rough sketch of the tower and all the modifications Argonox had made. It looked like he'd transformed what once had been small, closed off armament storage rooms into cells, installing those large, rune-infused doors and blocking off several of the passages leading to them with more barred gates to prevent breakouts. Judging by the scale and the markers for stairwells, Garnett was correct. Those high-security, magically reinforced prison cells were far beneath our feet now.

So ... had we passed by it on our way here? Had we gone by Thatcher and the others when Lukani set fire to that central chamber and not even known it? Gods, what if we'd cut off their exit point? What if they couldn't escape now because of the fire? Or the rush of enemy forces to that area?

"Looks like the floor below this one has some of the vaults." Reigh muttered under his breath as he ran his fingers over the pages, skimming them for details. "There's more down closer to the level where the elevator used to stop. I guess it was easier to have them there, in case he needed to remove them from the tower quickly. Hmm. You know, I'm betting that's where the mirror will be—close to the unloading dock where crates and supplies were taken off that elevator. The Mirror of Truth was huge. They had it on this rolling frame just to move it, and so they wouldn't be able to transport it up the stairs."

He went on, rambling about possible locations, but it was only muffled noise. My thoughts wouldn't stop racing, and I couldn't tear my eyes away from that place where Garnett had suggested Devana might be held. I wracked my brain, trying to remember what we'd encountered down that far. Had there been fighters pouring out of those doorways? Were they having to fight their way to the holding cells to find Devana? Or had they all just burned alive?

"Murdoc?"

I jerked at the sound of my name, looking up to find all three of them staring at me. O-Oh. What had I missed? I should have been paying attention. I needed to—

"Go find them," Garnett said suddenly. Reaching across the desk, she pointed to that spot on the map ... the one I'd been staring at.

The place where Thatcher, Phoebe, and Isandri might be.

I took a step back from the desk. "I-I can't, I have to—"

"Listen, love. We can take it from here. It's a simple matter now," she insisted. "But those three ... I think we both know that if things should go badly, sweet Phoebe is going to be caught up in a battle between gods. And if she or Thatcher get hurt, Isandri can't get them out on her own. They need you more than we do."

My mouth clamped shut as my throat seemed to close around everything I should say—all the reasons I shouldn't just abandon the three of them to handle this on their own. But, Gods and Fates, she was right. Thatcher had come a long way with combat training, but he was far from being ready to take on the brunt of a long battle by himself. Phoebe couldn't fight at all. Isandri handled herself well, but she couldn't protect all of them.

Reigh crossed his arms and gave me one of those smug, know-it-all looks that made me want to punch him in the neck. "She's right and we all know it. We got this. It's just moving some furniture around right? Go, Murdoc. We'll see you at the top of the tower."

I stumbled a little as I took another step back—another step toward the door. They weren't serious, were they? What if something happened here? I looked between the three of them, searching for anyone who might object or have second thoughts.

No one did.

Grabbing the hilt of my longsword, I pulled it free again and ran for the door. My focus narrowed straight ahead as every corner of my mind went silent, every sense and instinct drawing as taut as bowstrings. That hunting instinct quickened in my blood, stripping away every shred of doubt as I bolted back out into the hallway without ever looking back.

PART FIVE

THATCHER

CHAPTER TWENTY-SEVEN

"This ... this is it," Phoebe whispered brokenly, standing before an arched doorway at one of the floor landings in the tower. "My workshop was this way."

Behind us, the echoes of combat and the bellowing of what I could have sworn sounded like a dragon made my stomach spin like a whirlpool. That wasn't possible, though. There couldn't be a dragon anywhere in this tower. How would it have gotten in? And why? Unless Queen Jenna had launched her attack early, in which case, we were all going to be incinerated long before we ever found Devana.

I panted and wheezed, barely making it to the landing right behind Isandri. We must've run up four flights of stairs and zig-sagged down a dozen halls, only to slip along some smaller flights of spiraling steps just to get here. We'd gotten rid of most of our armor a long time ago, though. It made running this far a little easier, and a lot less noisy. So far, we'd managed to duck and dodge our way past the groups of armed men moving through the tower. Most of them seemed normal enough and were headed down to whatever commotion was happening below. But others moved strangely. Their eyes glowed blue, and they didn't speak to one another, or even react to anyone around them. Their expressions were empty of all emotion. It was just like Phillip had said before—they were in some kind of trance.

And I had a good idea who was responsible for it.

"Come! We cannot stop now," Isandri urged, her tone becoming more frantic as she darted past Phoebe into the hall beyond the doorway. It curved in a broad circle, just like all the other floors had. But the Tibrans had altered so much of the interior of the tower, it was difficult to tell what it might have been before the war. Barracks? Or a training area? Gods only knew.

It didn't matter now, though.

We moved fast and low, sneaking along the halls while Phoebe peered at every door, her lips moving as though she were quietly talking to herself. I tried not to focus on the petrified, almost catatonic look in her eyes, or the way she'd begun to shake like she was freezing, as we came to the far end of one of the halls. A large black door made of solid iron loomed before us. There was no handle, just a hole where it should have been, and a tiny window with a sliding panel over it that sort of reminded me of the slot I'd had to feed dragons through in the Deck back in Halfax.

Phoebe's face drained of all color as she stared up at it, seeming to shrink before it as though it were a looming beast about to devour her whole.

She didn't have to say it out loud. That look of petrification was enough.

This had been her workshop.

Only, it didn't look at all how I'd expected. I'd assumed it might look something like the Porter's workshop—open and inviting—where everyone could see whoever was working the forge and bellows, crafting new weapons, and meeting with customers.

This was a glorified cell.

"There is no handle?" Isandri asked, narrowing her eyes at the triangular-shaped hole.

"No," Phoebe whispered, her voice still shaking as she curled back away from it with her hands in fists against her chest. "I was not ... free to leave. The guard who was charged with supervising me had the knob. Only he could put it in and open the door. It was something Argonox asked me to make."

I stared at her, totally bewildered. "He forced you to make a lock for your own door? Just so he could trap you inside?"

Her mouth mashed up as her expression skewed with grief. Tears welled in her eyes as her chin trembled. "Y-Yes."

Something warm thrummed in the back of my mind. A heat like the comforting glow of firelight in a cold night. It spread over my brain and buzzed through my chest, bringing with it a sense of calm I couldn't understand. It didn't matter what it was or where it came from, though. It just felt ... right.

"Do we need to go in?" I asked her, keeping my tone soft and gentle as I put a hand on her shoulder. "Phoebe, do you need to see it?"

Right here, right now might be her only chance, and if this was the closure she needed, we could make time for that. Isandri could go on ahead of us if she didn't want to wait. But Phoebe's peace mattered, too.

"No," she answered softly. Closing her eyes sent fresh tears spilling down her cheeks. "It's enough to stand here ... on *this* side of the door."

I gave her shoulder a reassuring little squeeze. "Okay. Let's go, then. It's time to get this done, and go home."

"Okay." The corners of her mouth twitched upward,

tugging into an exhausted and strangely relieved smile. As though she had waited a lifetime for this moment. To walk away from that room on her own, without a Tibran guard on her heels like a guard dog, or the threat of death and torture in the back of her mind.

She'd been free before we ever set foot in this place, thanks to Queen Jenna absolving her at the Court of Crowns. But somehow, deep in my heart—the same place where all that buzzing, radiating warmth seemed to resonate from—I knew this was the first time she had actually felt free.

"Ishaleon ..."

I stiffened, my breath hitching as a voice, faint and fleeting, filled my mind like a rush of cool water. A swell of cold tingles shivered over me, starting at my toes and climbing all the way to the top of my head.

I whipped around, looking down the hall behind us. But there was no one there. No movement. No sound of anyone or anything coming closer.

But how was that possible. It had sounded so close, like someone leaning in to whisper right against my ear.

"Devana?" I heard myself ask, but it sounded so far away. Like I was hearing myself through a long tube or muffled beyond a door.

Isandri's head snapped around to stare at me, eyes wide. At first, I thought maybe she had heard it, too. But then she rushed toward me, searching my face with a frantic urgency. "What is it, Thatcher? Are you hearing her? Is she calling out to you?"

"I-I think so," I stammered, still barely able to hear my own voice.

Phoebe sucked in an alarmed gasp. "Isa, what's wrong with his eyes? Why are they glowing like that?"

What? My eyes were ... *glowing*?

"Listen to her, Thatcher," Isandri pleaded. "Perhaps she can help us find her."

I didn't know about that. If it really was Devana calling out to me, her voice had been so weak. Was she suffering? Was Iksoli doing something to her?

I turned away some and closed my eyes, trying to pull my focus back in away from everything else. My consciousness drifted, skirting the edge of that thrumming warmth that seemed to resonate from somewhere deep in my chest. Closer—I needed to get closer to it. To focus on that. I drew all my concentration there, trying to gather in around that buzzing heat like someone hugging the edge of a campfire.

"Devana?" I called to her—not out loud. I tried to do it in my mind, with my thoughts, the same way she did. My pulse gave an excited skip when it didn't sound muffled and distant like it did when I spoke out loud.

No answer.

I frowned. Why wasn't this working? It felt like it should. It felt right. So why didn't she answer me?

Oh ... maybe *that* was why.

In all the time I'd been aware of her, the times before when I'd heard her call my name, and the things Phillip had said about her calling out for me as well, she never once called me Thatcher. She never used my mortal name.

She had only ever called me by my divine name.

"Eno?" I tried again.

"Ishaleon." Her answer was immediate, and a lot louder than before. I could feel it, the answering echo of her divine presence close by, like ripples on a pond spanning outward. Her voice shook with emotion, halting and catching as though she were crying. *"Ishaleon, please ... please find me."*

I opened my eyes slowly, sensing the direction of those ripples of divine power. My gaze fixed downward, focusing on that point. And somehow, I just knew.

Two floors down. The hallway to the left. Two right turns. Then a sharp left at the place where the corridor split. There—a door in the dark, covered in runes.

That's where Devana was.

"I'm coming," I told her in my mind. *"Just hang on a little longer."*

"Ishaleon," she begged, her tone growing higher and more frantic. *"Hurry—hurry, please! She is ... she is coming!"*

BAM!

Everything snapped back into focus suddenly as a crash made all three of us jump and look up just in time to see every doorway up and down the hallway behind us burst open at once.

In a matter of seconds, a company of men in full battle armor, brandishing swords, scimitars, and spears, blocked our only exit. They stood shoulder-to-shoulder, staring straight ahead with eerily blank expressions, and their eyes glowing with an unnatural bluish light.

My stomach dropped and I lifted my crossbow, staring in horror at the small army blocking the passage. Gods and Fates, had they all just been standing in those rooms waiting this whole time? They hadn't made a single sound!

All their mouths moved in perfect unison, the crowd of fighters all speaking together like one, loud, disharmonious voice. *"We meet again, my darling little brother. Let's play again, shall we?"*

I set my jaw. Iksoli. So, this is what she'd been planning all along—to pin us down without a way to escape. I'd expected a fight. Sooner or later, I knew we'd have to cross blades with someone in this tower. That was a fact we all knew going in. But this wasn't at all what I had hoped for. And worse?

The person we'd come here to fight wasn't even in the crowd of armored fighters in front of us. Not really. Iksoli was hiding, as usual. Pulling her strings and making her puppets dance from afar.

It had to stop.

I spat on the ground, lowering my crossbow and shouting, "Why don't you face me yourself? Or did losing last time make you even more of a coward?"

All the soldiers suddenly erupted with laughter, leaning on one another and chuckling. They slapped each other as they cackled and pointed at me, then immediately snapped back to attention. Their expressions went totally blank again and they spoke as one, *"Ishaleon, my dear, you always were my favorite fool. I have dreamed of nothing else since last we met. Came to rescue our sweet sister, did you? Very well. Let's see if you are truly worthy."*

I ripped my xiphos free of its sheath and held it out, that heat roaring from my chest in waves down my arms, back, and across my face. I heaved in slow, heavy breaths as I sank down into a defensive stance.

"I will take the ones on the left," Isandri purred, stepping in next to me with a flourish of her hand. A flash of silver light lit up the hall as her staff materialized in her hand and she whipped it into a blurring spin and held it firmly out before her. "You can handle the ones on the right?"

I nodded once. "Absolutely."

Blood roared in my ears as I clenched the hilt of my sword, bearing in hard with every strike and parry Murdoc had ever taught me. My heart pounded, throbbing in my palms and kicking fiercely against my ribs, as I surged through the swarming soldiers with Isandri right at my back.

I dove forward, dropping to a knee and thrusting my blade in a blitzing slice across one of the soldier's legs. He staggered, immediately crumpling. I pitched backward just as

Isandri's staff whirled over my head and smash his helmet to bring him the rest of the way down.

Isa and I kept up the pace, carving our way forward, and moving in perfect unison. All the while, that radiant heat swelled in my chest. It sizzled through my veins, making my mind go completely silent and everything around me seem to slow down. I didn't have to think. I didn't have to worry about whether or not I could pull off that strike or handle parrying that blow. The impact of my blade locking with another didn't make me flinch. I felt no fear. No hesitation.

Only primal instinct ... and the heat of divine power.

"Shield!" Isa shouted.

I sprang backward, throwing up my empty hand and calling down a rush of that divine energy. A globe of golden light spread from my palm, enclosing me and Phoebe inside it an instant before Isandri cracked the crystalline head of her staff on the floor before us.

VOOOOM!

A shockwave of her power like a tidal wave of sterling light spread out from that point in every direction. The force of it sizzled against my shield and blew soldiers off their feet, sending them all flying back like ragdolls.

"Crossbow," I called back to Phoebe, keeping the shield up long enough for her to scramble in closer and unclip it from my belt. She had pretty good aim with it, after all. It'd serve her better than that Tibran sword she still had on her belt.

Isandri wasted no time. She rushed forward, stabbing her way through as many of the fallen soldiers as possible before they could get back to their feet. Once Phoebe had my crossbow in hand, I sprang in to help.

Six more down. Then ten. The hallway rang with the clash and clang of blades, the concussive booms of Isandri's divine attacks, the thunk of crossbow fire, and the gurgling cries of the soldiers as they fell one-by-one.

I whirled through another parry, kicking forward into a roll and coming up behind two more. A speedy stab to the place where their breastplate met their helmet put them on the ground fast. Isandri let out a yowl nearby as she sprang forward, shifting into her feline form and pouncing on another one like a furious winged tiger.

Then I could see it—the way through. We'd nearly cut through the entire crowd of Iksoli's fighters. I spun to the side, narrowly stepping around the swing of an enemy's blade as it hummed past my head. Gritting my teeth, I set my gaze on that exit point.

A shout of pain tore past my lips as something suddenly jabbed against my side. My vision went white and I staggered, reaching for whatever had hit me. Before I could find it, a soldier ripped the end of his spear free of my side with a gory yank. Leering at me with his eyes gleaming that ominous, misty blue hue, he bared his teeth and reared back as though to make another strike.

"Thatcher!" Phoebe cried out in alarm.

But everything went strangely ... dim. I couldn't feel it— any pain from the wound. It vanished in an instant as I stood, watching him advance on me again. He moved so slowly it was almost funny. The flutter of his clothes and hair, it all wavered in slow motion as he drove the point of his weapon in my direction again for another stab.

I blinked, watching it slowly inch toward me in amazement. Weird. What was happening? Had I done this? And why wasn't there any blood on the tip of his spear? Something about his posture, the way he moved as he thrust that weapon toward me, was like watching time repeat itself— only very slowly.

I looked down, realizing that I could still move normally.

The world hadn't grown dim. I was ... *glowing*. My body radiated golden light like a beacon, and when I reached out to touch the slowly advancing spear, it lit up, too.

The spear shattered into a thousand tiny shining sparks. Immediately, everything sped back to its normal pace. The soldier staggered and nearly fell, floundering away as his weapon exploded in his hands and vanished in a flash of golden light. He didn't even have time to be confused, though. The tri-dagger end of Isandri's spear suddenly punched through his torso, making him go stiff and fall limp as she stabbed him through from behind.

She looked at me, half in shock and half in concern that I might be mortally wounded now.

I reached down to my side, touching the place where the spear had stabbed me. But there was no wound. No blood. No evidence that I'd been struck at all. Wait, had that actually happened? Or ... had I just ... known it would? Had I glimpsed the future somehow? Had I known what that soldier was going to do before he did it? Was that even possible?

I had no idea, and right then, I didn't have time to figure it out.

"Go!" Isandri called, motioning for Phoebe to make her dash past the few remaining soldiers.

I fell in step beside her, seizing Phoebe's hand and pulling her close to my side to make sure no one made an easy slash at her as she dashed by. Isandri, her beautiful robes now torn and spattered with blood, ran up behind us in her human shape again. With her staff clenched firmly in hand, she stole a sideways glance at me, and I could have sworn there was the tiniest hint of bewildered fear in her eyes.

That's when I knew—whatever I'd just done, Isandri had seen it.

And she had no idea what it meant, either.

CHAPTER TWENTY-EIGHT

"Are you kidding me? Is that *dragon fire?!*" I yelled as we approached the bottom of the stairs in the tower's base level.

Yep. It definitely was. I'd been around dragons long enough now to know that dragon venom, burning or not, put off a very acrid stench that stung my eyes and throat. No mistaking it.

"Has the attack started?" Isandri said, throwing out an arm protectively in front of Phoebe as we all smashed together in the stairwell, staring out into the crackling furnace that was the base level of the tower.

I didn't know. Maybe it had. I'd lost all track of time while we were underground in those tunnels. And this tower was a little short on windows to the outside in order to check.

"It doesn't matter," I decided. "We've come this far. I'm not turning back now. You don't have to come with me, though. You can go up to the top of the tower and wait for the others."

I knew that wouldn't fly far with Isandri. She wasn't about to turn heel and run now.

"We're with you, Thatcher," Phoebe insisted.

Isandri's lips thinned with a determined glare and she nodded. She was coming, too.

All right, then. Only one way to do this.

I sucked in a steadying breath before I shut my eyes tightly and stoked the coals of that heat still simmering in my soul. Stretching out a hand, I unleashed that globe of energy again, letting it stretched down around us like a translucent curtain of golden light. Then, I started to walk forward.

"Stay close to me," I warned, taking it slow as I descended the last few steps into the smoldering dragon flames. I didn't know if this would work, or even how long I could sustain it. The effort made that heat in my chest grow more intense, like someone slowly pressing a hot branding iron against my clothes. It started out as just ambient warmth, then it grew more and more uncomfortable as we stepped into the crackling flames and made our way through the inferno. Bodies lay strewn, smoldering and melting under the heat and acidity of the burning venom.

I tried not to look at them too closely. What if I'd been wrong about thinking I heard a dragon down here? What if it had been an explosion, or some sort of Tibran weapon that had detonated? I knew they liked to use dragon venom—they'd filled orbs with it and fired them from catapults during the war.

Gods, what if Murdoc and the others had gotten caught in the blast.

No. I clenched my teeth and tore my gaze away, back toward our goal. I couldn't think about that. They weren't here. They were somewhere safe, maybe even already waiting for us at the top of the tower.

They had to be.

Sweat drizzled down my face as I watched the flames lick the outside of my shield, but none crossed through it. Not even a spark or a whisp of smoke touched us as we descended the stairs and crossed through the chamber to the hallway on the left—the same one I'd sensed before. Up ahead, the flames hadn't spread more than twenty yards or so down the hall. There wasn't much there to burn, after all. The stone floor, walls, and ceiling were bare of anything that might catch fire.

Staggering the last few feet past the flames, my arm dropped to my side and my shield dissolved. I wheezed and caught myself against the wall, fighting for every breath. The heat in my blood subsided, but not as quickly as it had before. It thrummed and pulsed through me, making my muscles draw tense and my lungs constrict like they were shriveling up inside me. I curled my hands into fists and pushed away from the wall, steadying myself before I dared to face Isandri and Phoebe again.

I had to get it together. We were nearly there. Just a little farther.

"Take it easy, Thatcher," Isandri whispered as she stepped over quickly and grasped my arm. She studied me, her expression tinged with worry, as she used the sleeve of her robe to wipe some of the sweat from my face. "You're not used to using your power this much. I spent years at my temple training to withstand the physical strain, but our mortal bodies were not meant to bear it for long."

"I-It's not like we have a choice," I gasped hoarsely. "I'll be okay."

"I, um, I think it's this way." Phoebe ventured a few steps ahead, pointing down the passage. "I remember—yes! It's this way!"

"She's right. We've got to hurry." I stumbled a few steps and had to catch myself against Isandri's side before I felt steadier on my feet. Managing a clumsy jog, I tried not to think about the fact that my feet and hands were tingling and numb. Flexing my fingers helped, a little, but the residual burn of that power left my head throbbing.

Isandri was right. I couldn't afford to push myself too far. Not if I still had Iksoli to contend with.

These tunnels and halls spanning out beneath the tower were smaller, but no less dark and ominous as we sped through them. According to Phoebe, they were all original to the construction of Northwatch tower—a place where the Maldobarian soldiers had stored their armor, weaponry, and other extra supplies. They didn't stretch out terribly far, and they formed almost a grid with numerous interconnecting halls lined with small storage rooms.

Or at least, they had been storage rooms once.

Now, every door was reinforced with iron plating and a heavy locking mechanism. They'd turned rooms meant for storing gear into prison cells, and by the look of things, a lot of those rooms were still shut tight. Gods and Fates, were there still people in every one of those rooms? My heart wrenched, pulsating with that heat at the thought. Surely, after being trapped in there this long, they'd all be dead, right? For their sake, I hoped so. There were hundreds of cells, and we didn't have time to check them.

We jogged to a halt at the end of a long corridor that split off two directions. I glanced to the left, then to the right. Both passages looked equally dark and potentially life-threatening. But I knew which way we had to go.

"I-I don't remember this part," Phoebe confessed, her face flushing as she looked frantically back and forth between the two halls. "I'm so sorry, I don't know which way to go."

"It's this way," I said, nodding to the left.

She stared up at me, eyes wide with amazement. "How do you know that?"

"I, uh, don't know. Just a feeling." I looked down, to the side, up—pretty much anywhere to keep from meeting her mystified gaze. I didn't know if she could tell when I lied, but I wasn't willing to chance it.

"You're hearing her, aren't you?" Isandri asked, her tone accusing.

I winced and nodded. "Before, when Iksoli sent those men in armor to fight us, I could hear her in my head. She knows we're coming for her. But ... obviously, so does Iksoli."

A few seconds of awkward silence passed before I dared to look either of them in the eye again. I turned around again, intending to continue on in awkward silence, but Isandri snapped a hand out, suddenly catching me by the wrist.

"Wait!" she whispered, as she yanked me to a halt. "Listen."

I stood perfectly still.

"What is it?" Phoebe whispered, too. "I don't hear anything."

Isandri's grip on my wrist tightened. She stared straight at me as terror crept over her features like a winter evening's chill. Her lips barely moved as she slowly uncurled a finger, pointing upward as she breathed the word, "Exactly."

I DIDN'T GET IT AT FIRST. IT WAS QUIET DOWN HERE, YES. Why was that a problem? It just meant we weren't being chased by more mind-controlled men with swords who wanted to kill us, right?

Wait a second.

If Iksoli's mind-puppets weren't down here ... then where were they?

My gaze tracked upward, following Isandri's gesture as the

faintest sounds of thuds and thumps resonated from somewhere far overhead. Footsteps? No. They were more distinct and consistent. Rhythmic, almost. A dull *whoomp—whoomp—whomp* sound.

All the feeling drained from my face. Oh. Oh gods. I knew that sound.

Dragon wingbeats.

"Queen Jenna has launched her attack," I realized in horror. The dragonriders were here, right now, flying somewhere far over our heads. They would start burning Northwatch to try and run out all these criminals and cutthroats so they could retake the area.

We ... we were out of time.

"We'll be trapped!" Phoebe whimpered, her eyes welling as she clung closer to my side. "Once they reach the tower, there's no other way out from this level!"

I didn't reply. Seizing her by the hand, I took off down the final, dark hallway. My jaw ached as I clenched my teeth, breathing in hard against the dull pain that pulsed through every muscle as I ran. I could bear it. I wouldn't give up. I wouldn't fail—not when we were this close.

"DEVANA!" I shouted as we ran. No point in keeping quiet now, right? Iksoli knew we were here. "WHERE ARE YOU?!"

No answer.

With Isandri running right alongside me, she gave a crack of her staff off the ground that sent up a current of her power to the crystal affixed at the top of her staff. The big, raw mineral lit up like a small star, lighting the way ahead and revealing the doors we passed. Each one of them had been crafted to look like a thick, metal vault instead of something you might store stuff in. The black iron surfaces were etched with patterns and spiraling designs, just like Phillip had described. Close—we were getting close.

My heart thumped like mad, my eyes searching frantically for the one I'd seen in my vision. The one that felt right. Would I even be able to tell? What if I got it wrong? How were we going to get it open?

"Ishaleon!" That fragile voice cried out in my mind so suddenly I nearly tripped and fell-face first on the stone floor. Skidding to a halt, I stared up at one of the doors. My hand slid out of Phoebe's. Wild energy began to buzz in my fingertips again as my gaze roamed the wicked black surface of the metal. Every inch of it covered with glyphs carved into the metal, like a patchwork of interlocking circles and sharp, jagged lettering in a language I couldn't read. All of it stemmed from one silver, dinner-plate sized, rotating dial right in the center. No handle. No knob.

Fates, it really was like a vault.

Stepping forward, I ran my fingers over the surface to trace along some of those rune marks. The instant my fingertips brushed the cold metal, a sting of pain hit the back of my mind like I'd been bitten by it somehow. I snatched my hand back with a hissing curse. What the—? What was that?

"It is heavily warded against divine magics," Isandri seethed bitterly as she held her staff closer, the light from the crystal giving a much better view of all those runic designs.

"Then how do we open it?" I growled, still shaking the lingering sting from my hand.

"It's a puzzle," Phoebe gasped, her pale blue eyes shining in the light as she stared up at the circular, silver dial in the center. "Look there, see the symbols around the edge of this part? I think the whole thing rotates and you have to find the right combination to deactivate the runes and unlock it."

Hmm. I hadn't noticed the tiny symbols etched around the edge of the silver dial. She was right, though. Gods, I'd never seen anything that complex.

"Can you figure out the combination?" I pressed.

Phoebe nibbled her bottom lip. "I-I—maybe? I did work with these kinds of runes some, but they're extremely complex. It will take me a few minutes, but I think I—"

A shower of dust poured over us as the ceiling shook, rattling the tunnel around us with a low groan like an earthquake. Phoebe shrieked, and I dragged her in close to try and shield her in case the whole place caved in on top of us. After a few seconds, the shaking stopped. Everything went hauntingly still again.

Isandri stood, staring upward again as the blood seemed to drain slowly from her face. "It's just like before," she gasped faintly, her voice shaking with terror.

"Like before?" What was she talking about? What did that even mean?

Isandri crept closer with her staff raised protectively. "The dragonriders attempted to retake the city while I was held captive here, in these very halls. The earth shook and groaned over us, and many prayed that we might be crushed so their suffering would finally end." Her gaze shifted slowly, panning back to look at me with her features drawn tense into a haunted expression. "There is a battle waging."

"A battle?" I barked in disbelief. "Against the dragonriders? No way! There aren't enough people here to wage that kind of resistance ... are there?"

"Oh, little brother. Do you think I would dedicate my efforts simply to trifling with you and your pathetic mortal companions?" A feminine voice giggled. It wasn't just in my head this time, though. Her excited laughter echoed down the hallway behind us, coming from somewhere in the dark beyond the swirling clouds of dust still hanging thick in the air.

My heartbeat skipped. Her name slipped from my lips like a hushed curse. "Iksoli."

Isandri tensed, her lip curling in a snarl. Her knuckles

blanched as she gripped her staff harder, her vivid yellow-and-lime eyes searching the gloom for the source of the voice.

I didn't see her, either. Not at first. Then, something moved in the gloom. Squinting down the passage, I could barely make out the silhouette of a figure prowling toward us.

"As if I would ever be so boring," Iksoli snickered again. *"Tibran soldiers stumbling around like sheep with no shepherd, and so many of their delightful war machines—all courtesy of that brilliant little mortal you've got tagging along there, of course. I really should think of a way to thank you, personally, Phoebe. None of this would have been possible without you, now would it? And to think, all of these delightful toys you made were just left to spoil. I couldn't allow that."*

Beside me, Phoebe shrank back and clutched my crossbow tighter to her chest. Her eyes welled, expression twitching as though she were a breath away from a full mental breakdown.

"Stop it," I growled as I drew my blade again. "Leave her and everyone else out of this. You've wanted to lure me here from the beginning, right? Now you've got your wish. So why don't you show yourself?"

Iksoli's laughter was venom. It reverberated off the halls all around us, seeming to come from everywhere at once, as that figure stalked closer. Through the curling wisps of dust still sparkling in the light from Isandri's staff, the figure finally stepped into view, eyes glowing like two blue stars in the gloom.

My heart stopped. My breath froze in my chest.

M-Mur ... Murdoc?

"You know, I've worn a lot of mortals over the eons. Usually, it's so cramped and confining to be packed into their meaty, heavy bodies —like a shoe that's too small." Her voice sighed through his lips with a blissful smile. *"But I rather like this fellow. He fits nicely, wouldn't you agree?"*

My sword slid from my hand and hit the ground at my feet with a clatter. "N-No," I stammered.

"Oh yes," she sneered with delight, manipulating his body into drawing the longsword from the sheath at his back. *"Now then, pick up your little sword, and let's have a rematch, shall we? Winner takes all."*

29

CHAPTER TWENTY-NINE

A million questions took my mind like a raging winter storm. How had this happened? How had she gotten control of Murdoc? What about the others—Garnett and Reigh? Were they okay? Had she killed them? What was I supposed to do now? How could I fight him?

I tipped my chin down some, never breaking eye contact as I slowly bent to pick up my sword again. "Open the lock," I murmured to Phoebe, trying to keep my voice low enough that Iksoli wouldn't be able to hear.

She gaped at me, still frozen in fear.

I gave Isandri a quick, hard look. Hopefully she would understand. This was their only chance. I didn't know how long I could hold Iksoli off. I didn't even know if it was her I would be fighting, or Murdoc. But as long as I had her attention, that freed them up to get through that door and rescue Devana.

It was now or never.

Stepping forward, I squeezed the hilt of my blade hard to try and get my hand to stop shaking as I stared into the glowing blue eyes of my best friend. I didn't know if he was okay, or if she'd broken his mind already. Surely she needed his thoughts intact to fight, right?

I didn't know—and the not knowing was enough to make my stomach swim and my knees feel weak.

"Why are you doing this?" I demanded, forcing my tone to stay steady. I needed to keep her focus on me so Phoebe and Isandri had time to work.

Murdoc's chest heaved with a bored sigh. *"Oh, you know, family issues. Oh wait, I suppose you don't know—not in this form. You can't remember anything about who you really are, can you? All the lives you've lived. All the things you've done. A shame, really. This is, by far, your least impressive manifestation. If not for the dragon, you'd be downright pathetic."*

"We'll see, won't we?" I growled. My throat burned as I surged forward, my blade swung wide in an assault Murdoc himself had taught me. Straight in, then a fast, sideways feint.

My feet flew, pulse booming as I dipped in a swift sidestep and slashed upward.

CLANG!

Our blades clashed as he blocked my blow without even looking my way.

Oh no.

"Tsk, tsk. You'll have to try harder than that," Iksoli taunted. *"Go on, try again."*

I gave a frantic shout of frustration and bore in harder, trying to shove him off balance as I moved through another sequence. Parry down, strike to one side, another swift sidestep with a heel hook to try and trip him.

Murdoc moved with me, matching my attacks and parries in perfect form. The clash of our weapons, of metal ringing against metal, resounded through the hall. The weak light from Isandri's staff cast Murdoc's twisted, sneering features in eerie relief. Each slam of our weapons rattled my bones. I could do better. I knew that. I could use my power. But ... but what if I hurt him, by accident? I had to find some way to pin him down, to immobilize him so I could focus and try to pull her out of his mind like I had with Phillip.

But how?

"Too slow!" she hissed as Murdoc sliced his sword across my chest. It sparked and scraped off my breastplate—the only piece of Tibran armor I hadn't discarded.

I dropped to a knee and kicked into a sideways roll, trying another fighting sequence he'd only just taught me. Roll sideways, try a flanking strike, interlock hilts, and disarm.

Murdoc was on me before I could even bring my sword around. He lunged like an attacking lion, blocking me immediately and shoving me backward. I lost my balance, arms flailing wide. I rocked back onto my heels, floundering to throw up a protecting parry as he brought his longsword down with bone-crushing force.

I didn't have a choice.

I thrust my empty hand forward, drawing from that raging heat that blazed through my chest and sizzled over my tongue. A flash of golden light burst from my open palm. Iksoli gave a shriek. Murdoc's blade slammed against my shield and the force of my power immediately threw him back. He staggered, barely managing to stay on his feet.

"Better, better," Iksoli seethed excitedly.

My body sagged, feeling the pull of that heat like an anchor had been tied around my heart. Every muscle ached and burned. My pulse throbbed, making my vision go bright with each beat. I was pushing it too far. I knew that.

I dove after him, a frantic grunt leaking through my clenched teeth as I let that power take over again. It surged through every part of me, pulsing down my arms and legs. The blade in my hand began to glow brilliant gold, just like the rest of me. Flames of power crackled between my fingers.

Every nerve screamed in protest, like I was slowly being torn apart from the inside.

But I had no other choice.

Just like before, I could see her presence entangled in his mind, ensnaring him like a twisted, gnarled black briar. She'd taken root more deeply, spreading her poisonous roots through his thoughts and emotions, trying to choke out every trace of reluctance and memory associated with me. She wouldn't let him feel anything, except the seeds of hate and bloodlust she'd planted.

"LET HIM GO!" I thundered, wailing my sword down against his as hard as I could.

Light exploded through the hall on impact. She shrieked again, more startled this time. With my free hand I reached for his face, stretching to press my glowing palm against his forehead. One touch. That's all I needed.

"NO!" She screeched in rage.

Murdoc drove his knee into my gut.

All the wind rushed out of me and I pitched forward, nearly falling.

He cracked the hilt of his blade across my face and sent me sprawling sideways onto the floor. I hit hard, barely managing to keep my grip on my weapon. Up. I had to get up. I scrambled to my knees as I wheezed in gulps of air.

Murdoc kicked my face again, harder this time.

Everything went white. Blood exploded into my mouth, and I flopped sideways. My body met the cold stone floor with my ears ringing.

"Did you think this would be easy? That you'd make it here, unlock our dear sister's chains, and simply walk away?" Murdoc's head rolled back with a deep laugh as his arms spread wide. He gripped a bloodied blade in each one—a longsword and another, much shorter sword I'd never seen him use before.

"I've waited an eternity for this moment! Are you watching, mother? Do you see me yet? Are you proud of your little girl?"

His head snapped forward again, leveling a wicked grin at us that curled slowly up his lips. His eyes gleamed like azure embers, empty of any sense of the person I'd known before. My stomach cramped and clenched. I couldn't stop myself from searching—hoping—needing to see some trace of his soul still in there, fighting to resist her.

But there was nothing.

Only malice ... and sadistic pleasure.

"Our parents have spurned me for the last time. Too long they have sneered at me from their lofty thrones. They have called me an instigator. A meddler. An unworthy imposter. She who was born without her own divine magic and can only survive by leeching power from her betters." Iksoli's voice boomed, making the hall shudder as Murdoc took a step forward with the blade still held out wide. *"They find me disgusting. They refuse to speak their own daughter's name, and so the mortals do not know me. They build no temples in my name. They make no pleas for my favor. They call me a cautionary tale. A figment of a nervous imagination. But now they will know ... I am all too real. I will carve my name into their history, and they will know that Iksoli is the goddess who broke the strongest of them. They will pray for my favor, and beg for my mercy. And with your power finally mine to wield ... I will give it to them. Their minds will bend to me entirely. Their hearts will love me and crave my attention."*

"Y-You're ... insane." My voice scraped with agony and my body shook as I sat up again, still holding my sword.

"No, brother darling," she cooed as Murdoc leaned down to touch the point of his blade to my throat. *"I am chaos."*

Pain like a white-hot spike drove through my head as something—like a tether forged in the foundations of my soul—suddenly snapped. My mouth opened wide, but I couldn't draw a breath let alone scream. M-My skin, my head, my eyes, e-everything—it ... it burned! Blisters welted upon my skin like I'd been lit on fire, but in place of blood and flesh beneath there was only blinding golden light.

I dropped my sword, clutching my head and trying to make it stop. That heat raged up like an erupting volcano, making my spine curl and every muscle convulse at once.

Murdoc stumbled back, that sneer of amusement faltering as he stared down at me in shock. Then his brows snapped together. His mouth twisted into a vengeful snarl. He swung in with his blade, slashing like he meant to cut my whole head off in one clean stroke.

Everything froze, like time itself had come to a grinding halt. His blade hung in the air, falling a tiny fraction of an inch at a time. I saw it—felt it—like it was a dance I'd already done a thousand times.

My hand snapped forward, catching his weapon in my fingertips. Just like before with the spear, the longsword glowed with that blistering light that traveled from my hand, up the length of the blade, all the way to the hilt. As soon as the light consumed it, the metal dissolved, vanishing into nothing but a cloud of tiny glittering sparks.

"Enough." The voice that came from my mouth wasn't mine. It was older, more mature—deep and smooth with a confidence I'd never had before. It flowed from my lips like a cooling rain upon parched, cracked earth, bringing with it a calm that resonated through every part of me. "You will not have him, nor will you take another mind within this mortal world."

I stood, my form seeming to grow and swell to greater height above him. Reaching down, my hand passed through the surface of Murdoc's physical form as though it were nothing more than an illusion—a mirage. Within it, though, I felt my fingers strike against something solid. I seized it. It writhed and struggled in my grasp, hissing and clawing at my arm as I ripped it free and held it out at arm's length.

A little girl made of shining blue light hung from my grip. Only, I knew she was no child. With my fist clenched hard around her neck, the goddess writhed and hissed like a caught viper. She bared her teeth, her nearly translucent form wavering and flickering as she tried to vanish, to flee again into the shadows of the world.

But I would not let her go. Not this time.

"You cannot do this!" Iksoli screamed in fury. *"You'll die now, you fool! Your mortal body will perish, burned away by divine power. You'll perish here in the dark, and all of your mortal pets along with you!"*

I frowned and tightened my hold on her. She stiffened, eyes going wide with sudden panic and realization. I leaned in closer, holding that look with my own steady, unrelenting glare. "There are things far worse than death that even gods might fear, dear sister. When you meet them, think of me and do not beg for mercy. You will find none."

Fear—whole and final—filled her eyes as the power swelled within me. The heat scorched along my arm, crackling toward her like a tongue of golden lightning. It caught her right between the eyes and Iksoli went rigid in my grasp, letting out a final, shrill scream that hung in the air even after her body began to dissolve into shining mist.

Gone. She was ... finally gone.

The world around me suddenly spun out of control, becoming nothing but a spiraling smear of color as I dropped to my knees. When my body hit the cool stone off the floor, I felt smaller again. Normal-sized, I guess. I couldn't be sure though. I-I couldn't see anything clearly. Everything was blurred and whirling. Every sound was faint and fuzzy, muffled like I was hearing it from underwater.

I didn't want to die. Not here. Not like this. I'd known it was a possibility from the beginning. But I'd hoped, somehow, I'd wind up on the other side of this horrible nightmare alive, wiser, and stronger.

Still, the others—Murdoc, Phoebe, Reigh, Isandri, and Garnett—would all be okay. I still believed they would make it. They would be safe from Iksoli now. No more schemes and dirty mind-control tricks. Northwatch would be reclaimed. Maldobar and the rest of the world would continue to heal. Everything would be right again.

And that ... was more than enough to make it all worth it.

PART SIX

MURDOC

CHAPTER THIRTY

My eyes flew open, everything suddenly clearing from the foggy, distant nightmare I'd been trapped in only seconds before. Lying sprawled on the floor in the middle of a dark tunnel, I bolted upright. My head throbbed sharply as I squinted around, trying to figure out where I was. Before, it had all been so ... chaotic and garbled. Flashes of images like shattered bits of a nightmare. How much of it was real? Or had it all been a dream?

I looked over to my right, and a sudden, primal shout ripped from my lungs.

Lying on his side, his body smoking like he'd just been pulled from a furnace, Thatcher lay motionless.

I scrambled over the floor toward him, seizing his shoulder and rolling him on to his back. His skin was pink and pocked with open sores, like he'd been in a fire. His eyes were bloodshot, and his lips were turning blue. He blinked up in my direction, but I could tell by the faraway look on his face that he couldn't actually see me.

Oh no. Not again. What had happened? H-Had I done

this? Us fighting, and me cutting him down, and—Gods, had all of that been real?!

"Thatcher!" I called as I tried to prop him up against me. "Don't you dare do this to me again, you idiot! Not again! Why—why do you always push things too far?!"

"M-Murdoc?" His voice crackled dryly. His eyes focused up at me with a little more clarity.

I clenched my teeth and bowed my head. "I'm here, Thatcher."

"D-Devana ... is she?" he croaked.

I looked up, staring through the open door of the cell. All I could see from there was the glow of sterling light from within. "I don't know. Just relax, okay. We'll get you out of here as soon as—"

His jaw stiffened and he started pushing away from me and trying to get up. "I-I have to s-see her."

Seriously? He was an inch from death, and he wanted to go in there? I growled a curse under my breath as I seized his arm suddenly and looped it over my shoulder, hauling him up to his feet. I basically had to drag him the whole way into that cell, his legs trailing behind as limp as overcooked noodles.

Rounding the corner into the tiny, shadowy room, I stopped short when I found them. Crouched on the floor before us, Isandri and Phoebe were wrestling fiercely with the chains connected to an emaciated female figure lying on the floor. She was so thin you could see every rib, joint, and tendon pressing against her ashen skin. Fates. I hadn't seen someone in that state since I'd been with the whelpers in the Ulfrangar. They had her arms and ankles shackled, and she didn't have a stitch of clothing on. If not for the ragged, halting rise and fall of her chest as she breathed, I would have assumed she was already dead.

But that wasn't what made bile rise in my throat as I stared down at the woman in horror.

Her entire head was locked inside some kind of egg-shaped device. It had no eyeholes, no way to see out of it, and only a tiny hatch door where her mouth might have been. Was that ... a mask? Gods, why did they have that on her? How long had it been there? How was she even still alive at all? The tarnished bronze surface of it reflected the light from the crystal on Isandri's staff, revealing a network of odd geometric designs and shapes, adorned in runes, and inlaid with what looked like silver. Powerful warding spells, probably.

"Murdoc!" Phoebe sobbed, looking up at me with tears making clean streaks in the ash and dirt as they rolled down her face. "Please—please help her!"

I carefully lowered Thatcher to the ground and rushed over, taking the small sword she'd been trying to use as leverage to break the chains on the woman's arms. I cracked them off easily, just as Isandri managed to do the same to free her ankles.

But the mask ... that was going to be a problem. There were no holes or places to put in a key that I could detect. No seam where I could wedge a dagger point in and crack it open. I couldn't understand how they'd even gotten it on her to begin with, let alone how to get it off.

"Here." Phoebe pressed something into Isandri's hand, a worried smile ghosting over her features.

Isandri hesitated, staring down at the little, palm-size cylinder made out of the same type of bronze as the mask. The same sort of marks had been etched onto it, inlaid with silver, and arranged in the same way.

"How did you ...?" Isandri's voice faded as her gaze slowly drifted up to stare at Phoebe in mystification.

"I've been working on it since we left Halfax," she said

quietly. "I don't know if it's going to work, but it needs a source of divine power to activate it—your divine power, Isa. Then if you hold it close, it should negate the ones keeping the mask locked on."

Ahhh. So that explained all the late nights she'd spent tinkering away on her own. She'd been working on this —the key.

Isandri's hand closed around the key-box. Her eyes shut tightly for a moment. Then she scooted closer to Devana's side, holding it close to the front of the mask. Her brow creased with concentration as all those silver inlaid marks began to ignite across the surface. The closer she held it to the mask, the more of the lines on the mask glowed in the exact same way. The marks sparked to life inch by inch, spreading over the mask and filling the air with gentle, radiant light. Behind us, Thatcher let out a grunt as he sat up to watch.

Click.

I sucked in a sharp breath as one panel of the mask popped ajar like an orange slice and fell away. Then another. And two more. Sliver by sliver, the mask opened up and fell to the floor with a *clang* like a flower bud opening. With every piece gone, more of the woman's head came into view.

Thick hair as black as raven feathers was matted around her neck and slender, pointed ears. Darkly tanned skin without a single freckle bore the same sort of markings that Isandri's did across her forehead. Her cheeks were sunken from malnutrition, and her lips cracked and dusky from dehydration, but her wide eyes of startling turquoise green were clear and lucid.

This was her—the Tibran witch we'd been sent to hunt? The one the Tibrans had struggled to subdue? A Rienkan elf? Those eyes were a dead giveaway. The sea elves of the south all had eyes the same hue of the warm waters that flowed through their homeland. I'd only met one or two before this, when their sleek and beautifully crafted trading ships made port in Saltmarsh.

The woman lay perfectly still and stared up at Isandri. For a moment, neither one of them moved or said a single word. Then Isandri gave a stammering, broken gasp. "D-Devana."

The woman's eyes squinted a little, as though confused. Then a faint, weary smile tugged at her lips. "Isandri ... my sister."

Isandri let out a cry and threw herself down, embracing the woman and sobbing against her. Devana must have been too weak to return the gesture. Not surprising, given her state. Her whole body trembled as she barely managed to lift a hand to touch Isandri's shoulder. "I knew you would come."

"I'm sorry it took me so long. I had to find him, I had to —" Isa pulled back suddenly, looking over at Thatcher who was still sitting close by. Her face paled some when she saw the state he was in.

Devana looked at him, too. Lying on her back, she smiled at him with a warmth and affection I'd never seen before. The hand that'd been resting on Isandri's shoulder now drifted out, reaching toward him. "Ishaleon," she called gently. "The mask held me here. T-Trapped me in this body. But now, I ... I can see you. I can see you and grant her wish."

Thatcher's eyes went wide. "Wh-What?"

She blinked slowly, the words seeming faded and fragile, like an old forgotten prayer, as she murmured, "Please, Ishaleon. I have to give it to you. Th-There isn't much time left ... and I promised her I would."

Isandri's frown was tinged with worry. "Promised who, Devana?"

The woman's smile softened as the clarity and light in her turquoise eyes began to fade. "His mother."

Thatcher's expression went completely blank.

His *mother*? Did she mean his divine mother, or ...?

Thatcher had never spoken about his birth mother. Not to me, anyway. In fact, I'd never heard him say anything about her whatsoever. No fond memories. No off-handed references. Nothing. Until now, I hadn't given it much thought. I'd assumed she had passed away, and the memory of her must be too painful for him to want to speak about it. Thatcher talked almost as constantly as Phoebe, and I reasoned if there was something about his mother he wanted me to know, he would tell me.

Now I had to wonder ... if I should have asked.

I glanced between them, trying to figure out what Devana meant by that, and why it had Thatcher looking pastier than ever. Granted, he did look nearly as awful as she did. Every breath he took made his chest shudder and quake, and he could barely keep himself sitting upright. Dark dusky circles hung under his severely bloodshot eyes, and his skin looked like it was still slowly searing away in places.

"Th-that's not ... she's not ..." he began to object as fear crept over his features. "She's—" He stopped short and looked at me, his mouth clamping down hard as though he didn't want to finish that thought while I was present.

"She's dead?" I guessed.

He didn't answer except to slowly nod.

"It's okay, Ishaleon," Devana murmured. "It wasn't your fault. She wanted you to know that. She didn't want to go. But she had no choice. It wasn't your fault. It was Iksoli. She touched your mother's mind and planted the seed of chaos. Your mother resisted it for years." Her hand opened, thin, nearly skeletal fingers slowly uncurling to reveal two small objects resting in her palm. A tiny scrap of folded paper, and a tiny gemstone that sparkled in the light. "Her love for you burned so brightly. So beautifully. I felt it, even from afar. She pleaded for me to give you this ... and I promised her that I would."

I watched, unable to speak as all the color drained from Thatcher's face. He wasn't close enough to reach out and take those things from her, and his jaw locked as he began trying to move—to crawl closer. His body shook, practically convulsing with every movement.

Isandri snapped her arm out, blocking my path when I started to help him. She slowly turned her face to stare at me, a grim understanding passing over her expression like an encroaching rainstorm. She didn't have to say a word. I understood. Thatcher had to do this on his own. I couldn't interfere.

He let out a groan, half agony and half relief, when he finally got close enough to take those two objects from her palm. As soon as he did, Devana moved with startling speed to grip his fist. All of her fragile, emaciated body trembled with the effort as she gripped his hand fiercely. Urgency took her features as she yanked him down and wrapped her other arm around his neck. She hugged him hard, her eyes suddenly shining a vibrant scarlet as they filled with tears.

"I-I am ... so proud of you." The voice that left her lips and filled the room with a harmony of echoing whispers didn't sound like hers. It sounded much older, and brimming with an emotion that made my heart sit like a lead weight in my chest. The whispers grew, seeming to penetrate my mind and body like arrows through soft cotton. Each heartbeat made my breath catch.

Devana's eyes glowed like two scarlet stars as she stared up, still holding onto Thatcher as though she were in some sort of trance. Her brow drew up, her expression skewing in grief before she turned to press her lips against his cheek with a final, fading murmur in that same, resounding voice, "I will always ... love you."

Devana's arm slipped away and she sank back against the floor, motionless. Her breathing stopped, and her expression became distant as the light faded from her eyes ... and her life along with it. Her skin seemed to rapidly turn ashen as the same sort of burns that had been on Thatcher suddenly bloomed across her. The same dark circles formed under her eyes.

And then everything went perfectly still.

Thatcher still sat, bent over her in shock. He didn't say a word as he gripped that tiny note and gemstone in his fist. Just as those wounds seemed to appear across Devana's body, they slowly faded away from him. The burns on his skin dissolved away. The circles under his eyes faded. He stopped shaking, and took in each deep, slow breath without shuddering or flinching.

Gods and Fates—had she *healed* him?

No. Not healed. She'd taken his injuries on as her own. And that, I could only guess, was more than her already fragile body could withstand. Her last breath given to spare his life.

The truest act of love.

Thatcher stretched out a hand and carefully brushed her forehead, closing her eyes and folding her arms over her chest. Then he slowly got to his feet. Tucking the two objects she'd given him into his pocket, he turned around to face the rest of us. I expected to see anguish and grief when he finally looked up to meet our stares. Sorrow and tears heavy in his eyes. But instead, there was only ... calm. Peace like a morning sunrise over the gently swaying prairies outside of Dayrise.

"Her time imprisoned in the mortal world is over now. She's back as she should be. We'll see her again when it's our time to return," he said as he reached to take Isandri's hand. "But for now, we need to go. The others need our help."

Isandri stared back at him, tears still streaming down her cheeks. She shut her eyes tightly, leaning in briefly to touch her forehead against his. "O-Okay."

31

CHAPTER THIRTY-ONE

It was a mad dash to the top of the tower. My second one, actually. And this time, I was definitely beginning to feel it in my calves and thighs. This would hurt tomorrow.

Phoebe, Isandri, Thatcher and I ran like the hounds of hell were at our heels, me bringing up the rear of the group to make sure we didn't have any stragglers. We dodged past the few lingering heaps of burning dragon venom that hadn't extinguished yet on the sublevel, and made a break for the stairs again. Not ideal, but I wasn't willing to risk taking that elevator when the entire structure rattled and shook, taking blows from whatever was happening outside. The chances of us getting trapped between floors on that thing were substantial.

Phoebe began to lose steam about halfway up, lagging farther and farther behind and finally stopping to lean against the wall. She panted and gasped, clutching her chest. I was willing to bet it was probably a lot more exertion than she was used to. Until we'd met, she'd probably done significantly less long-distance running for her life.

On my way by, I grabbed her around the waist and threw her over my shoulder, carrying her like a caught lamb. She squeaked and clung to my back, protesting a little—but only because she thought it was too much for *me*.

Hah.

The only other person who wasn't used to this much running had that determined scowl on his face like an angry teddy bear as he huffed and puffed. Thatcher began to lag about two-thirds of the way to the top, growling angrily under his breath and cursing himself.

Not that it was his fault, really. Farriers' sons weren't exactly renowned for their endurance sprinting abilities. At least, not that I'd ever heard of.

Isandri didn't miss a beat. Shifting forms mid stride, she seized the back of his tunic in her teeth and basically tossed him up onto her back. She bounded ahead with her glistening wings filling the narrow corridor as it spiraled around the tower, sloping upward to the pinnacle.

"I'm fine!" Thatcher growled. "Put me down, I can run!"

"Yes, but you're too slow," she snapped back.

"Well, excuse me for having shorter legs!"

"It's got nothing to do with your leg length!"

Well. It seemed like they'd worked out the sibling dynamics now. Great.

"Would you both just shut up and run," I shouted up to them.

BOOOOM!

The tower shuddered again, nearly shaking me off my feet. I stumbled and caught myself against the wall, feeling the stones vibrating under my palm from impact. Gods and Fates—what was happening out there?

"Murdoc!" Someone shouted from behind me. "You're not dead yet? I figured you were toast for sure!"

I turned, still carrying Phoebe over my shoulder, and

spotted Reigh, Garnett, and Lukani bounding up after us. Or at least, I assumed the grinning shaggy, yellow-eyed dog loping along beside them was him in another one of his animal forms.

I gave him a deadpan stare. "Oh. You're alive, as well. Wonderful. I'm so relieved."

He scowled and made a rude gesture as he ran by.

I smirked. Too easy.

Waiting until the lot of them passed by, I took up the chase and followed again.

BOOOOM!

We all came to another staggering halt as the tower rocked, taking another impact from somewhere outside. Phoebe screamed and gripped me harder. Up ahead, Reigh yelled a string of curses as he lost his footing and nearly fell face-first on the steps.

"What the heck is going on out there?!" he fumed as he stumbled back up and kept going.

"Iksoli's forces are using Tibran war machines—they're trying to shoot down the dragonriders!" Thatcher yelled back.

"How do you even know that?" Reigh shouted.

"I saw it in Iksoli's thoughts! Long story! Let's just go!" Thatcher called.

BOOOOM—BOOOOM!

Isandri screamed over the noise. "I thought you killed her!"

Thatcher braced himself against the wall. "I banished her beyond the Vale, but that doesn't mean the people who actually *chose* to fight for her are just going to give up!"

Right. Some people were wicked enough on their own without any divine encouragement.

"Almost there!" Reigh called back as he rushed ahead, bounding to the front of the group and steering us along until we came to a landing that must have been one or two floors down from the very top. "This way!"

I hesitated, glancing back up the central stairwell we'd been climbing for gods only knew how many floors. I'd lost count at forty this time up. Ugh. Whatever. I'd just have to trust that Reigh knew where we were going. If anyone knew how to get us out of here, it was him.

He led us down a few side passages, smaller halls blocked off by more of those ironwork gates. Garnett made quick work of them, though, and we slipped through easily. At the far end of a cramped side passage, a lone door stood looking like it might be nothing more than a broom closet. Only the door itself was made of solid plate iron, with a pair of heavy crossbars blocking it to prevent anyone or anything from coming through. It took Garnett and Reigh working together to lift the massive bars and toss them aside. Then Reigh pulled the door open with a creak and groan of the old, rusting hinges.

I guess no one had used this exit in quite some time.

The smell of cold, fresh air filled my nose as we plunged into the darkness of the steep, narrow staircase beyond. It sloped up steeply, completely unlit, and ended abruptly at the ceiling where a small hatch-door was also barred closed. I put Phoebe back on her feet and seized her hand, keeping her close at my side. Thatcher climbed down from Isandri's back, as well, and we all clumped together while Garnett and Reigh worked on prying the hatch open.

BANG!

I flinched and Phoebe shrank against my side as the hatch door suddenly caught the fierce wind outside and ripped open. Frigid wind rushed in, as well as the low, droning boom and roar of combat. Fire lit up the night sky, giving off enough of a glow for us to see as we scrambled through the hatch door, one at a time.

As soon as my boots struck the roof of the tower, I stood frozen in shock at the battle that spanned out from around the tower like a roiling, boiling sea of fire. Northwatch burned like the abyss itself as dragonriders sailed low, gliding just above the flames in groups of two and four. Their bellowing cries rumbled like thunder, interrupted now and then by the *SNAP—WHOOSH—BOOM* of a Tibran catapult firing at them.

Men brawled in the streets, appearing as hardly more than ant-sized specks from where we stood as they locked blades with what I could only assume were dragonriders or Maldobarian infantry. Honestly, from this height, it was impossible to tell. Whatever the case, they clearly had the upper hand. The enemy lines were broken and fleeing. All they were dealing with now were the stragglers who refused to surrender.

"Merciful Fates, Jenna," Reigh gasped as he stood next to me, the light from the inferno below reflecting in his light brown eyes.

The shrill note of a whistle made us both turn, spotting Thatcher as he stood right on the edge of the tower's staggering fifty-floor drop. He blew blast after blast into the whistle hung around his neck. I grinned when I saw him pull his goggles out from beneath his shirt collar and slide them on. His hair blew around his face as he looked down, around, and out across the city—giving that dragon of his directions to find us.

I turned, staring back out across the blazing battlefield as the distant sound of a familiar roar rose above the ambient symphony of chaos all around us. Through the plumes of smoke and columns of rising flame, the shape of three dragons flew straight for us, their saddles empty. Vexi led the way, her green scales shimmering electric in the firelight. Fornax flew right off her wing, following her sound and smell through the air as he rushed to answer his rider's call.

Last in line, and smallest of the three, a young drake with scales as black as onyx and a flashing red blaze down his back, steered straight for me. His big, blue eyes were intent and his wings flapped furiously to keep pace with the others. As soon as he spotted me, his mouth opened and his tongue lolled like an excited puppy, his hind legs paddling in the air like he was trying to go faster. Blite gave a few crowing calls of greeting, almost like he was relieved to see me.

I smiled back.

That ridiculous, troublesome beast. What would I ever do without him?

The dragons circled, holding in a pattern above, while one landed at a time on the top of the tower. The space was narrow, and time was short. The battle was already spreading to the base of the tower. Judging by a few dark scorch marks marring the stone, it had either taken some catapult fire, or a few errant blasts of dragon venom. No wonder it had felt like we were being shaken around inside a tin can before.

Fornax landed first and hunkered low as Thatcher rushed through getting himself and Garnett buckled into the saddle. As soon as they took off, Vexi touched down, and Reigh did the same with Phoebe while Isandri paced in her feline form, her wing feathers ruffled anxiously as she eyed the battle below. The only dragon who could manage the landing easily, thanks to his much smaller size, was mine.

Sitting astride Blite, I quickly tethered myself to the makeshift saddle before we took off. After all, my passenger was significantly easier to manage. Lukani wriggled deeper into my pocket, his long mouse-tail poking out. He was having a harder time holding his forms now. Getting tired, I guess. He hadn't been sure he could hold a large animal shape long enough to make it clear of the city. Better safe than sorry. I just hoped he didn't suddenly revert to his normal, boy-sized shape mid-flight and simultaneously cause us to crash while he ripped my pants off.

I might just have to let him plummet to his doom for that.

We took to the air and joined in formation with Vexi and Fornax, rising over the roaring heat of the fires and chaos still boiling far below. We kept in close and stayed far above the fray, well and clear of any of the dragonriders' battle maneuvers going on down below. Halfway across the city, however, a monstrous shape burst from the flames below and surged upward like a comet, beating mighty black wings and sending out a shattering cry that made Blite's hide shudder under my hands. The fire flashed across the king drake's body as he zoomed low, throwing down another incinerating line of flame before veering upward toward us. The orange glow of the lashing flames wavered off his midnight blue scales and obsidian-black horns, and flashed off the polished metal helm of the man riding on his back.

"You're late." King Jace signaled, using the dragonrider code of hand signals to communicate in the air.

"It's done," I signaled back. Naturally, I'd been taught this code as part of my Ulfrangar training, but this was the first time I'd used it while also riding a dragon. *"Going to Osbran."*

"Meet you there. Don't die," he replied, and then waved us off.

I watched, unable to keep myself from smirking again as he sailed back down into the battle and Mavrik breathed another long, blistering spray of burning venom. It was hard not to envy his speed and strength, and even harder to suppress the childish excitement that stirred in my gut to think that I was doing anything even remotely similar to that. Never in a million years would I have guessed I'd be sitting astride a dragon of my own, destined to follow someone like that upon a road of honor and valor.

But here I was.

And the path before me, a road lit by dragon fire and blazing with purpose, was clearer than ever before.

DAWN LIT THE HORIZON, TURNING IT MOLTEN RED AS WE prepared to touch down in Osbran, back outside the tavern we'd left behind scarcely a day and a half before. Somehow, it seemed much smaller and more secluded now. Like it might as well have existed in a completely different world compared to the utter pandemonium we'd left behind in Northwatch. Villagers scattered beneath us as our dragons landed one by one, cupping their broad wings and stretching out their hind legs to catch the ground like massive eagles. They cheered when we dismounted, crowding around to help us down and clap us excitedly on the back and shoulders. I knew they were probably just assuming we were official dragonriders returning from glorious battle, and simply didn't know any better, but it still felt ... good.

Granted, a few of them did take some cautious steps back when a mouse crawled out of my pocket and immediately turned into a green-skinned boy with strange yellow eyes. Lukani ducked behind me some, seeming equally unsure about them. I put a hand on his head and ruffled his hair in what was probably a horrible attempt to reassure him. He gave me a nervous smile, though, so maybe it worked.

It didn't take long for other, far more official dragonriders, to land around us. More and more came until there were about ten altogether, forming a circle and forcing the villagers back so we could make our way into the tavern and out of the open. Once we were all inside, and the tavern owner had been ordered to lock down his establishment and not let anyone else in, the dragonriders—probably on orders from Jace—

began to question us. Not that they were holding us captive, necessarily. But there was a sense of urgency and concern in the way they spoke. Caution, too, like maybe they were concerned one or all of us might still be under Iksoli's control. They pressed us for information, asking if there was anyone else who'd been left behind that might need help, if any of us were injured and in need of a healer straight away, or if there was anything we'd seen in the tower that should be noted for the soldiers making their way through it.

Garnett and Reigh swapped a meaningful glance at that last question and both shook their heads. Hah. I guess they'd found the mirror, after all.

Luckily, as for the rest of it, there really wasn't much to tell. Most of us had superficial injuries, cuts and shallow sword wounds, and were spattered in varying degrees of filth and blood, but we were alive and whole. Nothing a bath, a few simple stitches, and a long night's rest couldn't fix.

Hmm. For the most part, anyway.

As soon as most of the dragonriders withdrew back outside, keeping a perimeter around the tavern to keep the locals from harassing us further, Isandri drifted away almost immediately. She stared around at the tavern's dining room, her expression utterly lost until, through the anxious company of lingering dragonriders and medics still checking a few of us over, I saw her lock eyes with Reigh. He'd been exchanging hushed words with one of the riders, but as soon as their gazes met, his mouth snapped shut. He started for her with urgency in every step, muscling his way through the people gathered around until he got to her. He caught her in his arms, grasping the back of her head as she seemed to fall against him. With her face buried against his shoulder, I couldn't see her expression. But I didn't need to. Her whole body shook as she clung to him, all of her steely fortifications seeming to dissolve into grief the instant he touched her.

My soul went numb at the sight, and I couldn't tear my gaze away. Reigh gripped her fiercely, turning to guide her into a corner where no one else would see as he whispered something against her ear. Her head bobbed some, but she never looked up, and kept her face hidden against his shoulder as he went on cradling her tight.

We'd walked away from this. We'd stayed alive, and completed the mission just as we'd intended—for the most part. But the price had been great, and the scars would remain. They always did. Long after the battle ended and the embers died, the memory endured, deep and cutting.

Eternal in the hearts of the ones who'd carried the flame.

CHAPTER THIRTY-TWO

What happened next was inevitable. It came at the end of every grand heroic tale I'd ever heard. Feasting. Celebrating. Hazardous amounts of drinking followed by a parade of poor life choices. Typical hero stuff, or so they say.

Hah. I suppose the dragonriders likely did those things. But for us, the recovery was much more subdued. Quiet, even. We were alive. We'd completed our mission. But beyond that, there wasn't much else for us to celebrate. We hadn't been able to save Devana. I wasn't even sure that had been possible from the outset. In her state, she was only being kept alive by that gilded helmet they'd locked her in. To free her was to also kill her, but she'd been reunited with Isandri and had made contact with Thatcher before the end. She'd also given him those items—things I hadn't seen since he'd slipped them into his pocket—and a message from his mother. Maybe it was all worth it. Somehow, it didn't feel like my place to be the one to say whether it was or not. Life and death had always seemed like very simple concepts to me before all of this. Now, I wasn't so sure.

King Jace arrived the following morning, still filthy from battle, and looking like he might drop from exhaustion. He and Reigh spoke quietly, occasionally glancing in mine and Thatcher's direction. I guess I could have gone over and demanded to know what they were going on about. We were a little past all that shadow and secrecy nonsense now. Deep down, though, I knew it didn't really matter. The decisions being made now were out of my hands, and sweet Fates, I'd never been more thankful for that.

We spent nearly four days at the tavern getting patched up, under the careful supervision of King Jace—until he couldn't take the public fascination with his presence anymore and departed for Halfax. He said it was to deliver the details to Queen Jenna about our little adventure, but I couldn't help but notice how a little angry vein throbbed in his forehead more prominently with every day that went by. That probably had something to do with all the villagers that thronged around the tavern, peeking in all the windows, and ogling anyone in armor. I didn't know what he'd expected, though. Arriving on the back of the most famous dragon in all of Maldobar in shining armor hadn't exactly been inconspicuous.

A few of the other dragonriders had taken a shine to our tavern, though, and he commanded them to hang around and offer us assistance or security if we needed it until he returned. It made me snort and roll my eyes. Assistance? Security? Why didn't he just call it what it actually was—disaster prevention—and be done with it?

Lucky for him, we were all fairly satisfied with our recent disaster experience and weren't raring for more just yet. Garnett had trotted off to fill Arlan in ... and drag Lukani back by the end of one of his long, pointed ears. Something told me we'd see him again, though. Like it or not, he struck me as the kind of kid that even a man like Arlan would have a hard time containing.

"You think she'll come back?" Thatcher moaned into his cup of cider, leaning against the bar. He'd been moping ever since she left.

"If you want to see her so badly, go to Arlan's place and look for her," I muttered as I sipped at my own mug of spiced ale.

"That just makes me look desperate, though, right?" he grumbled.

I sighed. "Well, right now you look pathetic, so which is worse?"

He didn't reply.

We both looked up as a pair of figures came in from the biting cold, stamping the icy sludge from their boots and throwing back their heavy, fur-trimmed cloaks. A familiar pair of dragonriders wandered in, jabbering loudly and waving when they saw us. I forced a smile and nodded back, if only to at least appear friendly. Maybe they'd leave it at that and go on their way instead of—

Nope. Of course not.

Sam and Kellan, the two dragonriders I'd bumped into at the military compound outside of Osbran, swaggered over and leaned against the bar right next to where I sat. They laughed and pulled off their riding gauntlets, taking turns patting me roughly on the shoulders. "There he is! The Not-Porter!"

"Hey," I managed through my teeth, still forcing that agonizing smile. Ugh. Being social was excruciating. "What brings you two out this far? I thought the dragonriders were working on sifting through the ashes now?"

"Heard there was a nice *restful* babysitting post here in Osbran, but I didn't realize it'd be watching over you," the taller one, Sam, glanced me over with that suspicious look. "You mean you're not even a dragonrider?"

"Not yet," Thatcher piped up, still staring mournfully into his cider. "We both got chosen, but we have to go through training now."

"Aaaah. So that's it," Kellan mused. He leaned on the bar top beside me and waved a hand, trying to get the tavern-keepers attention. "Well, looks like we're going to be watching you lot for the next few days."

"Fantastic," I muttered and looked away.

"I didn't catch your real name before?" Sam pressed. "You sure you're not like a ... Porter cousin? Once removed, or something?"

I took another drink to hide my scowl. "I seriously doubt it."

He leaned in a little, close enough I could see him squinting at me and feel his breath puffing on my cheek. "What's your *real* name, then?"

"Fred," I growled. Putting down my mug, I left a few coins on the bar and turned away. "I'm going upstairs."

Thatcher just nodded, still sighing forlornly and not seeming to notice I'd left him alone with the idiot-brigade, as I retreated up the steps to my room. I'd scarcely made it halfway down the hall before the sound of scuffling beyond Reigh's door made me stop. I listened, almost certain I heard bags or heavy objects thumping against the floor right inside.

I rapped my knuckles on the door. "Reigh? You in there?"

It opened immediately. Reigh paused where he'd been lugging two saddlebags along the floor and stared at me in surprise. "Oh. Hey. I was just on my way down."

I studied the bags. "Going somewhere?"

He dropped them with a thud at his feet and straightened with a groan. "Yeah, actually. Isandri's decided she's ready to go to Halfax and talk to my sister about everything. Seems like the right time to, you know, come clean about what was really going on with Devana in there?"

Ahh. Well, that explained why he'd apparently packed up every bit of his gear like he wasn't planning on coming back. "Right. Where is she? Already gone?"

"No, she's uh, saying her goodbyes to Phoebe." He combed his shaggy mess of dark red hair away from his eyes and let out a heavy breath. "I actually thought about seeing if she wanted a lift back there, as well. It's probably pointless to ask, though. She's not going to want to go anywhere without you."

I stared at him, wondering how many of his bones I could break before he managed to call for help. Hmmm. Probably six. Seven, if I really pushed myself.

Reigh shifted and cleared his throat, almost like he could sense my violent thoughts. He looked away and quickly changed the subject. "So, uh, where will you go next? Back to Halfax, too. Can't stay here forever, right?"

No. I guess I couldn't. "I'll probably head that way with Thatcher when he's ready."

"Back to shoveling horse dung, eh?" He chuckled.

I shrugged. "If no one throws me in prison first."

"Well, in the event no one does, I guess I'll see you at the academy at some point, right?" He arched an eyebrow, as though silently asking me if I was still considering taking that path.

I smirked. "Worried about that little promise I made about sparring, aren't you?"

Reigh balked, "No! Definitely not!"

Suuure. Liar.

I stuck a hand out for him to shake. "See you there, then."

He eyed my outstretched hand like he was afraid I might pull a fast move and punch him in the throat, instead. Not that it wasn't tempting. Finally, he grasped my hand and shook it. "See you there."

OUR ROYAL SUMMONS ARRIVED FOUR DAYS LATER. QUEEN Jenna didn't spare anything on ceremony, and sent a grouchy but familiar face to hand deliver an intricately adorned letter bearing the royal seal. Southern Sky General Haldor graced us with his presence, bearing her invitation to return with him to Halfax and meet with her about what happened in Northwatch ... and what would be happening to us next. Not that I wasn't ready for a change of scenery, and anxious to get this over with, but finding out what the queen planned to do with me put an uneasiness in the pit of my stomach like sea sickness.

"It'll be fine, I'm sure of it," Phoebe coaxed as she followed me down the steps to the front door of the tavern. We'd already packed our things, and now we just had to load them onto Fornax and Haldor's dragon so we could go. Thankfully, between the three of us, Phoebe was the only one who had anything in the way of actual items to carry. I traveled light, and Thatcher could carry everything he owned on his person. Easy.

"I hope you're right," I admitted quietly as I helped tie a few more of her bags of crafting equipment and tools onto Fornax. "But if not, it is what it is. I never expected to walk away from this at all. The fact that I am is ... good. I'll take a lifetime in prison over a lifetime as an Ulfrangar any day."

"You deserve a lot better than that, Murdoc. You *are* better than that." Her smile was as sad as it was worried as she stared up at me, those big raindrop-blue eyes pulling me in like a vortex.

I had to look away. We hadn't spoken much since, um,

that conversation after the confrontation with the Ulfrangar. I didn't know what to say to her now. I didn't know what any of that meant. I didn't know where we went from here, or what she expected from me. I knew what I wanted, what I felt, but that was irrelevant. I wasn't in a position to go launching off into personal fantasies about my future when I had no idea what truly awaited me back in Halfax. I'd gotten a hero's welcome here, yes. But I wasn't ready to bet on that same reception when I faced Queen Jenna again. Since the last time I'd seen her, my presence had been the cause of personal injury and nearly death to several people she cared deeply for—including her own brother. Somehow, I doubted that was something she would just brush off.

My gaze drifted over to where Sam and Kellan strolled by, carrying their own bags slung over their shoulders as they laughed. They spotted us and waved, grinning broadly. Heh. They must've been happy to finally get back to doing something useful. A few days of being cooped up with us in that tavern and the luster of getting an "easy babysitting assignment" had worn right off.

As he sauntered by, Sam threw his head back, whistling merrily to the open sky as he made his way toward his dragon.

My heartbeat gave a frantic skip. I froze. Phoebe's bag slipped out of my hands and hit the ground at my feet with a *thud*.

"Murdoc? What's wrong?" Phoebe must have noticed my expression go blank.

I stared at Sam's back. That ... that song. I knew that song. Didn't I? I did. I'd heard it before.

I sprinted away from Phoebe, leaving her standing there with her things as I bolted after him. "Wait!" I shouted, barely managing to catch Sam by the back of his long blue cloak as he began to climb up onto his dragon's back.

He slid his helmet visor up and frowned down at me. "Something wrong there, Fred?"

Oh. Right. Curse it, I'd forgotten about that. Ugh. Never mind—not important.

"That song ... the one you were whistling just now," I panted as I gripped his cloak to keep him from brushing me off and flying away. "What's it called? Where did you hear it?"

He arched an eyebrow. "Oh, that one? It's just an old sailor's tune. Heard it all my life. I expect most people growing up around the docks at Dayrise have, though."

Docks at Dayrise ... Oh. That's where I'd heard it. I must've forgotten. Or just hadn't paid enough attention to it at the time. "R-Right. Oh. I just, uh, it sounded familiar."

He waved a hand dismissively. "Ah, I'm sure it's not uncommon. Funny you should ask, though. Mr. Porter used to have all of us whistling it while we worked the bellows for him as kids. Keeps you on the right rhythm."

What? Mr. Porter had taught him that? But he was a swordsmith, not a sailor, wasn't he?

"Murdoc!" Phoebe called after me, running over with her red curls and skirts flying "Murdoc, what's going on?"

Sam barked a laugh. "Murdoc? I thought you said your name was Fred?"

I scowled and looked at the ground. "It was a joke," I lied.

"Which one was a joke? Fred or Murdoc?" He sounded genuinely confused.

Curse it, this was stupid. I was stupid. Wasting my time over something like this ... "Murdoc," I lied again, purely out of spite and humiliation this time, and let go of his cloak.

He cackled like that was absolutely hilarious. "Thought so! As if anyone would name a kid after that place!"

Every muscle in my body locked up solid. My pulse came to a frantic, hammering halt. Slowly, I lifted my head to stare up at him. "That's ... that's a *real* place?"

"Oh yeah! Course it is! Everyone who grew up around there knew about Mur-dock." He slid his visor back down and shrugged. "At least, that's what the locals call it. The real name is Hamourlow Dock, but the lettering on the sign for it's been worn away for, gods, probably forty years. No one's bothered to fix it, and all that's left of it now is M-U-R-D-O-C-K. The K's starting to look a bit iffy now, too, though. It's sort of a local joke, I guess."

My ears rang, blocking out anything else he might have said as he gave his dragon's neck a pat. My legs shook, wobbling dangerously as I took a few steps back while they took off into the sky. Everything went numb. I dropped to my hands and knees in the cold dirt of the road. Th-There ... there was a place. A place called Murdoc. A place I'd even been to before.

It was where I'd heard that song before, whistled like a lullaby that cut me straight to the core.

It was where a family lived ... the ones Sam and Kellan said looked like me.

A family that was also ... missing a son.

The Porters.

"Murdoc? What happened? Snap out of it and talk to me!" Thatcher's voice shouted right in my face.

I jerked back, falling onto my rear end and blinking at him in shock. My head whipped around, looking for—curse it, where was he—where was Blite?!

Go. I had to go. Right now.

I scrambled up and ran for my dragon, Thatcher and Phoebe still shouting and chasing after me. There wasn't time. I couldn't stop. I couldn't explain it all to them now. Later—I'd tell them everything later. Right now, I just had to go.

"WAIT!" Thatcher hollered, finally grabbing the back of

my tunic and dragging me to a halt right at Blite's side. "What is wrong with you? Why won't you talk to me?"

I whipped around to stare at Thatcher with my thoughts spinning out control. Something—I had to tell him something. Words. Speak, curse it! "Murdoc," I managed to sputter. "They knew ... he said ... he knows where it is, Thatcher! He told me! It's ... it's in Dayrise!"

His face paled. "S-Seriously?"

All I could do was nod.

Thatcher let me go and stumbled backward. He blinked a few times, then turned and ran for Fornax, seizing Phoebe by the arm on the way. "GO!" He shouted as he bolted away toward Fornax. "WE'LL CATCH UP!"

33

CHAPTER THIRTY-THREE

It didn't take long for Fornax and Haldor's large male dragon, Turq, to catch up and fall right into formation on either side of Blite and me. We were at a slight disadvantage when it came to size and speed, after all. For now, anyway.

I pushed my young dragon hard all the way across the open prairies and rolling hilltops to the east, soaring between the towering plumes of clouds until the city of Dayrise appeared far in the distance. Thankfully, we didn't have all that far to go. It was a similar distance from Northwatch to Osbran. We had the wind in our favor this time, too.

As the city appeared before us, glittering in the evening light like a handful of jewels cast upon the dark, craggy shoreline, I looked out beyond it to the dark ocean. It shone and rippled, like a deep midnight blue blanket spread out along the steep sea cliffs. The smell of those cold salty waters carried strong on the wind, even this far away.

I shut my eyes and let that smell wash over me, seeping down into the very foundations of my soul. Gods, no wonder everything about this place felt so familiar. No wonder the sounds and smells of it had felt like I belonged there. It couldn't just be a figment of my imagination or hopeful thinking. No—it had to be real.

The sun had barely slipped beyond the mountains at our backs as we touched down in a large, familiar courtyard where we'd housed our dragons before in a nearby barn. I didn't waste a second. The instant my boots touched the ground, I spun to press my lips against Blite's scaly nose, and took off for the Porter's house like an absolute mad man.

Once again, Thatcher and the others called after me, but there wasn't time to wait around for them to get down. Besides, Thatcher had to be able to guess where I was heading now, right? Yeah. He wasn't a *complete* idiot. He'd figure it out.

My legs wobbled dangerously as I dashed down the sidewalk and onto the avenue that led in front of the Porter's sizable old house. It stood like a grand monument on the street corner, old and distinguished, but not too elaborate to be called noble. Staggering to a halt, I sucked in ragged breaths as I stared up at it. Lights glowed in the windows on every floor, and smoke floated up from both chimneys. They were home. Oh gods, they were home.

Fear took my mind like gnarled, clawed fingers as I started toward the front door. Oh no. I'd ... I'd come all this way. I'd flown all the way here on a whim. And why? Because some doofus thought I looked like a Porter? Because he'd whistled a song I recognized? Because a dock nearby had a name similar to mine?

Gods and Fates, what was I doing?!

Knock, knock, knock.

I hadn't even realized I'd reached for the big, brass knocker on the front door until it was too late. I snatched back, almost tripping over my own feet. Run—I should run. I should go back. This was stupid. I didn't know these people, and they certainly didn't know me. This was madness. I-I was—

The door cracked open just enough for one big, hazel eye to peer up at me. Then, with a creak of the hinges, a familiar young woman pushed it open the rest of the way and sighed. Aria Porter.

"Oh. It's you again." She didn't even try to hide the disappointment on her face as she glanced around, like maybe she was hoping to see someone else standing there with me. "Where's the rest of your friends?"

I shifted some and rubbed the back of my neck. "They're, um, they're not ..." My voice hung in my throat. The suspicious arch in one of her eyebrows almost made me forget why I'd come. "It's just me, for now, actually. Can I come in for a moment?"

Her lovely features sharpened, eyes narrowing some as she gave me a wary look. "I suppose. Is there something you needed?" She pushed the door open a bit farther and stood aside, motioning for me to enter. "The shop isn't open for customers this late if you're wanting work done."

"Oh, I-I ... no. No, that's not why I came," I stammered, unable to keep myself from staring at her. Was this really my —could she actually be my ... *sister*?

I let out a curse of alarm as I tripped over the doorstep on my way inside. Staggering, I barely managed to catch myself on the frame. Fates, what was I even doing? Why had I come here? This was ridiculous. I should go. Right now, before I humiliated myself any further.

"Then did you forget something? We didn't find any gear or personal items left behind after you left," she said, watching me flail with an unmistakable look of subdued bewilderment.

Gods, I must've looked like a complete idiot to her.

"A-Actually, I was wondering if I ... could I speak with

your father? Or ... or, um, your mother. E-Either one. If they're available." I went on stumbling over my words, my face flushing as I tried to hold her gaze and force a smile.

I guess it came out as panicked and borderline insane as it felt. Fates preserve me.

She took a cautious step back, as though she expected me to snap at any moment and try to rob her or something. "Ah, well, yes. What for, exactly?"

I let out a heavy sigh and hung my head, rubbing my forehead with the heel of my hand. The longer I stood there, the more idiotic it seemed. I'd come here on a hunch. That's it. I had no evidence—no good reason at all to think I might be related to these people.

"Look, there's just something I need to ask them. It won't take long. And I already know what the answer will probably be, but if I don't ask it's going to drive me crazy."

Aria glanced me up and down, her eyes narrowing distrustfully. Great. She really did think I was nuts. And I guess she wasn't entirely wrong about that. "Oookay. Wait right here for a moment, then."

I held it together until she had disappeared upstairs, then I threw my head back and groaned. Why—why had I done this?! I'd come all this way on some stupid, totally unfounded hope that two random idiots were right about me looking like these people? Had I completely lost my mind?

Now that I was here, I couldn't even see much resemblance to myself in Aria. Maybe our hair and eyes were a similar color, but there must be thousands of people in Maldobar with black hair and hazel eyes. I mean, yes, there was the name of the dock to consider. I hadn't been able to find anywhere else on any map of Maldobar called Murdoc. But still, that wasn't conclusive. I could have come from anywhere in the kingdom or even other lands beyond it. Not even Rook had known where the Ulfrangar had gotten me, right? Unless he'd gone to great lengths to figure it out somehow—which I doubted. It wasn't like they kept a logbook of it. I shouldn't be here. I should just go, right now, before they came down here and I had to—

"My daughter tells me you've a question?" A deep voice called down as heavy footfalls thumped down the steps.

The tone of it, deep and steady, confident but gentle, made my mind go completely silent. I froze. My heart gave a frantic, painful thud. Slowly, I forced myself to turn around.

I FELT ABOUT TWO INCHES TALL AS I MET THE GUARDED stare of a much older man coming slowly down the stairs. His dark hair fell loosely over his brow, flecked in silver at his temples, and framed his hard, angular features. His sharp jaw was dusted with silver stubble, and the creases at the corners of his eyes deepened as he looked me over from head to foot. His gaze had the same intensity of a lion inspecting an intruder that had wandered into his domain. It made me tense and take an instinctive step back.

When the man stopped at the base of the stairs, I spotted Aria and another slender woman who looked like she might be somewhere in her forties following close behind him. Mrs. Porter, maybe? I hadn't met either of these people, but the woman looked so much like Aria, it seemed like a decent enough guess. Her long hair hung in a silky black braid over one of her slender shoulders. She gasped at the sight of me, and latched onto the man's arm as though to stabilize herself. Her wide green eyes studied me with a look of silent terror as all the color drained from her soft features.

"Well?" Mr. Porter asked again.

"I, uh, yes. I do." I glanced between him and his wife a few times, scrambling to collect my thoughts. "I-I apologize for the intrusion. I just ... well, I heard about your son. The one that you lost, that is. And I wanted to know ... what happened to him?"

Mr. Porter's eyes narrowed dangerously. "What did you say your name was?"

I hesitated, biting back all the stupid lies I'd used a hundred times before to dodge that question. They were all far more palatable than the truth. But I hadn't come here to skirt honesty again. I hadn't come to deflect and make excuses.

My voice shook some, every word tangling up in all my fear and doubt as I stared back at all three of them. "I-I ... I don't know."

Aria gave a bewildered frown. "What do you mean? Before, you told me you were—"

"I know. I-I ... well, it's sort of complicated. When I was an infant, I was .... taken," I said quickly. "A group of people who called themselves the Ulfrangar stole me and a lot of other kids from our families all over the kingdom. They took us far away, and ... and didn't tell us where they'd gotten us." I tried to explain, to keep my voice calm, but every breath made my chest shudder and my hands shake. "They gave me a name after the place they took me from."

All traces of suspicion and foreboding intensity slowly drained from Mr. Porter's face as he watched me. His scowl softened. His dark brows rose. Beside him, his wife gripped his arm like a lifeline as her lips parted.

"And ... where was that?" he asked softly.

The words hung in my throat, burning and aching as I forced them out. "Somewhere called Murdoc."

Mrs. Porter gasped.

Aria went pale and clapped a hand over her mouth.

But Mr. Porter frowned—not angrily or bitterly, though. The soft furrow to his brow and squint to his eyes, and the way he tilted his head to one side a little, seemed more ... confused. Worried, even. He took a few steps closer and stopped right before me, leaning in to look at me eye-to-eye. "What do you remember?" he asked quietly. "Do you remember anything from before those people took you?"

Staring back at him, it felt like my brain had suddenly tangled into a thousand knots. What did I remember? "For the longest time I thought I didn't. I was really little when the Ulfrangar took me. And everything after that was so ..." My voice trailed off as my gaze wandered, drifting past him to the woman, Mrs. Porter. She stared at me like she was seeing a ghost—as though she might bolt back upstairs at any moment.

A heaviness settled in my chest, like an iron block sat right where my heart should have been. It made every breath a fight as I continued, "But when we came here before, with Jaevid and the others, I ... I heard something. A song. A lullaby, I think. I knew the instant I heard it ... that it wasn't the first time. I've heard it somewhere before, a long time ago. I just can't remember where."

Closing my eyes, I focused on that tune and started to whistle it. I couldn't sing it. I didn't know the name of the song, let alone the actual words. Fates, I didn't even know if it meant anything to them.

But what if it did?

I flinched and stopped whistling when something warm touched my face. Opening my eyes, I looked into the face of a man I knew I'd never seen before. He grasped my chin in his fingers, lifting my head so he could look me over carefully. His brows drew up when he brushed some of my hair away from my face, and his chin trembled as he ran a thumb over a spot on my cheek right below my ear where I knew I had a small dark freckle. Usually my hair hid it, and I'd never given it a second thought before now.

But Mr. Porter's eyes welled at the sight of it.

"Could it be?" he whispered hoarsely. "After eighteen years?"

I held perfectly still. Or, I tried to. I couldn't stop myself from shaking as Mrs. Porter came closer and joined him in studying me. She took one of my hands and began slowly unlacing my vambrace and pushing up the sleeve of my tunic. Her lips parted in another hushed gasp as she touched another place on my elbow where, amidst the dozens of scars that marred my forearm, I had a second small, dark freckle right at my elbow.

H-How had she known about that? Unless ...

"Rylen?" she whimpered, tears already sliding down her cheeks as she cupped my cheek.

I shuddered, unable to keep a sob from breaking past my lips. "M-Mom?"

They never answered.

Mr. and Mrs. Porter dove at me at once, flinging their arms around my neck and nearly dragging me off my feet. Sandwiched between them, I buried my face against my mother's shoulder and squeezed her as hard as I dared. She wept and kissed my cheeks and forehead. My father cried against my hair as he held both of us tightly against his chest.

We stayed that way for a long time. But I could have lived in that moment forever. Finally, my father pulled back long enough to shout to Aria, "Go! Go and get your brothers right now! Fenn is in the workshop. Derrin and Dorian are upstairs. Hurry!" he urged, his voice caught somewhere between tears and laughter. "Tell them Rylen has come home!"

She didn't waste a second, and took off upstairs as fast as a startled doe. I could hear her screaming their names as her footsteps thumped along the floorboards overhead and she opened and slammed doors. Then more voices joined hers, all repeating that name like bewildered echoes throughout the house.

"I-Is ... is that m-my name?" I stammered, my voice quaking as my chest seized with every broken breath.

My mother pressed her lips to my forehead, her eyes shining with the same deep green color as rose leaves. "Yes," she murmured as she went on petting my hair, as though she thought I might suddenly disappear at any moment. "Gods have mercy, you look just like your father."

I did?

Glancing back, I found him smiling proudly. He turned his head to the side a bit and tapped a place right below his ear. A bolt of emotion I didn't have a name for shot through me like cold lightning when I saw he had the same freckle on his cheek that I did. Tears filled my eyes again and I buried my face in my hands. All this time, all the years I'd spent searching, and there it was ... a tiny speck of evidence that no one could refute.

And I looked like my father.

"But you've got your mother's lovely dark hair," he said as he put a comforting arm around my shoulders. "And your grandmother's eyes."

"We all got that much," a voice called from behind us.

Looking back, I stared in silent awe at the four people gathered around the base of the stairs. Aria stood alongside two identical young men who seemed to be close to her age, or maybe a few years older. The sight of them hit me like a punch to the throat. They ... Gods and Fates, they all looked just like me! They had the same black hair, a similar face shape, and even hazel eyes like mine and Aria's. They were a little taller and maybe a little stockier, too. But the family resemblance was unmistakable.

The last man, who seemed to be the oldest, was the only one who had a more brownish hue to his hair. But apart from being somewhere in his thirties, that was the only stark difference I could see. He wore a spot-stained leather smithing apron and gloves, still holding a pair of heavy iron tongs in one hand like he'd ran straight over from the shop. Fenn, then? Did that mean the other two—the twins—were Derrin and Dorian?

My head spun as I gaped at them, leaving me breathless and lightheaded. I stumbled a little, but my father held me on my feet. I-I ... gods, I had *siblings*. I had three brothers, and ...

My eyes locked onto Aria as realization hit me so hard I nearly doubled over. That day in the street—when I'd first met her while she was chasing down her papers—she had been hanging up signs for *me*. She had been trying to find me, even eighteen years after the Ulfrangar had stolen me. Long after everyone else, including me, had stopped daring to hope ... she had still been searching.

My sister had still believed she would find me.

I took a staggering step toward her. I opened my mouth, wanting desperately to say something—to thank her somehow. But nothing would come out. I guess it didn't matter, though. She cried out and rushed for me, throwing her arms around my neck and hugging me frantically.

It didn't take long for everyone else to join in. They all gathered around me, closing me in from every side. My mother and father, three older brothers, and my sister. The family I had searched for, longed for, and thought I would never find again. The Ulfrangar had robbed me of so many things, but taking me from them was the cruelest of all.

But for the first time in my entire life, that past didn't matter. Nothing they'd done to me or forced me to do made any difference. There was only one fact—one truth—that meant anything at all now:

I was Rylen Porter. And I was finally home.

34

CHAPTER THIRTY-FOUR

There was a lot to figure out. A lot of gaps to fill in. And while I was eager to do whatever I had to in order to find my place here, with my family again, I had to admit ... I didn't really know what that meant. Fortunately, I wasn't alone in that.

Thatcher and the others came in not long after, and everyone moved into the living room and began to do a lot of explaining—including me. After a few hours, when we'd all calmed down a little, reality came crashing in for all of us. The truth of what had happened to me. The day I was taken, stolen from Aria's arms as a baby while she carried me to the market to meet our father, had nearly crushed the Porters. It'd hit her especially hard. She was only six years old at the time.

They'd searched for me for years. They'd scoured every city up and down the coast, and gone as far as Northwatch in search of anyone who knew what might have happened to me. But of course, I was long gone. And then the war had nearly torn the kingdom apart. They'd lost all hope of ever finding me again.

Well, everyone except Aria.

Talking them through my life was doomed to be every bit as difficult. I didn't know how much I should share. Right now, with emotions raw and my parents still in tears, I just ... couldn't tell them. The words hung in my throat like knots of heated metal. Thatcher helped, though. He told them how we'd met, sparing the details of me being an assassin, of course. He told them how we'd been working in Halfax at the royal stable, and that I'd been part of a mission authorized by the queen herself. He prodded me to tell them about Blite, and both my parents sobbed against me again when they heard that they had a dragonrider in the family once more.

They were proud.

But they didn't know the truth, yet.

"Right then. I suppose I should find lodging for our dragons, then. I'll send word to Jaevid and Queen Jenna to let them know we'll be delayed," Haldor said, standing and excusing himself quickly from the house.

"We should find a place to stay, as well," Phoebe suggested, giving Thatcher a little nudge with her elbow. "Wasn't there an inn nearby?"

"Nonsense! You'll stay here as our honored guests!" My mother protested. "Any friends of Rylen's are friends of ours."

My insides clenched up a little at the name. Would I ever get used to it? My *real* name?

"Thank you, but you would probably like a little privacy right now. We completely understand." Phoebe curtsied and grabbed Thatcher by the arm, practically shoving him out the front door. "We'll drop by in the morning for tea, if that's okay. Just to check in and see how you're all doing?"

"Oh. Oh, yes. We'll look forward to it," my mother agreed. Honestly, in that state, it seemed like she might agree to just about anything.

"I'll go and get your room ready," Aria announced,

standing and going to gently take her mother's arm. "Don't you want to help me? We can pick out a quilt for him."

Ah. I could see what this was. They knew there was something I wasn't telling them—information I was holding back. Things that my very delicate and emotionally fragile mother did not need to hear.

My father, brothers, and I sat in silence while Aria escorted my mother upstairs. Once they were well out of earshot, the atmosphere in the room grew heavy. All four of them stared at me, as though silently picking me apart to try and figure out what I might be hiding.

Fear prickled at my insides like spiders crawling around under my skin. I had to tell them. There was no way around it. And when I did, what if they decided maybe they'd rather not have me back? What if they found their long-lost son, only to learn he was going to prison as a murderer? What if they wished they'd never found him at all?

"You said the people that took you were called the Ulfrangar," Mr. Porter said at last, his tone quiet and firm.

"Yes," I answered.

"I've heard stories about them," Fenn spoke up, studying me with his head tilted to one side. He looked like he might be in his late twenties, or maybe very early thirties, at most. He'd taken off his metalworking gloves and apron, and sat with his thickly muscled arms crossed. "Rumors mostly. I always thought they were just something people made up—a drunken sailor's tale."

"No," I murmured. "In fact, they're the ones who set fire to the city square at King's Cross. They were ... trying to hunt me down."

"Hunt you down?" My father leaned in, visibly unsettled. "Why?"

I had no choice then. I had to tell them. Whatever

happened, whatever they did about it after—I couldn't keep this ugly truth from them.

So, I fixed my gaze on the floor between my feet, and I started at the beginning.

None of my brothers said a word the entire time. My father only asked a few questions. He wanted to know more about Rook, what specifically had happened in Thornbend when I met Thatcher, and where'd I'd lived while I was with the Ulfrangar. And I told him everything I knew. His brows went up when I mentioned the loose association I had with King Jace—Rook having been his pup, and so on.

Then he leveled a serious, unblinking stare on me that held me like a blade to the throat. "Did you kill people for them, son?"

"Yes." I swallowed hard. That word—*son*—hit me like a hammer to the chest. No one had ever called me that before. Not even Rook.

"How many?"

I bowed my head again. I couldn't look him in the eye as I answered, "Three hundred and forty-one confirmed kills, as commanded by the Zuer."

He sank back in his seat some, eyes going wide. "Sweet Fates."

"Wicked cool. Can you teach me how to fight like that?" one of the twins—I wasn't sure which—whispered excitedly.

Our father cut them both a punishing glare.

Fenn did, too. Then my oldest brother looked back at me again, his pensive expression impossible to read. "What has Jaevid Broadfeather said about all this?"

"He's been supportive of my decision to defect and leave that lifestyle behind," I answered, not really sure what to say beyond that. Jaevid had always chosen his words carefully around me. He had pushed me sometimes, but only so far. I guess in the end, he still wanted it to be my decision to follow this destiny or not. "I think he wants me to choose this path and become a dragonrider. I think he believes I can do it. I want to believe that, too. But ... I know there may be repercussions for what came before."

"Even if you were forced to do it against your will?" My father pressed, sounding more concerned than ever now.

I shook my head. "Murder is still murder."

"Do you think he will plead for you? Jaevid Broadfeather, I mean." Fenn asked.

To be honest, I hadn't really considered that. Maybe he would. He'd done a lot for me so far. King Jace, too. I didn't fully understand why either of those men cared anything at all about what happened to me, but if it came down to it, I had plenty of reasons to suspect they might try to intervene to keep me out of prison.

Even if I knew I didn't deserve that kind of compassion from either of them.

"Maybe?" I wasn't confident enough about that to say anything else. "But I already owe Jaevid a lot. I won't ask him for that kind of favor. I haven't done anything to deserve it."

"We'll just have to wait and see what word he sends back, yeah?" one of the twins piped up again.

"In the meantime, we can't tell Mum about this," Fenn warned as he rubbed at his jaw. "She's been through a lot. This would be too much, especially right now."

"Agreed." The twins nodded in unison.

"Then let's give it a few days," Mr. Porter decided with a heavy sigh. He looked at me, and I could see the weary lines of the years creasing his brow. Like each day spent in grief and worry, wondering where I'd been, had crushed down over him and left those marks. "Whatever happens, Rylen, I don't want you to doubt that we are glad to have you back. I know this is ... complicated. But we'll get it sorted. I have faith. The men you've walked with are world-changers. To have my son counted among them, working alongside them, I am truly proud. Whatever comes next, we'll handle it together, as a family."

I nodded, keeping my head down in hopes of hiding my face. I didn't want him to see how I was hanging by a thread—how desperately I wanted to believe all that. But with my fate now tossed to the wind for royals and powerful figures far beyond this threshold to decide, I had no idea what to expect.

And hope, I knew, was a dangerous thing.

I sat with my father and brothers for several more hours, talking quietly around the fire in the living room. They were eager to share more about their lives, our extended relatives, and the family business. Apparently, the Porters had been swordsmiths for generations, crafting the finest blades and weaponry in Maldobar. Our father, Bram Porter, took his sons to Blybrig Academy in the spring to craft in the dragonrider forges and outfit them for battle. A high honor for any craftsman in the kingdom, I knew. But, unfortunately, not an art I knew anything about—not when it came to the actual process of it, anyway.

My father's eyes twinkled with thought when I told him I preferred to dual-wield longswords. At my height, and with my inclination to agility and acrobatics, the weapons suited me better than most. I'd trained with many, though, and he seemed pleased at my extensive knowledge of the different types of blades and how they were used in combat.

My sister was a sharp mind when it came to the bookkeeping, apparently. She had a finesse for handling the various merchants, navigating intense negotiations, balancing expenses, and acquiring the finest materials. Somehow, that didn't surprise me. She didn't seem like the sort of woman who liked to take no for an answer.

"She keeps us in line." Father chuckled fondly as he rubbed at his chin. "I suppose it's only a matter of time till some fellow is knocking down the door to try and marry her. And may the gods guard him. Any man seeking Aria's hand had better have a will to match hers."

"I'm not sure anyone like that actually exists," Fenn muttered.

The others got a quiet laugh out of that. I couldn't really join in, though. I didn't know her well enough, and ... I had a feeling that iron will of hers had been the only thing that kept her motivated to search for me all this time.

We talked until the embers in the hearth died down, barely glowing amidst the ashes. Fenn stood and excused himself to go back to the workshop and close things up for the night. The twins reluctantly went back upstairs to bed, dragging their feet the entire way. Apparently, it was their duty to open the forge up first thing in the mornings and get things ready for the day.

"Come, I'll show you upstairs to your room," my father offered. He stood, stretching his back a bit before he gestured to the stairs.

My stomach spun and clenched as I climbed the steps, my hand sliding along the smooth wooden railing. The rich scent of clove and dried orange hung in the air. The stairs continued up to a third floor, but Father motioned for me to turn at the landing. The hall stretched on in either direction. On the right, he explained, was the washroom, study where Aria kept track of their books, and a small parlor. On the left, my room was next to the twins on one side of the hall. Fenn and Aria's rooms were directly across. My heart thumped as I walked along the rug that stretched over the wooden floor. A few brass sconces mounted on the walls illuminated old oil paintings of relatives, more proudly displayed weaponry, a few tapestries that looked like they must be a hundred years old, and some finely mounted antlers. All of it carried the feel of a long, proud family legacy.

"Try to get some rest, son," my father said as he stopped before the bedroom door—the room that was supposedly mine. "Tomorrow, we'll start figuring everything out. For now, let's be glad. It's been eighteen years since all of my children were safe in their beds. Let's be thankful for that."

He put a hand on my shoulder. I flinched some—an old habit. People did that to me a lot these days, and I still wasn't used to it. Kind and friendly touches were … strange and foreign. No one hugged in the Ulfrangar. No one shook hands, patted one another on the back, or gave playful punches. Any time someone else had touched me before, when I was with them, it was always to inflict harm. To punish. To assert dominance.

Sorrow flickered in my father's eyes, almost like he understood. I didn't see how he possibly could, though. He couldn't have known what it was like to walk with the pack, and I was incredibly glad for that.

Wrapping a hand around the back of my neck, he dragged me in suddenly and pressed his lips against my forehead. "I know this won't be easy. Not for any of us. But I want you to know, that your family is … very glad to have you back home, Rylen. Your mother and I have never stopped loving you. And we will be here to help you now in any way you need."

Tears welled in my eyes. I bit down hard and tried to blink them away. My father's hand slid away from the back of my head as he studied me carefully, probably noticing how I was fighting to hold it together. I wanted to apologize to him. No father wanted to find out his child was a murderer. But I was a monster shaped for destruction. And I didn't know if I could be anything else. I wanted to try, but that might not be enough. I might disappoint him.

"Goodnight, son." He gave my cheek a soft pat and turned away to go up the stairs to the third floor.

For several minutes, all I could do was stand there while his footsteps faded to silence somewhere overhead. Then my gaze drifted to the door—my bedroom door. I grasped the knob and twisted, pushing it slowly open.

Sterling moonlight bled through the large window directly across the modest, but well-furnished room. An armoire stood against one wall, and a washstand sat beside a tall dressing mirror. A large trunk under the window had blankets folded neatly and stacked on top, and an oil lamp flickered in a glass globe on the nightstand next to a decent-sized bed. When we'd stayed here before, this was the room Isandri and Phoebe had shared.

Now it was mine.

But I wasn't alone.

Aria sat on the foot of the bed, dressed in a long, white nightgown with a thick wool shawl wrapped around her shoulders. Her dark hair was braided over one shoulder like a long satin rope, and she cradled a small candle flickering in a clay bowl.

I hesitated, wondering if I'd come into the wrong room at first. Had Father meant the one on the other side of the hall?

I cleared my throat. "I-I, um, I apologize. I wasn't sure if—"

"Mother wanted me to tell you goodnight for her," Aria murmured without looking up. "I had to put her to bed. She's got a nervous illness. It makes her very weak sometimes and she can't breathe or speak."

"Oh. I didn't realize." I stepped into the room, watching the dancing flicker of the candlelight reflect on her eyes. "Is she alright?"

"She'll be better once she's had some rest." Aria looked up, her expression a mixture of apprehension and sorrow. "She ... she was never the same after you were taken. None of us were. Mother fell ill. Father hardly said a word for years. He drifted from job to job, working when he had to, but seeming almost like his mind had died and it was just his body moving on out of habit. The boys and I ... we had to carry on. We didn't have a choice. Fenn took care of us as best he could, trying to fill in the gaps so Mother and Father could ... grieve. But he was only fourteen."

"I'm ... I'm so sorry, Aria." I said as I sat down on the edge of the bed next to her.

"Don't be. It wasn't your fault," she murmured. "It was ... mine."

I frowned hard. "What do you mean? It wasn't your fault. You were a *child*. You couldn't have fought off the Ulfrangar, even if you'd been an adult." Fates, didn't she understand? She was lucky they hadn't taken her, as well, or killed her just for spite.

"*I* insisted on carrying you to the docks that day," she confessed, turning her face away. "Mother told me it wasn't a good idea. The dockside markets are busy in the middle of the day. But Father was waiting for us there. He'd promised to take us all to buy candied apples. And you were ... *my* baby. That's what everyone joked, because I loved taking care of you. Mother showed me how to wear you in a wrap. I helped her feed you, bathe you, rock you—everything. I could always make you smile and laugh. I taught you how to crawl and you'd just started pulling up and trying to walk. I even made Mother put your crib in my room so we could be close." She paused, her shoulders drawing up some as the hand holding the candle shook slightly. "Then you were just ... gone. They snatched you right out of my arms. They hit me across the face so hard I fell. By the time I got up, they were already getting in a wagon and speeding away. I couldn't stop them. I ran ... for miles. But you were gone. And I couldn't even remember what they looked like."

I held my breath, studying her for a moment. I knew what I had to do. I just, gods, I was no good at this. I steeled my nerve and reached out to rest a hand on her shoulder, the same way Father had when he spoke to me. "Don't blame yourself for someone else's wickedness, Aria. You didn't do anything wrong. What's wrong is that men like that, who do those things, walk free in this kingdom in the first place."

Her head turned slightly, peering at me through falling locks of her long dark bangs like she wasn't buying a word of that. "I missed you so much, Rylen. Every day. And now it feels like I've missed so many other things—parts of your life I should have been there for."

I pulled her in so she could lean against my side. "Sorry I'm not a cute baby anymore," I muttered. "If you've still got that crib, I can try to cram myself back in it."

A faint smile brushed her lips as she leaned her head against my shoulder. "Oh, gods. You've got Father's sense of humor, too, haven't you?"

"Maybe."

She puffed a deep sigh. "Great. Now Fenn and I are outnumbered in that respect."

I smiled back and gave her a little squeeze, hoping that was a consoling gesture. I'd seen other people do it, after all. Maybe it wasn't as awkward as it felt. "Thank you, Aria."

"For what?"

I closed my eyes and let my head lean over to rest on top of hers. "For not giving up."

She sniffled some and wiped at her eyes. "I would have searched for you forever. Every day until the end of time."

"Well, now there's only one thing I want you to do for me."

Her brow crinkled some, studying me with a hint of worry as the candlelight made all the tiny golden flecks in her hazel eyes sparkle. "What?"

I gave her another small squeeze. It'd felt good to hug her like that the first time—the sister who had never given up on me. "Be happy."

CHAPTER THIRTY-FIVE

I awoke late the next morning, lying sprawled in a bed that was mine, with sunlight peeking through the heavy drapes over the window. I found a set of new clothes, folded neatly and left on the bedside table. The dark green tunic looked a little worn around some of the hems, but it was clean and well made. The dark pants were, too, and they fit nicely despite my long legs that usually made everything I tried on a few inches too short. I smirked at my reflection in the mirror across the room as I finished lacing up my boots. I'd never had hand-me-downs before. Not like this, anyway. I liked it immediately, and wondered how many of my older brothers had worn these before. Maybe all three of them?

The house downstairs smelled of freshly brewed tea and the lingering aroma of a cooked breakfast. I'd slept in too late —a personal first for me—and had missed it, but Mom had made sure that a plate was set aside for me to have whenever I came downstairs. Mom and Aria sat at the table while I ate, asking me questions about myself that, thankfully, had nothing at all to do with my past as an Ulfrangar. They wanted to know where I'd traveled, what Queen Jenna was like, and if I'd seen Jaevid's wife, Beckah. They prodded carefully around the subject of my own romantic life, hedging at the question of whether or not I was courting anyone or not. I guess they were eager to have another woman in the house to even those odds, as well.

Mom patted my arm soothingly when I told her that, no, I was not courting anyone at the moment. "Don't you worry. My sons will have no trouble at all finding good matches."

My face burned and I looked away, trying to avoid Aria's teasing little grin.

It didn't work.

I could still feel it like the prick of needles on my skin as she very casually commented, "Oh, I know. How about that lovely girl who came along with you yesterday? I think her name was Phoebe, wasn't it? She's quite pretty, isn't she, Mum?"

My mother immediately launched into a hearty agreement, approving thoroughly of Phoebe's manners and how beautiful she thought her red hair and dainty blue tunic were. All the while, I could have sworn my hair was on fire because my head grew hotter and hotter until I knew I must be sweating.

"Sh-She's, uh, she's very nice," I agreed, nearly choking on my own spit.

"Is anyone courting her?" Aria pressed, feeding the fire like her life depended on it. "She seemed awfully attached to that cute, blond-headed boy with her. Are they a couple?"

I licked my teeth behind my lips, feeling that rising urge to inflict some manner of physical pain on Thatcher, purely on principle. "No," I managed stiffly. "They are definitely not a couple."

They'd better not be.

"So, she's available?" Aria was grinning wolfishly.

Gods, please save me from this. "I-I ... don't ... I guess she is, yes."

"Then what are you waiting for?" My mother joined in.

I opened my mouth, but before I could get a word out to defend myself, Aria jumped in again. "Well, if you're not interested in her, maybe Derrin or Dorian will be. I spoke with her a little before, and she seemed quite bright, too. She would be good to have in the family, I think. Mom, we should have her in for afternoon tea, don't you think?"

I could feel my pulse throbbing in my ears as I stared at her, my mouth still hanging open like an idiot. Seriously? Did she ... did she know that I—well, maybe not *loved*. Love is a strong word. But I certainly preferred Phoebe.

A knock at the door spared me from having a full-blown cardiac episode. We all leaned over to peer out into the hall, watching as one of the two servants working for my family answered it. The familiar voices coming from the doorway made me sink down in my chair with relief. Haldor, Thatcher, and Phoebe had come back at last.

But they weren't alone.

As they all filed into the dining room, smiling and greeting us with a mixture of curiosity and hesitance, a much older man in formal Gray elven robes followed at a distance. I'd have known his ominous, focused scowl from miles away. King Jace spoke a few hushed words to the servant, who tripped all over herself to dash away into the house.

I frowned. Why had he come? How had he found us here in the first place?

Oh. Right. He had spies all over this kingdom, thanks to Judan's hard work.

Aria and my mother began to rise when he entered, offering shocked, scrambling curtsies until he waved a hand and offered a gentler smile than I'd ever seen touch his features before. "Please, ladies, it's all right. Continue with your meal. We've come to speak with you and your family." His gaze landed on me with intent, that smile fading from his eyes to let the tiniest bit of cold pressure bleed through. "*All* of your family."

Ah. So that's what this was about. He'd come with word from Jenna, then. Maybe even Jaevid, too. The decision about me had been made.

I tried not to let my apprehension show as I sat alongside my mother, waiting while the servant collected the other members of my family from around the modest estate. Father and Fenn came from the workshop. The twins, Derrin and Dorian, wandered in from the courtyard, each carrying wooden practice swords. They all stared in shock at our new collection of guests sitting around the long dining table.

Not that it was the first time King Jace had been there, but they hadn't shared a meal with him the last time.

While everyone got settled in, Thatcher immediately rushing over to take the seat on my other side like it was some kind of competition, I watched Aria's gaze fix onto Phoebe like an eagle on the hunt. The corners of her mouth curled into a cunning, conspiring little grin, and I could practically see the machinations brewing in her eyes.

Then *he* sat down.

Haldor settled into the chair next to Phoebe, his smile more awkward and uncertain, like he wasn't sure why he'd been invited to this little gathering but was too polite to question it. Dressed in gleaming dragonrider armor, that royal blue cloak trimmed in fox fur clipped to his pauldrons, he sat straight and graciously accepted a servant's trembling offer for tea. I'd only met him in passing—including the night when he'd arrested Thatcher and me in Thornbend—but I'd heard a little about his family. They were rich Damarian merchants with strong holdings in Southwatch, apparently.

I watched the smile gradually dissolve from my sister's

face as she stared at him, probably noting those vivid, golden Damarian eyes. He was a bit older than she was, probably in his early or mid-thirties, but with that smooth, light brown complexion, who could tell? Not that I was any kind of judge, but there were probably a lot of women who would find his shoulder length black hair and sharp brow attractive.

Aria did, apparently. I couldn't think of any other reason for her to be blushing like that. Granted, dragonriders tended to have that effect. The flashy armor and reputation as the superior fighting force under the royal banner were considered a very potent and desirable mix among the noblewomen at court.

Hmmm.

Once the rest of my family arrived, taking their seats and staring nervously at their new guests, King Jace cleared his throat. "First, let me dispel any concerns so we're not all sitting here in suspense. Jaevid and Her Majesty won't be coming, although they do send their greetings and gratitude to your family for your support, especially over the last few weeks."

My father gave a nod. "We are honored to serve Her Majesty however we can."

Jace returned the gesture, although I could see him sizing my father up from across the table with that practiced, Ulfrangar speed. "They also wish to extend their condolences for what your family has suffered these many years. As do I. As a father myself, I cannot imagine what you've endured. I must admit, I was shocked to hear that Murdoc had—"

"Rylen," Aria interrupted suddenly. "His name is Rylen."

I stared at her in shock. Had she just ... interrupted a *king*? For my sake?

My reaction was nothing compared to our parents', though, who gaped at her in total mortification.

Even Jace seemed a little surprised. He blinked a few

times, then gave a light, snorting chuckle. "Rylen it is, then. At any rate, I was quite shocked to learn he'd located his family. For someone in his situation, I hope you can appreciate how incredibly rare that is. Children who are lost to the Ulfrangar never break free of them, and certainly never reunite with their families. Now, I cannot confirm this as he's no longer with us to speak of it, but I suspect that Rook may have chosen his Ulfrangar name in the hopes that this would happen. To select such a unique name tied so specifically to one location is not typical. I have reason to believe Rook chose it hoping that, eventually, Rylen would find his way back here."

My heart gave a hard, wrenching jerk. Rook had wanted me to come back? He'd been the one to give me that name yet, and until that moment, I hadn't realized ... by calling me that, he'd also given me a clue. The only clue that would lead me straight back home.

My eyes watered as I looked down again, fighting desperately to keep my emotions in check. Not now. I couldn't do this right now. Not in front of everyone.

"Unfortunately, simply locating and reuniting with his family is not enough to absolve Rylen of his past crimes as an Ulfrangar. I know many of you likely have no idea what that means, fully. I'm more than willing to explain it in greater detail, as I have a very ... similar history to your son. Like him, I was brought up within the ranks of the Ulfrangar. I also managed to escape. Granted, my own journey to freedom did not see me finding the trust and loyalty of friends until much later. Your son has been very fortunate to have met so many people who were willing to speak for him and stand at his side." King Jace's expression darkened some, and he tapped his fingers on the table. "But nothing they do or say can erase what was done while he still walked with the pack.

Rylen knows this. There is only one person who can truly offer him a clean slate going forward."

I swallowed hard.

Next to me, Thatcher shifted in his seat like he'd sat on a pinecone.

"I've spoken with Queen Jenna at length concerning your history—the same history you know that I share. She was ... reasonably shocked and dismayed. But hearing what you've done since your defection, how you've attempted to alter the course of your life and atone, was also surprising to her. I won't make light of the path you've been forced to walk, Rylen. I told her what pups like us were made to endure, and how we earned our place and survived. I told her plainly when I first met you, I feared what you might do to these people. I didn't believe you could be saved or salvaged from that life. I believed you were well and truly lost to the darkness of the Ulfrangar, and it goes without saying that those who have done what we have to survive their brutality are not worthy of mercy in any form." Jace's gaze shifted, catching on Thatcher who still sat right beside me. "But mercy sometimes finds us anyway. And I have never been so glad to be proven wrong. I put my word before Queen Jenna to vouch for your worthiness. I told her of your dragon, as well. And so, she has passed her judgement."

I stiffened in my chair as he reached into the breast pocket of his robes and pulled out a fine square of golden parchment, sealed with a blue and gold ribbon and the crest of an eagle. He placed it on the tabletop and slid it across to me with a knowing smile.

"Queen Jenna has given you official pardon, young man. But on one condition. You must walk the path I walked to redemption. Your sword must now serve Maldobar, as a Dragonrider formally trained under the supervision of Academy

Commander Broadfeather," he said, holding my gaze as I slowly reached out to take the letter. "What do you say?"

My hand halted, still holding the heavy piece of thick, folded parchment. It felt like it might as well have been a lead weight in my hands. My life, my future, was bound to this letter. What I chose now ... it was the path that would define me forever.

I glanced down the table toward my parents, my sister, my three brothers, Thatcher, and Phoebe. They all stared back. No one made a sound.

I looked back to King Jace, his brow now arched expectantly. "Well?"

Sucking in a deep breath, my voice shook as I finally answered, "It would be my greatest honor, Your Majesty."

THE HOUSE WAS PURE CHAOS AFTER THAT. THE GOOD KIND, though. My mother was frantic to serve wine and celebrate, even if it was far too early in the day for that. My siblings thronged around Thatcher and Phoebe, curious about the two companions I'd been traveling with all this time. Granted, I had a feeling Aria was still up to no good in terms of Phoebe. I'd have to address that soon.

My father stepped aside with Jace and Haldor, exchanging hushed and likely far more serious words. My father stood with his hands at his back, nodding and rubbing his fingers together in an all too familiar nervous habit. Hmm. So that's where that had come from. He nodded emphatically as he listened to Jace, and I had a feeling there was a lot to be said there—details about me, and what he might expect going forward. I probably needed to hear some of that information at some point.

But right now, there was a much more serious issue at hand.

"You know, Mom, that man there is Southern Sky General Haldor Kal'Sheem," I said as I put a hand on her arm and motioned to the only armor-wearing dragonrider in the room.

Her eyes went wide and misty at the sight of him. "Is that who he is? My, he's quite handsome, isn't he?"

"Oh, sure. And single, too, I've heard," I added quickly. "You know, I could be wrong, but I'm pretty sure his family are the same Kal'Sheems who run that big merchant company out of Southwatch. Big fancy house. Lots of ships. Tons of money and connections. He must be very picky about who he's going to marry, I guess, with that kind of a business to consider. He's probably just biding his time for the right woman with good business sense and an honorable family to come along ..." I let my voice trail off, watching as my mother's eyes went from Haldor straight to Aria.

Bingo.

I made sure I was giving Aria the same wolfish grin she'd given me when our mother went straight to her, seized her by the arm, and basically dragged her over to meet Haldor. Good luck with that, sis. Two could play that little game.

With that little situation sorted, it wasn't hard to drift into the background of all the excitement and chatter in the dining room. The servants brought out tea and snacks, looking more flushed and disheveled than I'd ever seen them.

I took the first chance I got when I was sure no one would notice to slip out of the room. I made my way through the house, running my hands along the walls to feel the bumps in the plaster as I went. I passed through the door on the first floor that led out into the wide courtyard. It was the same place where I'd sparred with Thatcher and taught him more swordplay. I'd also argued with Blite here a few times, which was why it didn't surprise me at all when the little black and red drake came waddling toward me over the cobblestones. He made musical clicking and popping sounds and sniffed through my hair, nibbling at my boots until I pushed his big head away.

"Hey, none of that. These are the only pair I've got left, thanks to you," I reminded him.

Blite's ears perked, his head lifting suddenly as he focused on something right behind me.

"You're missing your own celebration in there, you know," Thatcher said.

I smiled to myself and turned around, studying him with my dragon's big scaly head right next to mine. "Yeah. I guess I am."

"The crowd getting to you?" he guessed.

I shrugged. "A little. Mostly just ... wanted to think."

He wandered closer, grinning up at Blite and offering a hand for my dragon to sniff. "It's pretty great, right? You've got your family back. And we even knew them basically the whole time! I keep trying to wrap my mind around it," he laughed, but it was all wrong. Forced and almost frantic. "I guess you'll be staying here with them now, right? I'm really happy for you."

"Thatcher ..."

"No, I *really* am. I mean, yeah, it's kind of out of the blue. But you've been searching for them for a long time, and ... and they've been trying to find you, too. Your sister was telling us about it. Maybe it's a little weird for you still, though. I'm sure after a few months, once you've had a chance to really settle in, it'll get easier."

"Thatcher ..." I tried again. I wasn't sure who he was trying to convince—me or himself.

"And, you know, we'll still see one another at the academy, right? I know I'm a little younger, but Jaevid seemed to think I could handle it. We'll still—"

"THATCHER." I had to raise my voice to get him to stop.

He cringed and looked down, his mouth screwing up as he studied the toes of his boots like he'd found the meaning of life down there. Or rather, like he was desperately searching for it in a moment of pure and complete panic.

But I got it. He didn't have to say another word. I understood completely.

I had a family now.

And he ... was alone.

His home was still gone. His father was still dead. I'd been the only sliver of familiarity and safety left in his entire life. And now ... all of this had happened.

I couldn't go back to Halfax with him.

His eyes welled as he swallowed. "I'm okay. I'll be okay," he gasped, still sounding like he was trying to convince himself that was really true. "It's good that you're going to be here with them. It's where you should be."

I lunged at him, grabbing that stupid, ridiculous, troublesome kid in my arms and hugging him tight. He was a few years younger than me, a lot shorter and as scrawny as an alley cat—which I'd known from the beginning. But right then, it felt like he might as well have been six years old. A scared orphaned kid who was losing the only fragment of home he had left.

"I'm sorry, Thatcher," I growled through my teeth. "Gods and Fates, I ... I am so sorry."

"I-It ... it's ...o-okay," he started again.

"Shut up. Don't say another word like that," I growled again. "It's not fine. None of this is fine. You're such an idiot, you know that?"

"Y-Yeah ..."

I seized his shoulders and held him out at arm's length.

"I'll talk to my father. I'll ask him if you can ... I don't know. It's a big house. They've got plenty of room for ..."

I saw the answer in his face long before he ever spoke. That broken goodbye smile and hollow, quiet voice put a pang of pain through my gut as he murmured, "I don't belong here, Murdoc."

My chest heaved in slow, angry breaths as I gripped his arms harder. "Thatcher?"

"I've wondered a long time what it meant to be a God of Mercy. I worried about using my power to influence people into doing things they didn't really want to do. I've never felt very god-like. I don't even know what that means, really," he looked past me, up at Blite, and his smile widened some. "I think I get it now, though."

What? What was he talking about?

Thatcher took my hands off his arms, then carefully pressed his hand into mine to grasp it tightly. "It isn't about flashy powers or incredible miracles. It never was. It was about finding the lost ... and showing them the way back home. Not because they deserve it, but because deep down, we're all lost people. And we're all just trying to find our way home."

I frowned down at the way he was gripping my hand, almost like he was ... saying goodbye.

Then Thatcher held up his other hand, showing me where he held the tiny crystal between his fingers. It sparkled and shone in the sunlight, no bigger than a sunflower seed. "I've got one more miracle to do. It's waiting for me in Halfax," he said quietly. "I'll wait until you come to visit, okay? Don't take too long, though. I promise, this is one you won't want to miss."

PART SEVEN

THATCHER

CHAPTER THIRTY-SIX

"I think that about does it," I said, groaning as I bent backwards a little to stretch. I'd been helping Phoebe pack up her workshop in the undercrofts of the royal castle for almost a week. Today was the last day, though. Tomorrow, there would be a ship waiting in the port with her name on it.

"Thank you, Thatcher. You won't get in trouble with the stablemaster, will you? I know this took a lot longer than we thought," she worried. "I can go and explain to him personally, if I need to."

"Nah. I'm sure it's fine." I turned around to sit on one of the freshly-packed crates and wipe the sweat from my face with my sleeve.

"Are you going to the ball tonight?" she asked as she came over to offer me a waterskin.

I took it and gulped down as much of it as I could without choking myself before I answered, "Yeah. Queen Jenna invited me, so I can't exactly say no, right?"

She giggled. "No, I guess not. Are you excited? Rylen is

coming. And Prince Judan, Kiran, Jondar, and even Duke Cromwell!"

"Yeah. I am actually. It'll be good to see everyone again." Hearing her say it like that made me realize just how long it had been. Three months now, if I was remembering correctly. And in that time, a lot had happened, to say the least.

First, I'd gone back to my old job working for Stablemaster Godfrey. Not because I had to, necessarily. Queen Jenna was allowing me to stay at the castle as her esteemed guest, so I could have loafed around if I wanted to. But sitting on my hands and eating pastries was only fun for a few days. Phoebe had gone immediately back to working down here, designing new things and consulting with all of Maldobar's finest engineers. I wanted something to keep me busy, too.

And, well, stable work always was one of my finer skills.

Granted, the look on Godfrey's face when I told him I wanted to work in the Deck with the dragons was priceless. I guess he hadn't seen that one coming. But it let me be near Fornax so I could keep working with him, perfecting our flying, and using all the new equipment Phoebe had made for us.

Her life had been a lot more interesting, by far, though. Not even a month after we came back, the Court of Crowns was called to a close and all the nobles and royals began making preparations to leave. During that time, a much older woman we'd seen sitting in the court during Phoebe's trial came down to her workshop with Queen Jenna. I remembered her instantly because of her hair. It looked a lot like Phoebe's, although it was turning white around her temples and brow.

The woman had introduced herself as Orna, and explained she was the queen of a kingdom called Noltham, which lay far to the east. She believed Phoebe might be a relative of hers—a niece she'd believed was lost to the Tibran invasion years ago. The rest of her family had been executed, but due to the efforts of her castle guard, they had managed to smuggle some of her youngest relatives out. Many of them had been hunted down and eventually killed. But there had never been any evidence found when it came to her youngest niece, an especially bright little girl with wild red curls.

The whole time, Phoebe looked like she might pass out any second. She didn't say much, which for her, was sort of a big deal. In fact, I couldn't remember a time when she'd been quiet for that long. Eventually, though, she seemed to come to terms with the fact that this elegant, soft-spoken older woman might really be her aunt. Naturally, that made Phoebe a duchess, since she was now her only surviving heir.

And about the time Phoebe realized that, she finally did pass out.

It was a lot to take in. The queen offered to take her back to her homeland, Noltham, and let her see the place where she'd been born, tour the kingdom, and meet the few other members of her family who had managed to escape the Tibrans. There weren't a lot of them, and most were just distant cousins, but the queen sounded hopeful.

I guess finding out she had any close descendants left alive was more than she'd expected to find here.

Initially, Phoebe didn't seem to like that idea at all. She talked me in circles for days, explaining why it wasn't a good idea, that she really didn't want to be nobility, and that she liked her life here in Maldobar. But after a few days, Phoebe finally confessed that she really did want to go. She apologized over and over, almost like she felt bad for leaving. Maybe she thought she had to stay because of me. Like she was supposed to watch over me and keep me company now that everyone else had gone on their separate ways.

Of course, that wasn't true. My life was getting emptier by

the day, sure. But ... the silence and calm weren't so bad. There was peace in it. And deep down, I knew it wasn't over. I'd see them all again—hopefully tonight at the farewell ball.

Granted, there weren't a lot of nobles left now. Most of them had been all too eager to go back to their kingdoms and attend to rebuilding their lands and restoring everything the Tibrans had destroyed. But for the ones who had stayed, or were taking a bit longer to make their departures, Queen Jenna was having a grand celebratory ball in the royal castle. People from all across Maldobar and Luntharda would be there, as well. I'd never been one for dancing, but the idea of seeing everyone again, spending the night celebrating, and catching up on what we'd all been doing sounded great.

Also, lots of free extra-delicious food. That was always a bonus.

"You know, I think Jenna is right. I think you've gotten taller," Phoebe mused as she tapped her chin, staring up at me with a broad smile.

I groaned and rubbed my forehead. "Well, it's about time. Maybe everyone will quit assuming I'm twelve now."

She laughed again and petted my head consolingly. "I'm sure Garnett will be very impressed."

Ugggh. There it was. That joke was starting to get old now. I hadn't seen or heard from Garnett since we'd parted ways in Osbran. The fact was, I'd put myself out there in a big, embarrassing, and totally awkward way. I'd told her how I felt. I'd kissed her. And she had said ... nothing. She'd acted like it never even happened. I probably wasn't the most knowledgeable person when it came to girls, sure, but even I knew what that meant. Silence like this was a nice way of saying "no thanks."

"I really don't think she's going to come to something like this, Phoebe," I muttered as I stood. Time to go before she launched into all the reasons why I shouldn't give up hope. I couldn't listen to that again. It was completely humiliating. "I've got to head back to the stable, but I'll see you tonight, okay?"

Phoebe's mouth twisted to one side, looking at me with a heavy sigh and her hands on her hips. For once, though, she didn't argue. She just waved a little and murmured back, "See you tonight, Thatcher."

THE CASTLE WAS LIT UP LIKE SOMETHING STRAIGHT OUT OF a fairy tale. As the sun set and all the candles along the walkways, white cobblestone drives, and through every window and over every doorway were lit, the whole place sparkled like a field of stars. Wreaths of flowers and evergreen hung everywhere, filling the air with inviting smells. Music filled the night, mingling with the sounds of conversation and laughter as I stood against the wall in one of the massive ballrooms. All four of them were open tonight and filled with people in beautiful clothing. Men wore suits or flowing robes. Women displayed dazzling ball gowns or sleek fashions made of colorful silks embroidered with jewels. Dragonriders and infantrymen walked the halls with their ceremonial armor polished to mirrored perfection, and some of the international guests sported ensembles so elaborate and strange it made everyone stop and marvel.

I smiled as I watched the couples whirling on the dance floor before me, occasionally catching a glimpse of a face I knew. Reigh and Isandri twirled together, laughing and grinning like they were plotting something. They'd spent a lot of time together since they came back, and while they didn't visit as often now that Isa was serving in the court as an ambassador for Nar'Haleen, it was still nice to have them around.

Jaevid stopped by to say hello, introducing me to his wife, Beckah, before they went off to join in the dance, too. Jenna finally agreed to a dance with her fiancée, Phillip, who despite still looking like a monster straight from the darkest pit of the abyss, was a pretty decent dancer. It was easy to spot him, though, since he towered over everyone else and was the only one with a tail.

Judan strolled by with his mother, and they both said hello, too. I didn't spot Jace anywhere, though. Maybe he was hiding out in case someone forced him to dance. Somehow, he didn't seem like the kind of guy who enjoyed this kind of setting much.

"Quite a gathering, isn't it?" Someone bumped my shoulder suddenly to get my attention.

I looked over and up, meeting Ezran Cromwell's familiar roguish grin.

"Oh! Hey," I stammered in surprise. "Yeah, it's, uh, really big. And loud."

He laughed and leaned against the wall next to me, holding a glass of wine I suspected probably wasn't his first. "I always did hate these things," he admitted. "Say, where's that broody friend of yours? The one who stole my *favorite* hatchling right out from under my nose."

I cringed. "He's ... well, I don't know, exactly. He said he was coming. Maybe he's around here somewhere?"

Ezran made a miserable, growling sound into his goblet. "I owe him a good smack for that. So, Jaevid tells me you've been back to mucking stalls these days? Gods, boy! You're a bloody dragonrider now!"

I laughed, unable to hide the embarrassment that rose like tingling heat in my cheeks. "Yeah, well, I don't have anywhere else to go. And I don't like just sitting around doing nothing."

"Is that so?" He cast me a thoughtful sideways glance. "You like it, then? Living here and mucking stalls all day?"

"I-I mean, it's ... okay," I stuttered. When he said it like that, it did sound kind of miserable.

"I see. You're supposed to go to the academy next year, right? You getting a lot of training in?" he questioned.

Oh boy. Well, this was going to be a disaster. "Not really. I don't have anyone to spar with. Everyone's really busy, and I ..."

My voice died in my throat as Ezran stared me down, his eyebrows scrunching together like two angry little caterpillars. "Unacceptable," he pronounced. "Completely unacceptable. I won't have a rider chosen by a Cromwell dragon going off to the academy and making a fool of himself. Fates, Jaevid said you were out here wasting away, but I had no idea it was this bad. That settles it, then."

My eyes went wide. "Settles what?"

"You," he lifted his wine glass toward me. "You're coming back to the Cromwell estate with me. We'll start training you properly."

My mouth fell open. "But, uh, I have a job here and—"

"And you think someone else can't clean horse dung out of a barn? You're the only one qualified for that?" He scoffed and rolled his eyes, clapping his free hand on my back. "Nonsense. You're coming to stay with me, kid. You're good with dragons, right? Maybe my stable hands can teach you a thing or two that's a bit more to your liking. Place is pretty sparse these days, anyway. Just me and the servants. It'll be nice to have someone else to talk to. And we'll work on that training every day. You'll be fit for it when you start at the academy. Make no mistake, boy, that place is not for the faint of heart."

My whole face flushed as I stared at him, wondering if he really meant all of that ... or if Jaevid had put him up to it. "If, um, if you're really sure you want me there." I managed to rasp.

"I am." He looked back out across the ballroom and let

out a deep, resigned breath. "You're not the only one who arrived at the end of all this with nothing to go home to, kid. Guess that means we should band together, right?"

I smiled weakly and nodded. "I'd be honored, then."

"Okay," he grinned back, "Now, let's find that broody friend of yours. I'll never forgive him for taking my hatchling. He owes me at least one free punch, no flinching."

CHAPTER THIRTY-SEVEN

The night dragged on, and I managed to track down nearly everyone I'd wanted to see. I even danced a little with Phoebe, which was a lot more fun than I'd expected. I wasn't completely terrible at it, anyway. That, or she was just lying to make me feel better.

Yeah, probably that.

Murdoc arrived fashionably late, strolling in alongside his sister, Aria. Part of me wanted to run up and meet them, but even from a distance ... I could feel that things were different now. Murdoc was different. He was Rylen now.

He'd cut his hair short and wore finer clothes, a ceremonial breastplate, and matching bracers. He carried himself with much more distinction, looking perfectly at ease among the other esteemed nobles in the room. I wondered if that was something he'd learned in the Ulfrangar, or from his new life in Dayrise with his family. I wondered a lot of things, though. First and foremost, I wondered if he'd even want to talk to me at all now. We'd only exchanged a few letters over the last few months. Not that I didn't get it—he had a lot to deal with now. New family. New life. New everything. I wondered if he'd be upset if I accidentally called him Murdoc. It still felt strange to call him anything else. And lastly, I wondered if he was happy or not. It seemed like a weird thing to ask, though. Why wouldn't he be?

Walking in with one arm at his back and the other escorting Aria, he gave a small nod and smirk when he spotted me across the ballroom.

I waved a hand and smiled back. Part of me expected that would be it. He'd go off to mingle, and I might not even see him again for the rest of the night.

But Murdoc started for me at a speed walk, basically dragging his sister along the whole way. She scowled at him when she nearly tripped over her gown, and gave him a punishing elbow to the ribs.

"What's wrong with you?" she hissed. "Fates, Rylen. You planning on dragging me out by my ankles later?"

He snickered and winked. "Why don't you run off and find your beloved Haldor, eh?"

If looks could have killed, Murdoc would've dropped right where he stood. Aria pursed her lips and slowly shook her head, her eyes promising violence, like there were tiny burning villages inside them, as she slowly turned and walked away. Yikes.

"Haldor?" I had to be sure I heard that right.

Murdoc sagged on his feet and groaned. "Yes. Gods, I had no idea when I started that nonsense it would evolve into this. I thought it was just a prank. Just a taunt to pay her back. But they've been courting for three months and it's excruciating to watch. If he doesn't propose soon, we're all going to move out."

I laughed and shook my head. "You set your sister up with Haldor?"

"I didn't think she'd actually like him!" he flailed his arms like an angry puppet.

Well, so much for him not acting the same. Gods, I'd missed this.

"It's good to see you, by the way," I chuckled.

"And you," he sighed and stepped into his usual spot, standing right at my side with his arms crossed, like we'd never been separated. "You look slightly less pathetic than before."

"Phoebe thinks I've gotten taller," I announced proudly, straightening my collar a bit.

"She lied."

I elbowed him in the arm as hard as I could, but it didn't even make him flinch. Ugh. Typical.

We stood in silence for a few minutes, watching the dancing as the conversation of the hundreds of other guests roared on around us. I could tell by that angry little crease in his brow, right between his eyes, that there was something else he wanted to say. I guess he was just trying to figure out the right words.

"By the way, I'm going to stay with Ezran Cromwell for a while. He wants to help get me ready for the academy," I decided to break the awkward silence first. "He also wants to punch you for stealing his dragon, so, you know, be on the lookout."

"He is more than welcome to try." Murdoc's tone was ominous. Then his gaze panned down to study me out of the corner of his eyes. "Do you want to go there? To the Cromwell estate?"

My arms flapped against my sides as I shrugged. "I guess so. He said I could also learn to work with the dragons and hatchlings at his stable."

"Sounds like a good fit for you."

I bowed my head a little, smiling down at the floor. "Yeah. I guess it does."

Shifting where he stood, Murdoc cleared his throat and took in a deep breath. "Have you seen Phoebe?"

Theeere it was. The thing he'd really been wanting to say. I grinned and pretended to pick at my fingernails. "Yeah. Danced with her some. You know, she leaves for Noltham tomorrow."

"Yeah," he replied quietly. "I know."

"She's probably dancing in one of the other ballrooms. You should go say hello," I suggested.

His mouth pinched up bitterly and he tugged at his collar. "Maybe I will. Coming with me?"

I opened my mouth to answer, but someone else beat me to it. "Oh, no. He's got a previous engagement to attend to."

We both turned, looking down in shock to find Garnett standing behind us, beaming and wearing a beautiful emerald green dress with big bell sleeves trimmed in fur. All her ginger-blonde hair was tied up into an intricate plaited bun, and her lips were painted deep red. She flushed a little when she caught me staring, grabbing handfuls of her skirts and giving them a little twirl. "What do you think? Looks decent, yeah?"

"Looks ... beautiful ..." I managed to croak.

Murdoc seemed less enchanted by her beauty, though. "What are you doing here? I didn't think ... someone of your profession would be keen on making public appearances."

She winked one of her violet eyes. "Aye, well, you see that was before my employer suggested I make myself known to Her Majesty as one of the only survivors of my people, and appeal to her to help me find others. After hearing how she pardoned you, and was so avid to intervene for Phoebe, I decided it was worth the risk. So, now I'm officially being given the position as ambassador in her court. She's allowing me to use her resources to see if I can find any other dwarves who might have survived the Tibran scourge."

"And also passing along any other valuable information you happen to find along the way, I assume," Murdoc surmised.

Garnett nibbled her bottom lip innocently. "Only a little, here and there."

Suuure.

"But that's not why I came here tonight," she added quickly. Gathering up her skirts again, she stepped toward me and dipped into a graceful curtsy. "I came to talk to you, Thatcher Renley."

My hands got all sweaty and clammy as I led Garnett out onto the dance floor. I tried not to let how badly my knees were shaking show as I put a hand on her waist and guided her into a smooth, steady waltz around the room. We swayed gently to the rhythm of the music, me staring down at her and trying to balance my internal panic attack with remembering which steps came next.

"You dance pretty well," she sounded genuinely impressed.

"I practiced a little," I confessed.

"It shows." She smiled wider, making those dimples appear in her cheeks and her lavender eyes shine. Fates, I'd never seen anyone so pretty. "I have to admit, I was worried about you being here on your own. I wanted to come sooner to make sure you were okay." Her smile faded a little. "Are you?"

"Yeah," I managed to say without choking or wheezing. "I am. Knowing everyone's found happiness and a place they belong—it helps."

Her smile faded even more. "Everyone except you."

"Maybe so," I agreed. "But I like to think that just means my journey isn't over yet. The best is yet to come."

She laughed softly and moved in closer, dancing so near it made my heartbeat go nuts. "That's why I like you, Thatch. You always see the best in everyone. You see light even in the darkest places of the world. It's a wonderful gift."

"Some people think I'm just being naïve," I pointed out.

Her hand that was resting on my shoulder drifted over to touch my cheek. "Not naïve," she said softly. "Just good. Through and through. The best man I've ever met."

Again—she'd said it *again*. She'd called me a man instead of kid, boy, or any number of slightly dismissive words I'd been called throughout my life. I tried not to read too much into that.

But I wasn't successful.

"I hope you can forgive me for taking this long, but there's something I wanted to tell you. I just had to wait until I'd gotten all my stones in a row," she said as she slowly came to a stop. Still standing in front of me, the light from the chandeliers overhead making all the little pearls woven into her hair shine, Garnett put both hands on my cheeks and stood up on her toes so we were looking eye-to-eye.

Oh. Oh gods. What did this mean? What was she doing right here in front of everyone?

"I like you, too, Thatcher. And not as a friend. I think you're the kindest person I've ever met, and I *romantically* like you, as well." She leaned in and pressed her lips lightly against mine for a brief second. "And I'm only sorry it took me this long to say it, but I wanted to be sure I could be close. You deserve to be with someone who isn't always hiding in the shadows. It was scary for me, you know. I've been so worried about how the people here would receive me—especially the royals who would decide my fate. But you gave me hope, and a reason to want something better. Thank you for that."

All I could manage was a breathless, squeaky, "You're welcome."

She grinned and kissed me again, harder this time. "Let's dance some more, all right? Then let's go find the rest of your friends and see what kind of trouble we can stir up, yeah?"

I nodded. My heart still pumped wildly, making my head spin and my knees wobbly as I stepped in to dance with her again. "I, uh, I actually have a little sort-of trouble I need to, um, stir up."

Her eyebrows rose. "Is that so?"

"Yeah." I leaned down and whispered against her ear, making sure no one dancing around us might hear. "It won't be easy, though. You're a spy, right? How hard do you think it'll be to sneak something into Duke Phillip's wine glass?"

Garnett pulled back slightly, eyeing me with sudden uncertainty. "Like what, exactly?"

I slipped my hand from her waist down into my pocket, pulling out the tiny sparkling stone Devana had given me. "This."

"What's it for?" She sounded worried.

I gave her a wink as I pocketed it again. "Nothing bad, I promise. Let's just say ... I've got one chance to show him the greatest act of mercy the world has ever seen. So I can't afford to mess it up. Understand?"

Her eyes went wide, panning back and forth between my face and my pocket a few times. "You mean ...?!"

I nodded. "Think you can help me pull it off?"

Garnett's face lit with a smile that made her whole being seem to glow. "Without a doubt, love."

CHAPTER THIRTY-EIGHT

It wasn't nearly as difficult as I'd thought it would be. Not with Garnett's added help, anyway. She knew all the right things to say and ways to talk our way around the servants, making our way to the head table where Phillip and Jenna sat together. She made herself quite the spectacle, laughing and complimenting them on how beautiful the evening was, just long enough for me to lean over, using shaking Phillip's hand as an excuse to discretely drop the tiny fragment of crystal into his goblet before I leaned away.

Boom—mission complete.

We scampered off back into the crowds, hand in hand, and found Isandri and Reigh talking to Murdoc and Phoebe. In a matter of seconds, it was like I'd gone back in time. Like we'd never been separated. Like we might as well be right back in that tavern in Osbran, or in Ms. Lin's house near Dayrise. And in that moment, standing in the castle with the air filled with music and laughter, everything was right.

Everything was as it should be.

A few hours later, I noticed Duke Phillip make a face as he drank from his goblet. He smacked his lips and rubbed at his forehead, frowning into his glass before he took another sip. Boy, was he in for a wild night.

A wild rest of his life, actually. But a better one, I hoped.

When Devana had given me that crystal, and the note along with it, I hadn't realized what either of them meant right away. She'd whispered in my mind that this was the Gift of Grace—a fragment of pure love in physical form. It was all my mother had left behind to give me, and using it would allow me to negate one act of cruelty. I could undo something terrible someone else had done. I just didn't know what that should be.

But the note had a name written on it, and that was when I understood.

Phillip Derrick was a good man, too. He was destined to be our king. And what had been done to him by Argonox and the Tibrans was probably the cruelest thing I'd ever seen. He was cursed to live out his life like that—walking among his friends and family as a monster.

Or at least he had been before.

After tonight, all that would change. And by morning, gods willing, his life would be different. I didn't know if he'd go back completely to the way he had been before they experimented on him. I didn't know if that much damage could be repaired. But I believed. And sometimes believing is all you can do ... and all that matters in the end.

As dawn began to break over the kingdom, the ball finally wound to a close. Beautiful carriages rolled up to the front of the castle to carry all the shining guests back off into the night. But the six of us just sat on the front steps, watching the procession, and passing a wine bottle back and forth. It tasted terrible, but maybe that wasn't the point.

One by one, each of us started to break off and say our goodnights. Phoebe had a long day tomorrow, so she went first. Garnett volunteered to help Murdoc's sister find the room in the castle's guest wing where they'd be staying for the night. Isandri slipped away, giving me a wistful smile as she prowled away into the night and disappeared. Reigh went next, grumbling something about having to help with the departure arrangements for some of the vessels tomorrow.

Then it was just Murdoc and me, sitting on the steps, watching the sun rise.

"Hey," he muttered as he nudged my leg with the now empty wine bottle. "You know you can still call me Murdoc, right?"

Somehow, hearing him say that made every last bit of tension in my body about being around him, whether or not we were still friends like before, finally ease. I leaned forward and let my elbows rest on my knees as I drew in a full, calm breath for the first time in three months. "You're sure you're okay with that?"

"Yep."

"Good, cause it's really weird to call you anything else," I coughed a nervous laugh.

"Yeah," he agreed. "It's weird for me, too."

"Do you like it? Your real name, I mean?" I wondered.

He rubbed his fingers together—a nervous habit I'd seen him do probably a thousand times. "It scares me a little. It comes with a lot of expectations. A lot of weight and history, way more than I'd ever expected."

I showed him my best, most confident and resolute grin. "Yeah. It's a heavy name for sure. But you're a pretty strong guy, so I'm sure you can carry it."

"We'll see. I intend to try. By the way ... I saw you kissing Garnett out there again," he taunted with a sly twinkle in his eyes, even if the rest of his expression stayed stone cold and focused ahead. "Does that mean you're courting her?"

"I don't know," I admitted. "I didn't see you kiss Phoebe, though. Kind of running out of time for that, aren't you?"

He shot me the best impression of a shocked and offended stare I'd ever seen. Too bad I knew him better than that.

I snickered and looked back out across the castles front drive. "She's leaving tomorrow, you know. It's now or never."

"I hate you sometimes, you know that?" he growled through his teeth as he bowed his head.

"Nah," I countered. "Only when you know I'm right."

THERE WAS A CONSIDERABLE COMMOTION IN THE CASTLE early the following morning. Excitement, I guess you could say. Joy, even.

Naturally I knew *absolutely nothing* about the reason for it, or why there would be any cause for the royal family to call all their close relatives to come immediately to Queen Jenna's private wing of the castle.

Nope. No idea at all.

Servants cried tears of joy and whispered excitedly as they dashed through the halls outside the servant's quarters where I'd been given a modest room—at my own insistence, of course. Aubren had offered to put me up in his wing of the castle again. Reigh had even argued with me about it for days. But it felt weird to encroach on their family any more than I already had. Besides the servant quarters were clean and comfortable, so it wasn't like I was suffering at all.

A group of other stable hands went running by to see what was going on. One of them stopped long enough to stick their head in my doorway and ask if I was coming to see what was going on. "Nah, I'm sure I'll hear about it. I've got to talk to Godfrey about something this morning," I said, wafting a hand.

Okay, fine. It was kind of a fib. A really small one, though.

I did need to talk to Stablemaster Godfrey at some point about going to the Cromwell's. That could wait, though. I had more important things to attend to, first.

The courtyards were buzzing with activity as I made my way out across the castle grounds with Murdoc and the others. Servants, maids, stable hands, and guards all crowded together or ran around, trying to organize the chaos. Bells began tolling in the city streets of Halfax, and I had to duck my head some to hide my smile.

As soon as I set foot into the castle itself, the excitement intensified. The halls and parlors resounded with the sounds of happy crying and more maids rushed by with tears in their eyes. Halfway through the front vestibule, one of the servant girls who sometimes brought meals out for Stablemaster Godfrey rushed up and seized my hands, squeaking excitedly that Duke Phillip had been healed.

"O-Oh, yeah? Really? That's amazing," I sputtered nervously.

I guess she was too elated to notice my terrible attempt at a genuinely surprised expression, because she just went on shrieking with glee and skipped off out the door. I didn't even get a chance to ask for details.

Ah, well, if everyone was this happy about it, that had to be a good sign, right?

I couldn't hold back a proud smile as I continued down to the undercrofts beneath the castle. We'd all agreed to help Phoebe load the rest of the things into the wagons that would take them down to the royal port. Then, we'd say our goodbyes to her. Just for now, though. She'd promised to come back as soon as she could, repeating over and over that she loved it here in Maldobar, and she didn't want to live anywhere else. She insisted that her aunt understood, and had assured her she could come back whenever she wished. She could even live here if she wanted.

Of course, we all knew that was a lie. Not an intentional one, of course. Phoebe wasn't like that. But once she set foot in her homeland, we all knew she probably wouldn't want to be anywhere else. And who could blame her? There wasn't much tying her here now. We were all friends, yes. But family took precedence. And like Murdoc, she now had a chance to finally experience life with a family.

Who would pass that up?

Speaking of Murdoc ...

As we all gathered to heave the last crate onto the already overloaded wagon bound for the nearby port, he stared at Phoebe with a look like he might suddenly throw up at any second. I made sure I stood clear of him, you know, just in case. Better safe than sorry and covered in puke.

We could have ridden with the wagons down to the port. We could have flown on the dragons, too. But with only a few minutes before everyone went their separate ways for what could be a long time, it felt good to walk together on the long, gently curving road that led across the rocky grassland toward the port a few miles ahead.

Vexi and Blite were circling above us like massive scaly vultures, nipping at one another's tails and growling playfully. Even Fornax seemed to be relaxed and in a good mood as he lumbered along behind me, seeming to prefer sticking close today rather than joining in the aerial tussle. Garnett walked alongside him with her hand on his head, speaking to him like a mother cooing to a baby—a very large, fire-breathing baby that could have eaten her in one bite like a bon-bon. But he purred and seemed to enjoy the attention.

Up ahead, Isandri and Reigh strolled along making swats at one another as they bickered. Reigh was teasing her about her new, courtly robes that were a lot more extravagant than the ones she'd worn before. She wrinkled her nose and reminded him over and over that it was his fault for talking her into it in the first place. Squabbling aside, it was easy to see they were both in a much better place now. Happier, I guess.

"Did you see Duke Phillip?" Phoebe gasped up at Murdoc, who still looked a few breaths away from a full-blown mental breakdown as he walked quietly along with us. "I only caught a glimpse when I went to say farewell to Queen Jenna. Gods! It's incredible! How do you think it happened?"

Garnett and I exchanged a look. Oooh boy.

"I didn't see him," Garnett piped up, somehow executing a perfectly nonchalant and convincingly curious expression. "What happened?"

"He's human again! It's unbelievable, Garnett! It's like nothing ever happened. Every trace of what the switchbeast venom did to him just ... gone!" Phoebe bubbled with happiness and bounced onto her toes. "You should have seen him and Queen Jenna. I've never seen anyone so happy. They're all a bit nervous, too, I think. No one knows how it happened or if it'll last, but the medics were all flabbergasted. It's so wonderful!

"It's true," Reigh added, suddenly glancing back at us. "I saw him before we left. It's like the switchbeast venom never touched him at all. I knew him before all that, and he's completely back to normal."

Murdoc's eyes narrowed slightly, but he never looked my way. "And no one knows how or why it happened?"

Reigh just shook his head. "Nope. He wasn't feeling well after the ball last night, so he went to bed early. We all figured he just had a little too much to drink at dinner. But this morning—poof! It's like a miracle. They're all over the moon about it."

My throat went dry. He still hadn't even looked at me, but I knew just by the way Murdoc's jawline tensed ever so slightly ... Yep. He definitely knew.

CHAPTER THIRTY-NINE

While the rest of our group ran ahead out onto the long, busy dock of the royal port, a powerful hand grabbed the top of my head like someone picking up an apple. Oh gods.

"That was you, wasn't it?" Murdoc demanded in a low, ominous growl. "You did that to Duke Phillip, didn't you?"

I showed him a toothy, wincing smile. "Sorta, yeah, a little bit."

His eyes narrowed.

"I mean, I did tell you I was going to do ... *something*," I panicked.

His expression sagged with what I could only interpret as exasperation and general weariness. He let me go and rubbed at his eyes. "I'm not even going to ask. Plausible deniability. And don't you dare tell anyone I knew anything."

"I won't!" I promised. "Besides, it's not like they'll ever figure out it was me. I was extra-sneaky about it."

He moved his hand just enough to glare at me with one, bloodshot, very exhausted eye. "Thatcher, there is nothing even *remotely* sneaky about you."

I cleared my throat and tried smoothing down my hair. "It was good, though, right? They'll be happy now, don't you think?"

His broad chest heaved in and out with a long, exaggerated exhale. "Yeah," he relented at last. "I think they will be."

Good. That was enough for me.

Looking ahead again, I tipped my head back some at the warmth of the morning sun over the ocean. Gulls floated on the strong winds, and the massive ships rocked gently at their moorings. The swish and rumble of the waves lapping at the shore mixed with the shouts of the sailors and dockhands as they loaded cargo onto one especially robust looking vessel on the farthest end of the docks. With three large masts, windows all down the sides, and a gold-painted figurehead carved in the shape of an owl with its wings spread wide, I wondered at the flags flying proudly that bore that same insignia. The royal symbol of Noltham?

High upon the deck, a familiar older woman with long coppery red hair dressed in a deep purple gown and white cloak stood with a man who, due to his formal uniform and broad-brimmed hat, must have been the captain. She smiled when she noticed us, and Phoebe bounced up onto her toes again and waved excitedly.

We stood by watching while the dockhands rolled loading carts full of Phoebe's things onboard, an awkward silence passing over us almost like we were watching a funeral procession. When it was done and everything was loaded, then she'd have to go. She'd sail away over the eastern seas, and gods only knew when she'd be back.

If ever ...

"Oh! Fates, I nearly forgot!" Phoebe gasped suddenly. She swung her messenger-styled bag around to the front and opened it. Metallic objects clunked and clattered as she dug around inside, and finally pulled out a decent-sized black velvet bag. It was roughly the length of my forearm, and the object hidden inside seemed almost cylindrical as she handled it. Phoebe handed the bag off to Reigh with a secretive little smile, "This is for Judan. It's just a prototype. Tell him I'll send updated versions along very soon, but this ought to get him by until then."

Reigh took the bag cautiously, his eyes wide and a little alarmed as he studied it. "Okay," he agreed finally. "It's not going to explode, right?"

She giggled. "No! Not this one."

No one laughed with her.

She didn't seem to notice, though. "And then there's these," Phoebe continued as she dug around in her bag some more. She pulled out a bunch more velvet bags, each one only about the size of my palm, with a little drawstring tied closed. She handed one to each of us and stood back waiting, smiling from ear to ear.

"Oh, Phoebe," Isandri breathed in reverence as she poured the contents of her bag onto her hand. On a glittering silver chain, a thumb-sized pendant made of silver metal hung and sparkled in the morning light. It was a roundish, almost disk shape, and a tiny shard of a misty, purplish gemstone right in the center. The outside of the round silver disk part had been very intricately engraved with tiny rune marks that looked strangely familiar.

Hmmm. They were similar in style and shape to the ones on my goggles, weren't they?

"What are they?" Reigh asked as he held up an exact duplicate that he'd poured out of his own bag.

There was one for each of us—Garnett, Murdoc, Isandri, Reigh, and me—that were all crafted to be identical.

Phoebe clapped and squealed with delight, then pulled her own out from under the collar of her tunic. "Aren't they lovely? They're all connected! No matter how far apart we are, if any one of us ever needs help, all you have to do is press your thumb over the jewel. If you get it just right, it'll prick your thumb. Nothing too bad, I promise! But the runes need a tiny bit of blood to activate. When they do, they make all the other necklaces glow, so we know someone's in trouble." She calmed a little, her shoulders drawing up sheepishly as she fidgeted with her own pendant. "I just ... wanted to come up with some way for us to all stay connected."

"It's a good idea," Reigh said as he slipped his around his neck. "Thank you, Phoebe."

Everyone stayed quiet as we all did the same, sliding the pendants around our necks and tucking them under our shirt collars. The heaviness in the air was impossible to miss. Grief crept in like a poisonous fog, curling around us and sealing us in that silence. A low horn blared from the ship nearby.

It was time for final boarding.

Phoebe went to each of us one at a time, hugging our necks tightly and kissing our cheeks. She sniffled as she stood back, fidgeting with her hands and looking down at her toes. "I'm going to miss you all so much," she whimpered. "I'll come back as soon as I can, I promise."

"Don't rush, Pheobe," Garnett consoled with a knowing smile. "Enjoy your time with your people and learn about your home. It is a rare gift these days. We wouldn't dare ask you not to savor and treasure it."

We all nodded in agreement.

Well, most of us did. Murdoc stood disturbingly still, staring at her like he was stuck in some kind of trance. It didn't even look like he was breathing. I had to resist the urge to wave a hand in front of his face to make him snap out of it.

He probably would've snapped my wrist for that.

Phoebe's eyes darted up and hesitated on him for a few seconds longer than the rest of us as she gave a final, trembling smile. Then she turned and started walking away.

Garnett slipped her hand into mine and squeezed it, her eyes a bit misty as we all watched Phoebe climb the boarding ramp and make her way onto the ship's deck.

I stole another look at Murdoc. His chest was heaving fast now, drawing in rapid, heavy breaths as all the color drained from his face. His sharp features twisted into a look of pure, uncontrollable panic. But he didn't move. He didn't say a word.

As the sailors up and down the dock began withdrawing all the cargo-loading planks and ramps, untying the moorings from the dock, and raising the anchor, his jawline flexed like he was gnashing his teeth. His hands clenched in shaking fists at his sides. His eyes darted wildly between the dock and the ship.

"Murdoc," I snapped suddenly.

He jolted and stared back at me, almost as pale as a corpse now.

I gave him the very best annoyed glare I could muster. "What the heck are you waiting for?!"

His mouth fell open. That look of quiet terror shattered on his face. He looked back up to where Phoebe now stood next to her aunt near the bow of the ship, just as the last loading ramp was dragged out of reach.

Then, without a word, Murdoc bolted for the ship like a madman.

Reigh barked a laugh as Murdoc sprinted to the edge of the dock and leapt through the air, barely managing to grab onto one of the mooring ropes before the ship drifted out of reach. We all ran to the edge, watching and laughing as he climbed up the rope while the sailors onboard shouted at him, calling him a colorful variety of names that, given what he was doing, were probably deserved.

Murdoc made it to the deck of the ship, basically throwing himself over the rail and landing in a heap. He scrambled up immediately, disheveled but determined, and started shoving his way past the crew members who rushed him in varying degrees of anger and confusion. By then, the whole ship was aware they had an unexpected new passenger on board—including Phoebe. I guess she'd been watching the whole thing, because she started sprinting across the deck toward him. She cried out, but over the ambient noise of frustrated bewilderment now brewing on the dock and ship, I couldn't hear anything she said.

We all heard it when Murdoc shouted "PHOEBE!" at the top of his lungs, though.

They ran to one another across the deck. Phoebe hit him at full speed, her red curls and dainty pink tunic blowing around her wildly as she wrapped her arms and legs around him. He grabbed her out of midair and held her tight, pressing his mouth against hers in a desperate kiss like he couldn't hold it back for another second. The sailors who'd been chasing him began to laugh as they stopped and stayed back.

Murdoc gripped Phoebe tightly, kissing her deeply until she finally pulled back and cradled his face in her hands. I couldn't hear what they said—not from that distance. But I could see happy tears streaming down her face as she nodded and hugged him again with all her strength.

IT TOOK A LITTLE DRAGON-SHAPED HELP TO GET MURDOC back to the dock. Hard to turn a ship like that around on a whim, after all. But we all got a good laugh out of watching them sail off into the mid-morning sun a bit, holding each other. Then Blite soared over to pick him up, yipping and crowing excitedly as he zoomed around the ship. The sailors watching the sails and masts didn't seem to find it nearly as amusing, though. Maybe they were concerned about what a playful puff of dragon fire might do to their ship.

A valid concern, really.

Murdoc returned windblown and breathless at the far end of the dock. He stared after the ship, rubbing Blite's neck as the rest of us wandered up to meet him. He didn't look quite so sick and pasty anymore, though. There was a strange smile on his lips and a sadness in his eyes I understood all too well.

"Quite the show," Reigh jabbed with a snort. "All that and she still wouldn't come back with you, eh?"

"I didn't ask her to stay," Murdoc said quietly. "I'd never ask her to do that."

"Then ... what did you say to her?" Isandri asked, a curious arch to her brow.

"I told her that I loved her," he confessed without even the tiniest hint of shame or embarrassment. "And I promised that if she ever dared to set foot in Maldobar again, I'd find her ... and I'd marry her."

Garnett's mouth pinched into a thrilled little O-shape as she looked between the rest of us with wide, delighted eyes.

Reigh made surprised sputtering sounds.

I guess I did, too. Or maybe that was just me trying to breathe through the shock.

"You dashing devil, you," Garnett cheered as she clapped him on the back hard enough to make him stumble some. "How's a woman supposed to say no to that?"

Murdoc bowed his head and laughed under his breath. "She didn't. She said yes." He laughed harder and shook his head like he couldn't believe it. "She actually said yes."

"Well, congratulations then. Could be a while till she does come back, though, you know," Reigh reminded him.

Murdoc lifted his gaze back to the dark, retreating silhouette of the ship as it slowly slipped closer to the glow of the horizon. "I know. It's okay," he murmured. "Like every good thing that's ever happened in my life, I have no doubt ... she's worth the wait."

Almost a week passed like a blur. And like all good things, my time with everyone finally came to an end. Or, rather, a break. Yeah, that sounded better. Besides, it's not like we'd never see each other again. But life was sweeping us all in different directions now, and I'd come to accept that wasn't always a bad thing.

Murdoc went back to Dayrise to live with his family and continue settling in. He had a lot of catching up to do, after all. The Porters were elated to find out he was engaged, especially when they found out it was to Phoebe. I guess they really liked her. Somehow, that made me even happier to think about. I cared so much for both of them. Knowing they'd found happiness together was the best situation I could've ever imagined.

Reigh was probably the busiest of all of us. He and Aubren had taken the helm of handling all the departing dignitaries, making sure everyone was prepared and the exits of each royal and noble back to their homeland went as smoothly as possible. I honestly couldn't tell how much Reigh enjoyed the work, though. His time at the dragonrider academy was looming closer and closer, and maybe that's why he seemed more tense than ever. I didn't understand why he might be worried about it, though. Yes, dragonrider training was supposed to be brutal—mentally and physically. But he'd already undergone a lot of training, and he fought better than most people. Er, well, except for Murdoc, of course. Anyway, I seriously doubted Reigh was going to struggle through dragonrider training. What was he worried about?

Whatever it was, he wouldn't say no matter how many

times I asked. Eventually, I just had to let it go. Maybe someday he'd let me in on it, but for now, he was determined to keep his mouth shut.

Isandri and Garnett settled in to their courtly duties well, joining the growing council of international ambassadors who met with Queen Jenna and the soon-to-be King Phillip regularly. It kept them pretty busy, although Garnett always found time to come to the stable to visit. She didn't seem worried at all that I'd turned in my resignation to Stablemaster Godfrey so I could go and live with Duke Cromwell. In fact, she thought it was a great idea. I needed the preparation for the academy, and it wasn't all that far. I could visit her often.

Packing up the last of my few belongings—which amounted to a few changes of clothes, a sword belt, my xiphos, and crossbow—I buttoned up my only saddlebag and stood to look over the small room where I'd been living. The bed was clean and made. Nothing was left to tidy up. In a few hours, it would be like I'd never stayed here at all.

I sighed. Another chapter of my life had closed, and it felt like another one was just beginning. I just didn't know what to expect from this one.

Hopefully less fire and fewer poisoned crossbow bolts.

"Well now, you look ready to go," a deep voice observed from the doorway behind me.

I turned, facing the imposing figure of a tall, broad-shouldered man in a dragonrider's cloak and armor as he leaned in the doorway. Jaevid Broadfeather's smile was strangely cryptic, and maybe even a little nostalgic, as he asked, "Everything okay, Thatcher?"

I nodded. "Yeah. It is."

"Come on, then," he tipped his head toward the hall behind him. "I'll see you out."

We walked together from the servant's quarters, through the modest dining hall where the stable hands and other workers could share meals, and out into the open air of the broad courtyard between the royal stable and the Deck. The fierce wind tugged at Jaevid's long cloak, making the golden trim shine in the sunlight with every step.

"Ezran won't say it, but I think he's very pleased to have company in his house," he said evenly. "He's been alone there for quite some time. He's also a very talented fighter, so try to learn all you can."

"I will," I promised.

His toned quietened, becoming almost careful as he glanced at me briefly. "I must admit, I was concerned for you when I heard Rylen had chosen to stay in Dayrise with his family. I know it wasn't easy to leave him behind there."

"No," I agreed. "It wasn't easy. But ... it wasn't about me. Murdoc—er, Rylen—needs to be there. And he's my friend, so I need to support him. As long as he's okay, I'm okay."

"That's very noble of you."

I scrunched my mouth to one side, not sure if I agreed. Was it noble? Or was it just the right thing to do? Murdoc was still my best friend. Nothing about that had changed just because we lived farther apart. I wanted him to find the peace he'd searched for. Yeah, it hurt not to have him around. It was lonely sometimes. But part of being a friend is accepting that not everything is going to work out equally for both sides all the time. Sometimes, you have to give a little. And demanding that he come back with me, or trying to force my way into his new family, wasn't going to do anything but drive a wedge between us. I didn't want that at all.

I just wanted him to be happy.

As we approached the front of the Deck, Jaevid's pace slowed until he came to stop right outside the big, arched doorway. I stopped, too, and he turned to face me with a much more thoughtful frown. "I realize I should have told you this much sooner, but I wanted to let you know that I am proud of how you handled yourself through that ordeal, Thatcher. And I'd like to apologize for ever doubting you could handle it."

I grinned and jostled my bag some, balancing it over my shoulder. "I'm tougher than I look."

His smile was nostalgic again, almost like he was seeing a reflection of someone else standing in my place. "Yes," he agreed. "Yes, you are."

"I won't let you down in dragonrider training either," I promised. "I'll do my best."

"I know you will." Jaevid stretched a hand out to me, offering to shake. "If you ever need anything, please don't hesitate to contact me. I may be your commander, soon. But I'm also your sponsor. And more than that, I'm your friend."

Hearing that sent a little fluttering tingle of excitement through me. Never, in my wildest dreams, would I have dared to dream that Jaevid Broadfeather would consider me his friend—but he did. And as I grasped his hand and shook it once, I felt that connection like a seal stamped over my heart. I'd always assumed that being a dragonrider meant I'd be walking in the shadow of his incredible legacy, trying desperately to keep up and prove myself worthy.

I'd missed the whole point, though.

It wasn't about walking behind him or trying to match up to the heritage of his greatness. It was about both of us, turning to the same rising sun flung far upon the wild horizon, and walking our own, unique paths toward destiny without hesitation or fear.

"Have a safe journey, Thatcher," he said with a parting smile. "I'll see you soon."

"Until then." I nodded and jostled my bag, balancing it over my shoulder as I walked into the Deck alone. The musky smell of dragon filled my nose as I walked the sloping walkway up to the highest level. Sunlight hit my face with tingling warmth as I rolled open the stall door.

In the far corner of the stall, the huge mound of orange and black scales stirred. Fornax unfurled from where he'd curled himself into a ball, yawning widely and smacking his jaws. He blinked his milky jade-colored eyes in my direction, and purred when I ran a hand along his snout.

"Hey big guy. Ready to go home?"

He gave a deep, earnest snort as he got to his feet and stretched his wing arms one at a time.

"Good." I dropped my bag and walked around to where his saddle sat on a stand in a corner of the stall. A grin stretched over my face as I ran my hands across the smooth, sun-warmed leather.

Fornax's massive, horned head appeared over my shoulder, sniffing curiously.

"It's not going to be easy, you know. Ezran and the others are right—we're not ready for the academy. Not yet. We've got a lot of work to do." I reached up to slide my goggles down over my eyes.

He gave another loud, excited snort and trill of chirping sounds as we shared my sight through those goggles.

It was true, though. The academy was our next challenge. It might even be our greatest one. But whatever happened, whatever we had to face there, Fornax and I were in this together to the bitter end. Our bond was strong. And our strength was growing every day. As long as we held true to that connection, to that soul-deep oath we'd forged together, there was nothing we couldn't handle.

That was the path of the dragonrider.

And it was the only one I'd ever want to take.

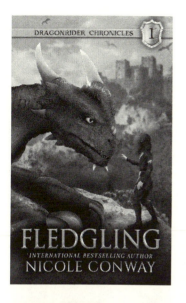

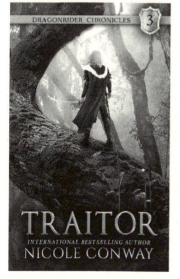

ACKNOWLEDGMENTS

First and always, I want to thank my wonderful super fans in the Dragonrider Legion! You guys keep me going with your enthusiasm for every release, and I can't wait to share what's coming next!

I'd like to thank my editorial team, who have gone above and beyond to keep things going over the last couple of years. It's been a difficult journey for many of us, but we made it.

To the wonderful folks at Dreamscape who have gone the extra mile producing amazing audio versions of these books. I wait with baited breath for each one, and Josh and the rest of the team have really done a fantastic job!

ABOUT THE AUTHOR

Nicole Conway is a graduate of Auburn University with a lifelong passion for writing teen and children's literature. With over 100,000 books sold in her DRAGONRIDER CHRONICLES series, Nicole has been ranked one of Amazon's Top 100 Teen Authors. A coffee and Netflix addict, she also enjoys spending time with her family, rock climbing, and traveling.

Nicole is represented by Frances Black of Literary Counsel.

Made in the USA
Las Vegas, NV
21 January 2023